You are walking in the forest.
With bare, naked feet,
You are treading the fragrant moss along the line of sun.
The forest is full of secrets, rustles…
…It is the strange wildwood of love.

Grażyna Chrostowska *(Ravensbrück, 8th March, 1942)*

Acknowledgements

With thanks to the Forensic Linguistics staff at the University of Łódź, and Aston University, but with particular thanks to Malcolm Coulthard and Krzysztof Kredens. I would also like to thank my agent, Teresa Chris for her invaluable support and belief, and my husband, Ken, for all the coffee, but mostly for just being there.

For Alex and Nadine

Chapter 1

Danané, Côte d'Ivoire, 2005

They were young men, dressed in a tattered array of battle fatigues, the leader lolling in the only chair, the others sprawled on the floor, enjoying the show. Their guns, polished, cared for, ready to kill, were propped across their knees. They were smoking and laughing.

Heat filled the air. The day was still, and since the soldiers came, even the barking dogs were silent. There was just the hum of the flies, drawn by the scent of blood.

They had stripped her naked.

Her legs were shaking. Her face was wet with the tears she didn't know she had cried. Her father's body lay in the corner of the room. They'd shot his face off when he tried to protect her.

She mustn't look at the cupboard. She mustn't think about the cupboard. Let them see her weakness. Let them see a pregnant woman, helpless and undefended. Don't let them see the secret.

One of the men on the floor prodded her belly lightly with the muzzle of his gun. The front sight dug into her. 'She's making a girl.'

There was laughter, shouts of agreement and dissent. They wrangled, waiting for the leader to decide.

His eyes were fixed, slightly glazed from the drugs they had all been smoking. He touched the tip of his knife blade to her stomach and moved it lightly across. She watched the trickle of blood follow it before she felt the sting. He spat on the floor. His teeth were discoloured.

'A girl?' He grinned loosely as he looked at the men. 'Do we need another girl? Shall I get it out?'

Their shouts that she and her child were dirty rebels, that it would take more than two of them to handle real men began to fade as darkness bloomed at the edge of her vision. She couldn't faint. She had to stay alert. She had two children to protect. Her baby was quiet inside her, maybe sleeping, maybe already dead. She was going to die. Her baby was going to die.

His fist drove into her belly.

She was on the ground, trying to protect the child inside her with her arms. She mustn't look at the cupboard. She mustn't think about the cupboard, but her gaze shot across in an involuntary glance. The cupboard was wood and painted white, a rough piece of furniture her father had made. It stood in the corner of the room with a plastic bowl on top. She had been pouring water into it when the soldiers came. Her daughter's small hands had been holding the jug.

And now she saw that the cupboard door was open just a crack, and the light, the light, oh no she could see the light reflecting from a child's eyes.

'No.' It was the first time she had spoken. She had screamed and she had cried, but she hadn't spoken. The leader's mouth stretched in a wide grin. 'Yes.'

She knew what they would do. She couldn't stop them. Now, she had to survive. Her baby had to survive. And her daughter. If they found Sagal...

If they find Sagal, if they do to Sagal what they are doing to her, then her soul will die. She will pour lamp oil over herself and her unborn child, over the house where her murdered father lies, and she will hold a taper to it and burn them all. Her only prayer will be that these creatures that used to be men will burn with her. She will take her own soul to hell, happily, if she can take their souls with her.

The men wait their turn, watching and laughing.

The drone of the flies is loud in the still, hot air.

Chapter 2

BBC news, UK, 2007

Q: *And the detention of children, minister. How do you respond to criticisms of government policy?*

A: *Let's be clear, nobody wants to see children detained. No one does, and certainly not me. But we do have an immigration system and we do have rules. When someone tries to break these rules – when they don't have a legal right to stay in this country for example, and they refuse to leave, then we have a duty to use all the resources we can to make sure they go.*

***

Dungavel detention and removal centre, 2007

Nadifa woke up. Every night, her dreams took her back. Two years lay between now and the day the soldiers came. It wasn't enough. It would never be enough.

She lay on the hard mattress, listening to the familiar sounds: feet moving down the long corridors, the jangle of keys, the slight echo of the voices, the wheeze in the breathing of the two-year-old child beside her.

She had given birth a few days after the attack, a month before her time. She had almost died. Her baby had almost died. They had tried to destroy her. They would have destroyed Sagal if they had found her. And if François, her husband, had been there when they came, they would have butchered him. It was François they had come for.

Instead, they had survived. They had escaped. They had won.

It didn't feel like winning. When she held her new son in her arms, she waited for the flood of love she felt when Sagal was born. But as she looked into his dark eyes, she realised what the soldiers had done. They had stolen the child from her belly and left this creature in its place. This wasn't the child she had carried all those months. This wasn't the baby she and François had made. This was a changeling, a child she had to care for, but one she couldn't love.

Her eyes burned with tears she couldn't shed.

She heard footsteps outside her door.

Beside her, the changeling child whimpered, and then began to wail. Instinctively, her hands moved to cover his ears. She could do this. She couldn't love him, but she could protect him.

In the corridor, doors opened and shut, voices shouted, and a child started screaming. She knew what was happening. The Congolese woman in the room three doors down was being taken away with her small boy. They would put handcuffs on the woman if she resisted. They would throw her into the van. They would put the terrified, hysterical child in their car. They would take them to the airport and force them onto a plane. Then mother and child would be gone.

Like François.

Like Sagal. Like her daughter she would never see again.

The light flickered, filling the room with its flat brightness.

It hummed, like the drone of flies.

Chapter 3

St Abbs, Scotland, 2007

Will Gillen woke suddenly. The bedroom was starkly illuminated, then thunder shook the windows and the light vanished leaving a blue-white afterglow. Rain clattered against the glass. The lightning flashed again followed almost immediately by another explosion of thunder. The storm was overhead. He could hear the sound of the waves surging.

But it wasn't the storm that had woken him. His fingers groped for the phone and he was already half out of bed, his response automatic. 'Yes?' He checked his watch, noting the time of the call – 5 a.m.

'Dad?'

'Ania! What's wrong?'

'Don't panic. I wanted to call you before you saw the papers.'

'The… give me a minute, Ania, I was asleep.'

'I know. I'm sorry it's so early, but we'll be boarding soon and I wanted to talk to you before…'

Boarding? He was getting out of bed as she spoke. 'Just a second.' He put the phone down and went to the basin. His face looked back at him in the mirror, unshaven with shadows under his eyes. His hair stood out in a wild tangle, showing the first strands of grey that were starting to weave through the black. He turned on the cold water, hard, and pushed his face under the tap, a trick he'd used often in the past to bring himself to quick alertness. He came back towelling his head. 'OK. Tell me what's going on.'

'The appeal. Derek Haynes' appeal. It's starting tomorrow.'

Now it was beginning to make sense. 'You think he might win?'

'They're challenging my evidence. It's going to get nasty.'

He sank down onto the edge of the bed. Ania's work as a forensic linguist sometimes took her into court as an expert witness. It was bad luck that had brought the Derek Haynes investigation her way. 'It was a nasty case full stop. You gave your opinion at the trial. If someone else disagrees, what's the problem? It happens.'

'It's not that simple. Look Dad, I'll have to be quick. They've called my flight.'

'That's OK – you can keep talking while you board.'

'I'll need a long wire. I'm using the phone booth.'

'Quickly then. Where are you going?'

'It's just a trip to Łódź.' Ania made regular trips as a visiting lecturer to the university in Poland's second city. Now, as he listened to her voice against the background of a busy airport departure lounge, he could hear something that worried him. 'Are you all right?'

She knew what he meant. 'I will be once I get there. Brown Jenkin's on my back today.'

Brown Jenkin was her shorthand for the recurrent depressions that had plagued her for years. His unease grew. 'Look after yourself.'

'I will. Look, you'll get a letter, OK? I don't want to take you unawares. You're around for the next couple of days?'

'Ania, what are you...?'

A note of impatience slipped into her voice. 'I haven't got time, Dad. Just watch out for the letter, OK? I can't explain now. I'm sorry to... I'd much rather... You'll be around?'

'Yes. I'm not going anywhere.'

'Good. They've almost finished boarding. I have to go. I'll call you.' The phone clicked off.

He put the receiver slowly back in its cradle and sat on the bed frowning in puzzlement trying to work out some kind of explanation for the call he'd just received. *Just watch out for the letter, OK...* What kind of letter did she need to warn him about?

He was too wide awake now to go back to sleep. He decided to make himself some coffee and start the day. He was taking his boat out for a day's sailing and he had plenty he needed to do.

The rain was battering the windows as he went into the kitchen. There was a scuffling noise under the bench and Keeper stretched her way out from her bed, yawning, her fronded tail waving a greeting. She thrust a welcoming nose into Will's crotch, then followed him to the door. She looked out into the black rain and gave him a look of appeal, but when he didn't relent, she vanished into the darkness returning five minutes later to shake the rain off her coat, spattering his trousers and slippers.

Will turned on the radio and listened to the shipping forecast. Last night's storm had passed, but the seas would be heavy. It would be a challenge to take the boat out on his own, and he found himself relishing the prospect. He needed to do something hard, something dangerous that required all his alertness and concentration.

The forecast segued into the news. He turned up the volume so he could listen as he packed the car. The Haynes appeal was the third item. Less than a year ago, Derek Haynes, a detention centre officer, had been convicted of child murder. Eight-year-old Sagal Akindès, the daughter of a Côte d'Ivoire asylum seeker, had been abducted from the centre near Manchester where she, her mother and her infant brother were then held. Her remains had been found several weeks later, dumped in a drainage channel that carried run-off from a field into the River Irwell a few miles from the centre. Now Haynes was appealing against his conviction.

The sky was just starting to lighten in the east as Will finished loading his Range Rover. Keeper, realising what was happening, held him up by dancing round the car in excitement instead of jumping into her place in the back.

It was only a short drive to the harbour. When they arrived, the small car park was empty apart from the van that belonged to Jack, the car park attendant. Keeper, once liberated, raced down to the jetty where she leapt into the water and swam back to the small shingle beach. Jack, one of the many dive enthusiasts who haunted these shores, came over as Will started unloading. 'Morning, Mr Gillen. Going out today?'

'Morning, Jack. Yes, it's about time. I haven't had her out properly since November.'

'It's heavy after the storm.'

'I'll be looking out.'

Keeper leapt into the water again. She was going to be frozen and sodden by the time he got her onto the boat. He called her sharply as she reached the beach and she came back, waiting until she was next to the two men before she shook herself.

The air was cold and filled with the smell of the sea. He tried to recapture the anticipation he'd felt about the day's sailing ahead of him but he couldn't shake off his anxiety about Ania. Before he negotiated his way out of the harbour, he called her. She should have been on the ground in Łódź by now, but there was no reply. He remembered she had called him from a public phone. Maybe her mobile had been out of charge. He'd have to wait.

Sailing always brought back memories of his children, twin girls, Louisa and

Ania. They'd spent most of their summers here. Louisa had never been interested in sailing, and used to spend her time on the boat crouched in the shelter of the cabin, her nose in a book. Ania loved the sea. She'd become adept at crewing and one of his enduring images from her childhood was of her tying off a coil of rope, her small hands gripping the line, her orange life jacket a beacon in the sunlight as they pitched through the choppy waters towards the calm of St Abbs harbour.

They had been peas-in-a-pod alike in appearance, so different in personality.

But Louisa was dead.

And Ania... *Brown Jenkin's on my back today*.

The Haynes case had been like a dark piece of the past coming to claim her. And it wasn't over. It would never be over.

Chapter 4

Gdynia, Poland 2007

Dariusz Erland shifted impatiently in his chair. He was in the small apartment in the port city of Gdynia where he had grown up, listening to the sound of his father shuffling round in the kitchen. He had arrived half an hour ago and had been waiting for over fifteen minutes for the tea the old man had insisted on making. 'I'll do it,' he called again, resisting the temptation to help himself to a cigarette from the packet lying open on the table. It was the third time he'd offered.

'No, no, no.'

Dariusz grinned to himself. His father was jealously proud of the domestic skills he'd developed after his wife's death. Before that, Dariusz could barely remember him going into the kitchen. He could hear the low mutter of *tea, cups, milk, sugar* as the old man aided his failing memory through the process. After another five minutes, he came through carrying the tray carefully and set it down on the table. It contained a battered tea pot, a mug, a jug of milk, a sugar bowl and a plate of pastries.

'I don't need all this,' Dariusz said, exasperated. 'Just...' He saw the light of pleased stubbornness in his father's eyes and gave in. 'Thanks.' He poured some tea which must have been left standing in the pot to judge from its colour then looked at the old man carefully. He was wearing a shabby pair of trousers and a jacket that had long seen better days. The collar of his shirt was frayed. The clothes hung on his skinny frame. As he breathed, Dariusz could hear the wheezing in his chest. 'You're supposed to be resting.'

His father dismissed this with a wave of the hand. He had always been an austere man. Life in Poland had been hard for his generation. He had spent the last years of his childhood under the Nazi occupation and most of his adult life under Soviet rule. He had worked in the shipyards and had been a leader in the unrest of the late 1970s and early 1980s, his activism landing him in prison more than once. He had been there in December 1970 when armed police opened fire on the morning shift coming into the Paris Commune Shipyard to start work. He still limped from where a police bullet had broken his leg. 'I was lucky,' he always said when he consented to discuss it. 'Others – they died.'

He would be eighty in three days' time. Dariusz' younger sister Beata was planning a party, when he and his four siblings would cram into the apartment where they had grown up, and celebrate in the traditional Polish way with good food and vodka. He could remember the celebrations from his own birthdays as he grew up, the voices singing: *Sto lat, sto lat, niech zyje zyje nam...* Then last night, Beata had called to tell him the old man was ill. 'The doctor wants him in hospital but he refuses to go. I'm worried he isn't even taking his medication.'

Dariusz was busy, but he took four days' leave and drove the 200 miles to the shores of the Baltic sea. He'd trained as an engineer in the heady days after the first Solidarity government. He thought – they all thought – that Poland was going to become a true workers' state, but with their eyes fixed on the future, they didn't see the corruption that was endemic in the old Soviet system as its tentacles ate into the roots of the new democracy.

He was his father's son and became involved at once in trades union activism which gradually took over his working life. After several years of fighting for the rights of his co-workers and finding himself mown down by people who had somehow emerged into the new democracy with their power intact and their wealth increased, he went back to college and took a degree in law. He still worked for the trades union, but he was disillusioned now. Too often he found himself defending workers against their own union rather than their employers.

The call came as he was loading his stuff into his car. It was one of the many bureaucrats he had to negotiate his working life around, Leslaw Mielek. 'What's this about leave? You can't go. I've got no one to cover for you.'

That was horse-shit. Dariusz had reorganised his case load so that all he had to deal with for the next few days was paperwork. He mentally subjected Mielek to an improbable sexual indignity and waited until the voice on the other end of the phone had stopped speaking. 'That's got to be your problem, Mielek. I can keep up with the paperwork from Gdynia. I'll be back on Saturday.'

'See that you are.'

Dariusz added a goat to the orgy and hung up. He put the matter out of his mind. He could deal with Mielek when he got back. His father was more important. Beata's call had worried him.

At first, his father had seemed fine and he thought Beata had been alarmist, but now he could see the unhealthy flush that minor exertion had brought to the old man's cheeks. 'What's all this about the hospital?'

'I'm not going. Once they've got you in there – my age – you're dead. I'm going to die in my own bed.'

'You're not dying anywhere, not yet. What about the pills they gave you?'

His father looked shifty. Dariusz stood up and went through to the kitchen. He rummaged in the cupboard where the old man kept all his medications until he found a packet of antibiotics with the pharmacy seal intact. He read the instructions, filled a glass with water and took it through. 'Here. You'll take these, and you'll keep on taking them, or I'm driving you to the hospital right now.' He looked into his father's stubborn eyes. 'If I have to, I'll carry you there. Now take them!'

There was a clash of wills, then his father capitulated. 'Lot of damn fuss,' he said as he accepted one of the capsules that Dariusz held out to him, and washed it down with a swig of water. Dariusz waited out the fit of coughing that he was pretty sure was simulated, then said, 'Right. Now you need something to eat.'

It looked like he was stuck here until the day of the party. He persuaded his father to go and lie down while he prepared some soup. He was in the middle of chopping the miscellany of tired vegetables he'd found in the fridge when his phone rang. He was expecting calls from work and he answered it without checking the number. 'Dariusz Erland.'

To his surprise, it was Ania. She usually called him in the evenings. 'I was just wondering where you are.'

'I'm at my father's. Where are you?' He dumped the vegetables into a pan as he spoke and put it on the cooker.

'In Łódź . I've come a few days early. I just called the flat.'

He cursed Beata for her untimely call, and his father for being a stubborn old mule. 'Shit. I wasn't expecting you until the weekend. My father's ill.'

'Is it serious?'

'It wouldn't be if he'd look after himself. Listen I can't get away until Friday now. Are you OK? Why did you come early?'

'To see you, of course.'

He could tell by her voice that something was wrong. 'Come on, *kiciu*. What is it?'

'Oh, it's just… A case. A case has gone wrong on me. I… Look, it can wait. You take care of your dad. I'll see you on Saturday.'

'Friday. I'll be back Friday night.' It would be a long drive, a good three hours. He'd have to fake the vodka toasts at the party.

'Will you?' She sounded better. 'I really want to see you.'

'And I really want to see you.' The soup was simmering now. He turned down the heat then went to sit in the living room. The smell of cooking followed him. 'We can still talk. What's the problem?'

'It's complicated. I…'

His father called from the other room, and started coughing in earnest.

'You've got things to do. I'll try later. When we're both in bed.'

He laughed. 'You do that.'

He was frustrated that she was here, in Poland, but she was still 200 miles away from him.

Chapter 5

The sea was calmer than Will had expected. He took the boat up the coast, keeping close to the inaccessible cliffs. In a few weeks, the kittiwakes would be nesting and the sky would be full of the sounds of raucous discontent as they fought for space on the narrow ledges.

The sky cleared, and the thin sun of winter warmed his face. Keeper nosed his hand then stood with her front paws on the gunwale, her tongue lolling as she surveyed the sea. It should have been a perfect day, except...

He'd had misgivings about the Haynes case ever since it landed on Ania's desk. Haynes, an ex-prison officer, had worked at the detention centre outside Manchester where the dead child, Sagal Akindès, had been held. Her father, François had sought asylum with his family, claiming government soldiers were looking for them. Instead, he'd turned out to be a jihadist who had hooked up with a local group suspected of terrorist links at the first opportunity. He had been summarily deported. His family had not gone with him because Sagal had been ill and deemed unfit to travel. When she disappeared, police had at first believed that the girl's mother, Nadifa had arranged for her daughter to be smuggled out and hidden by a well-wisher.

Then a farmer, trying to clear a blocked drainage channel into the River Irwell found the body of a child in an advanced state of decay. The investigation into Sagal's disappearance became a murder hunt. Derek Haynes, who had befriended the family, came under suspicion immediately. When police examined the computer in his office, they found photographs of the child, and a video. The video had been made in the basement of the detention centre, and it showed Sagal imprisoned. It had also recorded the voice of her abuser.

Ania was suddenly involved in the most high profile case of her career and her evidence had been pivotal in securing Haynes' conviction. She had found working with the video distressing, and the furore of publicity surrounding the case had

21

put further pressure on her. Ania presented a lively and vivacious front to the world and he was probably one of the very few people who knew about the black depressions that sometimes gripped her and threatened to drag her under.

Despite his attempts to put them to the back of his mind, his thoughts made a dark contrast to the brightness of the day.

The sun had set by the time he brought the boat back into the harbour. He followed the lights in to the calm of the sheltered water, applying a quick burst of reverse gear, a manoeuvre that was almost instinctive after all these years, to bring the boat alongside the quay. The small harbour was silent, apart from the gentle creak and suck as the moored boats rocked on the water. He jumped ashore and secured the lines then, calling Keeper away from some discarded food wrappings she'd found among the tangle of ropes and nets on the harbour wall, he headed towards the car park.

It was empty apart from his car and one other, a BMW X3. The policeman in him – the policeman he had been until a few short weeks ago – came alert. Strange cars were unusual at this time of year, and strange, expensive cars rarer still. It must have been left after Jack had gone – there was no ticket.

Whoever it was, it wasn't his business. He drove back up the hill through the village to his cottage. He checked the post with a sense of expectation, but the promised letter hadn't arrived. Then he saw the message light on the phone flashing, and felt the knot inside him release.

But it wasn't Ania. There were just a few seconds of hissing silence, and the caller cut the connection. It was probably a wrong number. He deleted it, then wandered round the kitchen, preparing food for Keeper, trying to stop himself from unpicking Ania's last call once again. *Just watch out for the letter, OK.* What letter? Why would she say that?

In the end, he decided he couldn't face an evening in the cottage staring at a silent phone like a jilted lover. He put his coat on and walked with Keeper along the cliff path to the hotel that looked out over the sea from the headland. It was run down but there would be food of sorts, there would be people and there would be a fire where he could sit with Keeper and enjoy a pint of beer. He tried calling Ania again as he walked but there was still no reply.

He ordered a sandwich and ate it at the bar, talking to the landlord who brought him up to date with the local news. The landlord was having trouble with some of the village youths who had very little to occupy their time during the winter months. 'It's no place for kids,' he said. 'Not any more.'

'Mine used to enjoy it,' Will said absently. Ania and Louisa had loved coming here.

The landlord started to say something, then stopped. 'Well, it was a change for them, wasn't it,' he said after a moment. He focused his attention on the glass he was polishing.

When he'd eaten, Will took his beer into the lounge and found a comfortable chair by the fire. He sank down into it, enjoying the moment of relaxation. Keeper curled up on the floor by his feet.

It had been a hard day's sailing but it had been a good one. Despite his worries, it had left him exhilarated. The torpor that had held him since he had lost the work he loved was starting to lift. He was too young at fifty-two to be idle. He was still ambitious. One career might be over but there was nothing to stop him taking up another. He started running some plans through his mind, but as the warmth began to seep into his chilled bones, the day caught up with him. His eyes were starting to feel heavy. He knew he should go back to the cottage, but he was just too tired to move.

Almost without knowing, he drifted into sleep.

He came slowly back to awareness and realised that Keeper's warm bulk was no longer pressing against his legs. He looked round and saw her at the other side of the room, sniffing the proffered hand of a woman who was sitting there. He clicked his fingers and Keeper came back to him. 'I hope she wasn't bothering you,' he said.

The woman smiled across at him. She had an attractive, bony face 'It was my fault, I'm afraid. I called her over. She's a beautiful dog. I didn't want to disturb you. You looked far too comfortable.'

He must have fallen asleep. He hoped his mouth hadn't been hanging open. 'I've been out on the boat all day. It doesn't take much to distract her if I'm not giving her enough attention.' He tugged Keeper's ears and she waved her fronded tail, panting up at him, her tongue lolling.

'What kind of dog is she?' The woman seemed to be on her own, a half-full glass of wine on the coffee table in front of her. A newspaper was untidily spread out on the seat beside her.

'It's a good question. She's her own kind, I suppose.' Keeper's ornate tail and rough coat came from her collie mother. Her exuberance and insatiable appetite came from somewhere else altogether. 'That must have been some night on the tiles,' Ania used to say when they speculated about Keeper's ancestry.

'A one-off. She's lovely.'

'She's hard work. Do you have a boat moored here?'

'No. I'm in Scotland on business. I thought I'd give this hotel a try.'

He grinned at her rueful expression. He loved the place himself, but he wouldn't dream of staying here. 'It's seen better days.'

'So far, the shower doesn't work, but if I change my room, I'll get a window that rattles so much I won't sleep. The TV has snowstorms on all channels and there's nothing to read.' She was counting the items off on her fingers as she spoke. 'The restaurant was freezing and I was the only customer so I'm spending the evening in the bar and the wine is lousy. Other than that, it's OK.'

He was studying her as she talked. She was wearing linen trousers and a chocolate brown jersey, the sleeves pushed up above her elbows. She seemed an unlikely candidate for any of the businesses that existed in the area. She certainly didn't look like the kind of woman who would normally stay in a run-down hotel in an out-of-the-way place like St Abbs that normally attracted only divers, walkers and bird watchers. He remembered the expensive car in the empty car park by the harbour wall. 'Can I get you a drink? I'm Will, by the way.'

'Sarah. Sarah Ludlow. And I'd love a drink.'

'What can I get you?'

She swirled the red liquid round her glass. 'I think I'll give the wine a miss.' She met his gaze and smiled. 'You choose.'

It was a challenge but one that Will could rise to. He knew the landlord kept a decent selection of malt whiskies. This was Scotland, after all. He chose a twenty-five-year-old Benromach and took the glasses back to the table with a small jug of water.

She tasted the whisky, her eyebrows lifting in surprise as she caught its quality. 'Thank you.' Keeper planted a hopeful chin on her lap, and she stroked the dog's soft ears as they began to talk. She was a lawyer, she told him, and she was in Scotland to see a client.

'A lawyer who makes house calls? I need the name of your firm.'

She laughed. 'I don't usually. This is an exception. Anyway, I got everything wound up this afternoon. I could have driven back overnight but I've never visited this part of the coast, so I thought I'd make a detour and take a look round.'

'Has it been worth it?'

'Probably not. It's beautiful, but it's a bit of a wilderness. Do you live up here?'

'I do at the moment.'

'How about a social life?' Her gesture encompassed the bleak hotel bar.

'There isn't much in winter. There's here, or there's a pub in the next bay at Coldingham. Otherwise, you have to drive out. You aren't seeing it as its best. You should have come in the summer.'

She looked doubtful and he felt an urge to defend his chosen home. 'When the commercial fishing went, people stayed on. They have deep roots here. It isn't as isolated as it seems. You can be in Edinburgh in an hour and it gets lively in the summer. People come here for the sailing and the diving.'

'Is that what keeps you here?'

'Partly. I've got a cottage up on the cliffs.' It had been the place that he came on holiday with the girls and his wife, Elżbieta. And then it had just been him and Ania. He didn't want to talk about that.

Before she could ask any more questions, he turned the conversation back to her. She was London born and bred, she told him, but she'd lived in the US for years. 'I went over there to finish my training and got involved with the work.' She'd come back to the UK five years ago. She didn't say what kind of law she practised. He didn't mention his own professional connection with the legal system. Lawyers and policemen should be on the same side but were frequently in bitter opposition.

She became animated when she talked. Her hands were small with long fingers and she used them to emphasise what she was saying. Her face wasn't beautiful, but it was expressive, and her eyes were bright as she laughed. 'And you?' she said. 'What do you do?'

'These days, I'm a sailor. Don't ever get a boat. Or a dog. They take your life over.'

'OK. Man of mystery, lives in the wilderness with his dog. Where next with the boat?'

He was glad she had the nous not to push it. His enforced retirement was recent enough and bitter enough to be a topic he preferred to avoid. 'I'm going to take her north, up the Norwegian coast in the summer. Have you ever been there?'

'Norway? No.'

As she was speaking, he glanced at the newspaper she had been reading. It was the Edinburgh Evening News. Derek Haynes' face looked back at him under the headline: DRAMATIC NEW EVIDENCE IN HAYNES CASE, DEFENCE CLAIMS.

He was suddenly aware of silence and pulled himself back. 'Sorry. You were saying…?'

'Scandinavia, I…' She followed his gaze to the photograph. 'Are you all right?'

'I'm fine. I haven't seen the news today. I just noticed the headline.'

She looked at the paper again, frowning slightly. 'It's an odd case. Apparently the expert witness got it wrong.'

Suddenly he wanted to be home. He checked his watch. It was after eleven. They'd been talking for almost two hours. 'I didn't realise how late it was. I have to get back.'

'Of course. I think I need to turn in as well. There's something about the sea air…' She looked at the paper. 'I'd let you take it, but it's the only thing I've got to read.'

He managed to smile. 'No problem. I'll say goodnight. Thank you for your company.'

'No. Thank you. You turned a dull evening into an entertaining one. It's been good to meet you.' She leaned forward and kissed him lightly on the mouth. The slight stickiness of her lipstick left a lingering trace. She smiled into his eyes. 'And Keeper,' she said, bending down to pat the dog's head, her hair, a dark honey blonde, falling forward over her face.

He walked back along the cliff path, the sea below him gleaming in the night. He could hear the sound of the swell as it washed against the rocks. The sky was clear, the stars blazing out with icy clarity. For a moment, he imagined he was walking back to the cottage with Sarah, still caught in the undercurrent of sensuality that had marked their goodbye, but then his thoughts moved elsewhere, troubled by the conversation he had had with his daughter that morning, and by the ominous headlines he had glimpsed in the newspaper.

Chapter 6

Keeper headbutted Will into wakefulness. He groaned as he checked his watch. It was just before seven on a cold, still morning. There were frost patterns on the inside of the windows and a thin layer of ice on the top of Keeper's water dish. Resisting the temptation to stay under the covers, he pulled on his trousers, boots and a heavy jumper then went downstairs and put a match to the gas.

The previous evening was coming back to him and the headlines he had glimpsed in the paper. He switched on the radio and angled the aerial for the best reception. The headlines were clones of those the day before and the day before that. More people had died in Afghanistan. There was trouble in the Middle East, unrest in the Palestinian territories.

And then…

'Dramatic new evidence came to light yesterday in the court of appeal where Derek Haynes, the man found guilty of the murder of eight-year-old Sagal Akindès, is appealing his conviction. Lawyers for Haynes declared that crucial evidence in the case against him was "in grave and serious error." We're going now to our legal correspondent, Mark Wallender. A worrying story, Mark.'

'Worrying and disturbing. An important plank in the case against Haynes was the identification of his voice on video recordings found on his computer. This identification was made in court by Dr Ania Milosz, an expert in voice analysis. But now an expert for the defence has not only challenged these findings, but has demonstrated deep flaws in Dr Milosz's original analysis. If that identification can't be made, then the case against Haynes is seriously weakened.'

'And what reactions do we have to this…'

Will listened, a sick chill growing inside him.

'We obtained what were supposed to be the original recordings from the police,' a spokesperson from the defence team said. 'These were the ones that came back after Dr Milosz had worked on them. Our experts subjected them to rigorous analysis and I am afraid there is no doubt. They have been tampered with. The prosecution has offered no evidence to challenge our claim. Mr Haynes has been the victim of a grave miscarriage of justice.'

Then Oz Karzac, Ania's boss came on. Will listened tensely, waiting for some kind of explanation. Karzac would defend Ania. He was media savvy, having worked in the film and sound industry before moving into the less crowded area of forensics. But Karzac confined himself to anodyne stonewalling. He was 'very concerned' and would be launching an internal investigation 'at once.'

'Do you want to challenge the defence contentions?'

'Until I've had a chance to study the evidence, I'm not in a position to...'

'You are accepting the defence case that the voice on the recordings is not that of Derek Haynes?'

'That's not what they're saying. They're saying the tapes don't confirm that.'

'Professor Karzac, they're making much more serious allegations. There are very grave questions to be answered about Dr Milosz's original work, are there not?'

'As I said, until....'

'Have you discussed this with Dr Milosz.'

'Not yet.'

'I understand she has left the country?'

'She's working with one of our overseas partners. This was a long-term commitment. Her absence isn't linked to this case. I plan to talk to her later today.' He would have done better not to answer an accusation that hadn't been made.

Will snapped the radio off. Ania had expected her evidence to be challenged, but this wasn't a challenge, it was far worse than that. Despite the careful wording of the reports, he could read the subtext. She was being accused of falsifying the evidence she had given to the court. Karzac, to give him his due, had supported her as much as he could, but his contribution hadn't helped.

He reached for his phone, making a quick time calculation. It would be just after eight in Poland. She would be awake by now, and she must be keeping an eye on the UK news. It worried him that she hadn't contacted him, and she apparently hadn't contacted Karzac either. He pressed the key for her number, and waited as it rang and rang.

This is the messaging service for…

'Ania. Call me. We need to talk about this.'

There was nothing he could do now but wait for her to phone.

The newspapers had loved Ania when Haynes was convicted. Her evidence had been sufficiently new, sufficiently sexy to attract their attention, and Ania herself was suitably photogenic. He'd dug out one of the many cuttings from the days of the Haynes trial. He smoothed it out and read it again.

'VOICEPRINT' CONVICTS MONSTER HAYNES

'Convicted out of his own mouth' took on a new meaning in court today. Ania Milosz, 29, helped to put monster Derek Haynes behind bars when she identified his voice as the one heard by the jury on the 'Sagal' videos.

'What I do isn't new,' the forensic expert told our reporter, 'But it's getting more recognition in the courts.'

The articles – and there had been several – were all accompanied by the same photograph, Ania coming out of the court in her tailored suit among the city crowds, her dark glasses creating a touch of enigmatic glamour, her fair hair, caught by the breeze, ruffled round her face. For once he had been able to look at her without seeing the ghost of his dead child looking over her shoulder. Despite his misgivings, he had been proud of her.

But now, these same papers were turning on her with all the savagery they were capable of.

He didn't know what to do.

Keeper burst out in a flurry of barking, and there was a sharp rap at the door. He went to open it, feeling the tug of anxiety. He wasn't expecting anyone.

A woman was standing there, her hand raised to knock again. Her eyes widened with surprise, and he realised it was Sarah, from the hotel the evening before. 'Sarah. I wasn't… Please. Come in.'

'Thank you.' She hesitated, then stepped into the room, pulling off her woollen hat. She was wrapped up against the icy wind in a sheepskin coat, a polo neck just visible inside the turned up collar. 'I hope I'm not disturbing you.'

'I'm just surprised you managed to find me.'

She was still staring at him. 'I just asked,' she said after a moment.

'Right.' The people of St Abbs were notoriously close-mouthed, but there was no reason not to tell her where he lived. Their evening in the pub would have been noted. 'Were you OK at the hotel last night?'

She smiled. 'Well... until about three. Then some drunks came in. What with that and the frostbite I gave up on sleep and did some work.' She didn't look as if she'd had a broken night. She looked fresh and alert in the cold morning air.

'Are you heading back this morning?'

She shook her head. 'I don't know yet. I haven't decided.'

'Coffee?'

'You're a mind reader. They only have instant at the hotel.'

He'd lit the stove so the cottage was warm, but she kept her coat on, looking round with some curiosity. 'You live here on your own?'

'Yes – it's just about the right size for one. I used to use it as a holiday cottage but now...' He stopped. He didn't want to start explaining his life.

She crossed the room and picked up one of the photos that stood on the shelf. It was one of him and Ania, taken about two years ago, the last time they had been here together.

'How do you like your coffee?'

She was still looking at the photograph, and didn't respond for a moment. 'Sorry. Black, no sugar.' She put the photo down. 'Your daughter?'

'Yes.' He was suddenly aware how little he knew her, and remembered his misgivings about journalists wanting a story about Ania. She wasn't like any journalist he had ever met – they didn't wear designer clothes and drive expensive cars, and they were a lot more direct with their questions – but he needed to be cautious.

'Does she come here much?'

'Sometimes.' It was Ania's bolt hole when Brown Jenkin had her in his grip.

She looked at him in surprise and he realised he had sounded curt.

'She's away at the moment.' He spooned coffee into the cafétière.

He saw her lips start to form a question and said quickly, 'She's in Poland. Business.'

'Whereabouts?'

'Here and there. It's an academic thing.' He didn't attempt to hide the irritation in his voice and was aware of her glance as he poured hot water onto the grounds. The conversation died.

He poured out the coffee and gave Sarah hers. She moved to the window that looked out over the sea. 'It's so lovely here. I'm tempted to stay on for a few days.'

If she'd said it last night, he would have been pleased. She was an attractive woman whose company he had enjoyed. He could have taken her out on the boat, shown her the hidden parts of the coast, explored the possibilities that had been there, unspoken, the evening before. Now it was different.

'Another time I'd have offered to show you around but I've got a lot on.'

'Don't worry about it.' She deftly turned the conversation. They talked about Keeper, about boats, about the weather, but they weren't able to recapture the rapport they had shared in the bar the night before.

She finished her coffee. 'I won't keep you. I can see you've got things to do and I've got a long drive ahead of me.'

'You're not staying then?'

She met his gaze and smiled. 'It doesn't look like it. Another time, maybe.' She fastened her coat and wrapped her scarf round her, pulling her hat low over her eyes. She held out her hand. 'It's been good meeting you, and thank you for the coffee.'

'It was my pleasure.'

He watched her head down the hill towards the harbour, then reached for his phone. He put it down again. Ania would call when she was ready. He picked up the newspaper cutting that was still on the table where he had left it.

'VOICEPRINT' CONVICTS MONSTER HAYNES.

Ania stood outside the Crown Court, her hand raised to her dark glasses, her hair stirred by the breeze. People were caught in the moment, moving between the pillars into the shadows.

And among the crowd, standing just on the edge of the picture, was a figure his eyes had passed over before. There was a ghost looking over Ania's shoulder, but it wasn't a ghost from the past. It was one from the future.

Sarah Ludlow stood in the shadows of the pillars, watching.

Chapter 7

Will made it to the car park in five minutes, held up by a delivery truck negotiating the narrow streets. Sarah Ludlow's car was gone. He saw Jack coming across and wound down his window. 'The woman... that car. Which way did she go?'

'Who?'

'The BMW. Which way did it go?' Jack shrugged and pointed up the hill. It was the only way out of the village.

'After that.' He realised his voice sounded curt. 'Did she say which way she was going?'

'I don't know. She didn't say. Nice car. Nice lady.' He could see the speculation in Jack's eyes, but he couldn't do anything about that. He stared out across the glittering water. She would almost certainly be heading south. He might be able to catch her up, but she had a powerful car. If she wanted to keep away from him, she could. And if he did catch her up, what then?

He was kicking himself for not making the connection sooner. He'd been tired, he'd been worried, but there was no excuse. The phone call the night before – it must have been Sarah Ludlow. Who was she? A lawyer touting for trade? Someone attached to the Haynes case? He realised she was probably a journalist on the track of a juicy story. How had she known that Ania had connections here? *I thought I'd make a detour.*

Detour, his arse.

She would have talked to other people as well, but he could be glad the news had broken when it did. He and Ania had long-standing connections with the village. The tight-knit community would have closed ranks and quietly, unobtrusively, stonewalled anyone who was digging around. But he had to put her out of his mind. He had to think about Ania now. He nodded a quick acknowledgement to Jack and drove back to the cottage.

Throughout the day, he watched the furore in the news reach fever pitch. The expectation was that Haynes' conviction would be quashed. The fight would centre on whether he was pardoned, or whether there would be a new trial. In the meantime, his lawyers battled to get him released on bail, claiming that the nature of their client's conviction put him in danger from people who would rather see him dead than free. Haynes was already in isolation. He had been attacked immediately the news of his appeal broke.

Deprived of their monster, the papers had turned on Ania. Haynes himself received no sympathy – most news reports, sailing skilfully close to the winds of the libel laws, implied that he was guilty as hell and was in danger of being allowed to walk free.

From Ania herself, there was nothing.

He tried calling her, more than once, but all he got was her answering service. 'For God's sake will you phone me!' he said in his last message. 'They're crucifying you. I can't help if you don't talk to me.'

But his immediate conviction that she was completely innocent of the accusations made against her was beginning to crumble. The police had been certain Haynes was guilty. They were less certain that they had enough to convict him. If she had been given access to evidence that showed Haynes' guilt, but evidence that wasn't admissible in court... Previous convictions? Previous accusations? Would she have done something to strengthen the evidence she had? Without her testimony, the case against Haynes could have gone either way.

He knew what it was like to be faced with hard decisions. In his own work, he had had to make judgements that might leave him hanging by his thumbs over the righteous blaze of the news media's anger, until he had made the one that had ended his career. But there were hard decisions, and then there were the decisions you should never make, and with the Haynes case, Ania had been too vulnerable.

They had been twins, Louisa and Ania, Ania the eldest by minutes. He had been twenty-two, not much more than a child himself. He could remember sitting by Elžbieta's bed feeling gut-punched with the shock of it – they were too young, they hadn't planned to start a family and they had had no idea that she was carrying twins. He hadn't felt the traditional paternal joy. He had felt fear, overwhelmed by the sudden responsibility and the realisation that his life – their lives – had changed beyond redemption.

It had been difficult. He was starting out in his career and it was a struggle to live on his salary. The demands of twin babies kept Elžbieta at home for longer than they had expected. They had been broke, and they both worked harder than they had ever worked in their lives before.

Q: *When and where were you happiest?*
A: *When my children were small.*
Q: *Who or what is the greatest love of your life?*
A: *My daughters.*
Q: *Both of them?*
A: *I love them both, but...*

It had always been Ania who had worried them most. She was the foolhardy one, the one who took risks and seemed to have no sense of danger. She would jump, climb, dive, leap into dangerous situations without a second thought; Louisa was quiet and thoughtful, a shy, bookish little girl who was scared of spiders and the dark.

But it was Louisa who had been abducted.

Will didn't want to go down that path. It had destroyed Elžbieta, leaving him and Ania alone, just the two of them bonded by tragedy and loss, and for him, the guilt that maybe he hadn't loved Louisa enough, maybe the bond he'd shared with Ania, the sheer joy of physical challenge had made him value his quieter, more introspective daughter less. If he had valued her enough, then surely, *surely* he would have been able to protect her.

But he hadn't. And he hadn't been able to protect his surviving daughter either. After her sister's death, after her mother's abandonment, Ania's life had been dogged by the depressions she came to personalise later as Brown Jenkin. Louisa became the topic they couldn't talk about – at first, her death, and later, her life. It was as if she had never existed.

Angrily he picked up the phone and keyed in her number. When he got her messaging service again, he disconnected and called the lab where she worked. 'FLS. How can I help you?'

'Professor Karzac, please.'

'I'm afraid Professor Karzac is unavailable at the moment.'

'I see. When will he be available?'

'Who's calling?'

'My name is Gillen. Will Gillen. I'm Ania Milosz's father.'

There was silence, then the woman's voice said cautiously, 'Mr Gillen. Perhaps... Just a moment.' The line cut off, then crackled into life again. 'Gillen? Oz Karzac. Have you heard from Ania?'

'No. She isn't answering her phone.'

'Jesus. What the fuck is she playing at?'

'I'm worried about her. She should be here.'

'Of course she should. I've told her. Well, I've left messages – call me, get yourself back. Nothing. She's keeping her head down.'

'She's probably as shocked about this as we are. She must be trying to...'

Karzac cut across him. He sounded angry. 'Listen. I'm very fond of Ania. We all are. But I can't go on defending her. If she did this – and it's beginning to look very much like she did – then it's unforgivable. It doesn't just put an innocent person behind bars. It undermines the whole credibility of the system, of what we do.'

'You think she fabricated that recording? Gave false evidence?'

'Believe me, Gillen, I don't want to. I've gone over it and over it. Just find me someone else who could have done it.'

Will made a decision. 'I'm going to bring her back. I'm taking the first flight I can get to this – where is it? Łódź? And I'm bringing her back.'

After Will put the phone down, he tried to drown his worry in anger – anger at Ania for not getting in touch, anger at Karzac for not believing in her, anger at the press for playing it this way before anyone knew what the true story was. He didn't know what to do, and the sense of impotence made him rage with frustration. All he knew was that Ania was behaving like a fool by trying to hide from all of this. It wasn't an empty threat he'd made to Karzac. If he didn't manage to make contact today, then he was getting on a plane tomorrow and bringing her back. If she was here, she could defend herself.

As it was, she was being destroyed.

Chapter 8

Gdynia, Poland 2007

It was just after nine. Dariusz waited until the sounds of intermittent movement and mutterings of discontent faded, and he knew his father was asleep. He'd managed to get another tablet down the old man's throat, and persuaded him to eat a bit. It was probably his imagination, but he thought his father looked slightly better. The old man was tough enough to fight off anything if he'd just take care of himself.

He opened a bottle of beer and stretched out on the couch. It had been a long day. He'd got up early and he'd spent his time running around to replenish his father's dwindling food supplies. The old man still lived as if he was in the middle of Stalinist shortages. He didn't have the mindset for the plenty that was promised by EU accession. He'd repaired the leaking water tank – the ancient plumbing needed replacing, but it was beyond even Dariusz' skill to find a plumber these days – and fixed the gaps in the windows that rattled and let in the cold. He'd checked the electric sockets and replaced two that were cracked beyond repair. He didn't dare look at the wiring – he didn't want to know. The flat was dilapidated. The best answer would be for his father to move. He'd have a talk with Beata, see if they could find a way of persuading the old man.

He was waiting for Ania to call. The news reports from the UK were getting worse and he was worried about her. There was no point in his trying to call her. She was trying to avoid the papers and was keeping her phone switched off.

'I'm getting hassle,' she'd told him. 'My boss and my dad both want to talk to me and I can't face them, not yet. My boss wants to bawl me out, and my dad's worried, I know he is, but that'll only make him bawl me out as well. I've had it up to here with all of that.' Her words were light, but there was a dead tone to her voice that told him it was getting to her.

'Are they giving you hassle here as well?'

'No. They're tiptoeing round me as if I was mystery parcel that had just started ticking. It's almost as bad.'

'They're worried about you *kiciu*.'

'I know. There's nothing I can do about it. I can't tell them anything they want to hear, so what's the point in talking about it?'

He bit his tongue on all the questions he wanted to ask, and turned the conversation to his planned trip to Manchester in the spring. By the time the call ended, her mood had lifted. 'I'm looking forward to Friday,' she said. Friday evening he would be driving back.

'Wait for me at the flat. I'll be home by midnight.'

'I'll be there. I'd better go. I'll call you from the hotel tomorrow – I'm working late again, so it won't be until after ten.'

He checked the time. It wasn't quite nine. He could relax for an hour. His eyes were heavy. He could feel himself starting to drift. He was jerked back to wakefulness by the sound of his father's voice. 'Dareczek!'

It was the use of the affectionate diminutive that he had barely heard from his father since childhood that alarmed him. He jumped up, wide awake at once. His father was sitting up in bed, looking worried, holding the sub-lingual spray he used to control his angina attacks.

'It's empty,' he said.

'You're ill? You need it? Don't worry, I'll call...'

'No, no, no. I just have a slight...' He touched his chest.

'Where's your new one?'

His father looked sheepish. 'I have the prescription, I just…' He fumbled for his dressing gown and started to get up. Dariusz sat him firmly back on the bed.

'Where is it?'

'In my pocket. In one pocket...' Dariusz went through the trousers and jackets hanging in the cupboard, and in the end, found the prescription stuffed in the bottom of a coat pocket. He cursed under his breath, but this couldn't wait.

It was twenty past nine. He just about had time to get to the 24 hour pharmacy and be back in time for Ania's call.

It was raining, and the empty roads gleamed in the streetlights. The pharmacy was by the station, and it was busy. He stood in a queue, fuming with impatience, and then had to argue the toss with the pharmacist who didn't want to fill the crumpled, barely legible prescription.

He got back just before ten by dint of breaking the speed limit and jumping a couple of red lights. He listened for the phone as he got the old man settled. As his father sank back onto the pillows, he said, 'That woman called. You know.'

He'd missed her. 'Ania. Her name's Ania. Did she leave a message?'

'What do I know about messages? She doesn't talk to me.' Meaning he didn't talk to her. His family was hostile towards Ania.

Before he met her, Dariusz had been seeing Krysia, a secretary in the firm he worked for in Łódź. It had been a fairly casual relationship, but Beata had met Krysia when she visited once and the two women got on well. Beata, the youngest of the family, had been spoiled by her three elder brothers, and she was used to getting her own way. 'I like Krysia. She's right for the family. I need a sister. Why don't you get married, Dariusz? It's time you settled down.' She'd given him the blue eyes treatment and shaken her curls at him like she used to when she was small which made him laugh. 'A sister, hey? I'll have to see what I can do.'

His relationship with Krysia had just about run its course by that time, and his meeting Ania had brought it to an abrupt end. Dariusz hadn't handled it well – he had thought that Krysia felt much the same way he did, but Beata hadn't only been working on him. Encouraged by her, Krysia had seen the whole situation differently. The fall-out had reverberated around his work and around the family. It had been months before he and Krysia were able to work together comfortably. Beata had still not forgiven him.

Instead of blaming Dariusz, Beata had chosen to blame Ania who had waltzed into her brother's life, dazzled him with her wealthy western European glamour and stolen him away. She encouraged their father in his instinctive hostility. He didn't like the British anyway – the betrayal of Poland after the war still rankled with many of his generation. 'What was wrong with that Polish girl?' he'd grunted, when Dariusz had told him that he and Ania planned to marry.

Things were no better almost two years later. Now wasn't the time to have a row, but he was going to have a serious talk with Beata. She was the one who was fuelling this antagonism. He had no idea what lay behind her continuing hostility, but it had to stop. He settled his father down for the night, then tried Ania's mobile, but it was switched off.

He left a message and tried her hotel, but she wasn't back. He left a message there as well. He felt anxious, as though he'd let her down, and told himself not to be stupid. She must have phoned as she was leaving work, and she would try again once she got back to the hotel.

He'd have to wait for her to call.

But she didn't.

Chapter 9

Łódź, Poland 2007

It was nearly three in the morning. The clouds that had filled the sky earlier had cleared causing the temperatures to plummet, and the wet streets to freeze. The air carried the scent of snow.

The university caretaker, Jerzy Pawlak was reluctant to leave the cubbyhole that served as his office. He wanted to be away from here, he wanted to go home, but it would be a few hours yet before the day shift came in to relieve him at six, and he had the rest of the dragging night ahead of him in a deserted building. It was freezing. The authorities saved money by turning the heating off at midnight.

He had to do another round. He pulled on his heavy coat and tucked his torch into his pocket. The building was dark and shadowed. The entrance hall was high-ceilinged and open, the staircase protected with ornate metal bars, the stairwell illuminated by huge windows through which the light flooded during the day.

He climbed the stairs slowly, stopping off at each floor where the corridors vanished into the darkness. He walked along each one using his torch to dispel the shadows, ignoring the creaks and taps, the sharp patter like the sound of feet, all the noises that plagued the hours between sleeping and waking.

The building lay still and expectant around him.

It took him almost an hour to reach the top floor. As he climbed the last flight of stairs, he allowed himself to feel the relief of a task almost finished. Once he had done this, the main work of his night was almost over.

He reached the top landing and stopped. He could feel a draught flowing round his legs like a river of ice in the cold air.

There had been no draught when he had come up here earlier.

For the first time, he listened properly. He could hear the drip of a tap, the occasional clink of the plumbing, the low hum of the residual warmth in the pipes as it fought its losing battle with the night's chill. He touched one of the pipes. It was tepid as it leaked the last of its heat into the night air.

The draught was flowing from his left. He turned towards it across the open landing and went to the door that led into the offices. He unlocked it and pushed it open. He was in a small lobby with three doors opening off it. The draught was stronger here and he could feel himself starting to shiver – with cold? He wasn't sure.

He tried each door in turn.

They were locked. The first one was an empty classroom. He shone his torch round the chairs and tables, and at the windows that were all closed. The next room was a computer room and the equipment was valuable. He went in and checked the room carefully. The windows were all tight shut.

His feet slowed as he approached the last room, a small office. As he opened the door, a flood of icy air engulfed him. He turned on the light.

The window was wide open.

His gaze moved quickly round the room noticing the phone on the floor, the chair pulled up against the sill, a shoe, a woman's shoe discarded by the chair.

Then he was at the window, his hand reaching to shut it. Instead, he looked out.

Far below him was the car park, a concrete space of outbuildings and shadows. The silver of the moon was dimmed by the light from the window. On the ground, below the window, five storeys down, a shapeless bundle lay in a pool of something that gleamed black in the moonlight.

Chapter 10

It was Keeper's bark that alerted Will. It was her deep, insistent bark, the one that said her territory was under attack from intruders. He was out of bed in a moment and on the stairs, a boathook in his hand as he saw the lights sweep across the cottage windows, the light that announced a car passing by. He felt himself relax as the minutes passed.

Then he heard the knock.

Keeper's bark became frantic. He put his hand on her collar as he opened the door. Two police officers were standing there with tense expressions that he recognised. They had bad news to deliver and they didn't want to do it.

He let them in, sat down when they asked him to and listened blankly as they said what they had to say, knowing the words that meant nothing now would return with full meaning later, no matter how little he wanted to hear them. 'Your daughter... in a fall. Late last night... University. So sorry... Anything you need.' They were deferential, aware of the status he had held until a few weeks ago, a status that he would never quite lose.

Ania had tried to cheer him up after he had conceded defeat and walked away from his work. 'You'll become a rent-a-quote for the BBC,' she had teased him 'You'll be on Question Time and the Today programme.'

'That's not my style,' he said, half smiling and found himself looking into the puzzled face of the young PC as she offered him a glass of water.

'Sir, do you need us take you anywhere? Is there anyone we can call?' The man, obviously senior, wanting to help or wanting to disengage.

Nowhere. He wanted to be... nowhere. He wanted to be asleep in bed for a few more hours of blank unknowing. He wanted to be himself two days ago, saying to Ania: *don't get on that plane.* He wanted...

He needed time to think. He needed to be alone. 'Thank you. I'll... make my own arrangements.'

They left awkwardly, shuffling in the doorway in a mixture of concern and relief. They didn't know what to do for him so they were glad to get away from their own impotence. He wanted to tell them not to worry. They hadn't failed him. There was nothing anyone could do for him now.

He sat in his chair. Keeper rested her muzzle in his lap. 'Ania,' he said.

Keeper whined.

Look, you'll get a letter, OK? I don't want to take you unawares. Her voice spoke in his head, and he realised that tears were running down his face. He didn't know when they had started, and he didn't know how to stop them. 'You never sent it,' he said. The last letter, never posted, never arrived.

His daughter was dead.

The limbo of shock held him. He didn't know how long he sat there. He felt as though he was about to slip into – not quite sleep, but another kind of unconsciousness. He welcomed it. He wanted the world to be gone. He felt as though a fragile web was all that protected him from some dark pit where the full understanding of Ania's death lay, that the slightest jolt would cause it to rip apart and he would fall forever.

Brown Jenkin.

Brown Jenkin's on my back today.

He closed his eyes and let the grey nothingness take him.

Then she was shaking him. He opened bleary eyes and he could see the urgency on her face. *Please. You've got to hurry. I don't want them to find it!*

He sat up, blinking in bewilderment. 'Ania...?' Then he was properly awake. He was in his chair in the cottage. The ashes were grey in the fireplace and the cold was eating into him. Keeper was watching him uneasily from where she lay on the floor with her chin on her paws. She whimpered when she saw he was looking at her and it all came flooding back.

Ania.

There were things he had to do, things she needed him to do. He had to get to Edinburgh, find a flight to Poland. His passport – he tried to remember where he had put his passport.

He didn't even know how she had died. The two constables had tried to tell him, but he'd barely heard them. A fall. They'd

45

said something about a fall. He should phone the consul. Someone there would be able to... But he didn't want to talk to anyone. He didn't want to hear anyone say the words.

He logged on to the internet and found the reports at once. They were as clear and as stark as he could have wished.

DISGRACED VOICE PRINT EXPERT DIES IN FALL.

Ania had fallen from the fifth floor of a university building in the centre of Łódź at some time the previous night. She had been found in the small hours by a caretaker doing his usual rounds. The police were investigating.

Which meant that they would, sooner rather than later, contact the British authorities and any investigation might move to the UK.

I don't want them to find it!

Her flat in Manchester. She needed him to go to Manchester.

Chapter 11

Will left St Abbs at four in the morning, unable to sleep and unable to bear the inaction. He took Keeper to the caravan where Jack, the car park attendant lived, rousing him by hammering on the door. He explained to the bleary-eyed Jack what he wanted and pressed a fistful of notes into the man's hand. 'I'll be back in a few days,' he said, and scribbled down his number. He could feel Keeper's eyes following him as he headed back to the car and knew he was leaving behind the last living thing in the world that cared for him. He didn't know if he would ever see her again.

He drove on automatic pilot, taking stupid risks until he remembered that it would do Ania no good if he ended up smeared across the motorway in the remains of his car.

The roads were empty apart from lorries travelling through the night carrying goods from Scotland down south and beyond. Cars began to appear as he neared Southways. He pulled in at a lay-by where a van sold hot drinks and snacks. He got tea and a sandwich and sat in the car staring into the distance. His hand reached automatically for Keeper's head, expecting to encounter a cold nose as she tested the air for the scent of bacon, but she wasn't there.

The road blurred in front of his eyes. He threw away the rest of the sandwich and resumed his journey, putting his foot down as he headed south.

The roads were filling up by the time he reached the outskirts of Manchester and for the last few miles, he found himself in stop go traffic. Fatigue made everything bright and distant and he blinked his eyes to clear them. His hand hovered over the radio switch, and moved away.

Are we nearly there yet?

It always used to be him driving, Elžbieta in the seat beside him reading the map, the children in the back, Ania soon impatient with the inactivity of travelling, her books and her toys scattered around her on the seat. The question had started before they were a mile from home and it had taken all his ingenuity to distract her.

'Are we nearly there yet?'

Louisa, reading, glanced up without interest and when she saw nothing to catch her attention, returned to her book.

He made his standard response. 'Not long now,' he said.

Ania's flat was in a warehouse conversion just off Piccadilly Gardens. If he tried to drive to it, he would get caught in the one way system. He followed the signs to a multi-storey, winding up and up in a seemingly endless spiral until he found a space. He could see the brightness of the day sandwiched between the concrete blocks as he locked the car.

His legs felt like lead as he walked down the steps to street level.

Piccadilly was still a mess of redevelopment. Like all urban centres in Britain, Manchester was promoting city living as the ebbing tide of industry left behind vacated mills and warehouses, high, Victorian and decaying. There had been a frenzy of renovation and for a few heady years, property prices seemed to rise by the day.

The demands of his work meant they'd lived in cities all of their lives. He and Elžbieta had squeezed their income to the limit and taken on more debt than they should to give the children a private education. He'd objected to paying for something that should have been available by right but he didn't feel able to abandon his children to the jungle that was local education where they lived.

Ania would have survived but he'd wanted better than that for her, and Louisa… She was like a wood mouse in the undergrowth, watching, alert, vulnerable to predators.

He hated cities.

After his suspension he had fled the cities. It had been a city that had taken the life of his other daughter. But Ania loved them. The centre of Manchester had been her deliberate choice.

He stood in front of the now familiar building, looking up at the windows rising in rows, tall rectangles on the ground floor, then high arches in doubles and triples, then smaller, narrower arches, then tiny square windows and finally the dormers crammed into the roof that marked the studio apartments. Ania's flat was on the fourth floor. She had sacrificed the huge windows of the ground and first floors for the views and added security of being higher up.

High windows.

She had fallen from a top storey window, plummeting helplessly to her death. Her fall would have lasted only seconds but those seconds would have been an eternity. They were her eternity.

He couldn't think about it. He couldn't bear it. He was here at the flat and there were things he had to do.

He used the key she had given him to let himself in through the main entrance. The lobby was silent and empty. When he had come here before, he had walked along corridors with odd corners and niches where the builders had worked to fit modern flats into the irregularities of an old industrial building. Each front door was closed on silence. The building felt devoid of life, the redevelopment a mask that hid the decaying, rat infested warehouse it had once been.

He pressed the button for the lift. He'd used the stairs the last time he'd come here, wanting the extra exercise. Ania must have seen him arriving because she had been waiting in the doorway of her flat for him, the light spilling out in a welcome burst of life and colour.

As he came out of the lift, it was as if he'd stepped back in time. The door of the flat was standing open as he remembered it, and she was there, her fair hair cut in a soft bob round her face, wearing a red skirt and a black jersey.

'I'm here,' he said.

She shook her head and he realised he was on his own in the corridor, holding the key in his hand. The door still stood open, but it was hard daylight that pushed the shadows of the corridor back. He was too late. Someone was already there.

He stepped into the lobby, blinking in the sudden brightness. The door into the main room was wide open and the winter sun poured through the window, flooding the space with its chill light. A woman was moving along the book shelves, removing books, flicking through the pages, shaking them and replacing them with expert efficiency. A small collection of items had been placed on the low coffee table. He saw a laptop, various files, some sheets of paper, some computer disks.

The filing cabinet that stood on the corner by the desk was open and the hanging files had all been removed and put on the floor. As he stood there, a man came out of the door that led into the bedroom, saying, 'There's nothing in there. Are you done?'

Then they became aware of Will. He knew who they were, but he wasn't going to accept anything without proof. 'Who are you and what are you doing?'

The man came across the room quickly and stood in front of Will, a bit too close, as if to exclude him from the place.

'What are you doing in my daughter's flat?'

'I'm sorry, sir, I'll have to ask you to wait outside.'

'And I need to see your identification. I'm asking you again: what are you doing in my daughter's flat? Come on.' He snapped his fingers, deliberately insulting, and held his hand out for the man's ID.

The man flushed, but the woman had come across now. 'It's OK Bryant. We've finished here. Mr…'

'Gillen.'

There was a moment of silence. 'Of course. I'm very sorry about your daughter, sir. Here.' She held out her ID, indicating to the man to do the same.

He checked the IDs they proffered, surprised at first to see that they were both detectives rather than civilian scene of crime technicians. Except this wasn't a crime scene, nor had it been treated as one. Then he understood: this wasn't an investigation into her death. It was part of the other investigation, the investigation into the possible fabrication of evidence, a criminal investigation into Ania herself.

I don't want them to find it!

He was too late. He'd let her down.

'What are you looking for?' He spoke to the man, suspecting he would be the weaker link. He recognised the practised stonewalling in the woman's courtesy.

She answered him. 'You understand there's an ongoing investigation. We can't discuss it with you. I'm very sorry, sir.'

She wasn't going to tell him anything. He could admire her professionalism, even through his frustration.

'Is it necessary to take her computer?' All her documents would be on there.

'The hard drive on her office one has been wiped. We need to see if…'

That was the man. The woman spoke quickly, giving him a quelling glance. 'We have to check everything, sir.'

'Of course.' The woman was about to speak again but he gestured her to silence. He didn't want to talk any more. There was nothing else to say. The man was packing everything into a large box to carry it away. 'When will I get these back?'

'Someone will be in touch with you. We've done everything we need to here. Is there anything…?'

'No. Thank you.' He waited until he saw them getting into the lift, then he went into the flat. They had done a good job. Apart from the hanging files on the floor in front of the filing cabinet, there was no sign that a search had been carried out. He wondered if he had arrived half an hour later, would those files have been put away? Would he have ever known they had been here?

Chapter 12

Dariusz Erland stood motionless at the large window as the technician on the other side drew the sheet over the face and covered the body again. It was a merciful concealment that came too late. Ania in his memory was overlaid by the smashed distortion he had just seen and had just confirmed was, indeed, his fiancée, Ania Milosz.

She lay on her back on the trolley in a strange parody of peace. Her hair had been brushed back from her face and looked soft and silky. Someone must have washed away the blood and dirt.

And someone had crossed her arms on her breast, maybe assuming – a logical assumption in Poland – that she was a Catholic. When the technician had pulled the sheet back, the first thing he had noticed was those slender fingers, still delicately beautiful on her left hand, bruised and swollen on her right.

She had been recognisably Ania, that was the terrible thing.

He'd missed her call. When she'd phoned, just before ten the night before, he hadn't been there. All she had was his father's unfriendly dismissal. The last time they'd spoken, she had said, 'I'm looking forward to Friday.'

And now it was Friday. 'I'm here, *kiciu*.' Now it's too late, now you don't need me any more, I'm here.

Hurdy-gurdy music was playing in his head and the police officer led him away.

Chapter 13

Will stood in the centre of the room, breathing in the smell. All he could detect was new carpet, the faintest smell of paint, and a lingering, intrusive fragrance that the woman had left behind.

There was a pile of post on the table. He checked through it quickly, but there was only junk mail. If there had been anything interesting, they had taken it. His mind felt like cotton wool. He went into the kitchen. There was no milk in the fridge, but there was coffee in the cupboard. He made himself a cup which he drank black of necessity.

I don't want them to find it... That wasn't what she had said. When she'd spoken to him, she'd told him to expect a letter. *I don't want them to find it...* She'd said that in his dream.

All he knew was that someone had ordered her flat to be searched, and the search had had high priority. Given the thoroughness with which the two detectives had done their job, he wondered if there was any point in his looking. He felt the shadow of defeat weighing him down, and braced himself against it. She needed him.

He had an advantage over them. He knew Ania, and if there was something she had concealed, then he knew the ways she might have hidden it. But he was reluctant to start. He didn't want to disturb this last place where she had been. Her books were on the shelves, neatly arranged, some modern fiction, some classics, a battered copy of Alice in Wonderland. A sudden image formed in his mind, him, lying on a bed with a child at each side, reading to them about strange creatures swimming in a sea of tears.

There was an unframed photograph propped against the books, Ania, Louisa and Elżbieta on the beach surrounded by sand, spades, buckets, the detritus of a summer holiday.

His wife and both his daughters.

All dead.

The sheer effort of drawing the next breath seemed beyond him. He stood still and let the pain wash over him, through him, and away, taking him with it, and leaving behind the professional, the detective who had worked on hundreds of cases, the detective who could work on this. Someone was dead, and he was here to find out why. He went across to the small office she had set up in an alcove and began his own systematic search.

He checked the empty filing cabinet drawers inside and out before returning each file, going through it carefully as he did so. All he found were her financial papers, her accounts, household bills, a copy of her will that he couldn't bear to read and a note with the address of her solicitor. He jotted it down for future reference then checked the desk. The desk top was empty and the drawers were neatly filled with stationery. In the back of the middle drawer, there was a small cardboard box with a pattern of cartoon ponies. It was battered and faded. He lifted it out and opened the lid, but it was empty.

He knew it should contain childhood memorabilia and he felt a flash of anger with the two detectives for taking it.

He checked every photograph and every picture, making sure there was nothing concealed in the frames, knowing he would find nothing, knowing the police would have found it first.

If there was anything to find.

She had been depressed when she called him. The probability of the public scandal must have been there in her mind, somewhere. There must be private things here, things she didn't want made available to a rapacious press. If the police had them – her diaries, her letters, her e-mails – then they would find their way into the public domain. He knew how it worked.

He was all too familiar with the system.

***

Birmingham, 2005

John Blaise, the Assistant Chief Constable for Security and Cohesion in the West Midlands, leaned back in his chair. 'What are you saying, Will?'

'You've read my report. Sir. There was nothing in that house. Nothing. It was clean.'

'And you... *We*, it wasn't just you, Will, *we* got it wrong.'

They'd been given the warning in the small hours on the day of the raid: a bomb factory was operating, the threat was imminent. They had to move fast, get in, and neutralise it. A textbook operation, except one person had managed to get out of the house before Will's team was in place.

'Sir, I need to know – the people on my team need to know – where that information came from.'

A faint line appeared between Blaise's eyes. 'I can't tell you, Will. You know that.'

'We killed a man. Someone on my team killed a man. Sir.'

'The intelligence came from a reliable source. That's all I can say.'

He looked at Blaise. 'You'll have my resignation tomorrow.'

And Blaise had smiled and shaken his head slowly. 'No, Will. We aren't doing it like that.'

Politically, the whole event had been a major embarrassment. There was no bomb-making equipment in the house and no evidence that there had ever been. Soon after the raid, Will had been suspended, his team facing an enquiry. Blaise had quietly moved to a different area of operations. At the time he'd said to Will, 'If someone had set out to damage us deliberately they couldn't have done a better job.'

***

He was right. Will, as senior officer, was left sitting out a long suspension; his team – a group of experienced, professional officers – was disbanded. Two of them had resigned through stress. Will had stayed, because the alternative was to be sacked and leave his team to face it on their own. Six weeks ago, the enquiry had made its findings public. No blame had been attached to his men. He himself had been criticised, but allowed to take early retirement instead of being disgraced.

The matter was closed, except for the memory of the 17-year-old boy who had been shot dead on a dank platform at Birmingham New Street station.

Chapter 14

Will came reluctantly back to the present. His head felt light and the sharp delineation of the room around him gave it a sense of unreality. The clock on the wall jerked through one minute. It was after eleven. He hadn't eaten since he'd taken a bite from that sandwich on his journey down, hours ago. He wasn't hungry, but he needed to keep his strength up. Ania still needed him. There were things he had to do.

He went into the small kitchen – when he'd first seen the flat, he'd made disparaging comments about the kitchen being designed for microwaving ready meals, so when he came to visit, she'd often cooked for him, making elaborate dishes that she served up with cool éclat.

He saw her again, just for a moment, standing at the work surface. It was summer and the evening light was flooding into the room. She was wearing a grey camisole and black trousers, her fair hair hanging forward over her face. He could see where it was cut short at the back, and the little 'v' of hair at the top of her neck. She turned round and smiled as if she were going to say something, and then the image faded.

They'd argued that day about the Haynes case. He had been worried that she was taking it on for the wrong reasons. In the end, she'd been angry with him. 'Haynes isn't just a sad pervert,' she'd said. 'The SIO on the case – that guy Cathcart I told you about – he thinks Haynes is part of an organised group, that the videos of Sagal were made to order. What we've got is just the tip of the iceberg. Haynes probably filmed her death. Cathcart thinks it involves influential people, people with money, people in charge. Someone's been getting in the way of the investigation. If I can do something to stop just one person…'

'You shouldn't get personally involved. You have to be dispassionate. The best expert witnesses are impartial.'

'I am impartial,' she said. 'I'll do the analysis and tell them what I find. That doesn't mean I have to feel any compassion for Haynes.'

But she hadn't been impartial. In a case like this she could never be impartial.

His eyes felt sore and he brushed at them with the back of his hand. He went to the fridge and opened the door. There was a loaf of bread still in its wrapper. It would be stale and dry, but he could toast it. There was some cheese, some salad leaves that were brown at the edges and an open bottle of white wine in the door.

He found a bin liner in the cupboard. He left the cheese and the bread on the work top, and dumped everything else. He made himself some cheese on toast, then went back into the main room carrying his plate. The low winter sun didn't reach the windows at the front, and he switched on the lamp to relieve the dimness.

As he ate, he tried to take stock. He had no idea what to do next – he had come here in the daze of shock, trying to fulfil some request he wasn't even sure Ania had made. He felt old. He had aches in his joints that he'd never noticed before. There were things that had to be done, but he was reluctant to leave the flat. It was a last haven, as if a trace of Ania's presence was still here, but once he left, it would go and he would have lost her forever. Slowly, he put the papers back into her filing cabinet. Whatever it was she wanted him to find, it wasn't here, not any more.

All he had to do now was check through her clothes. He went into the bedroom and opened the drawers in the tallboy. It felt wrong to be sorting through the silky underwear, all the lace and frills that reminded him his daughter was a woman, with a woman's life. There was a drawer full of carefully folded knitwear and tops, each one smelling of soap and cleanness. He found the grey camisole she'd worn last time he was here, and held it to his face, picking up the faintest fragrance that brought her vividly into his mind again. He couldn't stand it. He shoved it back where he had found it.

The bottom drawer contained miscellany: heavy walking socks, exercise sweats, a faded swimming costume, and, at the back of the drawer, another photograph. Two children waved at him from a playground climbing frame. One of them was sitting high up, hazardously secured by one leg hooked over a bar, the other was kneeling at the top of the slide. The sky was the pale blue of forget-me-nots.

He sank back onto the bed and closed his eyes. He was looking into a terrible emptiness. He didn't know what to do next. He didn't know, because now both his children were dead.

***

It had been one of those hot August days towards the end of summer. They were planning a holiday – a fortnight's camping in the south of France. They'd planned to leave that day, but then he'd had to work.

'You could go on ahead,' he'd said to Elżbieta.

'No way. It'll just give you an excuse to take on more work. Tell them you are on leave, as of tomorrow.' She'd tapped his arm with a peremptory finger and held his gaze.

He'd laughed. She was accusing him of not pulling his weight, but he was looking forward to the break. He'd planned to take Ania canoeing on the Orb. He'd tried to interest Louisa, but when he'd taken them to a stretch of the river one weekend where it was safe for beginners to learn, she had taken one look at the small boat and the wide river, at people doing rolls and retrieving themselves in the water, and refused to have anything to do with it.

He and Ania had ended up on the river together, while Louisa watched them from the bank. Ania's small face had been set with determination as she had steered the canoe, done rolls, paddled herself up and down the stream while Louisa read her book.

He'd been proud of Ania and hadn't attempted to hide it. Louisa had watched him, casting quick glances from behind the hair that tumbled across her face. She had known he was disappointed in her for not being braver.

He wondered afterwards if Ania had used that. Sometimes, they quarrelled, fought over the things that seemed so trivial to adults and so important to children. Maybe there had been a disagreement in the playground – Ania, white-faced and distraught over her missing twin, had never mentioned anything.

She had never said anything since, but it was after Louisa's death that the depressions she came to personalise as Brown Jenkin began to stalk her through her life.

Come on the monkey bars! Come on!

You do it. I don't want to.

You can't! You're useless. Can't do the monkey bars, can't canoe!

Shut up! Shut up!

Just a quarrel between children who were irritable and disappointed, children who were sometimes rivals for their father's affection.

And somewhere in the shadows of the trees, a monster had been waiting.

It was a figure that had lived in the back of his head since the day of Louisa's abduction. Then, he had believed that one day – and soon – the monster would be forced into the daylight of identification, exposed, convicted, destroyed.

More than anything, he wanted to look into the eyes of his daughter's killer. But he never had. All he was left with was the monster lurking in the shadows, Brown Jenkin who had come back and claimed his surviving child.

Chapter 15

Will realised he still had the photograph clutched in his hands. He looked at it, and saw with surprise the marks on the paper where tears had fallen. He wiped his hands over his face. He didn't have time for this.

Ania was standing by the window looking out over the city. As he became aware of her, she turned round and smiled at him, opened her mouth to speak.

The phone rang.

His head jerked up. He'd been daydreaming. He was sitting on the bed with the photograph in his hands, and he'd drifted away. The phone buzzed insistently. He located it on the dressing table. Ania's phone. Someone was calling her. He hesitated for a moment, then picked it up. 'Yes?'

'Will? Is that you?'

It was John Blaise, the familiar Yorkshire voice sounding firm and reassuring. The last time he'd seen Blaise was when Will had accepted the offer that Blaise had made him: no resignation, nothing to stir up the press. Retire under the conditions we are laying down and your reputation intact; or you and your team face the consequences.

The threat to the people who had worked for him over the past five years had made the decision for him. He had accepted.

'Yes.' He didn't bother asking how Blaise knew he was here. Blaise had probably known his movements from the time the news about Ania first broke.

'Will. I've been trying to call you all morning. Then I realised where you'd be.'

'My phone was switched off. I drove down from the cottage as soon as… early. I drove down early.'

'It's a bad business, Will. I can't tell you how sorry I am.'

There didn't seem anything to say.

'It's a tragedy,' Blaise went on. 'We all get over-enthusiastic at some time or another. She had strong feelings about the case, of course she did. How much do you know?'

'I know she fell. That's all.'

'I got on to the people over there.' Will heard a rustle of paper. 'They were very good. They've sent me copies of all the statements, everything they've got so far. It's early days of course. How much do you want me to tell you?'

'Everything.'

'OK. Now, the set up – well, you know that. This guy Karzac, her boss, he franchises a lot of their work over there. They knew Ania well – they're gutted. The man in charge…' There was a rustle of paper. 'Jankowski, Konstantin Jankowski. He says that they knew there was something wrong. She wasn't like herself. She was very quiet, very subdued. Now usually she organised her own accommodation, but this time she needed somewhere to stay – she arrived earlier than they expected so they put her up in the university accommodation outside the city. Pretty place by all reports, but maybe not the best if you're feeling a bit low. It's out in the middle of the woods, long way from anywhere. They said that she got straight down to work. That bit was fine – she got her head down and got on with it. Anyway, that evening she was working late – seems they had a bit of a backlog. This Jankowski character said he asked her if she wanted to go for a drink when he left. That was around eight. She said no, she wanted to get the stuff out of the way. That's the last time he saw her.

'The security guard that found her was doing the rounds in the small hours. He found the window open – she was on the ground below. Five storeys – it was a long drop. The police can confirm that was the window she fell from. Her prints were on the glass and on the sill. She hit her head on an overflow pipe on the way down. Cast iron. They found… Well, evidence. She was dead, Will. She probably died when she hit that pipe. She wouldn't have been conscious when she hit the ground, that's certain. The fall would have killed her instantly. Her neck was broken.'

Will shut the images out of his mind. 'So what's the progress on the investigation?'

The silence stretched for a moment too long. 'Will, you have to understand the set-up they found. The office door was locked. The key was in her pocket. And she left a note.'

His response was instant. 'I don't care what she left. She didn't do that.'

I tried to tell you. I did what I had to. Brown Jenkin was on my back.

Blaise's voice was gentle. 'I know it's not what you want to hear. I know it's hard to believe that Ania of all people… But she was in a bad mess, Will. When it all started coming out, I thought about you. I should have got in touch at once, but I thought you wouldn't want… reminders. I've seen the reports. She didn't make a mistake. She falsified the evidence. She would have been facing criminal charges for perjury. There's no doubt about that.'

Will remained silent. Everything in him wanted to reject what Blaise was telling him, but he had seen the start of the investigation himself.

'I looked for all the loopholes, Will. I didn't want to believe it any more than you do. But no one else tampered with that evidence – she worked with the originals. They were delivered to her under police seal. And she stood by that analysis in court. What she did was planned. She perverted the course of justice and she may have sent an innocent man to jail – or given a guilty one a way out. They were going to throw the book at her. The maximum sentence for perverting the course of justice is life. Now she wouldn't have got that, but five years? More? Will, that's what she was facing.'

Now he didn't have anything to argue with. One by one, Blaise had knocked down the arguments he was trying to put forward. Ania wasn't a quitter. She never had been. She could have faced down the public shaming. But jail. He didn't think Ania could have stood the prospect of going to prison – not if she was contemplating it when she was ill, tired and alone. And he'd been too dazed from sleep to hear the dread in her voice that must have been there.

She hadn't phoned to warn him it was going wrong: she'd phoned for help, and he'd let her down. *Brown Jenkin's on my back today.* Of course he was. And Will could have helped – he still had all his contacts, he could have got good witnesses to back her up. He could have got her the best defence. Medical witnesses – if she'd done what Blaise had implied, there must have been something wrong with her. He could have saved her from jail, he knew he could.

Why hadn't she asked him? 'I could have helped you!'

Her smile was rueful. 'There was nothing wrong with me, Dad. I was of sound mind, isn't that what they say?'

'Then… *why*?'

But her voice had faded and he could hear Blaise speaking again. '… anything I can do. You know that.'

'There is.'

'Name it.' Blaise sounded relieved.

'I want the contact for the senior officer over there. I want the introduction to come from you so they'll take me seriously. And I want to see the note she left.'

There was silence while Blaise considered this. 'OK. I'll do that for you, Will, because I trust you. But you've got to promise me you'll keep out of it. I don't want you barging in on their work, right?'

'I won't.'

'You're a relative, not an investigator.'

'I know.'

There was silence again then Blaise said, 'I can let you have a copy of the note. It was addressed to you.'

Just watch out for the letter, OK?

He couldn't breathe. The pain seemed to crush his chest. The letter. The letter that had never arrived – she was warning him what she planned to do. She had gone there to die. The letter she had promised him, the letter she had written to him… 'I want that. It…'

'It's part of the evidence Will. If you're sure you want it, I'll get a copy to you. I can e-mail it.'

'She left it for me.'

'OK, Will. OK. It's done. Now, you know where I am – if there's anything, I mean it…'

'One more thing. I want to see her.' The words were out before Will had realised he was going to say them.

'No you don't. You know what jumpers… What people who've fallen look like.'

'I want to see her.'

He heard Blaise sigh. 'Will, the overflow pipe stove her head in. Don't do that to yourself. Do you think she'd have wanted you to see her like that?'

She wouldn't.

Blaise recognised the assent in his silence. 'Call me if you need anything else.'

Will sat in the chair for a long time after he had put the phone down. The images were pouring into his mind unstoppably. He didn't even try to stop them. Ania, sitting in a room alone. He couldn't see the room. He had no image in his mind. All he could see was his daughter, sitting at a desk with her bowed head resting on her hand.

Thinking.

Round and round. It must have gone round and round.

No way out.

No way out.

She'd come to do this, but now she was here... Maybe she'd tried to call him at the cottage, maybe he'd been asleep and hadn't heard the phone.

She picked up the phone, keyed in a number. Listened, then put the phone back down.

It was getting dark and she was on her own with no one to talk to. Just an empty room in an empty building. Offices were lonely places after hours, the silence where there had been the bustle of people, the sound of her footsteps echoing along the corridors.

Perhaps she would have changed her mind, but all she had to go back to was her room in an isolated block in the middle of the forest, somewhere else to sit alone and think. She was exhausted from the stress and the worry, but the stress and the worry wouldn't let her sleep.

No way out.

The window was in the centre of her vision, the solution she had come here to find, the escape route her mother had used when she had left them, when her life became unbearable.

There would just be the drop, maybe a moment... then all her troubles would be over. If, *if* she made the final decision, then she didn't need to worry any more. Her gaze wandered round the room, passed over the window, closed and locked against the night, then came back.

Stopped.

Stayed.

She stood up and pushed the window open. The sky was dark and cloudy. Climbing up onto the sill didn't mean she had decided anything, it just meant…

Thinking about it. Just thinking about it.

The intensity of this moment took away the gnawing stress. This was something she could focus on. But each time she inched herself forward, just a bit, towards the drop, she came closer to the point of no return, the point when the decision was made for her.

The winter wind was strong up here, cutting through her clothes and chilling her fingers as they gripped the window frame. The brick wall dropped away below her, sheer, down to the dark and empty car park.

Her foot slipped and she grabbed frantically for something to steady her. The shock brought her back to her senses and she knew she didn't want to die down there. Her hand closed round the edge of the frame and she breathed again.

OK. It's OK.

But the metal frame was slick and her grip was failing. Her feet had no purchase on the sill that tilted away and down, worn smooth by decades of wind and rain. Time slowed as her hands scrabbled frantically for something, anything that would restore her equilibrium.

Then her foot slipped into space and the frame was torn from her grip.

After that, there was the fall.

'Ania!'

He sat upright. He must have drifted off into a twilight world between sleeping and waking. It was a place he never wanted to go again. 'Why?' he shouted. 'For God's sake! Why did you do it?'

But he had let her die in his mind, and there was no reply.

Chapter 16

*From **The Rules of Interrogation**, a paper presented to The International Conference on the Threat of Global Terrorism by John Martell Blaise, London, March 2003*

Finally, I think we can all agree that as a means of getting information, so-called robust interrogation – let's call a spade a spade here, we're talking about torture – is flawed. Personnel involved in questioning suspects don't want it and they don't need it. It isn't a useful tool. History teaches us that, over and over again.

There are, however, situations in which the judicious use of coercive interrogation can enhance techniques known to be reliable, and here I think our laws can be restrictive.

Psychological methods of interrogation are effective and we can prove that. In situations of national or even international threat, these should not be considered in the same light as methods of physical coercion. The lowering of an individual's threshold of vulnerability can only be desirable. Well-attested methods of disrupting sleep patterns, inducing unfounded fear, physical discomfort, isolation can lead a suspect to cooperate with the authorities. Until such methods are freely available to our own security forces, we shouldn't reject out of hand the possibility of, if you like, outsourcing (*laughter*) this work to interrogation teams who have more leeway. Carefully supervised, these methods can provide our own security forces with valuable, with life-saving, information.

<u>Q&A</u>

Question: I'd like to thank the speaker for a clear, lucid and rational account of the issues facing people working in our field. I would be interested in the speaker's view of the death penalty. Surely the threat of this is the ultimate psychological weapon?

Answer: As we know to our cost, the possibility of martyrdom can be an inducement rather than a disincentive. Death offers an end to any form of coercive interrogation that may, at the time, seem desirable to the subject. If we imposed the death penalty for parking offences, I'm sure we'd solve our parking problems overnight. Otherwise, I'm not impressed. (*Laughter*)

Chapter 17

The company Ania worked for was based in an old school building on the edge of the city centre regeneration area. It had been an astute move on the part of Oz Karzac – he had acquired offices on a premium site for a guaranteed low rent and as the regeneration bulldozer rolled over the area, the company became eligible for compensation to cover the expense of moving to the new, modern premises that were waiting for them in the city centre when the building was demolished.

Will had only been there once before. The old school was in the middle of a warren of residential streets, the red brick terraces that were typical of Manchester. The building itself was single storey, small, stone-built, with a glass and concrete extension that probably dated from the late 1960s. The playground had become a car park. Will found a gap and edged carefully in next to a Lexus LX, the incongruity of a high-end vehicle in these poor streets reminding him of Sarah Ludlow's BMW in St Abbs.

The company sign over the door partly obscured the word *Infants* that was carved in the stone lintel above the entrance. Ania had made a joke about it as she showed him in.

The faint school smell of chalk and cooking still seemed to hang around the place and the cream paint added to the institutional effect. He went to the small window in the wall marked *Reception* and rang the bell.

'I'm here to see Professor Karzac,' he said to the woman who answered his summons.

'Do you have an appointment? He's…'

'I'm Ania Milosz's father.' His voice seemed to echo around the bleak space.

The woman dropped her pen. 'Ania's… I'm so sorry. We all are. We…'

'I need to see Professor Karzac.'

'Of course. Yes. Just… Please. Take a seat. Can I get you…?'

He shook his head and waited while she made the call.

'Professor Karzac is on his way, Mr Milosz...'

He didn't correct her. 'Thank you.' He walked away from the window and looked at the notice board on the wall. Someone had put up a rogues' gallery of staff members with a brief outline of their expertise: *Darren Greaves, digital forensics; Oz Karzac (Director) forensic phonetics, CCTV analysis and enhancement, speaker profiling; Penny Jones...*

He stood in front of it, looking at the faces, looking at people Ania had worked with every day, most of whom he'd never met. Her picture wasn't there. There was a space where a photograph had been removed. A torn piece of paper stuck to the board as if it had been taken down in a hurry: *...eaker profilin...*

A door at the other side of the lobby opened and Oscar Karzac came through. Karzac was a plump man with a neat white beard and bright eyes. Ania had once described him as Father Christmas. He usually exuded bonhomie and a casual charm that must have served him well in the business world. His grip, as he took Will's hand, was firm, but his face was drawn and weary. 'I'm sorry,' he said. 'More sorry than I can say. Come through to my office – we can talk in there.'

Karzac led him into a small, cluttered room. The desk was barely visible under piles of paper and books, and the shelves that lined every wall were stacked high with boxes, books and envelope folders with papers falling out. 'Sorry about the mess,' Karzac said unapologetically. 'We're getting ready for the move and we're desperate for space.' He cleared a stack of folders from a chair and looked round for somewhere to put them, settling on the floor. 'Please. Sit down. Liz will bring coffee.'

Will didn't want to wait. 'What happened?' he said. 'The Haynes case. How did she get it so wrong?'

Karzac took out a pair of spectacles and settled them on his nose, then he studied Will over the top. 'How much do you know?'

'That my daughter was facing charges of perverting the course of justice.'

Karzac held his gaze then gave a single, abrupt nod. 'Yep. She probably was. If she'd talked to me, given me some warning, I might have been able to do something, but it just blew up in my face. The first thing I knew was when I got a heads up from our liaison guy on the investigation team – he warned me that Haynes' appeal lawyers were going after Ania's evidence.'

'When was that?'

'Monday. The day before she flew to Poland.'

'What else did he tell you?'

'That was all, but he sounded concerned.'

'So what did you do?'

'I went to Ania, of course, and told her.'

'And she…?'

Karzac held Will's gaze. 'I think she was expecting it.'

'Expecting…? How do you work that out?'

'She wasn't surprised.'

'Worried? Concerned?'

'No, not as such. Just… not surprised.'

Will filed that for further consideration. 'OK. Then what?'

'I asked her to check everything and write a report for me. She was leaving for Poland later that week, so I'd have to deal with whatever it was they thought they'd found.'

'How could she check? The police must have taken all the recordings.'

'No. We hold the evidence here. All the digital forensics in the area is handled by these labs. The rule is: you don't touch the original unless you have no other way of analysing the data, you work from copies. Voice analysis we have to do from originals, but Ania always took copies as well – you never know if something's going to be booby trapped. She was qualified to do that – all our staff are. This is...' He shook his head. 'The implications of this for us...'

'Ania did her checks on the originals?'

'No. Those are sealed. She was going to do her checks using the copies. She was getting started on it when I left that evening.'

'And then?'

Karzac's bluff assurance faded and he looked confused. 'I don't know. She said she would e-mail me at home if anything came up – you know, if she found any serious problems. Ania's a professional and defence lawyers – they'll grab anything. Someone farts on a recording and they think they've found the holy grail. I wasn't too worried but I'll admit I was relieved when she didn't send me anything. It was just another legal team having a go. Good luck to them. I expected to find her report on my desk when I went in the next day. *Nada*. First thing Liz tells me is that Ania had changed her flights. She'd left that morning. Gone, just like that, and she wasn't answering her phone. I was pretty pissed off by then. I went to her office to see if there was anything there, and when I switched on her computer, I found that she'd wiped it. The whole lot was gone. Even our technician couldn't retrieve anything and we employ the best. She'd cleaned out her filing cabinet – all her notes for the Haynes case and all the copies of the recordings.'

Will sat in silence. What he had just heard was damning. 'You're sure it was Ania?'

'Who else? This place is secure. The alarms were set and the CCTV didn't show anything, except Ania leaving the building that evening.' He took off his glasses and slipped them in his pocket. His gaze met Will's and held it. 'She was carrying a box that looked as though it was full of papers.'

And a few hours later, she had made that odd call to him from the airport. He wanted to go back in time, to be woken up again by the sound of the phone cutting through the storm.

Ania, tell me what's wrong. Let me help you.

'When did she change her flights?'

'Monday night. Look, I am truly sorry about what's happened to her. I didn't know she suffered from depression until Liz told me. If I had known, I'd have thought twice about giving her the case. Hell, I can understand what happened. Anyone would. But I can't protect her. That's with the DPP and the courts now. She didn't have to run away. We'd have helped her get psychiatric reports, all that stuff. I think they might have been lenient.'

Will didn't think so. Depression was no excuse. Even with Ania's background, the history she'd tried so hard to conceal, it was difficult to find extenuating circumstances. If she had fabricated those tapes, it had been premeditated and calculated. *If* she'd done it, she had stood by it in court and watched Haynes convicted. It couldn't be glossed over as the impulse of a moment, quickly regretted. And it *wasn't* understandable. Anyone would want a predatory paedophile convicted, but no

71

one would want an innocent man imprisoned for the rest of his life.

'If she did it…' He still wasn't prepared to accept that she had. He couldn't. 'If she did it, how could she have altered the recordings without the police spotting it?'

'The recording – it wouldn't have been difficult for Ania to replace it. Technically, it's no challenge at all. The difficult bit is making the new recording. It had to be Haynes' voice. She had to have enough recorded speech from Haynes to take it apart and put it together again to make an authentic sounding disk.'

'So where would she have got that?'

'She had about twelve hours of police interviews. They'd given her those for comparison. She must have faked the recording using those. That's the hard bit. It would have been a major job. It isn't just finding the words and phrases. They have to be the same volume and tone, people's voice quality changes – if your mouth gets dry, your voice sounds different, if you're anxious or tired, that affects it too, so if you put a recording together like that, you end up with a kind of aural Frankenstein – you can hear the stitches.'

'So…'

Karzac's face hardened. 'We have a technician here, Shaun, who's a genius with sound recordings. He's developed some software that can isolate stuff that we couldn't do before. While she was doing the analysis, Ania asked him to smooth something out for her. She said there was some fuzz – clicks and glitches – on something she was working on. He did it for her – why wouldn't he? But he was developing the software at the time so he kept recordings of anything he'd done. He checked them when the news broke. It was the Haynes material. I listened to it. It was almost perfect – there were just some bits where you could tell that there was something going on. If I hadn't known what I was listening for, I would have missed it. Of course, once you spotted it, it was a dead giveaway. She got Shaun to complete the last bit of the fabrication and now I'm going to have to work hard to convince the police he wasn't in on it.'

'Was he?'

'Of course not. He wouldn't even have listened to it. He'd just have taken out the bits she didn't want. I find it hard to forgive her for that. He's a talented guy and she implicated him in what she did. He's going to carry the Haynes debacle with him for a long time.'

And once she had that, she could load it onto the hard disc she had been given by the police, destroying the original evidence in the process. Will tried to picture her at her desk, working intently as she carefully put together fabricated evidence that would convict a man of a crime that carried a life sentence with an almost certain whole-life tariff.

She wouldn't have done that.

She wouldn't.

But you aren't sure, are you? Her voice in his head was sudden and shocking.

'Ania!'

Karzac looked at him with alarm. 'Gillen. Will. Can I…'

'Ania…' He calmed his voice with an effort. 'Do you think she would have done that?'

Karzac's hesitation was an answer in itself. 'She was very down on Haynes. She worked closely with the police team and she kind of got on board with their picture of the case. She said she didn't like paedophiles. As if any of us did. She worked late on it most nights – she said she didn't want that video playing when there were other people around. It wasn't healthy, her on her own here and that… thing, playing. I never wanted her to take the case. I told the SIO I'd do it, but I was away when it came in. By the time I'd got back, Ania was working on it and the police didn't want any changes. I should have realised how obsessed she was getting.'

Self-recrimination was an easy way out: easy words to say, with no penalties attached.

Had Sagal Akindès, the murdered child, become Louisa in Ania's mind? Listening to the recording, watching the video must have brought back that day in the park, must have filled in the gaps that none of them had wanted to think about. Would that have been enough?

Karzac cleared his throat. 'It seemed as though…'

Will didn't want to talk about it any more. He interrupted before Karzac could complete what he was going to say. 'If there's anything of hers left here, I'll take it with me.'

Karzac nodded. 'The police took some stuff. I asked Liz to pack the rest of it up.'

Will had to use his arms to push himself up out of his chair.

'Are you going to Łódź?' Karzac stood up as well.

'Yes. As soon as I can get a flight.'

'Do you want any contacts? If you let me know when you're going, I could…'

'I don't know. Yet. I'll be in touch.'

He collected the small box from reception that contained Ania's few possessions. Slowly, heavily, feeling like an old man, he left the building. He went back to his car and eased himself in behind the wheel.

'Why?' he said out loud. 'Why did you do it?'

But she couldn't – or wouldn't – tell him.

Chapter 18

DCI Ian Cathcart was a tall, energetic man. He had agreed to meet Will as soon as he had phoned shortly after leaving FLS. His old rank still had its privileges. 'We're gutted,' Cathcart had said when Will called to arrange a time to see him. 'She was one of the team. Just let me know how I can help.' He didn't seem to be angry with Ania, just confused.

He greeted Will with a vigorous handshake and took him into his office, a small room that was barely large enough for the basic desk, chair and filing cabinet it contained. It was meticulously tidy, the desk clear, the in-tray holding only a single sheet of paper, a list of tasks and dates written neatly on a whiteboard on the wall.

Cathcart pulled a chair in from the main office into the room, kicked the door shut behind him then said, 'OK. What can I do?'

'I want to know what happened.'

Cathcart shook his head. 'I've gone over it a hundred times. It doesn't make any sense to me.'

'Do you think she did it?'

Reluctantly, Cathcart nodded. 'She must have done. But I can't understand why.'

'Tell me about the case. Tell me about Ania's involvement.'

Cathcart sighed, blowing his cheeks out as he thought. 'It's hard to know where to start. We were investigating a disappearance, a kid. That makes everyone a bit tense. But it was an odd case. She was in Moreton. It's a detention centre south of Manchester. The family were waiting to be deported. The father had already been sent back, but one of the kids – the girl – wasn't well enough to travel. That gave the mother enough time to find a good solicitor and they were fighting it every inch.'

'Why were they in a centre?' As far as Will understood it, families with children were put in flats or houses.

'The father was involved with a radical Muslim group. He was arrested and the mother absconded with the kids, so they had to go into detention. It was after the father had gone that the little girl disappeared. It wasn't the mother that reported it – it was staff at the centre. The mother wasn't saying anything. We thought she'd smuggled the kid out to stop her from being sent back. We were worried – the kid was only eight – but it didn't look like an abduction, not then. It was a couple of weeks later when the paedophile unit found some photographs on the net – the missing girl – and there were some serious questions being asked.

'The location of the photos – it was a basement in one of the outbuildings of the centre. You have to ask: how much did the mother know? Someone's making kiddie porn using her daughter not a hundred yards from where she is. Some people reckon she had to know.'

'Why?' The logic didn't follow. 'The person who abducted her…'

'These pictures had been posted before the abduction. They were a kind of – I don't know – *aperitif*. Watch this space if you want to see more, kind of thing.'

Then there had been a long-term abuser at the detention centre.

'We didn't find the kid until a few weeks later. She'd been shoved into a ditch, covered up with branches.'

There was something horribly familiar about this story: an abducted child whose body had been hidden in a ditch. Louisa had been found in a drain by the river in the park, dumped like a bit of rubbish someone had no further use for.

'It was our paedophile unit that broke the case. They monitor the chat room scene and they found those first pictures. Here.' He pushed a folder across the table to Will.

Will picked it up reluctantly and slipped out one of the sheets. It was a print-out from an internet site, grainy images of a child dancing in a short, frilly skirt and strapless top, smiling flirtatiously at something just beyond the camera, enjoying the attention and the dressing up. Even with the poor quality of the print, he could see it had been taken by a good photographer. There was a real sense of movement in the image. The child had just completed a twirl, and the camera had caught the way her skirt had momentarily flounced up, revealing the edge of white, lacy knickers. It was a parody of a cheesy glamour shot, the partly clothed one before the real images that were to follow.

He saw that her feet were in sparkly party shoes. He felt sick. Louisa had had a pair of shoes like that. She had loved them.

The scene around the dancing child was incongruous. There was a brick wall behind her. Metal shelves ran along the wall and Will could see a box with torn flaps, a coil of wire, a lidless tin full of nails, the detritus of a place that was used for long-term storage, cold, damp and neglected.

He looked away. He didn't need to see any more.

'We knew someone in the centre had to be involved. Someone who knew how to bypass the security systems had taken her out. The kid's mother said it was Haynes, said he'd handed her over to someone in the support group, someone called Dave, she claimed.'

'Did you ever find Dave?'

'What do you think?'

'Wasn't that enough for a conviction?'

Cathcart grimaced. 'Haynes denied it, and the mother wasn't a reliable witness. That's why Ania's evidence was so important. The computer wasn't enough. Thing was, it wasn't his computer, not exclusively. It was in his office but other people had access to it. The files were hidden. It was conceivable that someone could have put them there without Haynes knowing. We had to identify him as the abuser. Ania told us she couldn't pin the voice to Haynes, not 100%, they can't do that yet, but she could eliminate the other users. And she could say if the voice was consistent with being Haynes'. That's what she did.' He frowned. 'I can remember when we found the recording, she came in and talked to the team. We'd heard the voice and we couldn't tell if it was Haynes or not. She listened to it a few times, and she gave us an off-the-cuff profile.'

***

Central Police Station, Manchester 2006

One of the DCs had bypassed all the modern equipment and had recorded the video sound onto an audio cassette using a machine he'd dug out of the back of some cupboard. It gave the recording an echoey, metallic quality. Cathcart, making a mental note to give the man a bollocking, could see Ania Milosz grimace as she listened to it. When it came to an end, she pressed the button and replayed it without comment.

Cathcart stayed where he was, sitting on the edge of his desk and waited. When it had played for the second time, she snapped off the machine and looked at him. 'OK. This is just a preliminary assessment. Your equipment is lousy, by the way.'

He grinned in rueful acknowledgement. 'What can you tell me?'

'He comes from Lancashire,' she said. 'There are some characteristics in the vowels and the way he pronounces the "l" that is very distinctive of that area – it's usually a feature that's gained in early childhood, and it tends to stay unless someone makes a real effort to change it.'

Cathcart felt depression settle over him at the prospect of working with another expert who went all around the houses to tell them what they had already worked out for themselves. OK, the guy was local. Big surprise.

If she was aware of his reaction, she didn't show it. 'Listen to the way he pronounces the "r",' she said. She let a small part of the recording play and the flat, dead voice spoke into the sudden silence:

...that's right...

...over here...

She played it again, and again. *That's right, that's right, that's right. Over here, over here, over here...* 'That's interesting. It's quite restricted, that pronunciation. You'll find it north of Manchester, Rochdale or Accrington if you're looking at urban centres. You'll find it in the country areas around Preston and in the north of the county. It's a feature that's vanishing. I'd be surprised to find it in a young man – I'd say he's thirty plus, possibly older.'

'OK.' That was better. It wasn't enough, but it was something.

She hadn't finished. 'Listen to the way he says *get* and *it*. He's saying them higher in the mouth than a Lancashire speaker – than any English speaker – would. And the way he says the vowel in *you*. That's diphthongised and coming to the front of the mouth.' She was speaking almost to herself, her head tilted in concentration as she played a section of the tape again. 'There. That's come from somewhere. For that to have stuck, I'd look at someone who has spent some time in Australia.' She looked up at him. 'That's as much as I can give you without taking it back to the lab.'

Now, Cathcart was impressed.

***

Cathcart looked at Will. 'She listened to that tape cold, and described the man I had just arrested. Derek Haynes, the man who owned the computer. He was 45, he came from Rochdale and he'd lived in Australia between 1986 and 1992. Her boss was going to take the case over when he came back from a conference. He's got a bit of a rep for hogging the limelight in high profile cases, but after that, I wanted Ania. I didn't know about your... about her history.' He frowned. 'The computer was sealed and went straight to the lab.' He nodded to Will's unspoken query. 'FLS. I've followed the chain of evidence. It went straight to Ania. FLS made a copy for us for our investigation. They got the interview tapes as well – they transcribe all our tapes for us, so she used those for comparison.'

'But you got the copy at once?'

'I've been looking at the evidence logs. We didn't get the copy for seventy-two hours. I went to have a look and there was a note from Ania apologising for the delay. She said they'd got held up in their system.'

Seventy-two hours was presumably enough time to collect what she needed for a fabricated recording. Will felt sick as he saw the pieces of evidence slotting together, and the picture that was forming.

'Anyway, a week later she was back. She couldn't say it in her report, but she told me that personally she was certain: it was him. By then, we'd found the basement where the recordings were made – in the detention centre where he worked. We'd got him. But now...'

'What about forensics?' If they'd found the location of the abuse, then traces of the abuser should be all over.

'Yeah, plenty. But Haynes admitted to using the basement. He kept some equipment there. He said he hadn't been in there much around the time the kid vanished, and he never saw anything untoward there. Everything pointed to him but there was nothing conclusive. And there were no forensics on the kid.

We found her too late and she'd been in the water too long. We don't even know how she died. We could put her in the basement and we could put him in the basement but we couldn't put them there together. The voice was the one thing he couldn't hide.'

His eyes met Will's. 'Haynes worked in that centre for five years. They detain kids in that place. I keep thinking about them.'

Locked up with a predatory paedophile, with few rights and no access to the law. And Haynes had used the basement a lot.

'Will he get off?'

Cathcart shook his head. 'Not if I have anything to do with it. We're going back over the evidence now. There has to be something – I just need one thing, one thing that will link him to Sagal, and I've got him. We never had any other convincing suspects in the frame. The mother's contacts didn't have access to the kid, not while she was in detention.'

'The father?'

'He was deported before the kid was taken. He's gone to ground. He never made any contact that we're aware of.'

'What happened to the mother?' She had been implicated in her daughter's abduction, Will recalled.

'We investigated her as well. We thought she had probably made a bargain with Haynes – time with the kid in exchange for getting all of them out of there – she's got another kid as well, little lad. The "Dave" story was probably some kind of cover up for that but we could never prove it.'

'What made you think…?'

'She was the one who'd cosied up to Haynes in the first place.'

'Where is she now?'

'She's still here, still in the UK. She's back in detention now – somewhere up north, I think. They were about to send her back but she's in luck. We'll need her here if there's going to be a retrial.'

The indifference in his voice made Will look sharply at him. Cathcart shrugged. 'That kid really drew the short straw. The dad was involved in terrorist shit. That's why they deported him. The mum was a prostitute before the immigration people picked her up. The staff at the centre said she was a cold fish. She had this little lad as well as the girl, barely looked at him, called him "the changeling" when she talked about him at all. What's to feel sorry for? It's those kids I care about.'

So did Will, but someone else's dead child wasn't – couldn't be – his main concern. He had been running the information Cathcart had given him through his head. 'Ania gave you a cold reading of that tape and it fitted Haynes. Why would she have needed to change anything?'

'I've been thinking about that, trying to make sense of it. The guy on that tape was local – we all knew that. But the rest of it – it was just what she said. It was "Can you hear this, can you hear that," but it was just a voice to us. I've been wondering… Did she know more than she told us? Did she have Haynes in her sights from the off?'

It would have been beyond coincidence anyway that a man with Haynes' profile but who wasn't Haynes would have had access to the machine. Cathcart's first account had made nonsense of Ania's fabricating evidence – if her initial analysis had been correct there would have been no need. But now… Haynes had been 'helping the police with their enquiries' by the time the video had been found. Ania would have known he was the man in police custody. In which case, why would she…? 'That recording you made, the audio cassette – it's the only copy of the original now?'

'It would be, if we still had it. Ania came by and picked it up.'

'When?'

'A few days ago. Just before the shit… Just before the story broke.'

'Where is it?'

Cathcart looked at him. 'I don't know. It's vanished along with the rest of her stuff.'

Another damning fact, another dead end.

Chapter 19

It was evening by the time Will left the police station. He'd had a vague plan to try and get a flight to Poland that night, but it was too late and he was too tired. He decided to go back to Ania's flat. He needed to rest, and he needed to think through what he had found out. He didn't want to sit among crowds in a restaurant, so he pulled in to a supermarket car park, negotiating shoppers pushing heavily loaded trolleys back towards their cars. He found a space next to a massive 4 x 4 that wouldn't have looked out of place driving across the plains of the Serengeti, and leaned his head back against the headrest. The idea of going into the supermarket and selecting things off the shelves seemed like an insurmountable burden.

He remembered taking the girls shopping when they were small. If he was on his own, he let them ride in the trolley pretending they were animals in a cage. As he watched the shoppers go past the car, he could see the small faces looking at him from behind the bars, little girls with blonde curls, giggling with excitement. He could remember the knitted cardigans they had been wearing, lumpy and home made, buttoned up to their chins for warmth. From somewhere in the recesses of his mind, the voices came back to him faint now across the gulf of time:

Daddy, Daddy...

Concealed between the Serengeti wagon and the wall, he felt tears stream down his face.

'Are you all right, sir?'

Will jerked upright. It took him a few seconds to reorient himself. He was in the car. The sheltering cliff of the 4 x 4 had gone, and the sky was dark. The bright yellow of street lights illuminated the car park. He checked his watch. It was after eight. He had been here for over an hour.

A man in the uniform of a security guard was knocking on the window. He pressed the button to wind it down. 'Are you all right, sir?' The man's face was tight with suspicion.

'Yes. Thank you.'

'Were you planning on doing some shopping?'

Will fought with the daze of confusion and fatigue. His face felt stiff. 'Yes. I'm just…' he made a vague gesture.

The man's face didn't relax. 'They'll be closing in five minutes.'

'Then I'd better get moving.' Will pushed the car door open, ignoring the man who moved away, speaking into his radio.

Cursing, Will walked quickly towards the supermarket entrance where attendants were already stacking up the baskets and lining up the trolleys. He stepped round a girl who seemed to be monitoring the door to keep new shoppers out. A blast of warm air hit him, followed by the chill of the coolers just inside the entrance.

He grabbed a bottle of milk, some bread and a paper and went to the kiosk to pay. He took his shopping back to the car, aware of the eyes of the security guard following him.

Chapter 20

This time, Ania's flat evoked no memories for Will. He was glad, as he let himself into the block and took the lift to the third floor, that he couldn't feel her presence, that he had no expectations of her waiting to greet him in her open doorway.

The flat looked almost clinically tidy. He was hungry, and tore a hunk of bread off the loaf he'd bought and ate it with some cheese while he waited for the kettle to boil. Coffee gave him an artificial boost of wakefulness. He knew he needed to sleep, but he didn't want to. He felt as though something malignant and watchful was close by and he was scared of what his dreams might bring.

Instead, he sat down to put together the information he'd gathered into notes. He was looking for inconsistencies. These were the weak places where an investigator could insert a wedge and start the process that would crack an entire case wide open.

Just over a year ago, FLS had been asked to analyse the recordings retrieved from a computer used by Derek Haynes. The work had been given to Ania as an expert in voice recognition and speaker profiling.

He jotted down his first question.

Did she tamper with the recording?

Everything he'd found, and everyone he had spoken to, said that she did. Cathcart had delivered the sealed laptop to FLS. No one but Ania had had access to it during the crucial period. If the answer to that question was yes, then that led at once to the second question: why? He stared at the page in front of him, but his mind was blank. He couldn't find an answer. He didn't have the information – yet.

He was puzzled that Cathcart, or someone on his team, hadn't noticed that the recording they sent was not the same as the recording that was used in Ania's analysis, but as he thought about it, he realised it wasn't so strange.

Cathcart and his team had heard the recording, but as long as what was returned to them was broadly similar in length and content, it was unlikely they would notice the changes. The child's voice hadn't been altered, just the relatively brief, terse instructions from the abuser. In twelve hours of interview recordings, it was probably possible to find everything needed to produce something that was almost identical in content to the original.

Then Haynes had appealed and Karzac was warned that there was going to be trouble. He had spoken to Ania. She hadn't been surprised, but she hadn't been worried either. She had gone over her report again, or at least she had told Karzac she was going over her report again. She had gone to Cathcart and collected the cassette. And then…

This was where it stopped making sense. She had destroyed any evidence remaining on her computer. She had packed up her files and notes and had taken a flight to Poland three days before she was officially due to leave. She'd run away.

Why?

Because she was afraid she'd be arrested? But she could be arrested in Poland just as easily. Everyone knew where she was.

To gain time? If she'd stayed in the UK, she would have been arrested and questioned more or less immediately. In Poland, she might gain a few days' grace.

Just watch out for the letter, OK?

He put his face in his hands. He was too tired to think, and he needed more information. Blaise had promised to send him the autopsy report and a copy of the note Ania had left.

He took his laptop out of his bag and switched it on. It found Ania's wireless connection and he was able to log on. She hadn't changed her password. He found himself hoping there would be something from her, some last message, some explanation, some indication that she had forgiven him for letting her down, but there was nothing.

There were messages from friends sent in the shock and aftermath of Ania's death. He opened them and scanned them quickly: *tried to call you… So very sorry… shock… can't believe… anything, anything at all.* And in all of them: *when will the funeral be?* He didn't send any replies. He couldn't cope with the grief of others, not now, but he felt the pressure of urgency again. He needed to be in Poland. He couldn't leave her there, a cadaver in a foreign mortuary. He had to bring her back.

Blaise's e-mail was there. Will read through it. It said the same things that Blaise had said to him on the phone, with a reinforcement of the warning: *you are not to get involved in any investigation*. This was Blaise covering his back. Will intended doing what he pleased, which he suspected Blaise already knew.

Blaise had honoured his promise. He had sent Will not just the autopsy report, but the witness statements the police had taken from the man who had found her, and from the colleagues she had been working with on the last days of her life.

Will read through the witness statements first. They all told the same story: Ania had been distracted and uncommunicative. She had immersed herself in work, starting early in the morning and staying long into the evening. She had refused offers of social contact, saying that she was busy and would catch up with people later. One statement used the word 'obsessed.' They all indicated that she had not been herself, they had all recognised a change in her.

Blaise had not sent the photographs that Will knew must exist, the photographs of her lying broken on the ground, photos of her on the autopsy table, but there was one picture. It showed a small, dingy office, sparsely furnished. There was a filing cabinet against the wall, and a desk under a window.

A phone was upended on the floor, trailing its cord, and a shoe lay on the desk top.

Above it, the window stood wide open.

The autopsy report was simple enough. The fall had broken her legs, her pelvis, her back, her arms and her neck. Her skull was fractured. The chances of surviving a fall like that were negligible. Occasionally some freak event occurred and someone walked away, but that was not the case here. She had been smashed to pieces.

Both his children, dead by violence.

Blaise had scanned the note Ania had left for him. He didn't want to read it, but he had to. This was what she had promised him, and this was a promise she had kept.

Daddy

I'm so very sorry. I wish I could think of a better way out but I can't. I can't face any more of this. Please tell everyone that I'm sorry about what I did. I thought it was for the best but I was wrong. Please forgive me.

Ania.

She hadn't called him Daddy since Louisa had died. His eyes felt dry and painful. Was that all she could say to him? 'Forgive you? How can I forgive you?'

He looked across the room and she was there by the window, her arm resting on the sill. He could see her silhouetted against the grey night. She turned her head away from him and the street light caught her face for a moment. She smiled, but her smile was sad. She shook her head.

And then he was awake, aware that he had lost time again, so tired that he had fallen into a waking doze even as he read his daughter's suicide note. He went to the bathroom and stuck his head under the cold tap until he felt some kind of wakefulness return, then he went back to his seat towelling his hair, cold water trickling down his neck.

He printed off the statements, the autopsy report and the letter, then looked to see what else was waiting for him. There was only an e-mail from someone called Walter Gilman, inviting him to become a friend on Facebook.

How old did they think he was? Sixteen? He deleted it.

A conversation with Ania came back to him. He had been complaining about the junk that was clogging up his e-mail now that he was no longer protected by the police systems, and she'd leaned over his shoulder to see what he meant.

'You need to upgrade your spam filter. God, what are these people like? "Want a larger penis?"' She made a gesture of typing in a reply. *'Depends…who's…on…the…other…end.'*

The recollection almost made him laugh.

Then he remembered her face as she watched him from the window, the way she had turned away from him, and the sadness of her smile.

Chapter 21

Will slept badly that night, an intermittent sleep in which Ania said something to him, over and over again, but he couldn't hear her. Then suddenly her voice was clear. 'Occam's razor,' she said. 'Don't forget.'

Soft footsteps moved around the flat and he sat bolt upright, his hand reaching for the light switch. The empty room looked back at him. He could hear someone moving in the corridor, footsteps coming to the door, closer, then fading away. Blaise sat behind his desk, his fingers steepled against his mouth as he watched Will striding backwards and forwards across his office.

You have no choice, he said.

No choice.

I have no choice.

And he was awake in the bleak chill of Ania's flat, a flat that had been empty now for almost a week and where all the traces of occupancy were fading away as if she had never been there.

He checked his bag, making sure that the print outs he had made were in the side pocket. He tidied everything away, folded up the bedding and bagged up the contents of the fridge. He would have to come back here and clear everything out, and he wanted the place to look impersonal and unlived in on his return. If he wasn't going to find Ania here, then he didn't want to find anyone.

He went down to the garage to collect his car and dumped his bags in the boot. He called Jack in St Abbs. 'It's Will Gillen.'

'Mr Gillen. Hi.'

'Listen, I'll be gone for a few days longer than I expected. Can you hang on to Keeper?'

'No problem.'

'She's doing well? She's OK?'

'She's missing you. She's been a bit off her food, but she'll be fine. Don't worry. Call me when you get back.'

He heard Keeper's bark in the background and Jack's voice, slightly muffled as he addressed the dog. For a moment, he felt a pang of longing to be back there, to be back in the quiet of the village, just him and Keeper and the coastal path to walk, or better still, the sea where he could turn the boat north and sail… anywhere. Anywhere would do. He shook himself and thanked Jack, promising to call with an update as soon as he knew more about his movements.

He felt like a betrayer.

The airport was to the south of the city. The roads were busy and the traffic on the motorway was heavy, but soon enough he reached the slip road to the airport and was following the signs to the terminal where the planes for the Polish carrier Lot departed.

He had two hours to wait after check-in. He wandered round the departure lounge aimlessly, avoiding the newsagents. He didn't want to see Ania's picture on any more front pages. He didn't want to hear any more bad news. He just wanted to maintain his equilibrium, to do what he thought she wanted him to do, bring her home, and then…

Then what?

His phone rang. It was Blaise. For a moment, he was tempted to leave it, but he answered. 'Gillen.'

'Will. How are you? I've been thinking about you.'

'I'm…' There was no answer to that question. 'OK.'

'Did you get the stuff I sent you?'

'Yes. Thanks. I… got it. I'm at the airport now. I'm going to Poland.'

'Right. You haven't forgotten what you agreed? About…?'

'I've no plans to get in anyone's way.'

'Good man. Have you seen the papers today?'

'No.'

'It's nothing new, Will, don't worry. It's just the same old stuff. They've granted Haynes a new trial. It's the best outcome we could hope for. They'll find something else. He won't get out. Then they'll forget about Ania. I think some people quite admire what she did – they can understand…'

'Yes.'

There was silence, then Blaise spoke again. 'You go and get her back, Will. Bring her home.' The kindness in his voice was more than Will could cope with.

'Goodbye.' He hung up.

Ania lifted her head and looked at him directly. 'You have to know where to look, Dad. It isn't that far away.'

'I'll find out. Don't worry. I'm getting there.'

The man sitting next to him looked at him uneasily and moved to another seat. Will wanted to laugh, but somehow he knew if he did, he would start crying instead. He sat in the sticky plastic seat until his flight was called.

Chapter 22

Four chimneys dominated the skyline as the plane dropped down towards the city. Will saw streets and buildings, the long constructions that indicated mills and, incongruously close to them, what looked like palatial residences.

As they broke through the clouds, he saw vast expanses of trees to the north that seemed to swallow half the city under their shade. 'It's beautiful,' he said.

'Łagiewniki. The largest urban forest in Europe. That's where I was staying – in the hotel in Łagiewniki.'

He smiled, pleased that she was here with him, then he felt the bump as the wheels touched down and he was on his own again. The sense of speed returned as the engines reversed and gravity attempted to push him out of his seat. Then they were taxiing towards the terminal, a tiny building that looked more like a bus station than an international airport. Just a few days ago, Ania had been here, had landed here, had waited in the aisle for the plane doors to open and to disembark to a city that was as familiar to her as it was strange to him. It was a city where she claimed she had been happy.

A city where she had died.

There was an air of decay and general shabbiness about the airport building, an air that was familiar to him from his excursions to eastern Europe as the countries threw off the shackles of Soviet dictatorship.

He found a line of taxis outside the airport and he asked the driver to take him to the Grand Hotel on ulica Piotrkowska where a room had been booked for him by one of Ania's colleagues. His Polish was rusty – Elżbieta had spoken it fluently and she had taught him and the two girls. He'd barely used it since she died, except occasionally with Ania, but he managed to make himself understood. The driver, delighted to find a visitor who spoke Polish talked all the way, turning round in his seat to observe the effect of something he'd said, taking both hands off the wheel to emphasise his points with gestures.

As the car made its hazardous way into the city, the sense of decay vanished as Will saw the evidence of regeneration: new building everywhere, apartment blocks ornamented with bright colours, new office blocks, signs to the Manufaktura, a huge shopping and cultural complex the driver explained, waving his hands in a vague gesture to his right as the car swerved across the traffic.

The taxi drew up at the side of the hotel. The driver carried Will's bags to the entrance, and a uniformed man from the hotel stepped forward to take them.

The street where the hotel stood vanished into the distance each way he looked. This was ulica Piotrkowska, Piotrkowska Street, the longest pedestrianised street in Europe. It was busy: people wandered in and out of the shops, and he could see hanging signs and boards on the pavement advertising restaurants and cafés. Bike-rickshaws plied a brisk trade up and down the road. There was something indefinably European about the scene – the variety of architecture, the ornamentation, the hanging baskets, empty now it was winter that spoke of cascades of flowers in the summer, and the entrances between the buildings that must lead to courtyards behind the frontages. If he had been here for a holiday, he'd be eager to dump his bags and start exploring.

He added a generous tip to the taxi fare, and the man pressed his number into Will's hand with enthusiastic promises to take him anywhere he wanted. Will stepped through the doors into the hotel.

It was like stepping into another century. The lobby was an open space of marble and polished wood. A stairway curved up from his left, a huge chandelier hanging above him. Despite its shabbiness, the hotel still retained the elegance of the days when it had been built, long before the wars and political oppression of the last century had brought Poland to a ruin it was still trying to escape.

'Will Gillen?' The voice came from behind him. A man stood up from one of the seats in the lobby. 'I have been waiting for you.'

'You are…?' His first thought was KGB minders, and he had to pull himself back into the 21st century.

'I'm Dariusz Erland. I am a friend of your daughter. Ania.'

He was a tall man, taller than Will, with a broad-shouldered, muscular build. His face looked creased and weary, with dark shadows under his eyes. He hadn't shaved. His clothes – a suit and a shirt, no tie – were crumpled as if they had been slept in. 'We must talk,' he said. 'There is a good café close by.' He didn't wait for Will's response but spoke rapidly to the receptionist. 'They know you are here. You can check in later. Leave your bags.'

Will was too tired to object. Keeping hold of his shoulder bag, he followed the man Erland as he led the way back out of the hotel into the rush of Piotrkowska.

Ania had loved this street. She had e-mailed him during her first visit, a detailed account of an evening spent here. There had been a festival in full swing, with musicians playing old Polish tunes on traditional instruments. She had been dancing in the street to a hurdy-gurdy in the late summer evening. *Na zdrowie!* she had signed off. She'd been happy.

Now, in January, it was dark and cold, and the people out on the street were moving quickly, grimly determined to get home. Will huddled more deeply into his coat and followed Erland down one of the small entrances that led off Piotrkowska into a courtyard where hanging baskets suggested that in summer it would be garlanded with flowers. They went into a café with a short counter and small, rather rickety tables. They were served with coffee that came in china cups. It was dark and rich, its aroma temporarily carrying away his fatigue.

'I met her the first time she came here,' Erland said suddenly. 'I thought she was a tourist, or a student maybe...'

***

Łódź, September 2005

The day Dariusz Erland met Ania Milosz was dull, with heavy clouds in a grey sky. He was on his way to work, taking a detour through the old Jewish burial ground. The leaves on the trees were starting to change colour and the grass was long and uncut. The cemetery had an odd, haunting beauty. It was a peaceful place – a place for the dead. Neither Catholicism nor Judaism allowed cremation, so flesh and bone fed the tangled grass and the overhanging trees.

Dariusz often took this route on his way to his office in the centre. Run down and neglected though the cemetery was, it held the story of the city's past. These days it was one of the stops on a path of holocaust remembrance, the rest of its history largely ignored, yet its tombs celebrated people who had shaped the city and whom the city still honoured and remembered.

The history of eastern Europe was a history of blood. Dariusz had grown up with the stories, stories his parents had told him, stories that inhabited the air he breathed.

He was walking along the path towards the imposing edifice of the Poznanski tomb where the great entrepreneur Izrael Poznanski was buried. His tomb attested to his importance in death, as the architectural heritage he left behind attested to the importance he had once had in life. As Dariusz approached, he saw the woman.

She was on the steps, the circular structure of the tomb looming above her. Columns and a massive pillar supported a dome with leaded windows that overlooked the family graves. The name POZNANSKI was emblazoned above the portico.

She was looking through the ornamental grilles at the huge sarcophagi that dominated the centre of the tomb and marked the places where Poznanski and his wife lay. There was something about her that suggested she wasn't local. The city was full of visitors for the annual festival. He almost walked on but he was curious, and he spoke on impulse. 'They didn't want to be forgotten.'

She glanced round at him. 'It's impressive.' She spoke Polish, with an English accent. She looked a bit wary – they were alone in the secluded place. Not wanting to alarm her, he didn't come any closer.

'I believe it's the largest Jewish tomb in Europe. You're here for the festival?'

'Is there a festival? I only got in last night. I'm here to work. I'm exploring a bit while I've got some time. Someone told me that Arthur Rubinstein's parents are buried here.'

'Yes – along that way.' He pointed along the path where the graves were crowded in. 'They're just ordinary graves. On the left along the row. There's a statue of him on Piotrkowska playing the piano.'

She smiled, suddenly warmer. 'Thank you.'

He watched her as she walked away, liking her slim build as she hitched the small backpack she was carrying higher onto her shoulders.

He stayed by the Poznanski tomb for a few minutes, studying the familiar structure with new eyes, then instead of following the path down to the gates, he found himself walking towards the far end of the cemetery, towards the Pole Gettowa, the field where the wartime dead of the Litzmannstadt Ghetto lay. It wasn't just the Jewish dead who lay here. There were also the less remembered, the Roma and non-Jewish Poles who had also been victims of mass executions. Somewhere here, his grandfather lay.

The Nazis had forbidden the use of stone grave markers, so burial sites were marked with metal bed frames or low cement posts. Visitors left small stones on the graves, like people marking their presence at a remote cairn: *we have not forgotten*. He picked a stone from the ground and placed it on the nearest marker.

As he walked back towards the gate, he saw the woman again. She was standing by the wall where memorial plaques had been placed, some by wartime survivors, some by the children, grandchildren and great-grandchildren of the victims.

She saw him coming towards her, and as he reached her, she began to walk with him. 'I found the Rubinstein grave,' she said. 'Thank you.' Beside the path there were deep pits in the ground. They lay in a line of six along the wall – rough, empty hollows that could have been freshly dug but for the grass growing inside them. 'What are these?'

'They're from the last days of the war. When the Nazis emptied the ghetto, they kept a few people alive to clear up after them. They made the men dig their own graves, but the Red Army arrived before they could kill these last few.'

Even now he found something chilling about their stark presence, as if the ghosts of the men who had dug them were standing there in silent witness.

'They were lucky,' she said.

'Were they?'

He saw her flush. 'To survive all that. In the end, they survived.'

'Survived to what?' He stopped. It wasn't her fault. 'I'm sorry. It's just that – in the west you see a happy ending to that war. It wasn't like that for us.'

'I know. My grandmother was a refugee. But surviving – isn't that better than dying? Isn't it a kind of winning?'

'In a way.' He was curious about her. Not many western Europeans came to Łódź to work. The traffic was mostly the other way. 'Now I know why your Polish is so good. May I ask your name?'

'I'm Ania,' she said. 'Ania Milosz.'

He held out his hand. 'Dariusz Erland. Let me show you the festival. It's the last night tonight – there's music on Piotrkowska.'

She'd smiled up at him. 'Thank you. I'd like that.'

And that had been the start of it.

Chapter 23

'She was going to move, to live here.' Erland lit a cigarette and Will looked round automatically for one of the staff to come and tell him to put it out, then realised that there were people smoking at other tables as well.

'When?' This was part of Ania's life he knew nothing about.

'Soon. We have an apartment in one of the new blocks they are building. It will be ready by late spring. She thought she would move then. She needed to make sure that her work could travel with her.'

'What will happen now?'

'I don't know. I haven't thought.'

'And the apartment?' It occurred to Will that Erland stood to do very well out of Ania's death if he now became the sole owner of the place they had bought together.

Erland let tobacco smoke trickle from between his lips and he stubbed the cigarette out. 'I'd stopped,' he said. 'She didn't like it. Now…' He met Will's gaze. 'I paid for the flat, Mr Gillen. She had a mortgage to pay already. It seemed fairer that way.'

Will realised his thoughts must have been clear on his face. He bit down on an apology. 'What do you do?'

'I'm a lawyer.'

'What kind?'

'I specialise in labour law. These days I do most of my work for one of the trades unions, the OPZZ.'

'You get a lot of work?'

'Yes. For a country that was part of the workers' paradise…' He gave the phrase an ironic twist, '… our people are not too well treated. The state has run things for too long in Poland. They still don't want to let go.'

A wave of fatigue engulfed Will. This was the man Ania was prepared to marry, sitting here discussing trade union politics, a day after her death. 'And did Ania know what…?' But he couldn't complete the question. He wasn't sure what he had planned to ask. He was here to bring his daughter home. That was all.

'Did she…?'

'I don't know. Nothing. It doesn't matter.' His head was starting to ache and the coffee was making his stomach churn.

Erland assessed him dispassionately. 'You need to eat.' He raised his hand and the waitress came across. He spoke in rapid Polish that Will didn't try to follow. 'I have ordered us *pierogi*,' he said abruptly.

Pierogi.

Sunday mornings, Elžbieta used to make *pierogi* using a recipe her mother had learned from her own mother. He was suddenly back in that kitchen. He'd just finished his morning shift and he'd followed the smell of coffee and fresh herbs from the front door. The sun poured through the window. Louisa was up to her elbows in flour as she mixed the dough, Ania was grating cabbage, her tongue caught between her teeth in concentration. Elžbieta glanced across at him when she saw him standing in the doorway and gave him the conspiratorial smile that parents share as they offer discreet help to children who are determined to go it alone.

Then he was back in the stark café, and the memory stopped his breath in his throat. He forced himself to concentrate.

'Tell me about Ania,' he said. 'Tell me what happened.'

Erland frowned. 'I don't know. I have contacts in the police and I've been asking questions, but it's been – what's the word? – stonewalling.'

'They know about you and Ania?'

'They know.'

'I saw the reports and I saw the note she left. It said – the police report said she wasn't herself, she was unhappy, distracted.'

'I didn't see her that week. My father was unwell. He lives in Gdynia and I took some time off to go and look after him. I wasn't expecting her till the end of the week. She told me it didn't matter, she was going to be very busy for the first few days, something important. Usually, she stayed with me but this time she stayed at the hotel. My flat is not so comfortable that she would want to stay if I am not there. So yes, she was distracted. And she was anxious.'

'What was the important work?'

'She didn't tell me. She didn't want to talk about it. I think she must have been working on those recordings. What else would have been important to her then? She had to clear her name.'

Working on the Haynes files. Doing what? He needed to know. 'Is that all she said?'

'I called her when the news broke. I said I would come back at once. She told me not to – I would be back in a couple of days and it would have been difficult to leave my father then. She sounded... OK.'

'Did she say anything else.?'

'Only that she couldn't tell anyone – tell you – what you wanted to hear.'

'Meaning?'

Erland shrugged.

'Did you ask her if she had done it?' *Why* she had done it.

Erland's look said everything he needed to say.

Will found it hard to continue. 'She had reasons – she would have had reasons. Did she tell you about her sister? About Louisa.'

'She told me. And you are saying she would send an innocent man to jail in memory of her sister?'

'No. I'm saying that she accepted the police case that Haynes was guilty. She knew they were having trouble making that last link. She knew the evidence wasn't conclusive. She couldn't risk Haynes going free.'

Erland was looking at him with an expression that was close to... what? Pity? 'So you are saying she believed she was helping the police when she took an action that will wreck what case they had? One that destroyed her career, damaged the company she worked for, damaged her profession?'

Will shook his head. He didn't know. 'She was carrying too much baggage from her sister's death. They never caught the man who did it. It never ended for her.'

'It never ended for her because she felt responsible. She believed it was her fault – her sister's abduction and then her mother's death.'

His denial was instant. 'You don't know what you're talking about!'

'I do know, because she told me. And she believed that you felt the same.'

It was like a punch in the stomach. 'That's not true!' He didn't know if he was denying what Ania believed, or what he had been accused of believing. 'Her mother – after Louisa… she lost her mind. *She* was the one who felt responsible. She left the children on their own in the playground.'

All she'd done was let the children play while she went to a café a hundred yards away, but she never forgave herself.

'And you?'

'I… I never blamed her. I blamed the man who killed our daughter.' But that wasn't true. Deep inside, hidden away where it could rot and fester, he had blamed Elżbieta.

Erland's shadowed eyes didn't leave his face. 'Ania had a fight with her sister. She was angry, so she ran away and left her. When she came back to the playground there was no one there.'

She'd never told him that. She never told anyone. The police hadn't been able to understand how the abductor had got Louisa away without Ania seeing him. They'd assumed that Louisa must have wandered out of the playground herself. They'd never known that it was Ania who had gone.

'And you see, as she grew up, she began to realise that if she'd spoken up at the time, maybe, just maybe they would have found Louisa before it was too late.'

Will stared at him. He couldn't think of anything to say. There was nothing to say. All he could think of was the guilt Ania had carried with her through her life, the guilt she'd never admitted to him.

'So you see the only person Ania had a motive to frame was herself.'

'You're saying that's why she…?'

'She didn't jump. Mr Gillen, did you know your daughter at all? She didn't jump.'

Chapter 24

It was midnight. For all his fatigue, Will was unable to sleep. He lay on the bed for a while, fully clothed, but the images the darkness brought were more than he could bear. He switched on the light and the reassuring normality of the hotel room returned.

He got up and found his bag. His laptop was stowed safely away in the central compartment. He put it on the desk and sorted out all the material he'd printed off back in the flat, the autopsy report, the suicide note and the witness statements, and laid them out on the bed. He read through them all again, carefully. He wanted to find something different, something that would change now that he read it with the knowledge Dariusz Erland had given him.

But nothing changed. If what Erland had told him was true, then it gave him more reasons to think that Ania had been driven to the point where she would follow her mother's example and kill herself.

And by the same method.

He had come home late that day – his work was taking him away for longer and longer. He had told himself that he was doing it for them, that his work would give them financial security, that he was doing what he should do as a father – providing for his family – for what remained of his family.

Now, far too late, he could admit that he had spent so much time at work because that was the place he preferred to be. It was the place he could get away from Elžbieta. She wasn't the woman he had married. She wasn't the woman he knew. In the year since Louisa's death she had sunk into a deep and unremitting depression. She drank. She became heavy and unkempt, the drugs slurring her voice and making her movements clumsy and uncertain. She'd stopped caring for herself and she'd stopped caring for Ania.

***

It was well after eight when he pulled up outside the house. He checked the time. He'd promised to get back early, but he'd let the various small distractions at the end of the day delay him. He felt a leaden fatigue wash over him as he climbed heavily out of the car and braced himself to face Elžbieta's reproaches.

The windows were dark and the house closed and silent. Elžbieta's car wasn't in the drive. She must be out. Maybe she'd taken Ania out to the Italian café in the small shopping centre half a mile away. He felt a slight lift in his spirits. If she'd done that, then maybe she was feeling better. Usually by this time, Ania would have eaten, and Elžbieta would be sitting in front of the television, channel hopping with blank eyes while Ania occupied herself in her room.

He left his car in the road and walked up the short drive, feeling in his pocket for his key. It had been a long day, and he was looking forward to a glass of whisky. This was the routine of his life – home from work, a drink, grab something to eat. He didn't like the mindless babble of the TV, so he would spend the evening in his study, catching up with work, reading the paper. At some stage in the evening, Ania would creep in and say goodnight.

'Had a good day, sweetheart?'

'Yes, Dad.'

Always the same colourless response.

At some level he was aware that his bright, bubbly daughter had changed, had become a silent presence on the edge of his vision. He kept telling himself he would do something for her, but then his own misery pressed forward and engulfed him. She was young. She was resilient. Time was her best support.

He was sorting out the key to the front door, when he realised someone was calling him.

'Mr Gillen!'

He turned round. It was one of their neighbours, waving to catch his attention as she came across the road. They'd moved here only recently in the aftermath of Louisa's death and barely knew anyone. He was surprised she knew his name. He forced a social smile onto his face. 'I'm sorry I don't…'

But this wasn't a social call. 'Celia Conway. I've got Ania with me. Your wife went out earlier this afternoon. I need to talk to you.' Her tone was peremptory. She turned and headed back to her own house as Will followed her, any irritation at her attitude swamped by his sudden anxiety for his daughter.

'Here's your father, Ania,' Celia Conway called as she came through the door. The house felt welcoming with warm lights and the smell of coffee and cinnamon. He used to come home to a house that welcomed him. These days, it felt cold and bleak and he realised with a sudden lurch of guilt that it was this way for Ania as well.

He saw her sitting at a table in the main room, books laid out in front of her. She looked at him nervously, and then her eyes slid away.

'She's doing her homework,' Celia Conway said. 'Ania, I'll just make your father a cup of tea, then he'll take you home.'

She confronted him as soon as they were out of earshot. 'I found her sitting on your doorstep. It isn't the first time. Do you have any idea what's going on when you aren't there?'

He shook his head, silenced by her anger, and his sudden awareness of his own negligence.

'I don't know what's wrong with your wife, but she clearly isn't capable of looking after the child. I'm not prepared to sit by and let this go on. It isn't fair.'

'I didn't realise…' He should have realised. And he had done the same – it was just that his neglect was less visible, was hidden behind the closed doors of the house while he pretended that her welfare was central to his life. He'd cared more about his next drink than he had about his daughter. 'Elżbieta's been ill. She needs…' She needed a husband who would care for her and she needed professional help. He felt the weight of his responsibilities settle more firmly round his shoulders. 'It won't happen again.'

She studied him in silence, then seemed satisfied with what she saw. 'I'm sorry I was so blunt.'

'It needed to be said. Thank you.'

He went into the other room where Ania waited for him, all pretence of working gone. Her face looked pinched and pale. 'Come on, sweetheart. We're going home,' he said, taking her hand. He wasn't going to make any big declarations. He was just going to make things change. Somehow, it was going to be better, for Ania, and for Elżbieta. He'd see to that.

***

But for Elżbieta, it had been too late. The knock on the door came later that evening. Elżbieta had fallen from the top storey of a car park in the city centre. Her car was parked close to the point of her fall. On the front passenger seat was a stuffed toy, Small Bear, a teddy bear that a friend had made for Louisa when she was a baby, that had been Louisa's constant companion. No note was ever found, but Will knew – and he suspected that even from the time of her mother's death, Ania knew too – that Elżbieta had jumped.

After that day, he had tried to do better. He thought he had convinced Ania that she wasn't responsible for the way her mother had abandoned her, that she hadn't deserved it in any way, that it had been the illness, not the way Elżbieta truly felt. What he hadn't known then was the secret that Ania had carried.

And now, once again, she was being made responsible for letting a child killer go free. Could she have born the repetition of that responsibility?

'It wasn't your fault. It wasn't you. You were only a child…'

'You said that before. It doesn't change anything. I was there. I know what I did.'

'It still wasn't your fault. You weren't…' But the voice had faded away. He had no answer.

He read through the suicide note again. It had been written on the computer she had been using earlier that evening. He checked the police report. They'd dusted the keyboard and found what they would have expected – lots of prints, most of them too smudged to be useful. There were two identifiable traces, one that was Ania's, one that belonged to a man called Konstantin Jankowski. He was the head of department and he and Ania had worked closely together. They'd both used the machine that day. Jankowski said he had spent a couple of hours with her the day she died, working through some analysis.

The metal frame of the window had produced one identifiable set of prints along the bottom as if she had clung on with one hand that last minute before she let herself go.

Or before her grip failed and she fell.

He put his face in his hands and forced himself to think. Dariusz Erland didn't believe that Ania had jumped. He seemed to despise Will for his belief that she had died at her own hand.

Erland didn't know Ania as well as Will did. He didn't know the poisonous legacy that Ania carried from her mother's death. He didn't know how completely the despair engulfed her when Brown Jenkin had her in his grasp.

So why was he here? If that's what he truly believed, why was he here? The funeral director could have organised the transport of her body home.

He was chasing shadows. He couldn't clear her name. He'd read through everything Blaise had sent him, over and over again. There was nothing there, or nothing he could find. When he went to talk to the police investigating her death, they could only show him what Blaise had shown him.

Dariusz Erland was insistent she had not committed suicide, but he was refusing to look at the facts. He was trying to absolve himself of the guilt of abandonment. She had needed him, and he hadn't been here. That was Erland's own agenda. Will didn't want to know about that. To anyone else, her death was explicable. Blaise had seen the logic at once. She was overwhelmed by the consequences of what she had done.

But he was her father. He knew her. There had to be a reason why she had tampered with the evidence, a good reason, a valid reason, even if it did leave her facing imprisonment and disgrace. That was what he was here to find out. He was here to clear his daughter's name of corruption for personal gain, for adulation and attention. She had done what she had done for a reason, a reason she had seen as honourable and sufficient, even if, in the end, it had driven her to her death.

He was here to find that reason.

Chapter 25

It was three in the morning. Dariusz Erland sat at his computer in the cramped studio flat that was all Łódź had had to offer for single men when he arrived in the city. At least the space was his own. When he was a child, the entire family had been crowded into the flat in Gdynia, not much larger than this. He could remember his parents sleeping on a pull-out bed in the living room, while he and his siblings had slept in the one small bedroom. As Beata grew up, she had shared the pull out bed with her mother and their father had slept with him and his brothers. It was the way people had lived in those days. No one was homeless but no one – or only the powerful few – had privacy and space.

Maybe that was why he had got out of the habit of sleep once he had left home. From his student days he had always thought that life was too good and too short to be wasted in sleep. He could remember long nights spent in crowded rooms, listening to music, drinking, talking, wandering back through the streets as dawn came, relishing the freedoms that the new Poland had brought to him and his contemporaries.

Polish people had launched themselves into the EU with an unprecedented enthusiasm, had travelled beyond borders that had been closed by politics and poverty and now they were returning, bringing the fresh air of new experience with them, shining a light on the corruption that linked Poland with its past. Western Europe was old and stagnating. The future was in the east, and this was the future he and Ania had planned together.

He lit a cigarette and watched the blue smoke curl up towards the ceiling. He had stopped smoking for Ania but now the self-denial seemed futile: the tobacco helped to clarify the thoughts that had been cluttering his mind since his meeting earlier with her father.

Will Gillen.

He had hoped that Gillen was here to defend his daughter, to ensure that her death was properly investigated. Instead, it seemed as though Gillen, tied in knots by different kinds of guilt, was all too ready to accept that Ania had died by her own hand. Gillen was caught up in his own past and his own obsessions, not able to see they were his, not Ania's.

Ania was more than her sister's death.

She had talked very little about her father. It wasn't the silence of estrangement. It was as if she didn't yet know how to bring her new life and her old life together. What Dariusz knew about Will Gillen he had gleaned for himself during the course of their relationship.

When the story that had ended Gillen's career had broken, there had only been a brief flurry in the Polish press: *British intelligence bungles again*. Now he had met Gillen, he wanted to know more. Ania's concerns had been for her father's welfare as press opprobrium landed on his head. *It won't last* Dariusz had assured her. British papers loved it when the authorities got it wrong and they could thunder out moral platitudes, but in this case, the victim was not likely to arouse their sympathy.

Gillen's team had been involved in the raid of a house in Birmingham, a house the intelligence services had pinpointed as a bomb factory. A seventeen-year-old youth who had escaped from the raid had been spotted an hour later in the city's main station, his rucksack bulking on his back, his eyes glancing nervously around. He had seen the police marksmen and his eyes had widened in fright. He had reached into his pocket with a jerky, panicky movement. Gillen's men had shot him dead.

In the end, no bomb-making equipment was found nor any evidence of radical activity. The house was one where asylum seekers were accommodated. The dead youth was an Iraqi Kurd who was destitute. He was living in the house illegally, given shelter by the residents who sympathised with his plight. The rucksack contained everything in the world he owned.

The dead youth had no family to act for him. They had been killed in the war. The story had faded into obscurity in a matter of days with the consensus that the occupants of the house had largely brought the disaster upon themselves. A system that normally moved with the speed of a glacier suddenly accelerated, and all the men in the house had been deported by the time the enquiry into the incident began.

The enquiry had released its findings just a few weeks before. It noted the unavailability of witnesses, and also queried the source of the misinformation that had led to the raid, but by that time, the news agenda had moved on. Gillen's early retirement after the enquiry was seen as the act of an honourable man brought down by events beyond his control.

Having met him, Dariusz was not so sure. Ania had suggested her father hadn't wanted to retire, but hadn't elaborated the point. Gillen himself looked worn down. Ania's death would have done that to him, but the weary anger in the man's eyes seemed to Dariusz to belong to an older wound. The death of his other daughter? Gillen had survived that, had gone on to be a success in his chosen field and as reasonably successful a parent as most.

There was something else eating him away.

Dariusz thought for a while, then scrolled though the numbers in his phone until he found the contact details for a journalist friend, Roman Strąk. He often worked with Strąk when he wanted to get stories about abuses of the labour laws into the national consciousness. Strąk worked for Zycie Warszawy, a national newspaper with a far wider circulation than the Łódź papers. If anyone in Poland knew the background to the story, he would.

Strąk's voice was blurred with sleep as Dariusz identified himself. 'Erland! Do you know what time it is? In case you don't, I'll tell you. It's three in the fucking morning. This had better be good.'

Dariusz glanced at the clock. Strąk was right. He'd forgotten the time.

When Strąk spoke again, his voice was less abrupt. 'I was sorry to hear about Ania.'

'The bastards have closed the case. I…'

'Look.' Strąk sounded embarrassed. 'I'd like to do a story, but I can't. There's no angle. 'Łódź police incompetent.' Big surprise. And no editor is interested in 'Foreign national jumps out of window.' Sorry.'

'Even if she didn't jump?'

The other man's voice was suddenly alert. 'You've got evidence?'

'Nothing much. Not yet.'

'Get me some evidence that will stand up, and I'll run with it, OK? Until then…'

'It isn't that. It's something else. I need as much information as you can get me about something that happened in the UK about eighteen months ago. I don't have the contacts.' He outlined what he knew, and heard the sound of a keyboard as Strąk looked the case up.

'Yeah. Got it.' There was silence as Strąk read through whatever it was he had found. 'Trigger happy bunch of dickheads… What's this got to do with Ania?'

'Will Gillen is her father.'

'*Is* he now?' Strąk's interest racked up a notch. Maybe Dariusz would get his story after all. 'OK, what do you want to know?'

'Gillen. He was suspended while they had an enquiry. He took early retirement a couple of months ago. What I want to know is did he jump, or was he pushed?' It was an unhappy analogy to use, but Strąk didn't comment.

There was the silence of thought on the other end of the line. 'Gillen's head rolled. That seems to have stopped the criticism in its tracks. From what I can see – this is just gossip, right, not official stuff but it's from a reliable source – the intelligence that led to the raid was dodgy.'

'Dodgy how?'

'It came via an informer.'

And informers, especially in these times, often had their own agendas. Whatever had happened, one of Gillen's men had been made a killer by that episode. Gillen's career had meant everything to him – Ania had told him that: *he cares about what he does and he cares about his team. After what happened to Louisa, and after Mum… they kind of became his family.* If that was true, then Dariusz couldn't see him accepting the comfortable berth of retirement with a good pension and no stain on his reputation, but that apparently was the deal that Gillen had made. Maybe Ania's view of her father was idealised.

'Thanks. That's… quite a story.'

'I wouldn't lose any sleep over it. I don't think Gillen has. Listen, this is getting interesting. If you find anything else…'

'You'll get it first.'

After he rang off, Dariusz thought about the call. Strąk hadn't been remotely sceptical that the police had not investigated Ania's death properly – he just wanted some evidence before he stuck his neck out. It was the way things were.

Corruption had been a problem in Poland since the days of the Stalinist era and its fungus threads spread through the entire system, sending up its fruits in unexpected places. Just a few years before, ambulance crews had been found taking bribes from funeral parlours in exchange for dead bodies, bodies that, in some cases, may have been helped on their way. The fallout of fear and anger from this had led to a loss of faith in the health system – as demonstrated by his father's refusal to go to hospital and his reluctance to take prescribed drugs.

Dariusz came across it every day in his work: laws about working conditions being flouted, health and safety laws blatantly ignored. The problem was, people took the system for granted. They accepted that bribing a doctor was the way to get treatment, to the point where some hospitals put up notices reading, "Doctors here do not accept gifts". But there were still hospitals where bringing gifts to the people who were treating you was an entry ticket to the ward. Everyone knew, but no one was prepared to take action.

His father told a story from his time in prison. The inmates had a way of distinguishing good wardens from bad ones. From the inmates' perspective, the good wardens were the ones who were out for personal gain, who would accept bribes in return for longer visits, more coffee, larger packages from home. The bad wardens were the honest ones, who tried to treat the prisoners equally and who wouldn't accept the bribes. 'The problem,' he had said to Dariusz, 'is that the country is being run by the good wardens.'

They had laughed, but the sad fact was the story was true, or true enough. And it wasn't just Poland. These days, the good wardens were in charge everywhere.

Chapter 26

When Will woke up the next day, he let the policeman he still was take charge. He wasn't Will Gillen, bereaved father taking stock of what he had seen and what he needed to do. He was DCI Gillen, senior officer in the West Midlands counter-terrorism unit. Today, he would see the last place where Ania had been alive, he would meet the people she knew. He had already met the man she had planned to marry, and had not been impressed. He would talk to the people who had investigated her death, then he would arrange for her body to be flown back to the UK.

After that...

For a moment, his head felt as though it was filled with cotton wool, his thought processes tangling up in a haze of weariness. All he wanted to do was lie down again and escape into sleep. He forced his mind back to the job in hand. He was here for Ania. Nothing else mattered. He would have all the time in the world to sleep once this was over.

It was 8.30 when he left the hotel. Piotrkowska was quiet. The shoppers weren't out this early in the morning and the rickshaw drivers had yet to set up their stalls. The opulent grandeur of the hotel dining room had offered only an indifferent buffet of tinned fruit, cold meats and dry bread. Swooping orchestral music had driven him out, breakfast virtually uneaten. He wasn't hungry anyway.

His appointment at the university wasn't for another forty-five minutes and when he made enquiries at the desk he found that the faculty building was only five minutes from the hotel. He couldn't face going back to his room so he hunched into his overcoat against the cold and started walking. He had no particular destination in mind. He just knew that he didn't want to sit in his room, staring at the walls.

He took one of the roads off Piotrkowska and stopped at a café with the improbable name of Coffees and Toffees, written outside in big letters in English. The girl behind the counter greeted him with a cheerful *Dzien dobry* and served him with a cup of good coffee that came with a piece of fudge.

Coffee and toffee.

'It does what it says on the tin.' Ania's voice. He turned round abruptly.

She was sitting at one of the tables. She probably came here often, maybe with friends and colleagues from the university which was, according to his map, just round the corner.

'Breakfast,' he said, knowing she would disapprove of such an unhealthy diet. The girl behind the counter gave him a puzzled look and he smiled at her and indicated the piece of fudge. She nodded in incomprehension.

He took his cup across to the table and sat down. The chairs were comfortable and upholstered in bright red. He felt old. He'd barely slept, and what sleep he'd had had been disturbed by dreams – not the dreams he'd feared, dreams of Ania falling, but a familiar dream, the dream where he was fighting his way through the crowds in a railway station, knowing that the minutes leaking away through the clock on the departure board were vital, that the cascade of seconds that raced past his eyes was counting towards something he had to stop, except he couldn't find his way past the people who stood in his way, meandered across his route and turned the straight line of his run into a jagged path with no clear way through.

Then he was in the mortuary, looking at the body of a youth, a boy of seventeen who had fled for most of his life, and had now come to the end of it.

In his dream, the dead eyes opened and looked at him. The boy's mouth moved and bled, but no words emerged.

You are responsible for this.

Ania's fingers touched his wrist. 'I never said that, and I never thought it. You did what you had to do.'

'I walked away from it.' Sweat broke out over Will's body and for a moment, nausea overwhelmed him. He felt saliva flood his mouth and he clenched his jaw, breathing deeply through his nose. He sat very still and gradually the sickness faded. He straightened up, aware that the girl behind the counter was watching him, her cloth moving mechanically across the top of the bar. He managed to smile at her and after a moment she smiled back. He looked across the table but now there was no one there.

He took several deep breaths and gradually he began to feel more calm. He needed to think about the forthcoming meeting he had with the head of department where Ania had been working. Konstantin Jankowski would have known Ania well – she had been coming here regularly for the past two years and had always spoken warmly of her Polish colleagues.

He wondered what plans Dariusz Erland had. He didn't feel any need to meet the man again. OK, Erland might well have become his son-in-law, become part of his life, his family, Ania and Dariusz, the father of his grandchildren, a man who Ania must have loved. To Will, experienced in these matters, Erland looked like a thug. He was angry that Ania had been planning to throw herself away on this man, this trades union activist turned lawyer. Erland's profession only helped to confirm Will's opinion. The law was the profession of choice for the spivs and barrow boys of this world. Erland had had the brass neck to ask him, *Did you know her at all?* They had nothing else to say to each other.

It was getting on for nine thirty. He finished his coffee and nodded to the girl behind the bar. '*Do widzenia.*'

She paused in her mission to polish the counter to flawless brilliance. '*Do widzenia.*'

The centre of Łódź was built on a grid system. The department of English was on a main road that ran parallel to Piotrkowska. It was busy. He had to wait several minutes for a break in the traffic that roared past at reckless speeds. The air was tainted with the fumes.

His footsteps slowed as he approached the university building. It was a tall, art deco structure with high railings and steps leading up to an imposing front entrance. Young men and women – students presumably – were going in and out through the main door. He let his eyes follow the frontage up and then down again to the wicked spikes on the railings that separated the building from the street. But Ania hadn't fallen here. She had fallen from the back. If he wished, he could follow the road round, locate the car park entrance, go and stand on the spot where his daughter's body had lain, see the stain that might still be discernible where she had smashed onto the unforgiving ground.

He walked up the steps and through the entrance.

The lobby was wide, high and light. Tall windows illuminated the space. A stairway curved up to his left, and straight ahead of him, more stairs led down to the basement. These were plain and utilitarian, lacking the ornamented iron balustrade of the main stairway. A sign on the wall directed him to the car park.

There was no reception desk, just a small kiosk at the top of these stairs. A man in the uniform of a security guard was leaning against the counter. He was leafing through a newspaper, but he shot a glance at Will. Their eyes met, and the guard looked away quickly.

The man who had found Ania had been a security guard – Jerzy Pawlak. This could be the same man. On impulse he crossed the lobby.

'Mr Pawlak? Jerzy Pawlak?'

The man hesitated, then nodded. He looked wary, as if he wasn't sure he should make the admission. He was small and wiry with a narrow face and bright, sharp eyes. He had a thin, wispy beard.

'My name is Will Gillen. My daughter died here a few days ago. I believe you were on duty that night. I'd like to talk to you.'

Pawlak stiffened. 'I talked to the police. I told them everything.'

'You were the last person to see her. I'd like to hear from you what happened that night.'

'I don't want to talk about it. I don't have to.'

'No. You don't have to.' Will trod hard on his impatience. It can't have been easy for Pawlak. He didn't deserve Will's anger. If anything, he deserved thanks. 'I can come back later. Are you working tonight?'

'No. I'm on now.' Pawlak pulled his sullenness round him like a protection, the seemed to relent. 'I'm working tomorrow night.'

'Can I come and talk to you then?'

'I don't know. I'll be busy. I don't want…'

Will took out his wallet. 'I don't want to make things difficult.' He took out a note for 100 PLN. 'Here. For your time now.'

Pawlak's eyes flickered to the money, then round the lobby before he slipped the note from between Will's fingers. 'My time now?'

'And I'll give you something for your time tomorrow.'

Pawlak hesitated. 'Nine. Here. Tomorrow evening.' His gaze moved round the lobby again. 'I've got to work.'

'Mr Milosz?' Will turned round. A middle-aged man in a rather shabby suit was standing behind him, holding out his hand.

'Gillen. Ania used her mother's name. I'm Will Gillen.'

'I am Konstantin Jankowski. I knew your daughter well. I – we all – admired her a great deal. I have to tell you how sorry we all are.'

It was necessary, this expression of grief, but it was what Will had been dreading. He let his breathing steady then he was able to say, 'Thank you.'

'Did you want something from…?' Jankowski gestured towards the booth, where Pawlak was no longer visible.

'No. Nothing.' He didn't want to discuss it with Jankowski. He didn't want his meeting with Jerzy Pawlak to become official.

'I want to help,' Jankowski said. 'What do you need?'

'I need to know what happened.'

'Of course. I'll tell you as much as I can. We none of us realised she was…'

'What was she doing? Here?'

'Please come up to my office. We can talk there.'

Jankowski led the way up the stairs to the fourth landing. The stairwell was lit by a huge window. The banister was made of wrought iron, delicate and ornate. As they approached the top floor, Will saw that here, the ceiling was lower and to the left of the landing, the proportions were destroyed by a partition wall that cut the space off abruptly, presumably to create extra rooms. Jankowski led him to a door opposite the stairs and unlocked it. 'My office,' he said, ushering Will in.

It was a small room, cluttered with books and papers, the office of an academic. Will was reminded of Oz Karzac's office back in Manchester as Jankowski cleared some papers off a chair for Will to sit down. Jankowski switched on a kettle and with a quick query to Will, made tea. He produced a bag containing pastries and small cakes – Will could remember Ania commenting on the Polish sweet tooth.

'First,' Jankowski said as he sat down, putting a cup of tea in front of Will, 'I must give you this.' He put a carrier bag and a small backpack on the table. 'These are the things she left in her locker. The police have checked – they don't want them.'

Will glanced in the carrier. It contained a magazine, a couple of paperbacks, some pens and Ania's iPod. The backpack contained a washbag and some cosmetics. 'Thank you.'

Jankowski nodded. 'Now I will tell you what I know.'

He explained that Ania was there to help them with an expansion of the forensic linguistics work done in the department. FLS contracted work out to the university, but they lacked equipment, and their specialists kept moving on. 'We can't match the salaries in other professions,' Jankowski said. 'Academics are not well paid here. We lost our expert on recorded sound recently which means we will have to return some of our work to Manchester incomplete.' He frowned, preoccupied with his own problems. 'Ania was planning to transfer here so we were setting her up with her own work as well.'

That fitted in with what Dariusz Erland had told him. 'What kind of work? Forensic linguistics for the local police?'

Jankowski shook his head. 'Our police don't use outside experts to do these analyses. They use their own people and I'm afraid the standard of the work is not good. No, Ania had started some research and she was doing some teaching for us.'

So this was to have been her future, teaching at a Polish university, surviving on a Polish salary, living in an apartment with a self-styled union activist, following the roots that led from her dead mother, the mother who had died blaming her… He stepped hard on the self pity he could feel welling up inside him. Ania had chosen a life she thought would make her happy. Wasn't that what he had wanted for her?

It was, but she had deserved better than this.

***

Łódź University

Konstantin Jankowski customarily started his working day early. He liked the quiet of the building in the morning before the students and the rest of the staff arrived. It was around six fifty as he reached the top of the stairs, his mind already running through the various tasks he had to complete that day, starting with his 8.00 a.m. lecture.

He noticed with surprise and some annoyance that the door to the computer room was standing open. Someone must have forgotten to lock it the night before and the caretaker must have missed it on his rounds. He went to check – they could ill afford to lose any equipment – and was surprised to see that for once he wasn't the first person at work. Ania Milosz was sitting at one of the workstations with headphones on, staring blankly ahead. She must have caught his movement in her peripheral vision, because she pushed the headphones back. 'Konstantin.' She clicked the mouse and the screen she had been studying closed, leaving her work screen open.

'You're here early.' He could see waveforms across the top of the screen and spectrograms across the bottom. She must be doing some comparison work on sound files, but it hadn't looked as though she was working. It looked as though she had been surfing the internet, indulging in the electronic wool-gathering they were all prone to from time to time.

'I brought some work with me from Manchester that I need to finish. Is that OK? I'll make a start on yours this morning.'

'That's fine. By the way, I had a call from Oz Karzac last night. He wants you to call him – he needs to talk to you.'

All expression vanished from her face. 'OK.'

'He said he's been trying your number. You left earlier than he expected. He sounded quite… upset.' Oz had sounded furious. Jankowski had never heard him like that before.

She sighed and swivelled round to face him. 'You'd better know that Oz and I are having a bit of a tricky time just now. He isn't happy about this case – the one in the UK, you know? I think he'd have preferred it if I'd put off my visit, but there

117

would have been no point. There's nothing I can do at the moment. I'd rather sit it out here.'

'I read about it.' They had all seen the toll it was taking on her, but he had issued his instructions: no one was to mention it until she brought it up. 'Is there anything I can do to help?'

Her face softened as she smiled. 'That's kind of you, Konstantin. It's OK. It truly isn't as bad as it looks. I guess I'm a bit pissed off with Oz for not trusting me.'

'He must be concerned about…'

'His business? Yes.'

'About you, I meant. He must be concerned about you. I am.'

Her eyes were suddenly shiny and he had the impression that she was on the edge of tears. 'I'd better get this finished.' She turned back to the screen and he went on to his office, more worried about her than he had been before.

***

'Do you know what she was working on?' When Karzac told him she had taken files from the labs, it had sounded sinister, but maybe she had simply taken work that she needed to complete.

Except that she had deleted everything from her hard disk.

Jankowski shook his head. 'I don't know for sure. I couldn't say. To be honest, I don't think she was working at all. She was surfing the net when I saw her.'

'Surfing the net?'

'She was looking at Facebook when I came in. She had some work on the screen, but I don't think she was doing much with it. She was listening to music as well. She borrowed an old Walkman from me. I lent her some tapes – traditional Polish music. She liked that.'

A Walkman? Why had she wanted that? She'd had her iPod. 'I'd still like to know what she was working on. Do you have it?'

'The police took it all. After…'

The police. He hoped Blaise had smoothed the way for him. He needed to be prepared for that meeting, but for the moment, he needed to concentrate on what he was doing. Jankowski was looking at him expectantly. Will made himself say, 'I'd like to see the room now.'

Jankowski put down his cup and nodded. 'I have kept it unused until your visit. But…'

'You'll need to use it again. Of course. I understand.' He was grateful that Jankowski didn't try and dissuade him from seeing the place where Ania had died.

Jankowski led Will across the landing to the partition wall. The door was open and students were milling round on the landings. He could hear their chatter and laughter, which faded to silence as he passed.

Jankowski led him through the door. He found himself in a narrow corridor that ran between the flimsy cream painted walls. There was no natural light, just the pale flicker of a ceiling bulb. Doors opened off the corridor.

'In here,' Jankowski said, opening one, 'is where she worked.' They were in a room where computer terminals were lined up on long benches. A couple of students sitting at work stations glanced up. Jankowski made to pull the door shut, but Will stopped him.

'One moment. Please.' He smiled an apology at the students and crossed the room to where windows lined the wall. They were large windows, the sills only about four feet above floor level. They were closed, locked by handles that turned to release them. He went to one and gave the handle a firm tug. It moved, stiffly. He pushed the window outwards, feeling the resistance of something that hadn't moved for a long time. Outside, a fire escape ran down the wall. Beneath it, the wall dropped straight down onto concrete.

He pulled the window shut and locked it again, then went back to where Jankowski stood in the doorway, his face wary and unhappy. Will offered no explanation or apology.

Jankowski continued down the corridor. 'This is the room where she… the last room.' He pushed open another door and a wash of cold air flooded out.

The last room.

It was small. There was a desk under the window and a filing cabinet against the wall. There was a phone on top of the filing cabinet, but otherwise there was none of the equipment Will would expect to find in an office, no computer terminal, no desk furniture. It looked bleak and unused.

He stepped through the door. The desk chair was pushed in. If it had been pulled out, the few items of furniture would more or less have filled the space. There was no sign of any habitation, no papers in the in-tray, nothing on the surface of the desk.

The window was behind the desk. It was smaller than the ones in the computer room they had just visited. The metal frame had collected dirt over the years and the paint was chipped and dingy. The flicker of doubt planted by Dariusz Erland faded. No one could have forced her out of that window, and no one could have lifted her up to it if she had been unconscious. It would take immense strength, and why try, when there were perfectly accessible windows in the room next door?

Two paces took him across the room. He had to lean over the desk to look out. The wall dropped away sheer, fifty feet or more down to a patch of waste ground where a few cars were parked. Pipes ran down the wall. A few feet away, the metal of the fire escape was visible. Blaise's voice spoke in his mind: *she hit her head on an overflow pipe on the way down. Cast iron… stove her head in…*

He turned away abruptly and stared at the floor until he could lift his eyes and look round the room again. Ania's story seemed to have been told in a series of just such cramped offices: Karzac's with its mess of papers, the clinically neat office of DI Ian Cathcart, Konstantin Jankowski's cluttered room. And now there was this one. It was so small it was barely viable as office space. He could see the dark marks of fingerprint dust on the desk, on the sill, on the phone, on the window frame. There was more on the door handle. The floor looked as though it had been swept clean – maybe the forensic people had been more thorough than he had anticipated. It seemed a bleak place to die.

'Who uses this room?'

'It's space we give our PhD students. Ania used it as an office when she came here'

'But she worked in the other room.'

'Yes, if she needed the analytical software we use. This room isn't on the network.'

'Was it like this when she was found?'

Jankowski nodded. 'The police asked me if anything was out of place. There were…' He gestured towards the floor,

'…papers scattered. The chair was pulled out.' He frowned, trying to remember. 'The phone was on the floor. And… there was a shoe, her shoe, just there.' He pointed to the desk.

'She wrote a note on the computer.'

'The police took it.'

'The machine?'

'Yes.'

'It was in here?'

'No. It was in the computer room. There isn't a terminal in here. We aren't as well equipped as we would like.'

There was nothing here for him. The police had taken everything. He turned away, defeated. Jankowski watched him. 'Is there anything else I can do?'

Will shook his head. He couldn't trust his voice. The two men walked silently back down the corridor.

When they reached his office, Jankowski studied Will, his face troubled. He looked at the bags Will was carrying, the bags containing the few possessions Ania had left behind. 'You can leave these here,' he said. 'Collect them later. I have a lecture now, so my office is free if you need any time to…' His voice trailed off.

'Thank you,' Will said again. He needed a place where he could close the door behind him. 'Thank you.'

Chapter 27

Will sank into the chair at Konstantin Jankowski's desk. Now he was alone, he could relax the fierce hold he had kept on his emotions. There was a pain in his chest as though something was gripping him tighter and tighter, and for a moment, he had trouble breathing. He sat very still until the grip loosened and his breathing steadied. He was glad of the silence, glad to be on his own so he didn't have to act a part any more.

He was beginning to get a clearer picture of what had happened. Ania had been sitting at her desk, surfing the net, listening to music. In the days of iPods, Ania had borrowed a Walkman from Jankowski, and to make her request less strange, she had borrowed some tapes of traditional Polish music. As far as Will knew, she couldn't care less about traditional Polish music.

She must have been using the Walkman to listen to the recording Cathcart's team had made. It was the only surviving copy of the Haynes original, the one she had taken from Cathcart, and that had subsequently vanished. Was she having doubts about what she had done? Was she having doubts about Haynes' guilt? If she believed she'd sent an innocent man to prison... He shook his head in disgust. All the paths he was finding led back to the same place: the room, the window and the drop.

There was a knock on the office door. Before he could respond, it opened and a man came in, a tall, heavy-set man whose grim face looked tired and drawn. It was a moment before he recognised Dariusz Erland. Today, he was clean-shaven and his clothes looked neat and freshly laundered. There was only his pallor and a weariness around his eyes that remained from the day before. He looked at Will. 'They told me you were here. What time is your appointment with the police?'

Will made a point of checking his watch. 'Soon. I need to get going.' In fact, it wasn't for another half hour and the central police station was on the same road as the university. It would take him all of five minutes to get there, but he didn't want to spend time with Erland, nor did he want Erland to accompany him.

What remained of Ania was his.

Erland looked at the notebook. 'What are you doing?'

Will gestured at the computer. 'Checking my mail.' He waited for Erland to say what he had come to say. He wasn't going to listen to any more accusations from this man – he knew what he had done as a father and he knew what he hadn't done. He didn't need anyone else to tell him.

Erland crossed the room behind his chair and stood by the window, his frame silhouetted against the light. He looked like someone whose response to adversity would be to shoulder his way through obstructions with a ruthless disregard for others, refuse to take no for an answer, continue doggedly to whatever end he perceived. He was probably excellent at what he did.

But he had some information Will needed. 'You said they stonewalled you when you asked about Ania.'

'Yes. No one wanted to tell me.'

'Because…?'

'Because I was with her, we were together?'

But Erland sounded unconvinced.

'Or…?' Will prompted.

Erland looked away and shrugged. He wasn't prepared to discuss it. He obviously trusted Will as little as Will trusted him. 'You were going to marry her and they wouldn't tell you anything,' Will persisted. 'Why?'

'I have told you. There's nothing else…'

'She was my daughter!'

He hadn't meant to shout. In the following silence, their eyes locked until Erland looked away.

There was a knock at the door, and after a slight pause, Konstantin Jankowski came in. He looked at the two men, a faint line appearing between his eyes when he saw Erland standing there. 'I'm sorry to disturb you. I need to get…'

Will closed his notebook and stood up. 'I don't want to be in your way.'

'We are going to the police station,' Erland said. 'I came to take Mr Gillen.'

'Of course.' Jankowski's lips were thin. He said something rapidly to Erland that Will's Polish couldn't catch, and Erland grinned.

'Don't worry,' he said in English. 'I will take good care of him.' He nodded to Jankowski. 'Cześć.'

As they left the room, Jankowski called Will back. 'Are you sure you want him with you?' he said, his voice low.

'I can get rid of him if I need to. Don't worry.'

'He and Ania were friends.' Jankowski's gaze wouldn't meet his. Will wondered if Polish society, with its strong adherence to the doctrines of the Roman Catholic church, was still prudish about relationships that wouldn't raise an eyebrow in the UK.

'I know.'

'Be careful of him.'

Will nodded, then left the room and crossed the landing to where Erland was waiting for him.

Chapter 28

Police stations were police stations the world over. The one in Łódź was no exception. It was a relatively modern building, its concrete brutalism reflecting the influences of Stalinism on Polish architecture.

The main entrance opened onto a busy street, where patrol cars were parked outside. Erland led Will through the entrance into a lobby that smelt of cigarettes and unwashed bodies. A few people sat on benches in the waiting area, their down-at-heel shabbiness creating a different impression of the city than the one Will had had so far, as if the new Łódź , the renewed, innovative city was a mask beneath which the poverty and corruption of the Soviet days still lurked.

There was a reception window at the far end where a man was filling in a form in a leisurely way, ignoring a cluster of people waiting for his attention.

Erland spoke suddenly. 'They won't tell you anything important.' He went straight to the desk, pushing through the crowd as if it wasn't there. He rapped on the counter and said, 'Commander Gillen. He has an appointment with Komendant Król.'

The man straightened up, his gaze first on Erland. He seemed about to speak, then looked at Will. 'One moment.' He picked up the phone and almost immediately, a man wearing the black, military-style fatigues and cap that were the uniform of the Łódź police appeared at a door behind them and addressed Will. 'Sir. The Komendant expect...' He began.

'I speak Polish,' Will said.

'Of course. Komendant Król is expecting you.' He looked at Erland and his jaw tightened. 'He isn't expecting...'

Erland shrugged. 'I'll wait.'

Will followed the uniformed man. He was led through a maze of corridors to a closed door. His guide knocked, then waited until a voice responded. He opened the door and led Will into another small office, lit by artificial light as there was no window. 'Komendant. DCI Gillen,' he said.

The Komendant stood up as Will came into the room. He was a big man, heavy set with the high colour that spoke of raised blood pressure, an occupational hazard for police the world over. 'Mr Gillen. I am Piotr Król. I'm sorry about your daughter's death. Now, how can I help you?'

The expression of regret was formal but sounded sincere. Will could see a certain wariness behind the Komendant's eyes. He could understand it. He wasn't simply a grieving relative to be told what the police chose to tell him. He had been an officer in the UK force, and his visit here had been backed by Blaise, a significant name in pan-European security. Despite Erland's warning, Will knew this man had no choice but to cooperate with him and give him what he wanted.

'Thank you for your assistance. I'd like the see the case files on the investigation, everything you can show me.'

'Are you sure that's wise? You understand that we have effectively closed the case on your daughter. She took her own life, Mr Gillen. I am sorry to tell you this, but there is no other conclusion we could come to. There is a lot of witness evidence to tell us that she was unwell, she was not herself, and, forgive me, there were the… unfortunate events at home.'

Suicide while the balance of the mind was disturbed. She had been upset and distracted while she was here – everyone he had spoken to had commented on it – except Erland. He had claimed she was much the same as always – a bit anxious, under pressure from work, but calm and in control.

'I understand, but I need to know everything I can. She seemed to be coping, from what I can tell and then something happened to tip the balance. I think it happened that night and I want to know what it was.'

'Who can tell?' In this deeply Catholic country, suicide was doubly shocking. The person who died at her own hand had committed the one unforgivable sin, the sin of despair, a sin that would condemn them to hellfire for all eternity.

'You can't repent, you see,' Ania had explained to him once, 'because you're dead. That's it. You're lost forever.'

Not Ania. Not his child.

Piotr Król was still speaking. 'There's very little more than you will have seen already.' He had a file in front of him. 'Before I show you this, I have to say something. All of this is confidential. It goes nowhere beyond these walls.' He held up his hand before Will could respond. 'I say this because the man you are with is known to us. Under the circumstances, I must ask for your assurance…'

Will nodded. He had come here accompanied by a man who described himself as a political activist. He could sympathise with Król's caution. 'I understand.'

Król apparently found this sufficient and he pushed the folder across the desk to Will. His gesture indicated that Will was free to browse as he chose.

Will had seen these reports. Blaise had sent him copies, but he read through them again, making sure that nothing had been added or changed since he last saw them, that nothing further had been identified.

The story they told was the same.

The security guard, Jerzy Pawlak, had done his rounds as usual. The last people had left, to his knowledge, at around ten that evening. Well after midnight he had been checking the rooms on the top floor trying to track down the source of a strong draught. He'd found an open window in one of the small offices at the top of the building, and when he'd looked out of the window, he had seen Ania's body in the car park far below. The man was adamant that the room had been locked – he had had to use his pass key to open the door. The key had been found later in Ania's pocket.

The office had been examined by a forensic team who had found various unknown fingerprints, to be expected in a room that was used by a number of people. Ania's prints were on the window sill and on the window frame. They were the only clear ones, though there were some smudges that her prints overlaid. There was nothing identifiable on the phone, the door handles or the desk. It sounded much as Will would have expected.

They had found no evidence of a struggle in that room, or in the computer room where Ania had been seen working earlier – no disturbance, no blood, no body fluids. The only slight anomaly was the phone in the small office. It normally stood on the filing cabinet, but it had been on the floor, the plug pulled out of the jack. It would have taken only minor force to do that, but there was no explanation other than a conjecture that Ania had done it herself.

He turned back to the folder, aware of Król's gaze on him as he turned the pages over. He'd seen the post-mortem report once. He didn't want to see it again. He knew his daughter had died in the fall and he knew what the fall had done to her.

He looked across the desk. 'Thank you,' he said. 'There's just a couple of things. I understood that the last person to see Ania alive was Professor Jankowski when he left the building at eight. Is that correct?'

Król shook his head. 'The professor was the last person to speak to her at any length. The caretaker saw her when he did his rounds between nine and ten. She was working in the computer room where the professor saw her. He asked her if she had a key to lock the room when she left and she said she did.'

'And after that?' If he was doing his rounds hourly, then he should have checked again before midnight.

'He didn't see her. He assumed she had left. We now realise of course she must have been in the small office. The man says he didn't check it because the door was locked.'

Will was still turning the pages of the file. There was a section of photographs, and he opened it reluctantly. The first one was of a room which he recognised at once: the room where Ania had fallen. The last room.

It was the same as he had just seen it except the window was wide open and the phone lay on the floor beside the filing cabinet. There was a shoe on its side on the desk under the window. It was the kind of shoe that Ania always wore, insubstantial, with an impossibly high heel and a filigree of fine straps.

'Not a shoe for running in.'

He looked up.

She was watching him again, standing by the exit. Her head inclined towards the folder in front of him, then there was just the battered wood of the door.

Still holding the picture, he started reading the notes, skimming them because they told him the story he knew – the time of the call, the location of the body – and focusing on the bits where the gaps appeared.

Two questions were clear in his mind, and he couldn't see that the investigation had answered them: what had she been doing so late at night, and why had the caretaker assumed she had left? She had been in the computer room when Jankowski spoke to her, and again when the caretaker saw her. He had asked her if she had a key to lock up, and she'd said she had. She wasn't there when he checked later. He'd assumed she'd gone, or that was what he claimed. If so, why hadn't he seen her go? There was no way out other than past his desk. It was Mickey Mouse security.

She must have locked the door to the computer room, or the caretaker would have noticed, and moved to the small office at the end of the corridor. Why? The office was poorly equipped. There was no computer terminal, nothing for her to use.

He looked at the photo again.

The phone. He was pretty sure there wasn't a phone in the computer room. Students had free access to the computer room during the day. The university wouldn't leave a phone with an outside line in a room where students could use it. She may have gone to the small office to use the phone.

When he had been in the room that morning, the phone had been on top of the filing cabinet. The filing cabinet was behind the door, out of the way of the desk and the window. It couldn't have got knocked to the floor accidentally. There was no reason for Ania to have gone near the line. But it was there, on the floor, with the plug pulled out of the socket.

He looked at the police officer. 'Did you take prints from the phone and the phone wire?'

'We took prints from everything.'

Will looked at the photo, then checked through the notes again. There was nothing that looked like a report from a scene of crime team. 'Do you have the forensic reports? I'd like to see the results of the fingerprint analysis.'

Król reached across and turned the pages of the file. 'The summary is there.'

'I'd like to see the original.'

Król's mouth tightened, but he spoke rapidly to the man who had brought Will to the room and who was standing by the door. The man nodded and went across to a filing cabinet, where he began flicking through files.

'There is nothing there,' Król said. 'But...' He shrugged, glancing not quite discreetly at the clock on the wall. Will ignored this. He needed to see the report. In his mind, there was the image of a hand gripping a phone line and pulling it out of the socket, of the wire coiled round the hand and held firm by the thumb pressed against the side of the index finger.

The man produced a sheaf of papers from the filing cabinet. Will held out his hand. The man hesitated then glanced at Król, who nodded. He passed it across. Will flicked through the pages as though he were searching for the images that would show the matching comparisons, but his eyes were scanning the pages as he went.

It was there. They'd found a partial print on the phone line, a thumb print that wasn't hers, but gave insufficient detail for identification purposes. The report gave no more information than that.

He kept his face emotionless as he flicked on through the pages. Nowhere in the file was there any reference to a cassette tape. He handed it back to Król. 'Thank you. What was she doing there? Do you know what she was working on?'

Król indicated a section of the report that Will's eye had skimmed over. The transcript of the Haynes recording had been on the desk where she had been working, and the disk was in the computer. 'But she did no work on it,' Król said. 'All she had done was play it, over and over. The computer records show that clearly.' His eyes didn't leave Will's face as he pushed another folder across the table. 'And this,' he said. 'So you have seen everything.'

Will opened it.

Her body was twisted as if the impact with the ground had shattered her spine. Her legs were sprawled out, looking floppy and shapeless. If he touched them, if he tried to lift her, they would drape and sag because the bones no longer held them together. Her head was misshapen, distorted and smashed. Her face was mercifully turned away from the camera, her hair stuck to it, the pale gold stained dark and sticky with her blood.

She was like a rag doll thrown out of the pram by a fractious child.

His daughter.

Chapter 29

Dariusz Erland called out to Will as he strode out of the police station. 'Gillen. *Gillen!*'

Will could feel the rage surging inside him. Evidence was there in the file and it had been ignored. They'd opted for the simple solution, that a distressed woman had killed herself. Only the evidence that fit the pattern had been considered. Everything else had been dismissed: *this room is much used. Of course there are prints.*

'Gillen!' Erland had caught up with him and was moving beside him now. 'What is it? What did he tell you?'

'That they don't give a shit what happened to Ania.'

'He told you...' For once, Erland's assurance left him.

'There was someone else in that room.'

'How do you know?'

The impetus of Will's anger had slowed, and only grief remained. He shook his head.

'This way.' Erland took his elbow and steered him round the next corner, where a small, run-down café opened onto the street. When they were sitting at a table, Erland said, 'Now. How do you know?'

'There was a thumb print on the telephone cord, a partial, as if someone had...' He made a gesture to show the action of gripping a cord and pulling it free.

Erland lit another cigarette. His face was white, but his voice was matter-of-fact. 'So now you know your daughter again. Now there is evidence, you know she didn't kill herself.'

'I have always known my daughter, and I know that she could... If the wrong things happened at the wrong time, she could have done that.'

'Once, perhaps. Not now.'

Will shook his head. 'Do you think I want to believe my daughter killed herself? It's you who didn't know her.' He stopped Erland before he could respond. 'That window, the one where she... She had to have done that herself. There's no other

132

way. All I know is they haven't looked at the evidence properly.' His daughter's death, and they had carried out a shoddy investigation. His daughter's *death*!

Erland's face was expressionless. It was impossible to tell what he was thinking. 'So what is this evidence?'

'Small things. Questions that any half-decent investigation would have answered. Why did she go into the small office? The windows in the computer room were more accessible. Why did the security guard think she'd left earlier? The fingerprint.' He shrugged. 'I don't know. I just don't know. It may mean nothing – probably does. But they should have checked it all before they closed the case.'

'What are you going to do?'

'I'm going to start with the fingerprint. I need to know why the police aren't chasing it up.'

Erland was frowning as he thought about it. 'Do they know whose it was?'

'The report just said there wasn't enough for an identification.' His first reaction to what he had seen was fading, and he felt the familiar weight of discouragement. A partial fingerprint in a room that was used by a large number of people was hardly surprising, and it was in a place where a print could have been left undisturbed for months. Even so... 'The phone wire was pulled out. They *have* to consider it, even if it's only for elimination purposes. And there's no evidence that they checked the phone. Ania probably went to that room to use it but there's no record of any calls.' He would check the phone himself when he went back.

Erland stubbed out his cigarette. 'She called me that night. I was out. I tried to call her back but her phone was switched off. I thought she must be on her way to the hotel. I thought she'd call me again, only she didn't. I didn't see her again until...' His mouth tightened and Will realised Erland must have been the person who had identified her body. Against his will, he felt a surge of pity for what that must have cost him. 'All the time I thought she was safe, but she wasn't, and I wasn't there.'

Will had no answer to that. He didn't want to allow Erland the luxury of guilt over Ania's death. That was his, and his alone. 'I have to go.'

He still had something to do. She had left him something. This was what she was trying to tell him. The tape. He would find it – if it existed, he would track it down. He could well be in the wrong place for that, because he had one lead left to follow.

Sarah Ludlow.

She had been outside the court when Ania gave evidence. She had come to St Abbs looking for Ania and had found him instead. He had told her that Ania was in Poland, and she had left. A few hours later, Ania was dead.

Chapter 30

The message light was blinking on his phone as Dariusz let himself into his flat. He'd kept his mobile switched off. He didn't want anyone to be able to contact him today. There were five messages, all from Krysia, the woman he had been involved with before he met Ania. He sighed. He didn't want to talk to anyone and Krysia was the last person he wanted to contact. He wanted to think about what Will Gillen had told him. Gillen's findings at the police station were no surprise to Dariusz. He had known from the start that they weren't doing a proper job on the investigation. What he didn't know was why.

But he couldn't ignore messages from work. There were people relying on him. He keyed in Krysia's number. 'Krysia. It's Dariusz.'

'Dariusz. I'm glad you called. How are you?'

'I'm OK. What's the problem?'

'Oh that. Mr Mielek's going crazy. I told him you'd phone as soon as… He's been on to me all day to get hold of you.'

It was typical of Leslaw Mielek to make trouble over what was a simple enough matter. 'Tell him I'll call tomorrow. Wait. Don't tell him you've spoken to me, just leave it with me. I'll call him.'

'OK… Listen, Dariusz, I'm worried about you. I don't think you should be on your own right now. Beata thinks…'

'I'm fine, Krysia. Thanks. I'll be back in a couple of days, OK? I'll call Mielek now.'

He put the phone down and took some deep breaths to calm himself. He was angry at his sister's interference. She'd obviously been on the phone to Krysia as soon as she heard the news about Ania.

He didn't want to deal with Beata's schemes for his future. He didn't want to upset Krysia again, but he couldn't cope with this on top of everything else. He picked up the phone and dialled Beata's number.

'It's Dariusz,' he said abruptly as soon as she answered.

'Dareczek!' The diminutive from his childhood usually had the power to disarm him, but not today.

'I've just spoken to Krysia…'

'Good. You need to have people…'

'She told me what you'd said to her. Stay out of my business, Beata. If I need people, I'll choose my own.'

'Dareczek, don't get angry with me. Krysia's worried about you. We all are.'

There was genuine concern in her voice. He felt weary at the prospect of an argument. Maybe he should just leave it. 'I know.'

She sensed his capitulation and pushed her advantage. 'Krysia cares about you a lot, Dareczek. You need someone who…'

'I need Ania.'

'She's dead, Dariusz. She killed herself. She didn't care about you, did she? She wasn't thinking about you when she jumped out of that window.'

'How many times do I have to tell you? Ania didn't kill herself.'

Beata sighed. 'Oh, Dareczek. You always were such an…'

He was glad they weren't face to face. He wasn't sure what he would do if she was in the room with him. 'Stop it, Beata.'

'You never want to hear the truth, do you? She wasn't right for you. You need…'

He lost it. 'Beata. Shut up. Just shut your fucking mouth and listen for once.' The obscenity silenced her, as he knew it would. 'Don't interfere in my life. And don't say anything more about Ania. I don't want to hear it.'

'How can you speak to me like that? I know you're upset, but…' She sounded close to tears. 'You phone me up and swear at me, and you don't even want to know about Dad. When did you last phone him?'

She was right. He was in a bad way, swearing at his little sister, neglecting his father. 'Is he worse?'

'Oh, so now you care. This has upset him, too. You know he isn't well. She called him that night, you know. It's preying on his mind.'

'She didn't call him, Beata. She called *me*. I was out at the late night chemist getting his prescription. I could have spoken to her if I hadn't…' He couldn't go on. 'I can't talk now.' He put the phone down on whatever she had been trying to say.

He was so angry he couldn't sit still. He paced the room, cursing under his breath. He was angry with himself, angry with Beata, angry with his father… And work. Fucking Mielek. He could do without Leslaw Mielek's shit just now. One day – and soon – they'd have a showdown. The way he was feeling at the moment, Dariusz wanted the showdown to be physical. He wanted the satisfaction of driving his fist into Mielek's face and feel the crunch of the bone breaking. Life had been a lot simpler before he became a professional.

He picked up the phone and dialled Mielek's direct number. He was ready for a confrontation. Ania would have counselled delay but his anger demanded action. *Wait until you've calmed down.* It was wise advice, but Dariusz was in no mood for wisdom. He was in the mood for conflict.

'Leslaw Mielek.'

'It's Dariusz Erland. What the fuck are you doing harassing my staff when I'm on leave.'

'What do you mean, harassing? Where the hell are you anyway? You were supposed to be in work yesterday.'

'If you check your records, you'll see I extended my leave to the end of the week.'

'You didn't clear it with me.'

'You weren't there, Mielek. I cleared it with Jan Stefanowski.' Stefanowski was Mielek's senior. 'You'll have a memo on your desk about it.'

The silence at the other end told him Mielek hadn't bothered to check. It took him a moment to rally. 'I don't like your attitude Erland. I'm making allowances under the circumstances, but…'

I don't give a flying fuck what you think about my attitude. 'I'll be back in two days.' Dariusz hung up. The exchange had done nothing to get rid of his anger. It had only made it worse. He needed to focus. He had more important things to think about than a lump of horseshit like Mielek. He wasn't angry with Mielek anyway, not really. His real anger was directed at himself, and, he admitted, at Will Gillen.

Despite the galvanic shot in the arm Gillen's visit to the police had given him, he still clung to his belief in Ania's suicide. Her own father wasn't going to fight for her. Dariusz was going to have to do this himself.

At least Gillen had confirmed – and this was the view of a professional – that Król's men had not investigated her death properly. Now Dariusz had to find out why. One explanation was simple inefficiency: they were short-staffed, they were always short-staffed, and he could see why Król would not want to complicate what looked like a straight-forward case. On the other hand, Ania was a foreign national, and one with friends in high places. Surely this was one case where Król would have pulled out all the stops.

The other explanation was that a suicide verdict would prevent anyone from looking too closely at what had happened.

If that were so... what was the secret? One of Ania's past cases, a case involving child abuse and murder, had blown up in her face. She was accused of falsifying evidence. Instead of sitting tight and defending herself, she had run, and later, she had died. She had left a suicide note and had fallen from a high window. The bare facts looked damning.

Dariusz knew she hadn't killed herself. He knew she had been murdered. OK, there were anomalies. Gillen's point about the window was one that Dariusz had seen himself. It would have been impossible to force a conscious, struggling woman out of that window, and unconscious? Ania wasn't heavy. She weighed about fifty kilos, but even he would have had difficulty lifting that unconscious weight to that height and then manoeuvring it out through the small window.

It must have been coercion, but even that presented problems. How could her killer have forced her out of the window? Ania had a thing about heights. Her mother had died in a fall. The killer couldn't risk using a weapon if he wanted her death to look like suicide. He couldn't risk knife or bullet wounds.

It didn't matter. It had to be possible because it had happened. It wasn't the how he was looking for, it was the why.

What was it about the Haynes case that had led to murder?

Chapter 31

It was dark by the time Will got back to his hotel. He went to the bar and bought a bottle of beer, then walked slowly up to his room. He still wasn't hungry, but he ordered room service, then stripped off his jacket and lay down on the bed. He stared at the ceiling. A winter fly circled the light fitting, round and round, round and round.

He'd learnt almost nothing from Król, except the investigation had been skimped. It was so obviously a suicide, they hadn't chased up what little evidence they had. He could do that, but despite what he had said to Erland, he didn't expect to find anything.

The only lead he had now was Sarah Ludlow.

He could see her clearly sitting in the bar of the hotel at St Abbs, her newspaper strewn on the seat beside her, her hands gesturing to emphasise something she had said. She claimed to be a lawyer and clearly earned a good income from somewhere. She drove an expensive car and dressed well. Who was she? Why had she wanted to know about Ania? Who was she working for? He remembered his race down to the harbour to try and stop her, the empty car park and Jack's puzzled curiosity. He must have thought he was seeing the aftermath of a lovers' tiff.

She had made no attempt to find out about Ania that evening in the hotel bar, had done nothing to arouse his suspicions. Their encounter had been relaxed and friendly and her farewell had been warm. She had managed to put him completely off his guard with that last appeal to his male vanity.

He switched on his laptop and Googled Sarah Ludlow. He got over a million hits. OK, he was looking for a journalist – or just maybe a lawyer. He knew which he would put money on. He tried +"Sarah Ludlow" +journalist. This time, he got forty-one hits, but only one journalist, a scientific writer based in Canada. Maybe she wrote under a different name. He tried again, replacing 'journalist' with 'lawyer', and found her at once.

It looked as though she had been telling him the truth as far as that went.

She worked for a company called Merchant Matheson. They were solicitors with offices in the City of London, and regional offices in Manchester and Birmingham. The Merchant Matheson home page showed a cityscape of towers, brightly lit against banking clouds. The firm offered corporate services and services for private clients. Their work covered conveyancing, matrimonial, personal injury, wills, trusts, probate, immigration, landlord and tenant law and employment.

He clicked on the link *About us*, and then on *Our team*. Sarah Ludlow was a partner in the firm, and the head of the Manchester office. This might explain her association with Ania. Merchant Matheson would almost certainly have had contacts with FLS from time to time. It was the biggest private forensics lab in the area.

But it didn't explain what she was doing outside the court the day Ania gave her evidence.

The site didn't give any details about her areas of expertise. Employment law? A lot of Ania's voice recognition work involved employment litigation. It was possible. Immigration? As far as Will knew, FLS only took this work on for the Home Office, using voice analysis to confirm or refute the claimed origins of refugees. They didn't do any work for individuals because, Ania had told him, Oz believed this would jeopardise their lucrative government contracts.

So why had Sarah Ludlow travelled to the Scottish Borders? It had to be connected to the Haynes case. The news about the falsification of evidence had just broken. For some reason, she had raced north, presumably in search of Ania, under the mistaken belief his daughter had retreated to the St Abbs refuge. Sarah must have known Ania quite well to have made that assumption.

She told him she had come to the Borders to see a client. He'd joked about lawyers who made house calls, and she'd been evasive: *I don't usually. This is an exception.* Could she be working for Ania? Had Ania taken legal advice when the Haynes debacle first broke?

He looked at the other pages his search for had found. He'd got seventy hits, and about fifteen of them related to the woman he had met in St Abbs. One site told him she'd been employed by a law firm in New Orleans that specialised in death penalty appeals. Another site referred to her as '...the human rights lawyer, Sarah Ludlow.' He remembered she had told him she had gone to the US to complete her training and had stayed to work.

It began to make sense. Why would a human rights lawyer be hanging round the Derek Haynes case? That was an easy one to answer. If the recording had been fabricated then Haynes was a victim and his human rights had been violated. If someone was convinced of Haynes' innocence and was prepared to put the money in to back that belief, then a human rights lawyer like Sarah Ludlow would be the person to go to.

If she was working for Derek Haynes, what had she wanted from Ania that day?

He stood up and moved around the room, trying to clear his thoughts. His mind wouldn't focus. The questions were filling his head and he couldn't begin to look at the answers.

'That's not important now.'

Ania was sitting at the desk where he had left his laptop. Her gaze was intent, focused on his face. 'That doesn't matter. You have to listen.'

'*Doesn't matter*? Ania, it matters more than...' He stopped speaking. All he really wanted to say to her was *don't go! Please! Stay!*

But there was no one there.

You have to listen.

He had listened. What was it he hadn't heard?

At the airport. She had spoken to him at the airport: *You have to know where to look, Dad.*

He'd missed something, that's what she was telling him. He turned wearily to his papers to begin the process of going through them again, when he looked back to where she had been sitting.

He went across to the desk and switched on his laptop. The hotel didn't offer wireless, not in the rooms, so he logged on using his phone. His computer began downloading e-mails. He checked everything, even the ones he had ignored before, the ones from people who had known Ania. He would have to reply to these sometime, but not now. Not now. *So sorry, dreadful news, can't believe… so sorry, so sorry…*

He was looking for something else, something…

He had downloaded e-mails before, in her flat in Manchester. He could remember impatiently deleting stuff he had dismissed as spam, but suppose it hadn't been… What if there was something in there he'd missed? Something was nagging at his mind. He remembered what Jankowski had said, and realised what it was. When Jankowski saw her, she had been on the Facebook site.

Facebook. Someone had sent him an e-mail from Facebook. He could remember deleting it. If he'd emptied the folder, it was irretrievable, at least via any system he knew of. Had he…?

And then he could breathe again. It was still there, the invitation to become a friend on Facebook, an invitation from someone called Walter Gilman.

Gilman. He'd missed the significance the first time, but now…

Gilman. Walter Gilman and Brown Jenkin.

He should have seen it earlier. Brown Jenkin was a witch's familiar in a piece of pulp writing Ania had enjoyed in her teens. Walter Gilman was the name of a character who wanders with naive blindness into Brown Jenkin's lair and pays a terrible price. Brown Jenkin was the hunter and Walter Gilman was the victim.

He clicked on the link to the social networking site.

The site wouldn't let him on unless he signed up for an account. He wanted to hit the keyboard in frustration. He knew about surveillance techniques and tried as far as possible to keep his life off-grid. He didn't shop online, he didn't subscribe to websites. He used Hushmail for his e-mail accounts and his favoured browser was Xerobank, slower, but more secure. Facebook, on the other hand, was as public as it got. It was the cyber equivalent of jumping up and down and shouting, 'Here I am!'

But he had no choice. He registered for the site, giving the barest minimum of information he could get away with. He called himself James Pearson. Once he had signed up, he was allowed to proceed to the link that someone had sent him.

The page was a profile of Walter Gilman. It gave very little information – most of the spaces were blank. It wasn't the details of 'Gilman' that interested Will. It was the photo attached to the profile that drew his attention. It was a picture of a child's pink teddy bear, rather battered and grubby.

He recognised it at once.

Someone had made it for Louisa when the twins were two. Ania had had one as well, a yellow one, but she had never been very interested in cuddly toys and hers had been discarded years ago.

Louisa had loved hers. She had named it Small Bear and it had been her constant companion. He could remember having to turn back en route to a holiday destination because she had left Small Bear at home. The toy had been in the front passenger seat of Elžbieta's car the night she died. If he had had any doubts about who had sent the message, the picture dispelled them. Next to the photograph were the words 'Small Bear has a secret,' and just above it, the words "*5 days ago.*" He couldn't tell when she had added the page, but the message had been put there the day before she died.

Ania was the only person who would know the significance of the bear, and of the name Gilman. She was trying to tell him something, but whatever it was, he couldn't read her code. *Small Bear has a secret.* He didn't know what she meant. The toy had been thrown out years ago, after Elžbieta's death.

Dead end.

You have to know where to look.

When had she sent the mail? He checked the date and felt something cold touch him – it had been sent at twenty-one thirty the night she died. This was her last message, not the suicide note. And it wasn't linked to her because it had come from the Facebook site, which had almost caused him to miss it altogether.

Quietly, without fanfare, another figure moved onto the stage that had held only Ania. Her killer emerged from the shadows, caught, just for a second, in the light.

Chapter 32

Dariusz went in to the office the next day. Mielek might be a hundred kinds of fool, but he was right in one respect. Dariusz' work was piling up after his absence, and there was no one else who could take it on. He could continue his investigation into Ania's death from his desk at work as easily as from his desk at home.

Krysia looked up as he came in. 'Dariusz. It's good to see you.' Her face flushed. 'I mean...'

'It's OK. It's time I was back.'

'Of course. I understand. I'm sorry about...'

'Yes.' He went to his office quickly. He didn't want to talk to her about Ania.

He needed something to do, and his office was clearly going to provide it. There was a pile of correspondence waiting for him, at least a morning's work here in front of him before he could get back to his cases.

Before he started, he called Roman Strąk. 'Got your watch working again?' Strąk said in sour reference to Dariusz' last call, when he realised who was speaking.

'Sorry about that.' Dariusz didn't feel particularly repentant. 'One more favour. I want information about the case Ania was working on – the Haynes case, you know?' It hadn't hit the papers in Poland, but Strąk would be aware of it.

'What's wrong with a newspaper library? Shit, Erland, I'm not your clippings agency.'

'I want the stuff that isn't in the public domain. I want the recording and I want the video.'

There was a long silence. 'The recording... I can do that. The other... that's not so easy to get hold of.'

'Even for someone with your contacts?'

'Don't bullshit me, Erland. That video is officially child pornography. It's linked to a murder. Do you know how much trouble you could get into, being in possession of that stuff?'

'I don't have a choice.'

'Yeah yeah yeah.'

'Can you get it for me?'

'Probably.'

'Send it to my web mail, OK?' He didn't want these files downloading automatically onto his system.

'OK. It won't come from me, though. I don't know anything about this one, got it?'

'Got it.'

Dariusz put the phone down. He wasn't sure where he planned to go with this, but Ania's death was inextricably linked with this case. He was hoping that somewhere in the evidence, there would be something to tell him what had happened to her.

***

Will was up and out early the following morning. His discovery of the night before had given him back his energy. He wasn't going to let Ania down, not again. He used the city guide he'd picked up to locate the internet cafés in the city centre. His suspicions about Sarah Ludlow had reminded him that Blaise was almost certainly keeping an eye on him. If Ania was trying to tell him something via the Facebook page she had sent, then she didn't want anyone else to see it. He'd carry out his search where it wouldn't be noticed.

There was a café on Piotrkowska, but if Ania had gone there, he didn't want to use the same place. Instead, he walked through the streets to the main railway station, Fabryczna.

Here, the streets had a more raffish air. The station, like all stations, attracted the poor, the itinerant, the drunks, the casualties of the Soviet state and the fallout from sudden prosperity. A man, smelling strongly of some kind of raw spirit, lurched into Will and muttered something that may have been a request for money.

Will evaded him and walked towards the station frontage. There was an open square crowded with taxis, mostly old and battered, touting for business. People pushed past him wearing backpacks or dragging suitcases behind them. It was easy enough to meld with the crowd and let it carry him into the ticket hall, a high, spacious area that was neither indoors nor outdoors, a transit space between the street and the tracks. Huge boards showed arrival and departure times, and people queued at a long wooden counter where the ticket windows were placed. This kind of thing was second nature to him. He positioned himself by a notice board and observed the people flowing in and out of the hall.

He could see no sign of surveillance. Everyone seemed to know where they were going and what they were doing. There was no one showing undue interest in their newspaper, or studying timetables for overlong. He joined a queue at one of the ticket windows and after a few minutes, he was as certain as he could be that no one had followed him.

He collected a timetable and left the station. A few streets away he found the place he was looking for, the Internetowa Kawiarnia Spadochronowa: the Skydiving Internet Café.

He had no idea what the link with skydiving was, but the interior of the café had been decorated to create a hi-tech feel, with tinny metallic finishes contrasting oddly with spilt coffee and cigarette butts in the ashtrays. In the middle of the room, a model helicopter took pride of place. Will paid for computer time and took his coffee across to the tables where monitors faced away from each other. There was only one other person using the equipment.

He was about to log on to Facebook, then stopped. The Walter Gilman page was in itself a dead end. He needed more information. He stared into space, trying to remember. Who was the writer of the story? Who was Brown Jenkin's creator? He typed 'H.P. Lovecraft' into the search engine, and found it at once: Dreams in the Witch House. With an odd reluctance, he clicked on a link that gave him the text.

He drank coffee while he skimmed it, making a note of the names of the important characters as he went. He'd read it years ago but he'd never liked it. It had always struck him as both trashy and distasteful, an opinion he'd made clear to the teenage Ania at the height of her enthusiasm.

A re-acquaintance with the text did nothing to improve his opinion. It was a piece of lurid pulp writing about nameless horrors and arcane mysteries, but what made it so disturbing was the sense of something truly evil that permeated the text. It was carried by the figure of Brown Jenkin, the familiar of the witch Keziah Mason. Brown Jenkin was a rat-like creature with a small, bearded, human face and human hands. The witch light of its presence flickered and glowed from the places it haunted. Will hated the idea of this thing personifying the depressions that had eaten away at Ania's mind. It seemed obscene that even as a metaphor she should talk about having it in her head.

He shook the images away and logged on to Facebook. He had hoped that his response to the e-mail might have signalled to someone else, someone Ania had contacted who might have been waiting for him, but there was nothing there. There had been no activity on his James Pearson account, other than that generated by the site itself.

He began searching the site for the names Keziah Mason and Brown Jenkin, but found nothing that fitted. He read through the text again more closely this time. In the story, Walter Gilman had tried to protect a small child the witch had kidnapped and was about to sacrifice. He had managed to drive off the witch, but not Brown Jenkin, who had killed the boy. The child's name was Ladislas Wolejko.

Louisa in the park, playing by herself on the swings. It was twilight, and as he watched, a sickly phosphorescence began to glow in the dimness. Louisa swung, slower and slower, her feet brushing the ground. Stay high, he wanted to warn her. Don't come down. Don't walk away through those shadows alone in the evening playground. Then she was standing there, barely visible in the darkness and the bushes behind her rustled as though something small and rat-like was creeping towards her.

Hardly breathing, he typed the name Ladislas Wolejko into the search box.

There was nothing.

He stared at the screen in frustration.

Then a number appeared at the bottom right of the page: 1. Next to it, there was an icon with the words "Online Friends." It was a moment before he understood the significance. The site was telling him that one of James Pearson's friends was now online. James Pearson had no friends, except for...

Holding his breath, he clicked the icon. A note popped up. *Walter Gilman is not available to chat.*

The screen went blank. Will blinked, back in the sci-fi fantasy of the café. The waiter came over to apologise. 'The connection,' he said. 'It drops off sometimes. I'm sorry.'

'No, it's OK. I'd finished. Thank you.' He stayed in his seat, feeling as though he had been punched in the gut. He knew the Facebook page was from Ania. She was the only person who knew the significance of the bear, and of the name, Walter Gilman. Someone else had accessed that account. Someone else had taken over the Walter Gilman persona. Everything Will knew about the site, this person now knew as well. *Small Bear has a secret*. What secret? Where?

He paid for his coffee and his time online, and took a tram back to Piotrkowska. As the tram clanged its way along the street, he saw a fair haired woman walking with a brisk, familiar step along the pavement. As the tram went past, she raised her hand in a salute.

Chapter 33

It was getting colder now as the day began to fade. Will wanted to get into shelter, but he had somewhere to go before he went back to his hotel. The streets were coming alive with night-time crowds as he stepped off the tram into the evening. The street lights cast a yellow glow and the air had the bite of winter. He pulled his scarf more closely round his neck.

Five minutes brisk walking brought him back to the university. It looked as though most students had left but there were still some stragglers on the steps standing round in groups smoking, laughing and talking.

There were lights on here and there in the building. This was a place where people routinely worked late so it wouldn't be a problem to gain access. He checked his notebook quickly and went up the steps past the students who moved apart politely to let him through.

The lobby was empty, a space of grey shadows in the twilight. The stairway opened up in front of him, the steps gleaming faintly in the last of the evening light. The stairs down to the car park were in shadow. Will could hear his footsteps echoing as he walked across the flagged floor to the small reception booth.

It was empty, but he could hear someone moving in the cubbyhole behind the counter. He rapped on the wood and after a moment, Jerzy Pawlak emerged. 'Yes? Oh, it's you. You said nine.'

'I was passing. Can you talk now?'

'I'm working. I don't have time for this.' Suddenly he was angry. 'I'm sorry about your daughter, but what do you think it was like for me? I found her. The police...' He broke off and looked at Will. His face was sullen.

'You saw her from the window. Did you go down to the car park?'

'Of course I did. I wanted to see if there was anything I could do.'

Will looked away. He wanted to disengage from Pawlak's distress. He should be sorry the man had had such a traumatic experience, but he didn't have the time or the energy to let it concern him. 'According to the statement you gave the police, you spoke to her in the computer room at around nine.'

'I asked her to lock up and she said she would.'

'What was she doing?'

'Working.'

'But what was she actually doing?.'

'Working on the computer.'

'What was on the screen?'

'Why would I look?'

Will told himself Pawlak was not being deliberately obstructive. 'Was she the last person in the building that night?'

'Yes.'

'You're sure?'

'No one came in after I locked up. It's not my job to search the place. Is that all? I need to get on.'

It would have been easy enough for anyone to have hidden somewhere in the maze of rooms and corridors. All the entrances were well observed from Pawlak's station, but anyone could have come into the building earlier and waited.

'A couple more things. You told the police you thought Ania had left. What made you think that?'

'I heard her. She came down the stairs and left by the basement door. I heard it close.'

This was new. This wasn't in the police statement. 'You heard her?'

'That's what I said.'

'But you didn't see her?'

'I was doing my rounds. I was along the second corridor. I heard her on the stairs, so I went downstairs to make sure the basement door was locked. I do my job properly.'

'What time? What time was it you heard her?'

'I start my round on the hour. So eleven thirty? Something like that.'

'And you told the police this?'

'I don't remember.' Sullen.

'Describe it, the sound you heard.'

'Someone on the stairs. What do you want me to say?'

'Like this?' Will picked up a pen and made a staccato rapping sound on the wood, the brisk tap of high heels. 'Or this?' This time he used the side of his fist: *pad pad pad*, a man's footsteps.

Pawlak shrugged. 'Footsteps. I heard footsteps.'

He wouldn't say any more.

Chapter 34

Back in his room, Will took stock. Despite his precautions, someone had found the Facebook site. And now there was something else: *footsteps on the stairs*... Someone had come down those stairs that night, someone who hadn't gone up them, not after Pawlak came on duty. Someone had been concealed in the building and knew when the security guard would be making his rounds, someone who had slipped out of the basement exit because there was something he needed to check in the car park, something he needed to do... Whoever that person was, he knew the university well.

It had been in the police report: ...*key to the room door in the left hand pocket.*

Maybe that had been her last moment, the feel of the key being slipped into her pocket, knowing that her death would be written off as the suicide of a guilty woman...

He trod hard on the emotion welling up inside him. He didn't know what to do. Pawlak claimed he 'didn't know' if he had told the police about the person he had heard on the stairs, the person he'd assumed was Ania. There had been nothing in the police records, or nothing Will had seen. Did that mean Pawlak hadn't told them? Was he lying now to get Will off his back? Or had Król concealed the evidence?

There was no reason he could think of for Król to ignore it. He would want the death to be suicide because that meant less work for a force that must be over-stretched. The fact the fingerprint on the phone hadn't been followed up was a mark of the kind of sloppy work that happened when a force was undermanned and overworked, but evidence of someone else in the building – no police officer could dismiss that. He made a note to contact Król, and went back to his notes. He read through his list of unanswered questions again:

1. ~~Did she tamper with the recording?~~
2. Why?

3.   Why wasn't the substitution noticed in the first investigation?
4.   Why did she run away?

Why had she done it? Why had she tampered with the recording? If he could answer that, he would know where to start looking.

Konstantin Jankowski had implied she was trying to find something that would clear her name, but that didn't ring true to Will. If she hadn't tampered with that tape, if she was innocent of that accusation, she would have sat tight and relied on the expertise of her colleagues to prove it.

He was slowly and reluctantly prepared to accept that she had done it, because he was beginning to see that she might have had a reason.

She, Louisa and Elżbieta had been the only people in the park the morning Louisa was abducted. Elżbieta had been in the café and had seen nothing in the crucial thirty minutes. The police had assumed that Louisa had left the playground and encountered her abductor elsewhere in the park. But no one knew until now that it had been Ania who had left, and she might, just might, have seen something, something that held no significance for a child. But later, as an adult, with the growing realisation of what her concealment might have done – a small childhood fib with consequences far beyond anything she could have conceived – she must have relived that crucial period of time, that half hour that had changed all their lives, over and over again.

When the photograph of the man helping police with their enquiries appeared in the papers, what had that face meant to her? Had she recognised him but known there was no way she could prove it after all these years, that it wasn't enough? Had she found her sister's killer? Or believed she had found her sister's killer.

If I can do something to stop someone like that…

He picked up the phone and dialled the number of Ian Cathcart's direct line. It was after six in the UK, but he might just catch him. Cathcart answered at once. 'Cathcart.'

'DCI Cathcart, it's Will Gillen.'

'Mr Gillen. How are you?'

'I'm OK. I'm in Poland dealing with – that's not important. I need some information about Derek Haynes, about the investigation.'

There was a beat of silence, then Cathcart said, 'What did you want to know, sir?'

'Remind me – when did Haynes emigrate?'

'Hang on. I'll check.' He heard the sound of a keyboard, then Cathcart came back. '1986. Autumn 1986.'

1986. Louisa had died that summer. 'OK. I need to know – you're re-investigating. Is there any evidence to suggest the killer might not have been Haynes, that it was someone else?'

There was a pause as Cathcart worked out his response. Will waited with growing impatience. 'Nothing.'

He released the breath he didn't realise he had been holding. 'Are you looking at any other cases of child abduction in relation to Haynes?'

There was a long silence.

'I'm talking about the Louisa Gillen abduction in 1986. I'm talking about my daughter.'

After a moment, Cathcart's voice came back. 'Yes, sir. I know. We didn't realise that Ania was…'

'She didn't want you to. That was why she changed her name. She started using her mother's name because she was dogged by the case everywhere she went.'

'They're going over several earlier cases. I understand your daughter's is one of them. I should have… I'm very sorry, sir.'

He should have known. Someone should have told him. Even Blaise had kept him in the dark. He knew they had found nothing. If they'd found the smallest thing, he would have been informed. But the one person who might have been able to give evidence against Haynes, the person who might have seen him in the park that day, was dead.

'Thank you, Inspector.' He put the phone down.

When the Haynes case started, she'd had only her childhood memories, an identification that wouldn't begin to stand up in court. What she had done wasn't about revenge. If she had recognised him, then she knew she was facing a dangerous, predatory paedophile who had killed at least once before. She'd done what she had to to get him off the streets but she must have known that her evidence could be challenged at any time.

Louisa and Ania had been in the playground while Elžbieta had a cup of coffee in the park café. When she returned to find the girls, Ania was swinging on the monkey bars alone.

There was no sign of Louisa.

Her body had been found four days later, stuffed into one of the pipes that channelled the river through the city. She had been raped and strangled.

Like Sagal. Same modus operandi.

The story of Sagal Akindès's disappearance had never quite made it to the front pages, not until her body had been found and the photographs had surfaced on the internet. Then the story gathered momentum. Photographs of Derek Haynes, the man *helping police with their enquiries* started to appear, first as a blurred figure between two police officers being escorted into the police HQ, then clearer pictures passed on by colleagues and acquaintances, stories about Haynes being *a loner*, being *quiet*, being seen in the road watching the children on the local sports field.

Derek Haynes was 50. He would have been 28 when Louisa was murdered.

He could have done it.

It could have been him.

What Ania had done – it had been a holding operation, a way of making things safe until she could... until she could come up with the evidence that would keep Haynes locked away for good.

That was why Ania had to stay out of custody – there was something more she had to find and she hadn't, not yet. She'd been aware that the police might already be watching her so she alerted him to its existence via the Facebook link...

He forced himself to stop. He was building a house of cards. He had to stay with the evidence. She had no reason to conceal her search from the police. They would have been as eager as she was to link Haynes with any previous killing. If there had been anything, she would have shared it with them.

He played with the idea that Haynes himself was behind this, that he somehow had a reach outside of prison and that was why

Ania had run. But if Haynes had that kind of reach, he would have been able to protect himself in prison, protect himself from prison in the first place.

But there was someone else, someone he hadn't considered.

He thought for a moment, then added a question to his list:

Whose voice was it on the original recording and where is he now?

Chapter 35

Dariusz got back to his flat after midnight. He spent the early part of the evening working, talking to someone who had information about a man – a very wealthy and powerful man – who had apparently bribed a government minister to amend a bill that might damage his media empire. Dariusz was trying to persuade the informant it would be safe to become a witness for the prosecution.

He needed proof of chicanery that would stand up in court. His contact could provide that proof, but the man was scared. He'd insisted on meeting in absolute secrecy. The talk had taken place in Dariusz' car on a back road close to the Jewish cemetery. Afterwards, chilled to the bone, he had called in at a bar.

Now he was feeling buzzed from a double vodka and from an overdose of cigarettes. It made him feel better for the moment, but he would pay the price in the morning. He cleared his desk and slipped his digital recorder out of his top pocket. He'd taken the precaution of making a recording as his informant had talked and he needed to transcribe it.

He switched on his laptop and waited for it to boot up. He entered his password, only for the system to refuse him entry. *Invalid password.* He put his face in his hands and swore under his breath. He'd loaded an illegal copy of some software a couple of days ago: that must be what was causing the difficulty. He was facing a classic chicken and egg problem: he needed to log on to remove the software, until he removed it, he wouldn't be able to log on.

He shelved it. He was too tired. He couldn't be bothered with the rigmarole of dealing with a recalcitrant machine. He paced the small room, lit another cigarette then stubbed it out. He switched on the TV and channel-hopped for a while, then turned it off again. He felt too restless for sleep, and too weary to do anything useful.

In desperation, he poured himself more vodka. Another drink should put him out and the hell with the consequences tomorrow. It wouldn't be the first time he'd worked though a hangover. He showered, then, naked apart from a towel wrapped round his hips, he sat at his desk again and stared into the night, lighting another cigarette. His mind was blurred and unfocused with alcohol and his mouth tasted of old rope. He wondered what Ania would say if she came through the door and found him like this, half drunk and smoked out.

You left me, kiciu. *You'll have to give me some time.*

***

Will's sleep was broken that night. Sometimes he was walking along the dark platforms of New Street station, the brick tunnel above him pressing down as he continued his futile search. Sometimes he was walking along narrow streets in an unfamiliar town, a street with high wooden houses and narrow alleys, where things scuttered in the darkness and a witch-light flickered and gleamed in the night. It was after five before he fell asleep properly.

The sounds of the street outside woke him. It was morning, the sky was light. He checked his watch. He'd slept until nine. He swore and dragged himself out of bed. The four hours' sleep he'd managed had left him drained. The world looked strangely clear and strangely insubstantial. He could feel the threads of exhaustion starting to wear him down.

Not long now.

He dressed quickly and went out into the day. He grabbed some coffee and set off towards the Manufactura that had been built in the heart of the city. It was in an old industrial campus that had housed a massive textile factory, the mansion of Izrael Poznanski, the owner, workers' houses, a school and a railroad station. Now it was an arts, leisure and shopping centre.

It was a short walk from the top of Piotrkowska. He went in through a high brick arch and found himself in a huge square where the red brick of the old buildings was complemented by airy constructions of glass and steel. He could see spouts in the ground where fountains would jet water into the sky. For a moment, he let himself pretend he was here with Ania, that she was showing him round the city she had planned to adopt as her own.

'It's just another shopping mall,' he said, deliberately contentious.

'Just a shopping mall? How can you say that? It's a whole cultural centre. There's a theatre, a museum, art galleries, *and*, by the way, one of the best restaurants in the city.'

He could take a hint. 'I suppose you want me to take you to dinner tonight?'

But he was alone. The open square stretched out around him. He could picture it in summer, busy with shoppers strolling in the sun, with children playing, running through the fountains, the sunlight prismed in the droplets. But he wasn't here to sightsee. He located an interior design store and a photographer's. From the first, he bought a roll of transparent self-adhesive wallpaper; from the second, a camera and a sheet of projection film. Together, these made an effective kit for lifting fingerprints. Some Scene of Crime officers preferred this method to the traditional one. He was going to lift the print on the phone wire in the room from where Ania had fallen. If the Polish police wouldn't investigate it, then he would do it himself.

He felt a bleak determination to finish what it was his daughter had started. He went back to the hotel where he put together his makeshift fingerprint kit, cutting a strip from the Cetafix wallpaper that he would use to lift the prints and a matching sheet of transparent projection film that would serve as a cover. He would only have one chance at this, and he had to get it right.

He knew he ought to eat but once again the lush swoop of strings drove him away from the door of the hotel restaurant. It was as if he was caught in some nightmare, some groundhog day in which he would live and relive his empty search with no promise of release and no hope of moving on. Where was there to go? What lessons remained to be learned?

He walked the short distance to Kościuszki, to the department of English Language. Here, the same sense of déjà vu wrapped itself round him as he went up the steps towards the main entrance.

159

It was after ten and the students were moving purposefully in and out of the building and the lobby was full with the bustle of the day. The sound of voices echoed off the high ceiling. He felt like an automaton as he crossed the lobby and went up the stairs. This would be his last visit. Once he had the fingerprint, he had no reason to come back.

There were no students on the top floor. There was no one around at all and the door of Jankowski's office was shut. Will hoped to complete what he had to do before Jankowski became aware of his presence. The figure that lurked at the edge of his enquiry was still faceless, still unknown. Whatever form this figure may take as the light crept nearer, he was too well informed already. Will intended keeping his own secrets.

He went to the end of the corridor. There was no daylight here. That night, Ania had walked down this corridor in the same darkness. He reached the door of the office and turned the handle with a sudden misgiving that it might be locked.

It opened. There was a draught from the ill-fitting window. Against his will, his gaze moved towards it, towards the metal frame where Ania's fingers had lost their last, desperate grip. The marks of the fingerprint powder were still visible. He turned to the filing cabinet behind the door.

The phone wasn't there. He looked round the room again. There was no sign of it. It was like the morning he'd arrived at her flat to find the police already there.

Too late. He was too late.

Slowly and stiffly, he walked back to the landing. He was about to knock at Jankowski's door when it opened and Jankowski came out. He was holding Ania's backpack, the one Will had left in his office the last time he was here. 'The porter told me you were on your way up. I was…' He stopped at the look on Will's face.

'I came to check the phone that was in the office.'

'Where she….? Of course.' Jankowski made as if to lead the way. Will stopped him.

'It's gone. The phone is gone.'

Jankowski made an impatient noise in his throat and muttered something that sounded like a curse. 'I'm sorry. Someone will have taken it. If I had known you wanted it… It's what happens here. We're always short of equipment so if something is not being used, it goes somewhere it will be used.'

'Do you know who might have it?' As evidence, it would be useless now, but it might still hold the information Will needed.

Jankowski shook his head. 'I can ask. But…' He spread his hands in a gesture that encompassed the building. It could be anywhere. 'I'm sorry,' he said again.

Will tried not to let his anger and frustration show. It wasn't Jankowski's fault. It was his, again. All through this, he'd let his emotions get in the way, let them make him careless and slow. As soon as he'd seen the prints he should have been here, should have made sure the phone was secure.

Jankowski shook his head with regret. 'I'm sorry,' he said again. 'I'm glad I saw you because I wanted to ask you…' His voice was careful. 'The funeral. When will it be? I would like to come if possible. I may not be able to but please believe that I would wish to be there. At least we want to send something in memory. She was our friend and we weren't there when she needed us.'

'I understand. I'll let you know.'

He took Ania's bag and went down the stairs against the flow of students walking up to classrooms and lecture theatres. Universities were places of hope and expectations, places where people with all their lives in front of them were just starting out. Oh, early adulthood carried as many miseries as any age, but it had the unquenchable hope of youth.

And he was getting old.

He was out in the street, walking aimlessly in the wind that was blowing down the long avenues of the city, barely aware of the cold cutting through his coat and chilling his hands to numbness.

'Dad. You need to look after yourself. You need to get warm.'

He saw that he was walking past the café he'd been to before, Coffees and Toffees. A hollow dragging feeling inside him reminded him that he still hadn't eaten. He went in. It was the same girl behind the counter and she seemed to recognise him, giving him a bright smile and a cheerful, 'Cześć.'

He bought coffee and, mindful of Ania's injunction, a piece of cake, then he took his tray across the room to a table in a corner away from the window. He didn't know what to do next. He didn't have the resources or the authority to investigate any further, and his chances of getting the information he needed to persuade the Łódź police to pursue the case were slim. Without the print, all he had was Pawlak's claim to have heard someone on the stairs. He could take that to Król, but he doubted it would do any good.

He closed his eyes and waited, and she was there. 'You've done enough. It's time to go back,' she said. 'You need to go home.'

He looked across the table to where she was sitting. The light didn't quite reach her and her face was in shadow. 'I've let you down.'

'You haven't. You've done everything you could. You can go home now.'

It was a moment before he realised the waitress had come across to him. Will looked at her blankly.

'You want?' she said in careful English.

'No. Nothing. I was talking to...' He shook his head. 'I'm sorry.'

'Is OK.' She moved away, watching him from the corner of her eye.

Maybe he was going mad. A part of him welcomed the idea.

Chapter 36

When he got back to the hotel, he called the airline. There were seats on a flight leaving at seven that evening if he was prepared to pay a steep fee for altering his travel plans. He dealt with the admin briskly and booked the seat, then he gathered up the few things he'd bothered to unpack and stowed them in his suitcase. His laptop and his papers were already in the bag he carried everywhere with him. At least with those he'd been careful.

He didn't know what to do with Ania's things. He was half tempted to leave them here for Erland to deal with. Let him have them if he laid such a strong claim to her memory. He picked up the backpack, weighing it in his hands, then emptied the contents out onto the bed.

He caught a drift of perfume, a fragrance that bought her vividly back to him. He saw her standing outside the cottage in St Abbs, Keeper tugging impatiently at the lead she was holding; he saw her in her life jacket throwing the ropes to someone on the harbour side; he saw her scrambling over the rocks under the cliffs, her hair blown about by a stiff breeze from the sea; and he saw a stream of grey ashes pouring into the water, drifting for a moment on the surface and then vanishing forever.

'I understand. I'll do it,' he said.

He shook the bag again and something rolled out, something he'd missed before. It was a pink teddy bear, faded and stained. The ears were uneven and the arms stuck out like starfish. He felt a stab of recognition that was so sharp it was painful as he picked it up

Small Bear. He'd found Small Bear.

He moved it in his hands, feeling its worn softness.

Elżbieta had had this on the car seat next to her, that day she made her last trip, as if the toy could stand in for the child she'd lost. He'd never found out what had happened to it. He hadn't cared. The police must have returned it with the bag of Elżbieta's possessions. He had thrown the lot away, but Ania must have retrieved the toy. She'd said nothing, but she had kept it all these years.

Small Bear has a secret. This was what the Facebook site meant. He had been looking too hard. There was no secret code, no hidden message on the page that he was unable to find. It was simply this, to tell him to look at the bear.

He had found what she wanted him to look for.

But as he turned it round in his hands, he could feel that it was loose and floppy. He checked more closely and saw one of the seams had been split open and the stuffing pulled out. He pulled out the rest, searching through it, pressing the empty limbs of the toy between his fingers, but there was nothing there.

The awareness cut through him like a knife. Once again, by the time he understood what she was trying to tell him, it was too late.

She had sent him to her flat and the police had got there first. He had tried to collect what was left at the university and lost it. His hands were working frantically as the anger and despair washed over him, testing again the fabric, the small arms, the reinforced head, looking for the secrets the bear held.

Nothing.

Whatever it was, it was gone.

The despair hit him like a tsunami. It was overwhelming, and it drove him to his knees. The pain in his chest was so sudden, so intense, he couldn't breathe. It was going to kill him. He struggled against it because he couldn't die now, not now, not when he was so close.

The abyss of nothingness reached out for him. He tried to speak but he couldn't find his voice. Then he was at New Street Station, out of breath from running, looking down into the dank oubliette where the tracks lay. A boy sat on a bench, the bulk of his rucksack telling the story they thought they knew.

And he was sitting on the bench looking back up towards the concourse, towards the men with their guns held ready. He reached into his jacket for the identity card, the card that would tell them he meant no harm. The bullet struck him squarely in the chest, driving red hot agony into the core of his being.

Then the blackness took him.

Chapter 37

His head was resting on something soft, and he could feel a cool touch on his forehead. 'Dad. Wake up. Wake up.' In the background, an electronic sound beeped with maddening regularity.

His hand was almost too heavy to lift but he reached up and felt her fingers as they entwined with his. He tried to say something. 'Ania. I'm sorry.'

It was more a breath than speech, but she seemed to understand him because he felt her squeeze his hand. 'It's OK. I'm OK,' she said. Relief overwhelmed him and he slept.

The relief stayed with him as he rose to the surface again. He'd been trapped in some terrible dream, but that was all it was, a dream. He thought he could hear the sea, and reached his hand out, waiting for the touch of Keeper's nose as she welcomed him to the day.

As his eyes opened, he saw something above his head, an odd shape that his brain couldn't decipher, until it suddenly became a drip stand with a bag of fluid hanging down. His gaze followed the line down, to the needle taped into his arm.

Hospital. He must be ill, must have had an accident, something... He struggled for recall.

He'd been shot... No, he'd... a hotel room. A child's toy ripped apart...

There was someone sitting by his bed. He heard the crackle of a newspaper as the figure moved. 'Ania?'

'You're awake.' It was a man's voice. Will forced his head to turn. Dariusz Erland was sitting in a chair by his bed, a newspaper folded carelessly beside him. 'I'll call the nurse. You're lucky I came to the hotel.'

'Lucky?' Reality came flooding back. He had known, of course, that the moment of relief was false, a trick played by his mind to allow him to rest, but it was bitter to relinquish it. The moment he had felt Ania take his hand was still there and his fingers closed round the memory.

'I was expecting you to call me. When you didn't I went to see what was going on. I found you on the floor. You were unconscious.'

Will shook his head. 'What happened?'

'They were concerned you may have had a heart attack but it seems you were just exhausted. You have been asleep for hours.'

Before he could say any more, the door opened and a man came in, a white coat open over his suit. A nurse accompanied him. 'Mr Gillen. You're awake. How are you feeling?' The man's English was excellent and Will didn't argue that he could speak Polish. He was too weary of strange places, strange voices, of straining all the time to understand.

'Tired.'

'No more pain? You were in pain when you came in.'

He was going to be in pain forever, but this wasn't what the doctor meant. 'No pain.'

'Good.' The doctor was testing his pulse as he spoke, presumably a bedside trick as a monitor behind him beeped reassuringly. 'Now, we aren't sure what has happened. We thought at first you were having a heart attack, but the results of your ECG and blood tests suggest you were not. We would like to do more tests because…'

Will struggled into a sitting position. 'No. I'm OK. I've been overdoing it, that's all.' He needed to take better care of himself. Ania was depending on him. 'I let myself get tired but I'm fine. I'll get checked over back in the UK. I can't afford time in hospital now. I have things I need to do.'

The doctor tapped his notes with his pen. 'You understand there's a chance this event does indicate problems with your heart? If you were to have another attack…' He spread his hands to indicate the potential seriousness of the situation.

'I had a full health check six months ago. My heart was fine. It's…'

'I know about your circumstances, Mr Gillen. I'm very sorry.'

Will nodded abruptly.

'It would be unwise for you to leave hospital without further tests.'

166

'Am I fit to travel?' He didn't know what time it was and he had to get his flight. 'I'm leaving tonight. My flight goes at seven.' He looked at his wrist, but his watch was gone.

Erland spoke from his chair. 'I cancelled it.'

'You did what? Call them. Now.' He could feel the anger starting, and the ache in his chest. 'I have to get back.'

'Do you want to kill yourself?' The question hung in the air, then Erland said, 'It's almost six thirty. You're too late.'

'I could…' He pictured himself pulling on his clothes, running into the street and hailing a taxi. Just for a moment, it seemed feasible. He could send for his luggage, he could… But the plane would be boarding. Even if he could get to the airport, get through security in time, the gate would be closed. 'Where are my clothes?'

Erland had produced a bag from somewhere before Will asked. 'They'll extend your stay at the hotel. It's never full. I'll call them and arrange it. I can drive you there.' His face was impassive.

'I want to check you over once more,' the doctor said, 'then if you choose to leave, it is up to you.' He waited until Erland had left the room, then said something to the nurse, who nodded and followed Erland out. 'She will see to your medication. I have prescribed a mild sedative.'

'Thank you.' Will had no intention of taking anything that would dull his alertness, but he wasn't going to argue. Then he realised that the doctor had another agenda. 'Your daughter,' he said, coiling his stethoscope into his pocket after a fairly cursory check of Will's chest, 'they brought her here that night.'

'Here?'

The doctor's fingers touched his wrist. 'This stress is dangerous. You must take that sedative if you are to continue.'

'Ania. They brought her here?'

'Yes. My colleague did an external examination, then the matter was turned over to the police pathologist.'

'Is that usual?'

'In cases where there is suspicion, yes. It becomes their jurisdiction.'

'So what are you saying? What are you trying to tell me?'

'Just that – maybe you should ask for another post-mortem. Their pathologist, to be honest, is not as skilled as the team we have here.'

'She died in a fall.' Working that out required little skill on the part of the pathologist. The question that Will needed answering was how she had fallen, not how she had died. The pathologist couldn't tell him that.

'My colleague had some concerns.'

'What are you saying? That it wasn't the fall that killed her?'

'No. Not that at all. He just thought there were some peculiarities that the police report didn't cover. It may be nothing.'

'Can I speak to him?'

'Not now. He's on secondment to a hospital in Poznan.'

'I need to talk to him.'

The doctor shook his head. 'I don't know that he would want... Perhaps I shouldn't have said anything.' His gaze met Will's. 'Get another post-mortem.' His bleep went, and he looked relieved. 'You must excuse me. Remember, you have to rest. Your body has given you a warning – heed it.'

Will dressed quickly, noticing that Erland had brought clean clothes, not the ones Will had been wearing when he was admitted. Erland must have taken his key, had full access to his hotel room. He felt angry at the thought of Erland going through his things, maybe reading the notes he had made, handling the stuffed toy, wondering what its significance was. There was nothing he could do about it. He had to think about what the doctor had told him.

Ania had died in the fall, but he should get another post-mortem... He tried to keep the information clinical and distant, aware all the time of the tightening in his chest, the way the tension restricted his breathing, the dull ache under his breast bone. Her body would be on its way back to the UK – the undertaker had arranged the transport.

He went along the corridor to where Erland was engaged in conversation with the nurse. They were laughing together as the girl, an attractive young woman with soft dark curls, put together a series of forms. She sobered as she saw Will. 'Mr Gillen.'

He spoke to her in Polish. '*Dziękuję.*' *Thank you.*

She handed him an envelope, and a box with a pharmacy label on. 'These are for you to take every morning and at night. The doctor says you must do this.' Her gaze sought out Erland.

'I'll make sure he does.' Erland smiled a farewell at her and led Will along the corridor following the exit signs.

'Did you get her phone number?' Will couldn't resist the dig. Ania was dead only a few days and Erland was already flirting with attractive women.

'Sure. They took Ania to this hospital first, you know,' Erland said, giving the information he must have had all along but had not until that moment chosen to share with Will.

'And you think she can tell you something?'

'Who knows.' It was already dusk as they headed through the car park. Erland led Will to a battered old Ford. 'I'll take you back to the hotel.'

He didn't speak as he drove them back into the city, weaving through the fast-moving traffic with the skill of familiarity. He pulled up in a side street next to the main entrance. 'You're in the same room. You didn't check out, so there's no need to check in again. I've sorted it.'

Will knew he should be grateful to Erland for the efficiency that saved him from all the tedium of unnecessary paperwork, but he still felt angry, and the anger made him churlish. He was aware of Erland following him in through the door and into the lift. 'I'll be fine now. Thank you.'

Erland didn't answer, just led the way to the room and, using the key he must have taken earlier, opened the door. He waved Will past him then followed him in and shut the door. 'We need to talk.'

'About?'

'About what you have been doing. I owe it to Ania not to let you kill yourself.'

'Ania's my concern now.'

Erland picked up the bottle of vodka that was standing on the desk, poured himself a large slug and tipped it down his throat. He looked the way he had the day Will first saw him, unshaven and pale with dark shadows under his eyes. His gaze met Will's. The hostility between them was overt. 'Look, Gillen, you don't like me. That's fine. I don't like you. But I want to know what happened. I want to know for Ania. She deserves that and there's just you and me now. It was almost just me, so we'd better start talking to each other before it's too late.'

He reached into the bag he had been carrying and took out a bundle. He opened it and the dismembered remains of a soft toy spread out across the desk. 'I could ask you about this. I know it. It was Ania's. She took it with her wherever she travelled.'

Small Bear.

Erland's smile contained no humour. 'You see, I didn't waste my time while you were ill.'

'You went through my things?'

'Of course. And I'll tell you what I found. I found that the fingerprint in the room is lost – for the moment. If you really think it is important, go to Król. Get it. He's an honest man. I know what Pawlak told you, about hearing someone on the stairs. If you'd talked to me, I could have told you about Pawlak. He used to work for Służba Bezpieczeństwa, the SB, the police of the Soviet times. There are many such – they did the dirty work for the state, and the state got rid of them when they became an embarrassment. Now, he lives by other means. One of them is selling information to the authorities.'

'You're telling me he was lying?'

'No. But he may have been.' Will didn't say anything. He could remember the satisfaction on Pawlak's face as Will passed money across the wooden counter.

'I also found a Facebook page that goes nowhere.' Erland indicated the remains of the toy beside him. 'And this, of course. Did you find anything? Was there anything hidden there?'

'You've been busy.'

'What do you expect? We lived together. She was part of my life. We were going to get married. It doesn't matter what you and I think about each other. We'll probably never see each other again once this is over. What matters is Ania, what really happened that night. We have to talk to each other, tell each other what we know. What else did you find?'

Will could feel his fists clenching. He didn't want to listen to this. Ania was his daughter. She'd come to him for help, not Erland. She'd sent the Facebook e-mail to him, asked him to go to her flat, she'd… come to him. If she wasn't prepared to trust Erland, then why should he?

After waiting out his silence, Erland sighed impatiently. 'OK. I'll tell you what I know. I'll tell you what I've worked out. When the Haynes appeal broke, Ania must have found something that scared her. She stopped using her phone. All her calls to me were on landlines. She didn't e-mail me. She didn't stay at the flat.'

Maybe it was you she was scared of. Will didn't say it, but he could see Erland reading the thought from his face. 'So who was she hiding from?'

'I think the security services were after her.'

That thought had crossed Will's mind as well, ever since he'd realised Blaise was taking a close interest in the case. He remembered her call in the early hours of the morning to tell him she was leaving. *I'll need a long wire. I'm using the phone booth.* He'd wondered why she was using a landline, but hadn't given it much thought. And the e-mail – she'd used the Facebook site because it was a way of sending an e-mail that wasn't linked to her.

He no longer believed the Polish police were incompetent. The evidence he had uncovered couldn't have been missed by them. They might have preferred Ania's death to be suicide, they might have been willing to ignore some inconclusive evidence, but what he had been told at the hospital showed that they had taken specific steps to keep the details of the investigation within their own domain. Someone had put pressure on them.

The only people who could exercise that kind of influence were the security services, and that made no sense at all. If they'd wanted Ania, if they'd wanted to question her, they had more than enough to arrest her.

And her death? He had no illusions about the people he'd worked with. They functioned in a hard world and they brought hard solutions to it, but they didn't carry out botched assassinations because a court case had gone wrong.

The security services hadn't killed Ania. They didn't need to. They had had the option of burying her alive.

He didn't share these thoughts with Erland. 'Why?'

'I had to ask myself why she sent this to you, not me.' He flicked the ruined toy on the desk in front of him. 'The Facebook page, the toy, all of that shit.'

'Because she trusted me.'

'Or because she knew the people who were after her didn't need to worry about you. You wouldn't cause them any trouble. You were already bought and paid for. You know what I'm talking about.'

'Tell me.'

'The Birmingham shooting. You walked away from that. What did you give them that they let you do that?'

Will felt a strange calm settle over him. In a way, Erland was right. Will had been offered a price for his silence, and he had accepted it. 'It's not that simple.'

'So tell me.'

Will had never talked about it, not even to Ania. She thought he had taken early retirement after the enquiry ended because he couldn't live with the fact his operation had killed an innocent youth. That was the public version and he had never contradicted it, not even to her. She'd never know, now. She was gone, and he didn't think he would see her again. He sighed. 'We had intelligence about a bomb factory.'

The intelligence had been sudden and urgent: the threat was imminent. They thought they'd got the house covered in time, the area quietly evacuated: a textbook operation.

And then one of the neighbours told them about the young man who had left the house during the night, slipping out through the yard gate as the sky began to lighten. He had been wearing a heavy anorak despite the mild weather, and he had been carrying a rucksack.

It was sheer luck – ill-luck as it turned out – that he had been spotted on CCTV, heading towards the station. There had been no time for an evacuation. They couldn't risk anything that would alert him.

He should have known. Will always believed – whether it was with hindsight or with justification – that he should have known. He had been a policeman for three decades. He should have listened to the voice of disquiet that had been speaking in his head, but in cases like this, you didn't act on hunches. You acted on evidence.

In his dreams, he was always running through the station, running through crowds to find the men he'd sent and call them back. In fact, nothing so dramatic had occurred. He hadn't even been there. He had been at the control centre. The young man had entered the station before they could intercept him. When he saw the police in pursuit, he had reached under the bulk of his anorak and they had shot him dead. When the body was examined, he was holding his identity card in his hand.

'The house was let to asylum seekers,' Will said. 'Landlords get contracts to take them on, and the rules are strict: you live where you're put and you don't let anyone else stay there. The lad that was shot – he was destitute. Someone in the house had befriended him and let him stay. They must have realised someone was watching them, so he had to get out of there without anyone seeing him. They probably expected a raid.' The Borders and Immigration teams always came in the dawn hours when their actions could be carried out unobserved.

'Where did the intelligence come from? Interrogation?'

Will knew what Erland meant, the men whisked off the streets from countries around the world and taken to places where they could be questioned by means that were – still – not legal in the west. 'No one ever confirmed it but that's what I believe. The official story was we were set up by a malicious informer. Whatever happened, we killed an innocent man.' The mop-up had been good. Blaise had been in charge and he knew what he was doing. By the time the enquiry began, there was evidence to show the young man had doubtful connections. It had been easy enough to find those in the life of a destitute youth. The only other people who knew the story, the men in the house who had befriended him, had been deported.

Erland's face gave no clue to what he was thinking. Will shrugged. 'I'm realistic. I know how these things work. But I didn't want it happening again. The men who pulled the triggers – one of them is still on sick leave. I don't think he'll ever recover, not really. I wanted a guarantee we'd stop using information that had been tortured out of people. I didn't get it.'

'So you retired. Fair enough.'

'I told you – it wasn't that simple. There were other people I had to protect, my team. That was the deal. I'd take the rap and keep my mouth shut, they'd clear the men on my team and let me take early retirement. I agreed.'

'Bought and paid for. If you speak out, they'll destroy you.'

'Not any more. I don't give a shit any more. They can do what they like.'

'So it was the security services after Ania.'

'I don't know. I think she believed that. She had to buy herself time. Don't you get that?'

'No. I don't. Because…' Erland reached past him and picked up the file.

'Because?'

'Because Ania didn't fold up under pressure. She didn't run away. She came here for a reason. I'll tell you what I don't understand. It's this.' He brandished the file. 'Messages on internet sites. Things hidden in teddy bears. It's bullshit. Ania has something important she wants to tell you, so instead of just telling you, she sets up a fucking website link, and instead of sending you whatever it is she wants you to have, she hides it in a stuffed toy. Christ, Gillen, you must think she was stupid, playing spook games when someone was trying to kill her.' His gaze met Will's. 'You accept that now, right? Someone killed her?'

Will nodded, once. He couldn't say the words. 'I don't think she was stupid. She thought she couldn't send me anything – she thought we were both under surveillance and it would never arrive. She had to improvise.'

'Why?'

'Because she knew someone was after her.' In his head, lightning flashed and the crash of thunder dragged him out of sleep to the sound of the phone ringing. 'She called me. Three days before she died. She knew the night before they were on to her about the fake recording. That's why she ran.'

'You believe she faked the recording?'

'No one else could have done it.'

'She told me she had done nothing wrong.'

'She thought she'd done the right thing. She believed Haynes was guilty and…' He saw Erland open his mouth to object and held up his hand to stop him. 'And she thought that he was the man who killed her sister.'

Erland looked at him. The silence stretched out. 'She thought…?'

'When you told me what had happened, that she'd left Louisa in the playground, I began to understand. It took me a bit of time, but I got there in the end. She must have seen him in the park that day, only she didn't realise what it was she'd seen, not then. That's why she felt guilty.' *You see? I know my daughter after all.*

For the first time, Erland seemed to be listening, not just looking for reasons to shout him down.

'Haynes left the country shortly after Louisa was killed. God knows what he got up to in Australia. When he came back, he took work in a place where he could get access to vulnerable children. The murder of that little girl – it was almost a copycat for Louisa's murder. He knew what he was doing. She was left in a culvert. The water destroyed all the evidence. They couldn't pin it on him.'

'So why destroy the recording? If it was him, why…'

'Because…' This was where the ground became less firm. 'I don't think it was conclusive.'

'If it wasn't Haynes' voice, whose was it?'

That was the question, the one that had been haunting him ever since he'd worked it out. 'I don't know. I think Haynes must have had an accomplice.'

'And she let that man go free?'

'No. She had to get Haynes off the streets. No one knew who the other man was. No one knew he existed. I think she was looking for him. I think she was working on that recording. I think she was looking for the other man.'

Chapter 38

Now, Will had Erland's attention. 'That means she must have kept the original.'

'I never believed she'd destroy that evidence. She must have kept it.' As he spoke, he could see how thin his theories were, how they were built on hope and speculation. The whole story he had created was falling apart like a house of cards as he told it. 'It's the only way I can account for what happened.' It was a plea.

'So the thing someone is looking for, it's the original recording? It still makes no sense. She had plenty of time to get it to you – she didn't have to play stupid games with the e-mail. Did you find it?'

'No. It was gone by the time I worked it out.'

Erland chewed his lip, his eyes scanning the papers in the file. 'It just doesn't… She left a trail, and they were onto it at once.'

'That's because I didn't see what she was trying to tell me.'

'How does it work? This "code" you're supposed to have. The one that you didn't see in time.'

The note of scepticism and challenge was back in Erland's voice. 'It's a short story. One she used to read when she was younger.' *When I knew her and you did not.* He took the print-out he had made in the internet café from his bag and passed it across.

Erland flicked through the pages, skimming the text. 'Her tastes changed,' he observed. Then after a moment, 'Brown Jenkin. Of course.'

Will knew it was unreasonable, but it hurt that she had shared this with Erland. 'I'm not saying she still read it. I'm saying she knew I would pick up the references.'

'You didn't.'

'I let her down. I know that.'

'No. I think she didn't care whether you picked up the reference or not. It wasn't for you. It was for someone else.'

Will stared at him. Erland was talking rubbish. Ania had left a trail and he'd followed it. She had been guiding him, telling him where to go. She had said, *You have to know where to look.*

'You were looking for the wrong code. She read this story when she was a teenager, right? What did you think of it then?'

'Trash.'

'And she knew that?'

'Of course.'

'So – that's what she's telling you. That's what the code says: this is trash. It never meant anything. It's there as a distraction, something to get them looking in the wrong places. If she had the original recording, it was never here.' He shook the bear and they watched as the remains of the stuffing fell to the floor. 'It's trash.'

Ania's voice spoke from behind him. 'Not all of it. I had to do what I could.' He turned sharply, but the room was empty.

Erland's gaze followed his. 'What?'

'Nothing. I thought I heard something. If she thought it was trash, why did she send it to me? She sent it the night she died!'

'Maybe it was the only way she had of alerting you that something was wrong.' Erland moved to the window and glanced out, using the curtain to conceal him. 'They took the bear apart. They must have found something.'

The Walkman. She'd borrowed a Walkman from Jankowski, telling him she'd forgotten her iPod. She hadn't been listening to traditional music. Maybe she'd used it to record something onto a cassette tape that she could conceal inside the stuffed toy. They'd found it, but they must know by now that they didn't have what they wanted.

That left him, and Dariusz Erland. Did it mean they were both in danger? He looked at Erland who was staring out into the grey evening, a brooding expression on his face. They didn't like each other, they'd admitted as much, but that didn't matter. Whatever happened, they were bound together by what they felt for Ania. As he looked at Erland, he understood for the first time that Ania had cared for this man, and that Erland had lost someone he valued as greatly, in his way, as Will had valued her. 'We should work together,' he said.

Erland looked round, surprised. 'That's what I thought we were doing.'

Not quite. Will had remembered something, and Erland's dismissal of what he had found – the website and the story – was going to keep him quiet. He wanted to check it before he told Erland, if he ever did.

After Erland had left, Will forced himself into action. He called the airline and found that they had a cancellation for a flight in two days' time. He booked it, then took stock of his situation.

Exhaustion was overtaking him. It was as if he'd used up all his reserves of energy so that even the short walk from the car to the hotel was more than he could manage. He could feel the ache starting again in his chest, and knew he needed to rest.

He wanted to be home. Ania had told him he could go home, and there was nowhere else he wanted to be. He didn't want to stay any longer in a country that seemed more alien with each passing day, but there seemed to be no way back now. He would have to wait.

The simple act of planning helped to calm him, but when he lay down on the bed, his mind refused to be quiet. When he closed his eyes, Ania was struggling with a shadowy figure in a cluttered space where her quick thinking and her agility were hampered by obstacles that kept blocking her routes of escape. The pain in his chest intensified and the blackness threatened at the edge of his vision…

…the basement was in darkness. His hands slid across the door to find the bolt then he drew it and stepped out into the night. The air was freezing and took his breath away. The ground was uneven under his feet

There was just a glimmer of moonlight to guide him. The huddled shape lay on the ground and he checked quickly to make sure no one was watching as he approached it. Her head was a bloody mess and a dark pool was slowly spreading around her. He stepped carefully to avoid contaminating his feet. He removed his glove to touch her neck lightly. No pulse. She was dead. He slipped the glove back on, and took a key out of his pocket, the key to the room. He looked up at the window still hanging open into the night. He tucked the key into her skirt pocket then walked quickly away.

Will's eyes snapped open. He felt cold all over. The images from the night time car park were as vivid as any memories he had.

Crazy. He was going crazy.

He got out of bed. He couldn't risk a dream like that again. He had to hang on to his sanity. For Ania's sake, he had to keep everything together. He reached for the box of sedatives he had been given at the hospital and checked the dose: one to be taken at six-hourly intervals. He opened the box and swallowed two then sat in the armchair by the desk. He wasn't going back to bed until he could feel them start to take effect. The last thought he had before he drifted into oblivion was that he had been angry. As he stood over Ania's body in the car park, he had been consumed by a blazing frustration and rage.

Chapter 39

Dariusz Erland spent the next morning at his desk. He told his secretary to hold his calls, and he raced through a backlog of work. He completed reports that were overdue, caught up with his correspondence, and spent an hour on the phone rescheduling appointments he'd had to cancel while he was absent.

He was pretty sure that Gillen had got it right. They were looking for the original recording from the Haynes case that Ania must have brought to Poland with her to work on before the law caught up with her. The trail of red herrings Ania had set up seemed to have worked. Where the actual recording was, where she had hidden it, he could only guess. It had to be findable. If she had hidden it too well, then she had done her killer's job for him.

He knew her – had known her – so well, he should be able to work it out. She may have been relying on him to work it out. She'd chosen not to go to the police in Manchester, and she certainly couldn't have gone to the police in Poland. The good wardens stood in her way.

Who could she trust? She could have trusted him, she could have told him. It hurt him that she hadn't, but he hadn't been there. When she had needed him, he hadn't been there. Who else? Jankowski? Her relationship with Konstantin Jankowski had been friendly enough, but they were just colleagues, and Jankowski was a systems man. He would always play by the rules. He would have given anything she had left with him to the police.

She had friends among the post-graduate students, friends among her colleagues but he doubted she would have wanted to put them at risk, and she must have known it was dangerous. Why else had she run away?

He closed his eyes, remembering.

***

The chapels were deep in the forest. It was summer, and trees were heavy with leaf. The paths Dariusz and Ania had walked had been in shade, but the clearing was full of sunlight, the timbers of the ancient buildings glowing with warmth, two wooden Baroque chapels dating back to the 18th century.

Ania dumped her backpack on the ground and stood in front of the nearer one, staring up at the minaret surmounted by a cross. 'It's beautiful. Can we go in?'

'They aren't locked.'

She looked at him in surprise, and tried the door. It swung inwards and she walked into the shadows. He followed her, pleased to be showing her this. The interior was tiny, a small space in which maybe eight people could have stood to attend the celebration of the mass. There was a pump in the middle of the space and the floor around it was wet as though someone had recently drawn water there.

Light shafted down from a high window illuminating an image on the wall where the all-seeing eye of God, an eye in a triangle with beams of light radiating from it, observed its scant congregation.

Ania looked at in silence for a moment. 'That's creepy.'

'That's what Catholicism is: God is watching you.'

'Why does it sound so threatening? My mother was a Catholic. Did I tell you?'

He stood behind her and slipped his arms round her waist. He already knew about her mother, the closeness of early childhood and the story of rejection and neglect. If she wanted to talk about it again, he was prepared to listen.

'She used to tell us, me and Louisa, that if we were good, God would watch over us like that, that he would keep us safe. When Louisa died, after they found her, I thought we must have done something wrong, because he didn't, watch over us I mean, which meant there was only us. I used to have nightmares. I thought that she had been alive in that drain, you see. I thought she had died in there and I used to dream that she was calling to me and it was deep and dark. I would have to crawl in there and then I would be trapped and die too. I'd hear her calling, and I was waiting because I knew He would come… only He didn't. There was only me and I couldn't save her.'

He thought about the children of the Litzsmannstadt ghetto who had been given up to the Nazis by their Jewish leader. *Give me your children*, he had said, and they had done it. Their parents had dressed them in their best clothes, as if they were going on holiday, as if they were going to a celebration, and watched them as they were loaded onto the trains and sent to their deaths in the gas vans of Chelmno. *Give me your children…*

'And with all of this, you still want children of your own?'

They had talked about it, their own children, hostages in an uncertain world.

'Since I met you… Yes. Maybe I do. These days, I put my faith in technology. And you.'

* * *

And you. When it came to it, he hadn't been there.

They had walked a long way that day, eaten Polish sausage and bread and drunk beer under the trees. It was a good memory. He still had the good memories. *Watching over*, she had said. *Keeping safe…* Could she have remembered the Chapel of St Roch, there under the trees of Łagiewniki, hidden something under the watchful, all-seeing eye?

He dismissed the idea. It was the same kind of thinking that lay behind the mystery website and the teddy bear. Whatever she had done with that recording, she had to be sure it would be safe – she wouldn't have left it to chance like that. *These days, I put my faith in technology.*

Technology hadn't helped her either. The Haynes case, with all its dependence on technology, had destroyed her. He could remember when she had started work on it, her distaste when she talked to him. 'Do you want to take this on, *kiciu*?' he had asked her, concerned about what it might do to her.

She had been adamant. 'That little girl – it's like Louisa,' she had said. 'Stuffed in a drain. Dumped and left to rot.'

Will Gillen had said the same thing as well. *Like Louisa.* That early tragedy had shaped their lives, still held them in its web and had slowly devoured them. Gillen thought that Ania had found Louisa's killer, and this was the reason she had died, because she had his voice on record, and she was the only person who could identify him. Dariusz had never really looked into the details of the case – like most people, he suspected, he didn't want to know too much about a paedophile killing.

He logged on to his web mail. He didn't use this address often. An e-mail was waiting for him, with a large attachment. He didn't have to open it to know what it was. It was the video and photographs from the Haynes case. Strąk had come through.

Dariusz locked the door of his office, and detached the computer he was working on from the network. He didn't want anyone sneaking glances at what he was doing.

He slipped a pen drive into the port and downloaded the files onto it, then he opened the drive to see what he had got. There was a video file, and a set of jpegs. It was the video that was the most important, but he hesitated before opening it, and clicked on the images instead.

And she was there, Sagal Akindès, the murdered child. The first thing he noticed was her smile. She was small, with thread-like arms and skinny legs. The photographs were accomplished, catching a real sense of movement as she danced. Her body was half turned away as if she had performed a pirouette for an observer. She was looking slightly beyond the camera, and she was smiling with the cajoling appeal of a child who hopes for treats. It could have been an innocent picture of a child dancing. She looked happy. It had never occurred to him that Sagal Akindès had been a happy child.

He moved his cursor to the video. He hesitated, but he couldn't start being squeamish now. Whatever was contained in the file, it had happened a long time ago, and it was over. He turned the sound down – he didn't want to listen, not yet, then opened the file and braced himself.

The image was dim. The camera wobbled round a damp basement, as if someone was levelling it or steadying it. Dariusz could see metal shelves lining the brick walls which were thick with flaking whitewash. The floor was flagged stone. He recognised the background from the photograph. The image steadied and brightened.

A child was sitting on the floor facing a chair, an old fashioned kitchen chair. Her ankles were tied to the legs.

Dariusz felt nausea in the pit of his stomach. It was the same child, but she wasn't smiling now. Her face was contorted, and tears ran down her cheeks. She was staring at the camera, straight at him, straight through the lens, as if she was pleading with him to help her. 'I can't.' He almost spoke aloud. She was beyond any help he had to give.

He wanted to turn away, but he kept watching.

He saw her lips move again as she said something then the image fuzzed and the screen went blank. Dariusz stared at it. He checked the file and played it again, but the same thing happened. He sat staring at the blank screen.

Was that it? The implications of what he had just seen were disturbing, but the actual video itself was barely... Then he realised the file must have got damaged in the course of the transfer. There was more. He just hadn't seen it.

He pressed the heels of his hands against his eyes and tried to think. Ania had told him she wanted to see Haynes convicted, not only because of the murder of the child, but because she believed he was part of a paedophile ring, kidnapping and abusing children not just for his own enjoyment, but to feed the depravities of other men: they in turn kidnapped, coerced and raped, spreading their poison and drawing yet more people in.

He closed the files down and slipped the pen drive into his pocket. It was after six, time to finish for the day. He could hear Krysia moving about in the office next door. She seemed to be waiting for him and he didn't want any company this evening. He wanted to get home and think about his next move. He packed his bag and left the office quickly, pretending he hadn't heard Krysia's call of 'Dariusz!' as he headed for his car.

Chapter 40

When Dariusz got back to his flat, he made himself a sandwich. Carrying a doorstep of bread, cheese, salami and pickle in one hand, he switched on his laptop and searched through his bag for the pen drive with the files Roman Strąk had sent him.

He had software on his system that might sort out whatever had happened to them in transit. Otherwise, he was going to have to go back and ask for them to be re-sent. He wanted to avoid that if possible. Strąk had been cagy enough the first time.

He typed in his password, remembering it hadn't worked last time, but the system accepted it. He must have mistyped it previously. He'd been drunk. He loaded the data onto his system and set the software running to try and descramble the damaged files. It would take a bit of time before he knew if it had been successful. He lit a cigarette and moved round the small room, stretching his legs.

The door of the wall cupboard was slightly open. The hinge was loose and he kept thinking he should repair it, but he'd never got round to it. The whole flat was in need of an overhaul, something he and Ania hadn't bothered with as they would be moving out soon to their own place. It was untidy as well. These past few days, he hadn't done anything. He'd left stuff out, dumping his things as soon as he got in rather than putting them away. He had always been organised – an essential skill for someone who had lived in the crowded conditions of his childhood. Ania had been the messy one, scattering her clothes on the floor, leaving her possessions lying around.

'Don't you ever pick up after yourself?' he'd said to her once in exasperation when he hadn't been able to find a clear surface to put his bag down.

She'd been sitting on the side of the bed changing to go out. She met his gaze and dropped her camisole deliberately on the floor. 'Are you going to make me?'

'If that's what you want.' He'd wrestled her down onto the bed and the memory faded into a blur of eroticism and sadness.

He poured himself a vodka and tipped it down his throat. On impulse, he pulled the cupboard door wide open. Maybe he could fix it now. Ania's clothes faced him, hanging in a neat line along more than half of the cupboard space. His own wardrobe was more modest: jeans, trousers, a jacket, an overcoat for the cold weather. Winters in Łódź could be bitter.

He could remember her wearing each one of the garments that hung here, and he slipped them off the hangers one by one, a dress in some soft fabric that had served if they went out, trousers, jeans, T-shirts, a blouse, a jersey. There was a shelf filled with underpants, bras, stockings, and on the floor of the wardrobe, a pair of insubstantial shoes, sandals with a high heel and fine leather straps. He could remember walking down Piotrkowska with her, window shopping for their flat. She'd worn a thin cotton dress, a gold chain round her ankle, her bare feet pushed into these sandals. Her toe nails were painted scarlet, and he hadn't paid any attention to the shops at all. He'd just wanted to take her somewhere secluded and make love to her.

He turned away. Ania was dead. She was gone. He was here and he had a life to pick up and get on with. Tomorrow, he would take all the clothes, all her things and throw them out. Keeping them was a pointless act of self-pity and sentiment.

Then he noticed something. The hangers on her side of the wardrobe were always lined up with the hooks facing inwards so it was easy to lift them off the rail. He'd teased her about this one bit of order within the chaos she tended to spread around her. Now, the hanger that held her raincoat was on the rail with the hook facing outward.

He looked at it. He hadn't touched her clothes since she died. He hadn't touched them since she was last here. It was the way they preserved their privacy in the tiny space, being meticulous about each other's possessions.

He shouldn't have had that last vodka. Something was flashing urgent warnings into his mind and he couldn't focus. He hadn't touched that hanger. Ania had not left it like that – he would have noticed.

Someone had been here.

While he was out, someone had been here.

He was moving round the flat as the realisation came to him, checking the window locks, checking the doors. There was no sign of a break-in.

He checked the desk drawers where he kept his credit cards. His wallet was still there, intact and apparently undisturbed. Something rattled as he swept his hand round the inside, and he pulled out a small bunch of keys on a leather fob. He stared at them blankly, then he realised what they were.

Ania's keys. She'd been here. While he was away, she must have...

But she wouldn't have left them here. They would have been in her handbag. They must be among her possessions, her effects that would be – where? With Will Gillen? But why would Gillen break into his flat? Gillen was so destroyed he could barely organise himself to walk around the streets of Łódź. With the police? Why would they break into his flat?

Or it could be...

He slipped the bolt across on the door. The adrenaline rush was starting to counteract the effects of the vodka. He stood very still, letting his breathing steady, making himself calm down and think. Someone had been here. It wasn't a burglar. His possessions were intact. They must have searched the flat, must have been looking for... what?

The missing tape.

His gaze moved to his laptop sitting on his desk. As a minor security precaution, mostly against the possibility of its being stolen, he'd booby trapped it. Anyone switching it on would see the user name and password already entered, the mark of a careless user, or someone who had nothing to hide. But if anyone clicked the login button using that password, the computer locked.

A couple of days ago, he had found his computer locked and hadn't realised the significance of what he'd seen. If the vodka hadn't made him careless, he would have realised at once what had happened. Someone had searched his flat, someone had tried to break into his computer. Beneath his anger, he felt a cold tension. He had seen Ania's body, seen how the fall had smashed and shattered her.

Who would be surprised if Ania's heartbroken lover followed her example to the grave?

His laptop. They'd tried searching that but they hadn't got beyond the password trap. Whoever was looking must have run out of time, and then, of course, Gillen had led them to the website and to the soft toy. The question was, had the searcher been on the right track? Was the missing recording – or a lead to its location – stored on his laptop? *These days I put my faith in technology.*

He opened the search facility. A cartoon dog wagged at him from the screen, an irritating and distracting piece of whimsy. He searched for document names first, trying the ones that seemed obvious, the ones she might expect him to try: Ania, Brown Jenkin, Louisa.

Nothing. Then he tried document names that linked to the case, though that seemed risky. She wouldn't have wanted anyone to spot the file: Sagal, Haynes, FLS, but that search came up empty as well.

He was going to have to look for something in the document that… Then he realised and cursed himself for an idiot. It wouldn't be a document. It would be a sound file, or even a video file like the ones Strąk had sent him. That was simple – he had few enough to check all of those manually. It was possible she had hidden it in plain sight where he would see it at once as an extra, as something that shouldn't be there, but no one else would be aware of its significance. He opened his audio and video folders, but there was nothing there he wasn't familiar with. He opened each file briefly to make sure that it contained what it said it contained.

Nothing.

OK. There might still be something. He set the search to check his C drive and asked for all audio and video files. The search ran for a few seconds and listed the results.

At first, he thought he had hit another dead end as he saw the list of the same files he had just checked, but then he spotted it. Hidden away in a Russian doll of folders, down among temporary files, under folders with cryptic number references – all stuff he never checked, stuff most computer users never checked – there was a video file.

It was labelled 'Dolls_4'. He felt a leap of excitement. The missing file – it was here. *These days, I put my faith in technology.* Except… there was something that wasn't right.

If Ania had put the file here for him to find, she had left it very much to chance. He could have used this machine for the next 20 years and never have known it was there. The name was strange as well. Dolls? It meant nothing to him.

Someone had been playing games with his computer.

Puzzled, he checked the activity on the folder. It had been downloaded from the internet. His stomach started to clench as he saw the date: three days ago, long after Ania's death. There had been other files here as well, files that had been deleted but had left their traces: Dolls_1, Dolls_2, Dolls_3.

They had got beyond the password trap. Someone had managed to log on without the password and download these files onto his system. A premonition gave him a feeling of sick dread as he clicked on the file. The media player opened, and the video began to play.

Later, he was glad he had left the sound turned down. At the time, all he could do was slam the lid of the laptop shut. He was at the other side of the room, as far away from it as he could be before he was conscious of taking any action.

The image he had seen was burned in his mind. A baby. A child of about six months old. He didn't know where, he didn't know when, but he knew from what he had seen that the child in those pictures would almost certainly be dead. He hadn't heard it. At least he hadn't heard it.

He closed the file. His head was spinning. Someone, somehow, had put that file onto his computer, put it where he would never look, left it there until… Until someone else found it, someone who had been tipped off it was there.

He could feel his heart hammering. His first instinct was to delete the file, but he didn't have the software to do that beyond all possibility of retrieval. And if he deleted it, he would be destroying the evidence that led to the person who had put it there.

Now he had to move fast. The file had been on his computer for three days. He didn't know why the police weren't there already. He had to get this to them before they came to him. It was his only chance of convincing them he wasn't responsible for downloading it.

He didn't like the idea, not at all. It was a high risk strategy. If he got it wrong, if he couldn't convince them – if he couldn't convince a jury – then he faced jail and disgrace.

His relationship with the city police was edgy at best. Several of his most high-profile cases had involved people facing the criminal law. On a couple of occasions he had got people off on what even he could recognise as dodgy grounds, making the understaffed, underpaid and overworked police look foolish. They didn't like him. Even if they believed him, they would relish the opportunity to give him a bad time.

He went into the bathroom and splashed cold water over his face. He was shaking. Then he went through his address book to find the number of the most senior, and most reliable officer he knew. Ironically, the name he came up with was Piotr Król's. Król detested him, but he had a reputation for honesty. Despite the debacle of the investigation into Ania's death, Dariusz believed he would get a fair hearing from Król.

Slowly, reluctantly, he picked up the phone.

He forgot, until he saw the police car pulling up outside the block twenty minutes later, about the files Strąk had sent him. They were still on his pen drive. He couldn't be found with these as well. He made a snap decision and pulled it out of the machine, opened the window and threw the small object out into the night as hard as he could.

Then he faced the door and waited.

Chapter 41

Will shut himself away in his hotel room, away from the press who had tracked him down and were bombarding him with phone calls. He told the hotel switchboard to refuse them all, and settled down to wait.

He'd done everything he could here. He'd contacted a pathologist he knew, someone he'd worked with often enough in the past, Euan Kingsley. He could trust Kingsley with Ania. If Kingsley found anything, then he could push for a coroner's inquest. It was the best he could hope for now.

He checked his mobile to see who had been trying to get in touch with him. Anyone he wanted to speak to would use that number, not the hotel. Among the messages from various UK news media, there was one from Oz Karzac at FLS.

Karzac deserved a call. Ania's actions had damaged the professional reputation of his company almost beyond repair, yet he had defended her even after he must have known she was guilty. He keyed in the number for FLS and was put straight through when he gave his name to the switchboard.

'Gillen. Will. How are you?'

'You wanted me to call you.'

'Yep. I wanted to let you know we've started a memorial fund. There's quite a sum. It's well into four figures. A lot of people admired your daughter. Someone suggested the money should go to ChildLine. Would you be OK with that?'

'Whatever you think.'

'OK. Thanks. I'll get it organised.' He was quiet for a moment, then said suddenly, 'I keep hoping it'll die down but there's a lot of stuff in the papers again today.'

'Not from me.'

'I know. Not from here either. We're closed up tighter than a… We're closed up tight. Are you OK? It said you'd been in hospital.'

'I'm fine. It was nothing, Just a check-up, really.'

'Oh. OK. What's this about a second post-mortem?'

The question came abruptly, catching Will off his guard. He didn't want to go into details. 'The coroner asked for it.' Not exactly true, but the coroner would ask for it if Will managed to provide enough evidence.

'Why would the coroner want to second guess the Polish police? Is there something I don't know about?'

Plenty, Will wanted to say. 'Nothing. It's just – a formality, really. That's all. Anything they find will be in the papers.'

'That's just it. Look, I know this sounds selfish, but the longer it's in the papers, all over the news, the more damage… Shit, Gillen, Ania cared about this business. She helped me build it up. She wouldn't have wanted… Sorry. It's not your problem. It's going to delay the funeral, isn't it? I'd like to be there. We all would.'

'It's still going to be on the sixth. I'll let you know if…'

'Thanks.' The call tailed away into silence. Karzac said, 'Keep in touch.'

Will called DCI Cathcart who sounded tired and harassed. 'Nothing,' he said abruptly to Will's question about progress. 'The bastard knew how to cover his tracks. It means he's almost certainly done it before. We'll get him. Somehow.' But he sounded as though he was speaking by rote, saying the right things but not believing them. The conviction that had been in his voice earlier was no longer there. 'This second inquest – it isn't helpful. It's muddying the waters.'

'How?'

'It's like we don't know what we're investigating any more.'

After he put the phone down, Will reflected that Karzac was wrong. It was very much his problem. He just didn't understand it.

Chapter 42

The police took Dariusz into town. They arrived on the attack, with an arrest warrant and a warrant to search his flat. They couldn't have processed the paperwork between his call and their arrival. He realised they must have been preparing to do this, they must already have received the tip off. He'd been only just in time.

As they came through the door, he'd moved away from the window, standing still with his hands slightly raised, knowing how quick they could be with their batons and their boots. Król wasn't there and Dariusz's requests to be taken straight to the Komendant were ignored.

He was arrested on a charge of owning illegal material, and he was handcuffed and loaded into the van with a routine amount of pushing and shoving. He did manage to find out that Król wasn't available until the next morning. Until then, he was at the mercy of juniors with a grudge to work off. He made a mental note of each breach of their code, and told himself he would sue the arses off them once this was over. In the meantime, he kept his head down and made no objections. He didn't want to give them any opportunity of charging him with assault or resisting arrest.

When they got to the police station, he was processed then thrown into a cell, underground and windowless, where they left him with his hands still cuffed behind him. He had fallen, unable to balance and unable to use his hands to defend himself. After a struggle he managed to get his legs underneath him and kneel up, then get to his feet, feeling a damp stickiness on his face where it had lain against the floor.

The cell stank. It smelled of sweat, of urine, of vomit. There was a faint light coming from the grille in the door, otherwise he was in darkness. He felt his way round and found there was a wooden bench just about wide enough to lie down on and a blanket that was thin and stiff with dirt. He lay on the bench, edging himself onto his side so he wasn't lying on his cuffed hands, and tried to suppress the panic that was bubbling up inside him.

They hadn't beaten him up. At least they hadn't beaten him up. His status as a lawyer might have stopped them, but if they found his pen drive... He felt a cold dread start to flood through him and trod on it hard. He had to stop thinking like that. He forced himself to start working on the problem of what had just happened. *Set it out, think it through...* He could feel the mantra start to work, feel himself start to focus. *You have to do this*, he told himself. *To save yourself, you have to do this!*

Who? Who had planted that file on his system? There was something else he hadn't considered. What if there was more to find? What about his work computer? Jesus, he hadn't thought about work. He hadn't thought this through at all. In his panic to get to the police before they got to him he'd missed the possibilities of what else the intruder might have done.

It was still possible the police had set him up. It had been a professional job, one that he wouldn't have known about if it hadn't been for the misplacing of one coat hanger. If the police had done this, he was finished.

He tried to reassure himself. It didn't make sense. His relationship with them wasn't the most cordial, but there was no reason for them to do something like this. And if they had, why hadn't they picked him up immediately? Why wait?

It wasn't the police. He knew who had done this. It was someone who had left enough traces, tenuous, but there – a voice on a lost recording, footsteps on the stairs the night Ania died, a fingerprint on a phone cord. This was the person who had put him here, handcuffed in a police cell.

The questions churned through his mind, less and less coherent as the night wore on. No one came to release the handcuffs. His shoulders were aching and a throbbing pain was starting in his hands as the blood pooled and they began to swell. He edged himself back onto his feet and went to the door. He shouted through the grille, then he kicked the wood in frustration as no one responded and no one came. All he could do was endure.

The hours dragged on as the pain got worse. He made himself as comfortable as he could on the bench and tried to lower himself into sleep, knowing he needed to marshal his resources for the following day. He didn't know how long he was there. They had taken his watch, and anyway, it would have been too dark to read its face. The long night dragged on.

Chapter 43

Dariusz must have slept in the end, because he jerked awake as the light in his cell blazed on and the door was pushed open. 'Morning.' It was an incongruously cheerful junior, carrying a tray that he dumped down on the shelf. 'Room service!' He looked at Dariusz sprawled on the bed. 'Those should have come off last night.' He reached for a key on his belt and released the handcuffs, tutting as he saw Dariusz' purple, swollen hands.

Dariusz couldn't suppress a groan as his hands throbbed with the pain of returning life. He moved his shoulders, trying to relax the frozen muscles. The young man went cheerfully off to deal with the inmates of the other cells, and Dariusz took stock. As his nose had told him the night before, the cell was filthy. There was dirt ingrained on the floor and stains on the walls. He was inured to the smell, but the waft of fresher air from the corridor reminded him it was there. He felt grimy and sweaty. He itched, and he longed to get under the shower and wash the place off himself.

He inspected the tray without much enthusiasm. It contained a cup of grey liquid that turned out to be coffee when he tasted it. It was thin and over-sweet but it was welcome and he drank it. There were a couple of slices of bread and jam which he ate. The sugar rush made him feel more alert, and he tried to think again about what had happened, concentrating on the events to take his mind away from the pain in his hands.

Someone had planted a file containing child pornography on his computer. Judging by the bit he had seen, it was the worst kind of material, brutal to the point of lethality, and involving very young children.

There was something nagging at him, something important that he'd seen and not seen, and he couldn't bring it to the surface. He sat quietly, not concentrating, just letting his mind drift, letting something elusive and intangible rise to the surface, slowly, closer…

The cell door clattered open again. This time it was an older man. He eyed Dariusz with some distaste and said, 'You'll be wanted upstairs in half an hour. Come on.'

'I want a representative.' He didn't need a solicitor – he could act for himself – but he wanted a reliable witness. His rights had been violated and trampled on. He wouldn't get any redress. The police defended their own. For the interview, he wanted a witness.

'She's here.'

Dariusz breathed again. He'd called Krysia's number last night, but he had no way of knowing if his message had got through. 'What time is it?'

'Eight. If you want a wash, you'd better get a move on.'

The man's attitude and distance told Dariusz he knew what the charges against him were. He focused on the toilet facilities available which were inadequate but very welcome. He washed himself all over in cold water at a small basin. His face looked back at him from the polished metal that served as a mirror, weary and unshaven, but he felt more equal to coping with what the day was going to throw at him. 'OK,' he said. 'Take me up.'

Chapter 44

Will slept late. He ordered breakfast, then packed his bags while he was waiting for it to arrive. He felt light-headed and detached, the result of the sedatives he had taken, but at least the lurking pain in his chest, the sudden fast beating of his heart and the breathlessness had gone. He kept his mind focused on what he was doing and tried not to think too much about what lay ahead.

He was ready to go home. His bags were still packed. He picked up the damaged toy from the desk where Erland had tossed it the day before. His fingers touched the worn fur. *This is trash. It never meant anything.*

He tucked it into his suitcase. Ania had kept it all these years. He would take over its guardianship now.

There was nothing left to do. He was impatient to leave. He expected Erland to arrive at any minute. Despite the hostility between them, he didn't want to go without saying his farewells. But the morning wore on, and there was no call. He tried Erland's phone, but it was switched off. Their last encounter had been too bruising. Erland had had enough. Will was surprised by a sharp stab of regret.

He went down into the street and took a last walk along Piotrkowska and towards the university. Round the corner was Coffees and Toffees where the same girl polished her counter. 'Cześć,' he greeted her. She gave him a bright, blank smile and he took his coffee to a far table. The person he had hoped to see wasn't waiting for him. He had no sense of her now at all. She'd gone, and it was time for him to leave as well.

Chapter 45

Dariusz was released at midday. 'The Komendant says you can go. You're lucky you've got friends, Erland,' the officer who had questioned him said as Dariusz prepared to leave. Dariusz hadn't seen Król, but he knew Król must be observing what was happening. His faith hadn't been misplaced.

'My things?'

'You can collect them at the desk. We're keeping your computer and your phone. And don't think about going anywhere for the next few weeks. We don't like your kind, Erland. We're watching you.'

The interview had been bruising. They'd gone after him with everything they had. Krysia had sat beside him, a silent witness to the proceedings. He had tried to catch her eye a couple of times, but she kept herself disengaged.

'Why didn't you report this break in?'

'I didn't know it had happened.'

'And you just happened to find the file last night? How?'

'I was searching my system. I thought my girlfriend might have left a message or me.'

'Why would you think that?'

'Because she was murdered. I think she found something and was killed to keep her quiet.'

'She killed herself, Erland. Maybe she had a guilty conscience. She shared your interest in… videos, didn't she?'

On and on it had gone, round and round, pushing and prodding, trying to confuse him in his fatigue, trying to make him lose his temper, anything that would make him talk. Through the endless morning he told himself he just needed to hold it together for a bit longer. He couldn't prove his story: without further evidence, they couldn't disprove it. Before too long, they would have to release him. And eventually, they did.

As Krysia, drove him back to his flat, he could sense her unease. 'Thank you.'

'I didn't do much.' He could see she was struggling with something, and it burst out. 'All this stuff about Ania. I know you don't want to think... Dariusz, can't you see this is destroying you?'

'Ania was murdered.'

'She killed herself, Dariusz. She committed a crime and she couldn't face up to what she'd done so she killed herself. Why can't you see it?'

He didn't reply and they drove in silence before she began again. 'Why didn't you report the break-in?'

'I didn't know it had happened. Shit, Krysia, weren't you listening?'

'It's just us now, Dariusz. You can tell me what's going on. You don't have to...'

'I told the police what happened. That's it. That's the truth.'

'How could someone break in and you not know? And how did you find the file? If you didn't know it was there, how did you find it?'

'What is this, Krysia? What are you saying?'

'It's just... Did you know the police got an anonymous tip off yesterday that you had illegal stuff on your computer? Then suddenly you're on the phone with a story about a break-in. It looks bad, Dariusz. That's all I'm saying.'

She pulled up outside his flat. He waited until she looked at him. 'Krysia, if you don't believe me, we can't work together. I need to know what you think I'm capable of.'

Her gaze was all over the place. He waited. When she finally looked at him, he could see the doubt in her eyes. 'I want to believe you, but I can't ignore the evidence. I wish you'd reported the break-in earlier. The police think you're lying. '

He felt a stab of anger. Was this what it was going to be like? 'And you? Do you think I'm lying?'

She wouldn't look at him. 'No. Of course not. If you say you were set up, I believe you.'

She was still angry with him. He couldn't tell whether it was her anger that was dictating her behaviour or if, deep down, she had doubts. He could taste something bitter in his mouth. But it was the best he could hope for. 'OK. Let me know what's happening. I'll be in touch.'

The police search had left chaos behind. He started picking up the papers and the clothes that were scattered across the floor, then felt overcome with weariness. The drawers of his desk had been forced open, the wood splintered beyond any easy fix. He surveyed the mess and wondered what his chances were of getting the police to pay for the repairs. Last night was catching up with him. He needed to sleep, but he didn't have enough time.

The message light on his phone was flashing. He played the voice mail. There were two messages. The first one was from Will Gillen. It was short and stilted. 'I'm leaving in an hour. If you want…You've got my number. Goodbye.' Dariusz felt a reluctant grin spread across his face. Fucking tight-arse Brit.

The second one was from Leslaw Mielek, the office manager, asking him to call immediately. He sounded agitated.

Dariusz knew he should have expected this. The police would make sure Mielek knew what had happened to him, and why he had been arrested. Mielek had been looking for reasons to cause trouble, and now he had them, in spades. He toyed with the idea of keeping his head down, but that would just play into Mielek's hands.

Mielek picked up the phone as soon as Dariusz keyed in his number. 'Erland. You're on leave as of now. Don't come near the office.'

'You don't have that authority, Mielek.'

'I do now. This doesn't come from me. It comes from the top.'

'On what…'

'You know what grounds. You're lucky they just want you on leave. If it was up to me, you'd be suspended. You'd be well advised to start looking for another job.'

'That's not your decision, Mielek, so don't…'

'You'll get paid up until I know whether I can sack you or whether I want you to resign.' He put the phone down before Dariusz could respond. He sank down into his chair, feeling as though he'd just taken a massive punch. He didn't know if Mielek truly believed what he was saying, or if he was just taking an opportunity as it arose, but Krysia… OK, there'd been bad feeling between them because of Ania, because of the crass way he'd handled it, but he'd thought he could rely on her for something like this. After what they'd shared, how could she believe…? He couldn't think of any way to respond to what was happening, because he wasn't sure he understood himself what was going on.

As his head began to clear, he could see how he had been corralled. Someone had placed the file in his computer and tipped the police off. What had saved him had been police caution. They'd been wary of picking up a high-profile lawyer without firm evidence. Before they'd made their move, he found the file. That bit of luck might save him.

Despite Krysia's doubts and Mielek's call, he was certain he had done the right thing going to the police. It was the action of an innocent man, and the fact they had released him suggested that in the absence of evidence to the contrary, they thought so too.

The danger wasn't over. They had asked him about Will Gillen, and they had dug deeply into his relationship with Ania. He and Gillen had been looking for a conspiracy. Dariusz had peered into its depths only to find conspiracy hunters looking back. If he couldn't find the person who'd done this to him, then he was well and truly fucked.

Just like… The elusive thought he had lost when he was locked up in the police station, the one that had evaporated as his cell door was opened, came into his mind full formed. Like Derek Haynes. What had happened to Derek Haynes had just happened to him.

Derek Haynes, condemned by all right thinking people, could be as innocent as he was.

Chapter 46

Will's plane landed in Edinburgh on a bleak January night. He could see the rain gleaming on the runway as the plane came down through the clouds. Ania's body had been flown back two days before, the day he should have returned. As he ran with his fellow passengers from the plane to the airport terminal, the rain hammered down through the grey evening. It seemed a fitting tribute to her death.

He'd left his car at Manchester Airport. He took a taxi into the centre of Edinburgh, to the bus station. The bus from the city to Berwick called at St Abbs. The journey was just under two hours and he had checked the timetables before he left. He could get a bus at ten past seven, and be in St Abbs before nine. It would be better than a long taxi ride, being stuck for over an hour with a driver who might want to talk. Will needed silence.

His departure from Poland had been low-key. There had been no sign of Erland and no communication from him. Will told himself he didn't care. It wasn't important – they'd said everything they had to say to each other, but in fact he was disappointed. His antagonism towards Erland had burned out at some stage during the past couple of days. In the end, he had wanted Erland's support, wanted his good wishes. He'd wanted to say goodbye.

The bus crawled through the black night, the journey accompanied by the scrape and swish of the windscreen wipers. The driver, high in his seat in front of the massive windscreen seemed more like a captain on the bridge of an ocean-going vessel as the storm battered them. The road was a circle of light held in the headlamps.

He was back in St Abbs. He was walking along the cliff top with Keeper beside him. It was a beautiful summer's day, and he was on his way somewhere, to something he was looking forward to. He could see the rise in the ground ahead, and he could hear, carried on the breeze, the sound of voices, of children playing. He smiled to himself. He was nearly there. But

Keeper suddenly danced off towards the edge of the cliff and he had to turn away to catch her. When he turned back to the path, the sun had vanished behind clouds that came rushing in, and the sound of children playing was gone. He looked round, confused.

'St Abbs!'

He jerked awake. The driver had pulled in by the side of the road. He was looking back at Will. 'St Abbs!' Will staggered to his feet, stiff from fatigue and hours of travel.

In the short walk from the bus stop to the cliff top, the rain soaked him to the skin. The downpour obscured his vision and he wiped his gloved hands over his face in a futile attempt to clear it. The prospect of his cottage that had seemed like a haven from the distance of Łódź felt grim and lonely as he battled against the wind down the road to the village.

The lane to the cottage was dark. He could just make out the wall where it jutted out to mark the end of the path. As he got closer, he saw a shape bulked against the cottage door as though someone was waiting there silently, concealed in the night.

He stopped, then something burst out of the darkness. He staggered back as something hit him in the chest, almost knocking him off his feet. He was engulfed by wet fur and frantic barks as Keeper welcomed him back.

The shape detached itself from the shelter of the wall and proved to be Jack, the car park attendant. Will put up his arm to defend himself from Keeper's frantic leaps. He couldn't bring himself to speak sharply to her. 'Thank you for bringing her. It's a foul night. I would have come down tomorrow and picked her up.'

'No problem.' Even in the depths of winter, in the thin light of his torch, Jack's face looked tanned. He had thrown a waterproof over his shoulders in concession to the storm, but he was still wearing cut-offs and trainers. 'Be a bit of a depressing homecoming spending the first night alone.'

This simple act of thoughtfulness caught Will unawares and for a moment he found it hard to speak. 'Yes. Thank you.' He knew it sounded abrupt but he couldn't trust his voice. 'Do you want a drink before you...?'

'No thanks. I'll be getting back unless there's anything else you need. Here.' He thrust a carrier bag into Will's hand.

'Shopping. You can settle up with me later.' He turned back along the lane and vanished into the darkness.

Will was home.

He fumbled with his keys in the lock then pulled the door open. It swung back silently, releasing chill, musty air. He stepped inside, shut the door on the storm and stood on the stone flags as he took off his coat and shook the worst of the wet off his hair and clothes.

Keeper shook herself thoroughly then started exploring, her nose fastened to the floor, snuffling along the skirtings and under the bookshelves. Her hackles were starting to rise. Every now and then she came back to Will to press her nose against him and brush more rain from her coat onto his already soaking trousers, then she returned to her search, growling deep in her throat.

'What is it girl?'

She paid no attention to him, but kept on searching until she came to the old sideboard. She looked at him and whined, then pressed her chest to the floor, trying to get her nose underneath the heavy piece of furniture. Will crossed the room and crouched down next to her. He reached under with his hand and pulled out a lump of dried mud. Keeper sat back, satisfied.

Will studied it. It looked as if it had fallen from someone's boot. There was part of a tread pattern, nothing that would give much away, but it didn't come from anything he owned. It was clay, not local soil. Someone had been careless. He looked round. Everything was as he'd left it, some papers scattered on the table, his coffee cup in the sink. He could see the dent in the cushion where he'd sat that night, after the police had given him their deadly message and gone.

It was cold. He lit the stove and turned on the water heater, then he peeled off his wet clothes. He pulled on the heavy jersey he wore when he was out on the boat, and a pair of old jeans, then emptied the bag of shopping Jack had left. Milk, butter, eggs, bread, beer, all the basics. He abandoned his plan to make coffee and opened a can of beer, wandering round the room as he drank it.

The storm was still blowing, rattling the windows and sending gusts of cold air through the cottage. Keeper had taken up her position by the stove, sitting upright and alert as her gaze followed him.

He wasn't surprised someone had been here, and he was pretty sure he knew who it was. He still couldn't accept that the security services had been responsible for Ania's death, but he knew they were taking a keen interest. What he couldn't understand was why.

He checked the phone. Most of the messages were from friends wanting him to get in touch, expressing concern about his welfare. There was a message from Oz Karzac asking Will to call as soon as he got back and one from DCI Cathcart making the same request. He felt no sense of urgency to get back to them. He'd said everything he had to say in his last call. It could keep. There was a pile of post in the wire cage on the inside of the door. He checked through it but he knew there would be nothing there. If Erland was right, if Ania had hidden the recording somewhere else, she wouldn't have sent it here. If she had, then it was in the hands of the security services, for whatever reason it was they wanted it. He felt a curious urge to call Blaise and ask him.

Instead, he ran a deep bath and once he had soaked the ache and the chill from his bones, he went to bed. He propped a boathook against the wall within reach of his hand and let Keeper curl up on the mat on the floor beside him. It wasn't just the need for security that stopped him sending her down to her bed in the kitchen. She was the last of his family and he needed her with him.

He was waiting.

That night, he didn't dream.

Chapter 47

In the days after Gillen had left Poland, Dariusz let himself drift. He didn't challenge the decision to send him on leave. It was as if he'd lost the energy to fight. He changed the locks in his flat, getting a locksmith to put in the highest security system he could. He installed a burglar alarm. He couldn't think of anything else to do.

As the days went by, there was no further contact from the police. Krysia called him and told him they'd found nothing on the office systems. He had to assume the lack of contact meant they'd found nothing further on his laptop. Krysia's voice sounded wary as she spoke to him, as if she was speaking to a stranger.

His days stretched out in front of him, smooth, uneventful, dreary. He told himself it would get better. With time, it would get better.

For now, he was waiting.

***

The phone started ringing for Will the first morning he was back. He fielded calls from Ania's friends and from family friends, thanking them for their condolences, and telling them that he would contact them about the funeral as soon as he had news. He implied that a further post-mortem was a legal requirement. He wanted to keep speculation to a minimum.

He tried to avoid the press, refusing to give any interviews. As a result, when they reported the story, he became the man who bungled the Birmingham raid, and a grieving father who wasn't able to accept the truth about his daughter's death. The Haynes case was rehashed, with the news that there was to be a retrial and Haynes had been released on bail in the meantime.

He barely went out, just brief, monosyllabic visits to the village shop, and short walks along the cliff top with Keeper. The thin, persistent rain of winter made the ground treacherous. Once, close to the edge, his foot had slipped on the wet grass and he had seen the headlines in his mind, headlines that condemned him and his daughter as cowards who were unable to face the consequences of their actions. After that, he stayed indoors, living on bread and coffee. The level of the whisky bottle fell and fell.

It wasn't until the fifth morning that he heard from Blaise. 'How are you?'

'I'm OK.'

'You don't sound OK. I'm reading about you right now. Will, is this doing any good? Is it helping you come to terms with it?'

'Not really.'

He heard Blaise chuckle. 'Stubborn to the end. I had a call from Poland, from Król. You remember Komendant Król?'

'Of course.'

'He isn't happy with you, not happy at all. I thought I told you not to go investigating, not to get in the way?'

'What did you expect me to do?'

'Exactly what you did, Will. Exactly what you did. That's what I told Król. If he can't run a tight ship, don't expect one of my people to go in there and play along with it.'

He wasn't one of Blaise's men, not any more. 'What else did he say?'

'Not much he could say. Look, are you sure he got it that wrong?'

'He got it wrong. There was someone else there.'

'Based on?'

Will was pretty sure that Blaise already knew. There was no reason to keep it secret anyway. 'The caretaker heard someone in the building that night, and there was a print on the phone cord. No one investigated those'

'They did. He's not as incompetent as you think. That caretaker is ex-SB turned informer. He used to make a good living selling information to the police, but he got greedy. Król looked into the footsteps story – there was no evidence of anyone else there. And a partial fingerprint in a room that's used by any Tom, Dick and Harry? None of it adds up to murder, Will. You know that.'

An account of footsteps on the stairs didn't sound like a lucrative informer's story, and even though Pawlak had managed to make some money out of it from Will, he wasn't convinced. 'Why come up with something like that?'

'Just trying it on. Now, aren't you going to tell me about the second post-mortem?'

'Let's just say I'm hedging my bets.'

He heard Blaise sigh. 'OK. As you like. I'll be honest with you. I think you're clutching at straws. Don't get me wrong, I understand why. Maybe you're right. If you are, I'll do everything I can to make them follow it up. If you're wrong – Will, I don't want you to spend the rest of your life as one of those conspiracy obsessionals. Promise me one thing: once the post-mortem is done, bury her. Don't leave her in the morgue.'

He rang off, leaving Will staring at the phone, puzzled. He'd expected something different. He picked up the whisky bottle and poured himself what was probably a triple measure of Scotch, the start of an evening's drinking that was the only way he knew to make the hours pass into sleep, or at least into oblivion. Ania had tried to explain it to him once when she talked about her depressions, about being in the grip of Brown Jenkin's claws. 'The seconds are too long. There doesn't seem to be any way through them.' He picked up the glass, and Keeper came and laid her chin on his foot. She whined.

He looked at her properly for the first time in days. Her coat was matted, her eyes dull. Since he retired, she had been used to going everywhere with him, taking long walks on the cliffs or across the fields where she could chase rabbits and play with other dogs. Her life and his had been spent outdoors. For the past week, she had been shut up here with an owner who was rapidly becoming a drunk, curled up for long hours in her bed while he slept off the whisky he'd used to bring about sleep in the first place. If he couldn't look after her properly, he didn't deserve her.

He found her brush and spent half an hour gently grooming the coat he used to brush every day until it was smooth and glossy. 'OK. That's you done. What about me?'

She studied him intently, her head cocked to one side.

'A bit of a scruff?' He looked in the mirror. His hair was a wild tangle and it was so long since he had shaved that he effectively had a beard. His eyes were bloodshot. His clothes were dirty and crumpled. He reminded himself of Dariusz Erland the way he had appeared that evening in the hotel when Will had first seen him.

He stripped off his clothes and dumped them in the washing machine, then went upstairs to the shower. There was no hot water, so he doused himself in cold, then shaved off five day's growth of beard. The man who looked back at him as he ran the comb through his hair was pale and hollow cheeked, with the shadows of stress and sleeplessness under his eyes, but he no longer looked like a vagrant, like someone who had lost all interest in living and all pride in himself.

He put on clean jeans, a shirt and a heavy jersey, then pulled on his waterproof and called Keeper. If he was going to drink, he'd do it at the hotel where pride at least would stop him from drinking himself into a stupor.

Keeper's pent-up energy made her dance round his legs as they set out through the village in the moonlight. When they reached the cliff path, she snaked her way into the undergrowth, coming back with a stick that she laid at his feet, watching him with bright eyes. He threw it a short way for her and they made their way along the path like this, Keeper bringing her stick back, Will throwing it in the kind of mindless routine that had marked their walks in the years since she first came to him as a boisterous, undisciplined puppy. The rain had stopped but the ground was still wet. Will walked slowly, watching the clouds as they rolled across the moon.

The bar was its familiar self, the threadbare carpet and smoke-stained walls comforting in a way that Will couldn't explain. An open fire had burned down to embers and the room was warm and welcoming. There were a few other customers: one or two gave him a quick nod of greeting, their eyes avoiding his.

The embarrassment of bereavement – he had become too familiar with it in his life. He took his whisky over to the chair by the fire where he usually sat and sank down into it. Keeper stretched out on the rug, groaning with pleasure as the warmth flowed over her.

He knew he wouldn't be disturbed. The people of St Abbs had a strong sense of privacy. They preferred their own not to be breached, and respected that of their fellow villagers. Will was still a bit of an outsider for all the years he had been coming here, but he knew that no one would intrude on him.

Last time he had been here, he had spent the evening talking with Sarah Ludlow. He wanted to find her, but he was waiting for the results of the new post-mortem before he challenged her. He wanted to be on unassailable ground before that confrontation.

He had two singles of malt whisky, making them last through the evening. As he stood up to leave, Iain, the landlord gestured him over with a jerk of the head. 'Good to see you back,' he said.

'It's good to be back.'

'You missed yon bawbags. We had them in here asking questions.'

'I'm sorry you were bothered.'

Iain's normally gloomy face lit up with a grin. 'No bother. There's no law against asking. Can't say the same about telling, mind, and I got some good money across the bar.'

If the invading journalists had swelled the hotel's profits for a night or two, then something good had come out of the whole business. 'That's OK then.'

'I got this for you.' Iain passed a bag across the bar, nodding at Will as he did so.

Will slipped it into his pocket. 'Good night.' He whistled to Keeper and stepped out into the winter night.

It looked as if the waiting was over.

Chapter 48

When Will arrived back at the cottage, he towelled Keeper off, wrestling with her as she attempted to shake her coat free of the rain, hung his waterproof on the back of the door and went across to the table, still carrying the small package that Iain had given him.

He turned it over and over in his hands. It was addressed to Iain at the hotel, and inside, there was a second package. This one had his name on it in writing he knew very well. William Gillen. It was scrawled as though she had written it quickly. Folded up in the package was a piece of paper. He unfolded it and spread it out on the table in front of him. Again, he saw the familiar writing and felt a sense of her presence so clearly that his breath stopped in his throat. He looked round the small kitchen, at the familiar stove, the flagged floor and the wooden shelves that ran up the wall. He knew she was there – just beyond the door, just on the stairs, maybe she had just stepped outside for a moment, but she was there...

And then there was nothing, just a package and a note written in black ink on a piece of notepaper headed with the logo of the English Language Department, the University of Łódź .

Dear Iain

Can you give this to my father the next time he comes into the bar? Don't take it to the cottage or give it to anyone else, just hang on to it until you see him. I'd be grateful if you could keep it quiet.

Many thanks

Ania.

So simple. Behind the dust cloud of websites and e-mails and things hidden in teddy bears, she had simply posted it, relying on the closed nature of the St Abbs community to get it to him. Her faith hadn't been misplaced. Iain had kept the package, waiting until Will came into the bar, handing it over almost as an afterthought at the end of the evening. He slipped his finger under the seal, and opened it.

An audio cassette tape dropped onto the table. A note was wrapped round it, held with an elastic band. Will unfolded it and her voice spoke in his head as he read it.

Dad, I'm sorry for all this cloak and dagger stuff but I've got a better idea of what's going on now. I can't get this done here – my mistake. If it goes through official channels, I'm afraid it might disappear. I'm working on the other stuff, but in the meantime it would help a lot if you dealt with this for me. Can you give it to:

Sarah Ludlow
Merchant Matheson
The Cotton Warehouse,
Merchants Quay
Manchester
M50 2DA

Tell her it needs to be <u>authenticated</u> and analysed. She'll know what to do.

Love, Ania

x

PS. See you soon.

The missing tape. It must be the copy of the original recording, the one DCI Cathcart had made that she had listened to and given the off-the-cuff analysis that had impressed him so much. He held it in his hand, puzzled. Why was it so important? It was a poor quality recording – Cathcart had admitted as much – that would have no value in court. Could it be the only extant copy of the original file? Even so, it had no value as evidence, none at all, and yet it had cost his daughter her life.

He saw a dark staircase in an empty building, and heard footsteps, soft and stealthy, climbing up towards a room where Ania sat staring at a computer screen, her head resting on her hand. When had she heard the sound, and when had she realised what it meant?

Will had not been impressed by what Blaise had told him. Pawlak couldn't have expected money for reporting an unseen intruder on the stairs. There was no reason to make that story up. That person would have been central to any investigation, not dismissed as an informer's fabrication.

He remembered his dream of opening the door to the car park, of standing above a huddled figure, consumed by rage and frustration because... Because he had failed to find the audio cassette, the cassette that was now in Will's hands.

He read her note again. There was something about the tone that disturbed him. It was dated the day after she had arrived in Łódź . She obviously didn't trust the authorities with whatever evidence this tape held, but there was no sense of the danger she was in. And there was something else. She addressed him as though he knew what she was talking about – *all this cloak and dagger stuff, a better idea of what's going on, my mistake, the other stuff* – as if they were half way through a conversation, except he hadn't heard the first part.

Then just on the edge of hearing, as if the sound was coming to him across a gulf of distance and of time, he heard the sea surging against the rocks in the storm, and the sound of thunder. Her voice was faint and far away. *Look, you'll get a letter, OK? I don't want to take you unawares. You're around for the next couple of days?*

The letter she had promised him. It wasn't the suicide note she had meant. It had never been the suicide note because she hadn't written it. She had sent him a letter about the Haynes case, explaining what was going on, explaining what she was doing. He'd never got it. It had never arrived.

The dried mud under the dresser – if the letter had arrived after her death, then Brown Jenkin had claimed it.

He had no choice now but to work with what he had, which were Ania's instructions, clear and simple. They gave him a direct line to Sarah Ludlow but he knew things now that Ania did not. He knew that Sarah Ludlow had come looking for her, had come asking questions not openly but surreptitiously. She had found out what she wanted, and then Ania had died.

Ania might have trusted her. He could not.

He sat at the table, turning the cassette over and over in his hands. He knew it had to be important, but he also knew that it was impossibly contaminated. It was a copy made casually on poor equipment. The chain of evidence had broken as soon as Ania took it, and the fact that it had been in her hands, unsupervised, meant that whatever was on it would not be verifiable, would never stand up in any court.

And yet she must have known that herself. She was familiar enough with the rules of evidence. He read the note again: *I can't get it done here* – whatever 'it' was – *my mistake*. She'd taken it to Łódź with very clear plans, plans he might understand if he had received her letter. *Get it <u>authenticated</u> and analysed.* What did she mean by *authenticated*? It couldn't be authenticated, not now.

He switched on his laptop and looked up the Manchester offices of Merchant Matheson. The address Ania had given him was right. The offices were out at Salford Quays. He could call in the morning but he didn't want to talk to Sarah Ludlow on the phone. He wanted to be able to see the expression on her face when they met again without warning. He wanted to know if he would see guilt.

Chapter 49

Dariusz' arrest left him with a sense of anxiety and claustrophobia. He didn't know if he was being watched or if his calls were being observed. His flat felt like a stage, a stage that was illuminated by a single bright light. What he saw as walls was simply darkness from which eyes watched him as the spotlight sought him out.

He lived in a high-tech world, and now he was deprived of his resources. His phone numbers were stored in his phone. Until he got it back from the police, he couldn't contact Gillen easily. Gillen may well have tried to call him, but Dariusz had no way of knowing. He'd tried calling Król, asking for his phone at least to be returned, but there had been no response. He got the impression that Król was taking the opportunity of making his life as difficult as possible while he had the opportunity.

He still hadn't been able to look at the files from the Haynes case, the videos and images Strąk had tried to send him, the ones that had got corrupted when he first downloaded them. They were lost now with the rest of his data. They'd been on his pen drive, and though he'd tried searching the ground around his flat, there was no sign of it. He'd have to contact Strąk and get him to resend them, but he couldn't do it from his own systems, even if the police didn't have his laptop. His e-mail was almost certainly under surveillance, as was he.

He needed to get out of the flat and get to some public facilities, an internet café, a public phone. There were people he needed to contact before his pariah status spread and no one would talk to him or help him.

Król probably had someone watching his flat. He put on a dark jacket and stuffed a baseball cap and a lightweight backpack into the pockets. He went down to his car, not attempting to conceal what he was doing. There was no point. As he drove away, he saw a car pulling out into the traffic behind him.

He made no attempt to shake them off, just kept sufficiently ahead of them to give himself a bit of breathing space. He drove into the city centre and parked illegally at the back of the university, in the car park where, such a short time ago, Ania had died. He got out, went straight into the building through the back entrance. By the time he stepped out into the cold through the front entrance he was in his shirt sleeves, carrying a small backpack and wearing a baseball cap pulled down over his eyes. Anyone looking for him would be looking for a bareheaded man in a dark jacket. He was now wearing a red shirt and a cap. It wasn't much of a disguise, but it might make him hard to spot if someone were scanning the crowd from the steps of the university building.

The first place he went to was Al. Piłsudskiego, just off Piotrkowska where he could lose himself in the crowds of the Galeria Łódzka. He made his way through the shopping centre to the electronics store where he bought a new phone, a pay-as-you-go. He checked the street as he left the Galeria, then headed straight for the cinema complex close by where the café offered internet access.

He bought some coffee and found a quiet table where he could work unobserved. He needed a new e-mail account, one the police didn't know about. Will Gillen had a Hushmail address. Gillen should know about e-mail security. If it was good enough for Gillen, it would do for him. He logged on to the site and found he could set up a free account which didn't need an alternative e-mail address to verify it. The police would need a court order to access it, a Canadian court order. That was good. That was excellent.

He got Strąk's e-mail address from the paper's website and mailed a high priority request for Strąk to contact him. Strąk called almost immediately. 'What's going on? You've got that story for me?'

'Not yet. I'm working on it. I've got some problems.'

'I know. I've been hearing whispers about you.'

'About dodgy stuff on my computer?'

'Yeah. Was it the stuff I sent you? I warned you it was…'

'No. It was something else. It just… turned up.'

There was silence as Strąk absorbed this. 'Then you've got a serious problem. There's a well-organised police leak on the go as well.'

'Shit!' He felt a weary anger. The fact that the police were resorting to this meant they didn't have enough to charge him, which was good news of a kind, but it also meant that the story would spread and be impossible to suppress. Now, no matter what happened there would always be people who believed what was being said about him.

'So, talk to me, friend. What's been happening? What have you done to get up their noses so comprehensively?'

The ready way that Strąk dismissed the rumours lifted a weight from Dariusz' shoulders. After Krysia's reaction, he had been worried that everyone, given the nature of the accusations against him, would back away. 'I don't know. Not exactly. I'm trying to find out. It's got to be – look, we're talking business here, aren't we? This has to be off the record for now.'

'OK. For now. I'll be mightily pissed if someone else gets it first.'

'If I can give it to you, I will. It may not be my story to break. It's about Ania, that's where it starts.'

'I thought it must be. What do you want?'

'I want you to send those files again.' He spoke over Strąk's interruption. 'I know. But they must have got damaged last time when they were sent. I didn't get the complete file.'

'I sent it to you.'

'I know, but it didn't come through. Not all of it. Right now, I need that stuff.'

'Why?'

'Because whatever happened to Ania happened because of that case. I have to know why.'

'My contact's going to want to know why I need it again.'

'Tell him you're investigating Ania's death.'

'You don't have to tell me my job. OK. How do I get it to you?'

'How soon can you get hold of it?'

'Hour or so if my contact's around.'

'OK. Once you've got it, e-mail it to poorman30@hushmail.com.'

'You got it. Listen, mate, you need some help?'

'You'd be better keeping away from me until this is over. Get me this stuff, and you've given all the help you can. If you haven't sent it in a couple of hours, will you e-mail that address and let me know?'

Now all he could do was wait.

Chapter 50

Salford

Salford Quays was like a toy town in pink brick, steel and glass. The water was deep blue like in a child's painting. The dream-like quality – a child's dream – was enhanced by the emptiness. This was a landscape that was yet to be peopled.

Will had taken the train from Edinburgh the previous day. It had been evening by the time he arrived in Manchester. He'd gone straight to the airport to collect his car which had amassed huge parking charges, then driven back into the city to Ania's flat.

He was troubled by no memories as he walked up the stairs, saw no one waiting for him in the doorway. Inside, the flat was silent, with the musty smell of abandonment. He had hoped, as he opened the door, that she would be there to welcome him, to tell him he was doing the right thing, but the empty rooms were cold and anonymous now.

The next morning, he called Merchant Matheson early, at eight thirty, and gave his name as Walter Gilman. 'I need an urgent appointment with Ms Ludlow. Can she see me today?'

'Ms Ludlow has a full schedule. Can you tell me what it's concerning?'

'It's a matter relating to Derek Haynes.'

'One moment. I'll check with Ms Ludlow if she has any time.'

Five minutes later, he had an appointment for ten thirty. He stowed his laptop in his bag with all the information he had gleaned in Łódź loaded onto it. He packed the audio cassette still in its wrapping along with both of Ania's letters. What he planned to do with all of this, he hadn't yet decided.

As his car pulled out of the car park, he felt a sense of something closing, something coming to a slow, inexorable end. He couldn't see what the end would be, there were still things to do, but he knew that one way or another, it was nearly over.

When he got to the Quays, he left the car in one of the public car parks and walked along the water to the block where

Merchant Matheson had their offices. Despite the sun, it was cold. The light reflected off the water and off the glass of the buildings with a painful intensity. He felt a sharp pang of homesickness for the cliffs of St Abbs, the sharp calls of the sea birds and the restless surging of the sea.

He crossed a brick-paved courtyard to the entrance of a building signposted as The Cotton Warehouse and went in. The receptionist directed him to a waiting area and he sat in one of the comfortable chairs, thumbing through the kinds of magazines such places seemed to keep: Country Life, Vogue, New Statesman and a few professional journals.

'Mr Gilman?' For a telling moment, he didn't react, then looked up to see a young woman smiling at him from a doorway across the lobby. 'Miss Ludlow will see you now.'

He picked up his bag and followed her along a carpeted hallway to an office door. She opened it for him and let him precede her. 'Mr Gilman,' she said.

Sarah Ludlow stood up from behind her desk. She was smaller than in his memory, more formal and restrained. She was wearing a dark jacket and her hair was pulled severely back from her face. She wore glasses with a heavy black frame. 'Mr Gilman,' she said as she rose to greet him, then her smile of professional interest froze.

'Do you want coffee?' the secretary said behind him.

Without moving his gaze from Sarah's face, he said, 'Yes. Thank you.'

Her paralysis broke. 'Thank you, Alice. Give us a few minutes please.' She waited until the secretary had withdrawn then said, 'What are you doing here?'

'I didn't think you'd agree to see me and I need to talk to you.'

She regained her composure. 'I was very sorry to hear about your daughter, but I think this conversation would be better at another time and another…'

'I would have thought you'd have expected me sooner rather than later.'

'You can't ambush me like this.'

He shrugged. He just had.

'Why should I expect you at all? Listen, Will…'

'You came to St Abbs looking for her, didn't you?'

He mouth tightened, then she made a gesture of resignation and pointed at a chair. 'You'd better sit down.' She pressed an intercom button and said, 'Alice? We'll have the coffee now.' It buzzed a distorted reply. 'Yes, fine. Just bring the coffee in. Thank you.'

They sat in silence until the secretary brought in a tray with china cups and a coffee pot. 'Thank you,' Sarah said again. 'No calls for half an hour please.'

As the door closed, Will said, 'Is that code for "Call security and get him thrown out."?'

Her mouth twitched in a reluctant smile. 'If it was, I wouldn't tell you.' She looked at him, her gaze steady. 'Yes, I came to St Abbs to look for Ania.'

'And you found me instead.'

She held a lump of sugar above the coffee in her cup, letting the liquid rise up through the grains before she dropped it in. 'I didn't know who you were when I met you at the hotel.'

'You travelled hundreds of miles on the off-chance of seeing my daughter, and you "just happen" to bump into me in the local pub? You can do better than that.'

She didn't look up. 'What do you want me to say? It's the truth.'

He turned his head away in exasperation.

'I didn't travel all that way to see Ania. I was in Scotland for another reason when the news about the Haynes appeal first broke.'

'Convenient.'

'It was, or it could have been. I tried calling Ania at work but they told me she'd gone away. I knew she came to St Abbs sometimes – she told me it was where she came when she needed to get away from things – her bolt hole. It seemed a good bet that was where she'd be so I drove back that way. When I saw the cottage, it was obvious someone was staying there. I thought it was her. I tried phoning but I got the answering service so I went to the hotel.'

'And the next day? It was a coincidence that you came to my house and asked questions about her?'

'It wasn't until then that it dawned on me who you were. I didn't realise anyone else lived there. Ania described it as a holiday cottage.'

'It was until recently.' He didn't want to talk about that. 'You didn't say anything.'

'I could hardly discuss Ania's business with you. That was private.'

'She was your client?' That was one possibility that hadn't crossed his mind.

'No.'

'So you got the information you needed and left?'

'More or less. I might have stayed but I could see you had things on your mind.'

It could have happened like that. He had no way of proving or disproving what she said. He had every reason not to trust her. 'And your business with Ania? She died the day after you came looking for her.'

This time she met his gaze. 'I know. If I could have contacted her, maybe...' She waited.

He didn't give anything away. He wasn't going to tell her what he had found out in Poland. He wanted to see how much she knew. 'Go on.'

'I met her during Haynes' first trial. I heard her give evidence and I talked to her afterwards.'

The picture from the newspapers – the shadowy figure of Sarah standing between the pillars behind Ania. 'You were at the trial? Why? Were you part of Haynes' team?'

'God no. My client is a different person altogether. I was there for Nadifa Akindès, for Sagal's mother.'

***

...If they find Sagal, if they do to Sagal what they are doing to her, then her soul will die. She will pour lamp oil over herself and her unborn child, over the house where her murdered father lies, and she will hold a taper to it and burn them all. Her only prayer will be that these creatures that used to be men will burn with her. She will take her own soul to hell, happily, if she can take their souls with her.

The men wait their turn, watching and laughing.

The drone of the flies is loud in the still, hot air.

223

Manchester Crown Court Trial of Derek Haynes.

The barrister made a careful display of letting his disbelief show. 'It's a perfectly simple question, Ms Akindès. Did you or did you not offer to have sex with my client?'

'No.' The dead sound in Nadifa's voice wasn't helping her. Sarah Ludlow tried to catch her eye, but Nadifa's gaze was fixed on her hands. The barrister studied her with a detached curiosity.

'Your children were just commodities to you, correct? Useful for getting you into the country, useful for allowing you to stay.'

'No.'

He looked across at the jury. 'We've already heard evidence that you refer to your son as "the changeling." Is this correct?'

Nadifa shook her head.

'I didn't hear you.'

'I... Because...'

'Do you or do you not call your infant son a changeling?'

'Because...'

'Yes or no, Ms Akindès.'

'...yes.'

'What did you call your daughter, Ms Akindès? The goods?'

The cross-examination had been brutal. As the mother of the murdered child, she was entitled to the jury's sympathy but the barrister had been working very hard to destroy her credibility, and he was succeeding. He'd already forced her into the admission that she'd gone into hiding after her husband had been arrested for his Jihadist connections, and that when she was destitute she'd sometimes spent the night with a man in order to have a roof over her and her children's heads, and that she had accepted money the next day. She said she had done it to protect her children, but the barrister – who was good, Sarah couldn't deny that he was good – was making mincemeat of that claim.

He returned to the issue of prostitution. 'I see. You had perfectly good accommodation until your husband decided to repay the British state by working with people who planned to overthrow it. When the authorities quite justifiably decided he had to go, they tried to put you in a secure place where you and your children would be safe. Instead, you chose to reject this. By your own admission, you picked men up on the street, you had sex with them and they gave you money.'

He looked at the jury. 'Allow me to read to you the definition of a prostitute in the Oxford English Dictionary. In this country a prostitute is: *a woman who engages in promiscuous sexual intercourse for payment.* I think we can all agree that what you have just described to us fits this definition.' He waited for the slight shuffle from the jury that indicated agreement. He'd won them over. 'Now…'

He moved on to establish that despite her denials, Nadifa had tried the same thing, or something similar with Haynes, rather than the prosecution interpretation of events, that Haynes had gone out of his way to befriend the family. Sarah waited for the prosecution to intervene, but they were probably happy enough for a sexual link to be confirmed between Haynes and the dead child's mother.

'I thought he could help us.'

Sarah wanted to drag Nadifa out of the witness box and hide her in some safe place where they couldn't reach her. Nadifa, who had somehow escaped from the hell that had been Côte d'Ivoire during the civil war years, who had survived all that had been done to her, Nadifa who was facing the prospect of a forced return to a country that had swallowed up the rest of her family without trace, who had used her angry energy and courage in every way she could to protect her daughter, was finally being destroyed. By watching out for the danger ahead, she had missed the danger at hand.

Sarah looked at Haynes and wondered if he knew or cared what women like Nadifa had survived before they became vulnerable to him, but he wasn't looking at her. He was hunched over with his arms resting on his knees.

'You thought he could help you. Did he?'

Nadifa shook her head.

'I'm sorry. I didn't hear that.'

'No.'

'To whom else did you offer sexual favours in return for "help"?'

Now Sarah could see the direction the barrister was heading. If Nadifa was willing to use her own body as currency, what might she have done with the far more valuable commodity of her daughter's body? She saw the prosecution belatedly get the message and jump in with a series of objections. Even so, by the end of the session, Nadifa's reputation as a loving mother who had lost her child was in rags.

Haynes was going to be acquitted.

The next person to take the stand was a forensic linguist. Sarah had little hope that this evidence would help the case. It was to establish that the voice recorded on a video showing Sagal imprisoned prior to her death was that of Derek Haynes. It would be useful, but Sarah already knew that voices could not be identified beyond reasonable doubt.

The expert witness was a woman, Dr Ania Milosz. She clearly understood the theatre of the court. She was wearing a dark grey suit that emphasised her professionalism. Her fair hair was cut in a short bob. She slipped reading glasses out of her pocket when she took the oath, and kept them on as she gave her evidence.

She was good. She explained what she did and how her analysis worked in clear, comprehensible terms. She played bits of comparison tape, talked about the features of Derek Haynes' voice, showed how these appeared more than once in what was a relatively short recording. She matched acoustic profiles, saying that these were closer than any she had ever seen in her career as a forensic linguist. 'I can find nothing that is inconsistent with the voice of the defendant,' she concluded.

And that was the weak point. When he began his cross-examination, the defence barrister aimed straight at what must have looked like an open goal.

'It is correct, is it not, Dr Milosz, that there is no such thing as a voice print?'

'Yes.'

'And therefore it is impossible to say with certainty that two voices come from one and the same person?'

'But it is possible to say with certainty that a voice does *not* come from a specific person.'

'Please answer my question: you cannot say with anything close to certainty the voice on that recording is the voice of my client?'

'In this case, I can.' Before the defence barrister could speak, she addressed the jury. 'The computer in question was used by only a limited number of people. I can therefore say with certainty the voice was not that of any of these other users.'

The re-cross had allowed her to confirm again that she had not been able to eliminate Haynes. 'There were a limited number of people with access to that computer. Of those people, the voice on the recording can only have belonged to one of them: Derek Haynes. There is nothing in that recording that is incompatible with his voice. In the course of my work, I have never come across a closer match.'

It wasn't just the evidence, it was the calm certainty with which she gave it and the way in which she addressed the jury as intelligent people who could appreciate the issues. *We all know what he's trying to do* had been the sub-text of her evidence. *Don't let him fool you.* When she left the stand, Sarah followed her out and caught up with her in the square outside the court. 'Dr Milosz?'

'Yes?'

'I'm Sarah Ludlow. I represent Nadifa Akindès. Sagal's mother,' she added, in the face of Ania Milosz's polite incomprehension. 'I was there as a friend today, much good it did her. I just wanted to say how impressed I was by your evidence.'

Ania Milosz pushed her sunglasses up from her eyes and studied Sarah. 'I hope the jury felt the same way,' she said after a moment.

'You're sure it was him?'

There was a satisfaction in her eyes that had not been there when she was being the professional witness in front of the jury. 'I've never been so sure of an analysis in my life.'

Chapter 51

'Now it seems there was a reason she was so certain.' Sarah's gaze searched his face. 'I know you don't trust me, but I want to know what you think. Did she fake that recording?'

'I... think so. Yes, I'm pretty sure she did.'

'Why? She must have known...'

'She had strong reasons for believing that Haynes was guilty of another paedophile murder.'

Her teeth played with her bottom lip. 'One that the police couldn't touch him for?'

'Yes.'

'There was something she said... We didn't know each other very well, but we kept in touch. We met for a drink one evening and she started talking about the case. She wanted to know about Nadifa, if what they'd said about her in court was true.'

'Why did she want to know?'

'She was worried about something. She kept asking me if I thought another person could have been involved.'

The recording. 'And could they?'

Sarah shrugged. 'It's possible. Some of the male staff at the centre were quick enough to take advantage of the women held there. Another paedophile? Why not.'

'Did she tell you why she thought that?'

'No. She just said she had a "feeling" which was why I didn't take it too seriously, not until...' Not until the news about the fabrication came out. 'If it wasn't Haynes on that tape...'

'She was worried that she'd let someone get off.'

'Yes. And it was getting to her. She looked ill that night. She wasn't eating, and there was something – forgive me – there was something dead in her. She wasn't the woman I'd seen in court that day.'

Brown Jenkin. He knew the signs. From what Sarah was telling him, after the Haynes trial, something had made Ania deeply depressed. She hadn't talked to him about it. During that time, they'd barely been in touch at all, now he came to think about it.

For God's sake why didn't you call?

There was no reply. Since Poland, since Łódź, she had gone.

He was aware of Sarah watching him with a slight frown. 'Sorry. I was thinking about something. Is that all she said?'

'Yes. After that, she changed the subject. I forgot about it – it wasn't anything I could follow up. But when the news broke, I realised what she must have meant. I needed to talk to her because if she was prepared to admit that there was another abuser, someone who wasn't part of the system, then maybe I could get Nadifa off the hook. Get her deportation stopped.'

So in the end, Sarah Ludlow's concern had been for her client, for the woman who had apparently sold her daughter to a paedophile. He could remember Cathcart talking to him, the indifference in his voice as he spoke about the bereaved mother. *That kid really drew the short straw. The dad was involved in terrorist shit. That's why they deported him. The mum was a prostitute before the immigration people picked her up. The staff at the centre said she was a cold fish. She had this little lad as well as the girl, barely looked at him, called him 'the changeling' when she talked about him at all. What's to feel sorry for? It's those kids I care about.*

It was as if she could see his thoughts on his face. 'What happened in that court was a travesty. Nadifa would walk through fire for those children. She did, more or less. That barrister had to discredit her – the less sympathy she got, the more chance his client had. He couldn't go after Sagal – the jury wouldn't wear that – but Nadifa? She was an easy target.'

'Maybe. But if she hadn't gone into hiding, they would have given her somewhere to live. She wouldn't have been in detention at all.' And she wouldn't have had to make a living as a prostitute, exposing her children to all that that entailed. He couldn't find it in himself to sympathise with her plight. If Nadifa Akindès had looked after her children, if she had been a half-competent mother, his daughter would still be alive.

'If she'd taken the accommodation, she'd have been sent back. They'd all have been sent back. Anything she and the children suffered here was better than what was waiting for them at home. Let me show you something.' She stood up and went to a filing cabinet on the other side of the room. She flicked through some papers and pulled out a single sheet. 'It's part of the statement that Nadifa made when she claimed asylum. You should know that it's supported by medical evidence.'

He looked at Sarah who was watching him, her face expressionless. He started reading.

...I was pregnant and I was almost about to give birth. We heard shots and ran inside. I was at my father's house with my daughter. But the rebels came to our door. I hid Sagal in a cupboard. I kept her safe. They were looking for my husband. They said he was a traitor, but he wasn't there. They made me undress. They shot my father when he tried to stop them. They made me parade in front of them. They were mocking me, insulting me, They kicked me so hard, it hurt so much. They started putting their hands in me, said they will take out the child. I was crying. And they raped me. I was so afraid. I thought they would find my daughter and do that to her. They weren't men. They weren't human.

They were all too human. This was what humans did. There were too many stories like this in the world. He thought about the youth who had run away from his men in fear that they were Borders and Immigration police come to send him back to a similar hell. Instead, they had killed him. He had nothing to say.

'Nadifa was luckier than some. One of the village elders managed to bribe the soldiers. They were happy enough. She was just recreation to them. They had other business that day. They left her. She gave birth to her son a few days later. Her injuries were so bad she almost died. She'll never be able to have another child. But she'd managed to keep Sagal hidden and later her husband managed to get them out. She was never going to let them send her children back there, especially not Sagal – if they'd found her that day...

'It's still happening – not so much, not so widespread, but she knows she's a target and next time, they'll kill her and her son. But she didn't give Sagal to Haynes. She would have killed herself first.'

'With a story like this, why was her claim refused?'

'Because Côte d'Ivoire is supposed to be "safe" now. It isn't, not for someone like Nadifa. And there's no life there for a woman who's been raped. She's unusual in that her husband stuck by her – the men there usually reject their wives if they're raped. François Akindès is an exceptional man in many ways.'

He was a man who had put his political interests before the interests of his wife and children. 'So where is he?'

'In Côte d'Ivoire. He was arrested at the airport when he arrived back in Abidjan. There's been no news of him since.'

'What about her family?'

'All dead.'

'Where is she now?'

'In Dungavel. That's why I was in Scotland. She's due for deportation any day.'

He had to make a decision. He had to decide if he could trust her. Her anger at the plight of her client was what had tipped the balance. He held out the package with the two letters. 'Ania sent me this. I didn't get it until I came back from Poland.'

She opened the envelope and took out the cassette. 'The other man,' she said.

He nodded, and their eyes met as if they were forming an alliance.

Chapter 52

Sarah pressed the button on the intercom on her desk. 'Alice, can you get me Martin York at the university? And will you cancel my eleven o'clock meeting? Something's come up. I'm going to need…'

Will let himself slump back in his seat. He was wearier that he ever remembered being. He could feel some of the weight lifting from his shoulders as Sarah Ludlow efficiently mustered her resources.

'I've asked Alice to bring me Nadifa's file and some of our audio equipment. Let's have a look at what we've got here.'

'You're planning on playing the tape? What if it gets damaged?'

'I'm planning on making a copy. There shouldn't be any problem. Then I'll know what we've got.'

'Can you get it – what did Ania say – authenticated and analysed? Do you know someone who can do it? Not FLS.'

'It can't be FLS,' she agreed. 'I don't use them anyway. I've got a contact at the university who does anything like this for me. Alice is getting in touch with him. Authenticated…? I'm not sure what she means. I don't see how that could be done.'

'What have you got against FLS?'

'I don't like the work they do for Borders and Immigration. They claim they can identify someone's location from their language – if someone says he's from Liberia, for example, they will listen to a recording and give a decision whether that's true or not.'

He could see that there would be a clash of ideologies given the work she did, but lawyers were usually pragmatists. 'I don't see your problem.'

'They get a lot of government money for the service and they always – or almost always – give the answer that Borders and Immigration want. You can't be that specific. Take Côte d'Ivoire. There are eighty languages spoken there. It's the same across Africa. They can't do what they say they can do but they get a lot of money for doing it. It's what keeps them afloat. It's dishonest, so I don't use them.'

As she was talking, her secretary came in loaded down with some kind of sound equipment, trailing wires as she went. She had a folder tucked under her arm. Will jumped up to give her a hand and she smiled her thanks to him. She had brought a large, old-fashioned cassette player with a double deck and various cables and extensions.

Will began sorting out the cables, moving the player across to a power outlet. Sarah ran a line to a pair of speakers that stood beside a CD player on a low table by her desk.

She straightened up, wiping the dust off her hands. 'This hasn't been used for ages. We keep it, because stuff still comes in on audio cassette sometimes. Right.' She slipped the cassette into the first deck, put a blank tape into the machine to copy and pressed *play*.

The first thing Will heard was the fuzz and scratch of something recorded on poor equipment, then a click as the sound cut in. He could hear a child crying.

Not... Over here. Like that.

Please. Please. Listen. Please. I can't...

Atta girl! That's right.

I can't...

Great. Great. You're a star.

(Muffled crying)

Star.

(Crying)

Look you'd better be quiet. We're going to get into trouble here. I'm not telling you again.

Please. Please. I'm sorry. I can't...

Jesus. You don't listen, do you?

Some music cut in and then the sound stopped. There was just the hiss and click of the machine. Sarah switched it off. Will felt his head pounding. As he listened, he had seen Louisa, seen the images the audio tape mercifully concealed. He had heard her voice imposed over the voice on the tape, heard his own daughter pleading with a monster. He could feel Sarah's gaze on him but he couldn't look at her. His mouth felt full of dust.

233

Chapter 53

It was two hours before the files came through from Strąk. Dariusz had drunk five cups of coffee and was aware of the café staff watching him with curiosity. Once he knew the files were there, he had to decide what to do next. He couldn't play the video here, not in such a public place. He could download them onto a pen drive, but he couldn't guarantee his watchers hadn't found him. If they saw him downloading something, they would almost certainly search him. He couldn't be caught with these files in his possession. He needed an hour's privacy with a computer.

He had an idea. He checked the time. It was just four. He went to a phone booth and keyed in the number of Leslaw Mielek's phone.

Mielek picked up immediately. 'Mielek.'

'It's Dariusz Erland.'

'Erland. What do you want?' Mielek sounded hostile and suspicious.

'I'm prepared to do a deal, OK?'

'What deal? I don't need to do a deal with you, Erland. You're finished.'

'Don't be so sure of that. I want you to listen to me, hear me out. Then if you still want it, you'll have my resignation on your desk, no arguments.'

'It's easier for you than getting sacked, I suppose.'

'Easier for you as well.'

'OK. I'm listening, but this had better be good.'

He would enjoy hearing Dariusz plead. And he would enjoy the slow deliberation before he said no.

'I can't talk on the phone. I'll come in to the office.'

Most Tuesdays, Mielek went home early. Dariusz waited, barely breathing. 'I'm not there now. I could...'

He'd go back in for this chance. Dariusz said quickly, 'I'm not free this afternoon. Tomorrow?'

'Tomorrow.' They agreed to meet at midday.

'Am I going to run the gauntlet when I get there?'

'So far, all the staff know is that you're on leave.'

That wouldn't last. 'OK. Thank you.'

He hung up. Now he had somewhere he could go to download the data. Mielek wasn't there, and he was the only person who might try and stop him. He felt a moment's unease about Krysia. If she saw him, he'd just have to tell her he was picking up some stuff. She'd understand.

He drove to his offices and parked in the road, some way from the building. He didn't want anyone spotting his car in the car park. He went in, bracing himself for cold glances and overt hostility. Instead, the receptionist greeted him with a subdued but friendly *Hi*. 'How are you?' she said. 'We weren't expecting to see you today.'

It looked as though Mielek had told him the truth. At present, the staff didn't know anything about his situation. The receptionist must be assuming his absence was to do with Ania's death. He gave her a thin smile. 'I'm OK. I've just come in to collect some stuff.'

She nodded. 'Is there anything I can…?'

'No. I'll be fine.'

As Dariusz let himself into his office, a door opened further along the corridor. He saw Krysia put her head out. 'Oh,' she said. 'I thought I heard your voice. I thought you weren't… I mean, Leslaw said you were on leave.'

'I am. I just need to get some stuff I was working on.'

'Oh. OK.' She gave him a doubtful smile and seemed about to say something else, then she ducked back into her room. Dariusz breathed out and locked the door behind him. He could feel his hand shaking, just a little.

Everything in his room had been disconnected. The police had checked all his systems here. It took him twenty minutes to get everything back together and working. He linked the computer to the phone line, bypassing the office network. He didn't want anyone else seeing what he was downloading. He felt hot and sweaty by the time he was finished.

He switched on his computer and went online. The office had a broadband connection – still in short supply in the city – but it wasn't very fast or very reliable. Painstakingly he set up a second Hushmail account on this system – this way the data would remain encrypted. Once that was done, he began to download the files Strąk had sent him onto a pen drive. Encrypted or not, he didn't want them on this machine.

They were large files and the system announced it would take ten minutes. The numbers jumped around, moving from '10' to '40' then back to 10 again. Then the download bar began crawling across the screen and the numbers began counting down. It seemed impossibly slow. He could feel his shoulders starting to tense as he tried to will the connection to go faster, will it not to fail.

6 minutes and 30 seconds. 29, 28, 27, 26, 25... He drummed his fingers on the desk. Come on. *Come on.*

It was then he heard the sound of car wheels on gravel. He looked out of the window. Leslaw Mielek was pulling up outside the door.

Chapter 54

It was midday by the time Will left the offices of Merchant Matheson. He sat behind the wheel of his car staring out of the window. The sunlight was dazzling as it reflected off the water. He wanted Ania to come and tell him he had got it right, that he was on the right track now, but there was only silence. He was on his own.

For the first time since Ania's death, there was nothing he needed to do. He was dependent on other people. Euan Kingsley, the pathologist carrying out the second post-mortem had promised to call as soon as he had some results. The information the cassette tape carried was now in someone else's hands. Sarah Ludlow's contact at the university had asked for it and she had arranged to have it couriered across. All he could do was wait, and he wasn't good at waiting.

His phone rang. He didn't recognise the number. Maybe this was Kingsley at last. 'Will Gillen.'

But it was DCI Cathcart. 'Mr Gillen.' His voice was taut with anger. 'What's going on?'

Will felt the blankness of incomprehension. 'What are you talking about?'

'Why do Merchant Matheson want the machine I used to make a copy of the Haynes recording?'

Merchant Matheson? 'I don't know. Is there a problem?'

'Yes, there's a problem. We did everything by the book on that case. It was your daughter who screwed it up. My team aren't carrying the can for that. All we did with that recording was copy it.'

'They're looking at the recording again, but they aren't going after your people. That's not what this is about.' He hoped he was being honest. He didn't know.

When Cathcart spoke again, he was trying to sound more moderate. 'So what *is* it about?'

'I don't know why she wants the recorder. It's out of my hands now. What's happening with the case?'

'Haynes is out, in a bail hostel. The case goes back to court in a couple of months. They'll throw it out if I can't get more evidence. That's why I don't have time to mess about with some human rights lawyer who wants to start grandstanding about my team.'

'That's not…'

'Don't bullshit me, Gillen.' Cathcart's courtesy had been swallowed up by his anger. 'You know how that woman operates. It'll be bleeding hearts about Haynes and his human rights, she'll be all over the TV and the newspapers dumping on us. Just remember. She's the one who drives the BMW. She's the one with the apartment in Hale. My people don't drive expensive cars. My people can barely pay their mortgages.'

He couldn't tell Cathcart Haynes wasn't Sarah's client. He barely knew himself what was happening now, and he no longer had any idea of who he could trust. There had been a time when he trusted his own instincts, but ever since Birmingham, he'd begun to doubt himself. He'd decided he could trust Sarah Ludlow, even though he knew her main interest was Nadifa Akindès. Listening to Cathcart, he felt the firm ground of his decision start to shift and crumble. If he had been wrong…

He had no choice but to stand by what he had done. If the recorder was essential to the analysis of the tape then Cathcart could hold everything up if he wanted to be bloody-minded about it. 'It isn't your team,' he said. 'There's some evidence – some – that another person was involved in Ania's death. Merchant Matheson are following up the last lead I have.'

There was a long silence. 'Another person?'

'Possibly. This is not about your investigation.'

'I should be the judge of that.'

'I'll make sure they send the results to you.'

He could almost see Cathcart thinking about it. 'OK. I'll release the recorder.'

'If… I'd be grateful if you could do it without making a lot of noise about it.'

'I'll release it.'

Cathcart would follow procedures. That was the best Will could hope for.

Chapter 55

Dariusz swore out loud. As soon as Mielek came in, the receptionist would tell him Dariusz was here. Then he realised. The reason Mielek was here was because he already knew. Dariusz had no time left. He looked at the monitor. The download was close to complete. *3 minutes*, the window said complacently. He reached out to stop it. He needed to unplug, switch off and hide all signs of what he had been doing. If Mielek called the police, if they found him with this material... He had no illusions about what would happen then.

He hadn't saved the attachments online. If he stopped now, he might damage them or even lose them. Strąk wouldn't help him again.

He stood over the desk, willing the download to complete. *2 minutes and 10 seconds, 9, 8, 7, 6, 5, 4, 3, 2, 1... 1 minute and 59, 58, 57...* He couldn't lose it, not for less than two minutes

He could hear the sound of voices along the hall, the sound of Mielek's voice and then a lighter voice he recognised as Krysia's. Krysia. She was the one who had done it. She must have called Mielek as soon as she had seen him. He could hear them moving along the corridor towards his door. He switched off the monitor and moved away from the desk. He positioned himself by the filing cabinets as the door flew open, and pulled open a drawer as though he was going through some folders.

He looked round, letting his face show only mild surprise. He could feel his heart thumping and he was afraid his voice would give him away. Mielek was in the doorway with Krysia. She wouldn't meet his eyes. The receptionist was just behind them. She spoke first. Her voice was nervous. 'I'm sorry, Mr Mielek. I didn't know...'

Dariusz smiled at her reassuringly. Mielek could be a bully with the junior staff and he didn't want to get her in trouble. 'Don't worry, you haven't done anything wrong.' To his relief, his voice came out OK. 'What's the problem, Mielek?'

Mielek looked at the receptionist and said irritably, 'Get back to your desk. You're not doing anything useful here.' He waited until she was gone then tried to push Dariusz to one side so he could get further into the room. Dariusz held his ground.

'What's the problem?'

'What have you come in for? I know you haven't got any of your filth on our system. The police checked.'

Out of the corner of his eye, Dariusz could see the pen drive in the computer and the giveaway light flickering, showing that something was going on. From his perspective, it looked huge, unmissable, as if a neon sign was flashing above his desk: *look what he's doing!* He scooped a couple of files out of the drawer and moved across the room, keeping between Mielek and the desk, deliberately encroaching on the other man's space, allowing his size to intimidate. 'I came for these. I've got work I need to do.'

'Give.' Mielek snapped his fingers and held out his hand. Dariusz was aware of Krysia looking more and more unhappy.

'My clients, Mielek, not yours. Haven't you heard about confidentiality? I'm taking these back and I'm going to work on them.' He heard a muted tone that told him the download was complete and cursed himself for forgetting the sound. He quickly took his phone out of his pocket and checked the screen, nodding as if he saw something he expected. 'I've got people waiting for these,' he added, letting the files slide out of his arms and onto the desk. Using his body as a shield to obscure his actions, he switched the power off at the wall socket, then eased the pen drive out of the port and slipped it into his pocket.

Mielek jabbed a rigid finger at Dariusz from his stance by the door. 'You don't get it. You don't work here any more. I tried to do this the right way, let you take leave, gave you a chance to resign. As of now, you are suspended. You don't get to take files out of here. Do you understand me? Do you?'

'That's not your decision, Mielek.'

'Mr Mielek,' Krysia intervened. He ignored her.

'I've always thought you were no more than a thug. This country's moved on since the days your father was playing heroes down by the docks. Does he like kids as well? Is that what happened to you?'

A moment of wild joy surged through Dariusz as he pictured his fist smashing into Mielek's face. He forced the impulse away. Mielek wanted an excuse, and Dariusz was not going to give it to him. He looked Mielek in the eye. 'Don't make me do something I wouldn't regret anyway.' He tucked the files under his arm and headed for the door.

He heard footsteps behind him as he walked along the corridor, the brisk tap of heels that brought Ania back to him for a painful, blinding moment. 'Dariusz. *Dariusz*!' It was Krysia. 'I didn't realise he was going to… I had to call him.'

He didn't turn round. He strode past the reception desk, aware of the receptionist's eyes following him, and left the building.

Beneath his anger and frustration, an idea was forming in his head.

Chapter 56

Will left a message at Merchant Matheson for Sarah Ludlow to call him as soon as she was free. He was at a loose end. He had nothing to do. He didn't want to go back to Ania's flat and spend the afternoon alternately brooding and worrying. He decided to drive to the FLS offices. He owed Oz Karzac a visit.

Despite Sarah Ludlow's reservations, he had nothing against Karzac. Ania's boss had had faith in her and publicly at least, had given her as much support as he could. He phoned from his car and when Karzac's secretary assured him that Karzac was there and would be able to see him, he headed back towards Manchester centre.

The traffic was bad. He had got out of the habit of urban roads, living in the remote borders, and he found it wearing to keep up the level of concentration this driving needed.

When he pulled up outside the old school where FLS was based, he could see that the place was undergoing change. There was scaffolding running up one wall, a skip in the car park, and removal van was being loaded outside the main gate. Will went to the main entrance and passed under the half-obscured sign, *Infants*. A harried receptionist looked up and said, 'I'm sorry, the offices are closed today. You need to… Oh. Mr Milosz. Mr Gillen. I'm sorry.'

'Professor Karzac is expecting me. You look busy.'

'Yes. We're moving this weekend. We're starting in the new offices on Monday. We've had to do most of it on our own. I don't know how we're going to be ready.'

'I'll get out from under your feet. Where can I find Professor Karzac?'

'He's in his office. Can you find your own way? The door isn't locked.'

All the sensitive material must be off the premises as the security he had been so aware of last time had gone. He pushed open the door leading into the offices and went through, following the corridor round to the room he remembered from before.

This time, it looked more spacious as most of the furniture had been removed. Karzac, who was sitting at his desk, a laptop in front of him, looked as if he had been washed up on some empty shore, the detritus after a storm. He saw Will and pushed himself out of his chair. 'Will. Take a seat. I'll just go and...' He wandered off before Will could respond and came back a minute later carrying a stacking chair. He gestured Will towards the desk.

Will took the chair off him. 'I'll sit here. I won't keep you. You've got a lot on.'

Karzac didn't look busy. Will had got the impression as he came through the office door of someone filling in time, someone who, like him, had lost his role. Karzac's face sagged and the beard that Will remembered as neatly-trimmed was bushy and uneven.

Karzac shrugged. 'There's not much for me to do, to be honest. I'm just keeping out of the way. I'm catching up on a book review I should have completed a month ago. How are you?'

Will treated the question as rhetorical. He imagined the answer was written clearly enough on his face. 'Is there any more news about the case?'

'Haynes? We aren't dealing with it any more.'

'Of course. I just wondered if you'd heard anything.'

'I'm right out of the loop.' Karzac looked resigned. 'I'm trying to keep our other contracts going. I'm gutted about Ania, but I have to think about the business. I've got a responsibility to everyone here.'

'I understand.'

'Have you had the results from the second post-mortem?'

'Not yet.'

'Will you let me know if...'

'Of course.'

Karzac nodded and was silent for a moment, then he reached into his desk drawer. 'I wanted to give you this. Here.' It was a receipt and a thank-you note from the charity ChildLine, for a donation of £2,000 given in the memory of Ania Milosz.

'Everyone wanted to give something, even the police who'd worked with her.'

Will didn't know what to say. He was afraid to trust his voice. 'Thank you.' He pushed the receipt back at Karzac. 'You should keep it. Put it somewhere where people can see it so they'll remember her.'

Karzac didn't take it. 'I don't know. Maybe her name shouldn't be here. It'll just remind everyone...' His eyes were red-rimmed. Karzac's world had been turned upside down by this. 'She was the best, you know. That's why I recruited her. And she cared about what we do here. That's why it's been so hard.' He rubbed his hand over his face. 'That's why it's been so hard.'

Chapter 57

After his meeting with Karzac, Will drove back to Ania's flat. He didn't have the heart for anything else. Karzac's battered, defeated look had left Will feeling angry and caged. He wanted to do something and there was nothing he could do. He had tried calling Sarah Ludlow again, but she wasn't available. He felt uneasy. The call from Cathcart had unnerved him

'Miss Ludlow's in a meeting,' the secretary said, and again when he called later, and again, then at six she said, 'Miss Ludlow's gone home, Mr Gillen.'

He swore under his breath. 'She was supposed to call me.'

'I gave her your message. I'm sure she'll contact you tomorrow.'

I need to talk to her now! He'd get nowhere by losing his temper. 'Can you give me a number where I can contact her?'

'I'm sorry, Mr Gillen. I'll ask her to call you when she comes in tomorrow, first thing.'

He wanted to hurl his phone through the window. He'd had it, he'd had the tape in his hands and he'd let it go. All he had now was a copy that Sarah Ludlow had made, and something told him that a copy would be useless. For some reason it was the original that was important.

He'd made a decision to trust her, but now that it came to it, he didn't. Somewhere in the story she had told him, there was a hole, and all his instincts were telling him – too late – to be wary of her.

***

Dariusz turned his car in the direction of his flat, his mind working as he drove. He'd taken a gamble on finding something in the files Strąk had sent him, and now he couldn't view them. After he left the office, he'd gone back into town and tried to buy a new laptop before the shops closed for the day, but the joint account he shared with Ania was frozen and he couldn't access the funds. His personal account was empty and his credit card was maxed out. He'd been letting things drift in the aftermath of Ania's death and now it was all catching up with him. He could probably get his bank to give him more credit, but that was useless now. The stores were shut. He couldn't do anything until tomorrow.

The pen drive was in his pocket, small, featureless, with nothing to identify what it contained. He remembered the photographs of the little girl dancing, with her innocent, coquettish smile, the video with its as yet undisclosed images. He couldn't face going back to his flat, not now. He wanted to walk, to think things through. He had decisions to make about his life, about his work, about his future. 'I've been putting it off too long, *kiciu*.' All the plans he had made were for a world in which Ania was alive, in which he and Ania were together. He was in a different world now.

As he turned down a dimly lit street, he realised he was on Aleja Chryzantem, Chrysanthemum Walk, the road that ran by the Zmienna gate into the Jewish cemetery. This was the place where he had first seen Ania walking among the graves. He wondered what had drawn him here. Memories? There was no more Ania. He could walk along these paths for a year, and he wouldn't see her again. She was gone, but the shadows among the trees drew him in.

He got out of the car and stood for a while breathing in the night air. The sky was clear and the moon was full. It was a night for ghosts. He walked past the ornate façade of the funeral home and through the high brick arch of the inner gates.

Inside the cemetery, there were no lights but the moon turned the pathways into tracks of silver between the shadows of the long grasses that grew among the graves. Though the night was still, the foliage rustled behind him.

Ghosts.

He followed the path past the memorial wall and the grave pits that had been dug in the last days of the war. She had waited for him here and they had walked to the entrance of the cemetery together, agreeing to make contact soon as they parted at the gate. They had exchanged a cool handshake, a formal contrast in his memory to their next meeting when they had danced to the hurdy-gurdy on Piotrkowska, and ended the evening in his flat, in his bed.

He wanted his life back. He wanted a time machine to transport him to that day in the cemetery, when he would walk along the path through the graves, glance at the woman who was looking at the Poznanski mausoleum and pass on by. He had been offered a choice at that moment, and he had chosen a path that led to pain, suspicion, misery and death. If he had never met Ania, he wouldn't know what he had lost.

Even thinking it felt like a betrayal. 'I'm tired, *kiciu*. This is harder than I thought it would be.'

Hurdy-gurdy music started to play, and once again, it was the festival and they were dancing on Piotrkowska, spinning round and round, a still point in a blur of colour, the single focus of the universe.

He shook the image out of his head. He couldn't bear it.

He followed the familiar route towards the Poznanski tomb. He was walking through the land of the dead to find his lost love. She would follow him to the world of the living and as long as he didn't look back, he could reclaim her. The path widened and he was in the open space that surrounded the mausoleum. It loomed above him, a silhouette against the brightness of the moon.

A cloud drifted across the sky, and he was in darkness. The still air was icy and the cold was starting to eat into him. It was time to go back to his flat and pick up the threads tomorrow. Tomorrow he would follow the path the video files would show him. Tonight, he had had enough. 'I'm sorry.' He said it out loud, as if the ghost who was walking behind him through these graves would hear him.

He was so preoccupied with this thought he didn't realise at once that the sounds were not in his head. They were real. It was a gradual awareness that made him stop and listen.

Nothing. Only the stirrings of the night. It was his imagination after all.

Too many ghosts. He'd been thinking about too many ghosts. He remembered his fantasy about bringing Ania back from the land of the dead, and the stricture imposed on him not to look back or she would be lost forever. Superstitiously, he walked on without checking, and after a moment, the sounds started again.

247

He kept moving, turning his head slightly to listen. It was unmistakeable now. Footsteps. There was someone on the path behind him. Whoever it was had no good motive for being there. The follower had stopped when he did, was moving quietly, trying to keep his presence hidden. Dariusz felt the cold clarity of fear as the options raced through his mind. A mugger? What mugger would hang around a cemetery late at night in the hope of some passer-by? A derelict or a vagrant who was planning to make an opportunistic attack? Vagrants were usually drunks, and they weren't subtle. He felt in his pockets for a weapon.

All he had were his keys. He wrapped his hand round them and let the ends protrude between his fingers in an improvised knuckle-duster. He had had his share of street brawls and he knew how to fight if he must.

He measured the distance to the gate. It was too far to gain surprise by speed. He had to factor in enough time to get back to his car and away. He wondered when his stalker had picked him up. As he drove around the streets? He hadn't been watching for followers then. He had felt oppressed in the café as he waited for Strąk's e-mail, as though someone was watching him and had put it down to paranoia. Was it? He didn't know.

What mattered was someone had been stalking him from the time he left his car and began walking in the direction of the cemetery. He could remember the sound of the grasses rustling in the still night as he walked along the path. The follower must be waiting for him to go deeper into its expanse, as far from the road and any late travellers as possible.

As soon as he turned towards the gate, the follower would jump him. He stopped, and the sounds behind him stopped as well. He pretended to be looking at his watch, angling it to catch what remained of the moonlight. In his peripheral vision, in the shadows, something gleamed.

A knife. The person behind him was carrying a knife.

His decision was made in an instant. He was running down the path towards the memorial wall, relying on memory rather than vision. The undergrowth snagged on his clothes. He could hear the sound of someone running behind him, the feet pounding on the ground, no further need for stealth. His pursuer was moving fast. Dariusz had very little time. As he came out of the path leading through the graves and onto the grassy area, he had only seconds. He had to get away before the other man made it into the open. He headed for the wall and saw the black pool of the grave pits ahead of him, the pits dug by the men who were to lie in them, that had been left as a memorial ever after.

Maybe they could save him now. He threw himself in and pressed his body into the grass, trying to muffle his breathing. He heard the sound of running feet as someone came along the path, stopped a moment and then ran towards the inner gate. He pulled himself up to the edge of the pit and saw the figure as a dim shape against the light. Then he was out of the pit and running in the shadow of the memorial wall away from the Zmienna gate, towards the Ghetto Field and the main entrance on ul. Bracka.

His pursuer must have realised almost as soon as he ran through the inner gate that Dariusz hadn't gone that way. There was no way he could have made it across the open space to Zmienna before the pursuer got there. The man would be back in the cemetery now, looking. He risked a glance over his shoulder, and saw the beam of a flashlight in the darkness behind him. He dropped down as the light traced across the grass close by him, onto the wall above him, away towards the darkness of the graves.

As soon as it moved away, he stood up and ran again. He could see the entrance in front of him now. It would be locked, but the wall was easy enough to scramble over. Pain shot through his hand as he pulled himself up. A circle of light caught him, then went out. He stopped on top of the wall and looked back, but all he could see was the darkness. He dropped down onto ul. Bracka and ran back towards the corner with Aleja Chryzantem.

It was dark and overgrown, a country lane in the centre of a city. He moved fast, but quietly now. The street was silent and there were no sounds of pursuit. He kept a watch behind him as he moved forward, keeping to the shadows, keeping out of sight.

His car was there, parked on the right, pulled off the road into a small lay-by. It looked innocent and abandoned. He wanted to be in it and driving back towards the security of the city centre, but it was surrounded by deep shadows. Caution – fear – held him back, kept him glued to the spot as he peered through the darkness. Everything was still. Everything was silent.

He clenched his fist round his keys as he reached the car, expecting at any moment the sudden grab, the sharp pain as the knife drove in between his ribs. He had the car door open and was behind the wheel in a moment. His hands were sticky with blood as he fumbled with the keys, and then the engine fired.

It wasn't until he was driving through the empty streets on the way back to his flat that he started shaking.

Chapter 58

It was getting on for 9.00 p.m. when Will's phone rang. He grabbed it before the first ring had completed. 'Sarah! I've been…'

But it was Euan Kingsley, the pathologist who had carried out the second post-mortem. 'I'm sorry this is so late, Gillen, but you said you wanted it as soon as I could get it to you. I've been in a meeting, and then you weren't answering your phone.'

His landline. Kingsley must have been calling the St Abbs number. 'I'm not there. I'm in Manchester. I'm sorry. I should have…'

'No. My mistake. I realised that but I'd left your details at home so it had to wait until now. I've put a copy of my report in the post but I thought you'd want the details as soon as I had them. OK. Now, I don't know what you were expecting, but there's nothing definite I can add to what they found in Poland.'

Will felt the hope inside him start to unravel. 'Nothing.' He could hear the flat note in his voice.

'I don't know what that hospital doctor was trying to tell you. He only carried out an external examination and you know as well as I do that those can be misleading. She was badly smashed up, a fall from that height.'

'I know.'

'The window of the room – did it have anything she could have hung onto? Bars? A frame?'

He thought about the small metal window above the desk with its sloping sill. 'Only the bottom of the frame. They found her prints there as if she'd clung on, but she couldn't have held herself for long – seconds, maybe.'

'Right… Could she have got her fingers round the frame, clung on like that?'

It was hard to talk without the images forming in his mind. 'No. Why?'

'The fingers of her right hand are dislocated. The problem is, they aren't just pulled out of place, they've been twisted. I

251

thought it might have happened if she was trying to grip round a frame – the weight of her body could have done it.'

'She couldn't have got her hands round it.' He could see her fingertips pressing into the metal, slipping, slipping…

'Could she have grabbed something on her way down?'

She'd smashed her head on the outflow pipe not far below the window. It was unlikely she was conscious after that. 'I don't think so. What are you saying?'

'I don't know. Maybe nothing. It's unusual, though.'

'If you were doing the PM for an investigation over here, what would you do?'

'I'd mention it in the report and I'd expect the investigating team to account for it.'

'And the original report?'

'They missed it, or didn't see it as significant.'

'So what do you think happened?'

'That's not my remit, Gillen. You know that. You're asking me to speculate without the facts. It isn't my job to hunt around for explanations. I link my findings to the evidence the police give me, and point out what doesn't fit. I can think of several ways it could have happened, but…'

'Euan, I'm talking about Ania, about my daughter. Privately, not part of your report, what do you think?'

There was silence on the other end of the line. When Kingsley spoke again, his voice was cautious. 'Listen, I don't want you to off half-cock, but one of the scenarios I would have to consider is that these injuries were pre-mortem. If they didn't happen in the fall, and I don't think they did, then I can't account for them.'

There it was.

At last.

Chapter 59

It was getting on for midnight when Dariusz got back. He parked by the side of the road and approached the main entrance to the block aware of the shadows and the darkness where the lights had failed. No one accosted him. Inside the block, the lights were on a time switch. He went quickly up the stairs, checking each landing, but there was no one there.

He let himself into his flat, locking and bolting the door behind him. Once he'd done that, he felt more secure. He was tired, but his mind wouldn't let him rest, churning over and over what had happened, and what he needed to do.

Someone had tried to kill him. He had no illusions about the intentions of the man who had followed him. It was still possible that it had been a vagrant. Łódź, like most Polish cities had a problem with the casualties caused by the social changes of the past decade, but broken-down alcoholics didn't stalk with calculated intent.

It had to be because of Ania. There was no other reason. Ania must have been killed to keep her quiet. Whoever was responsible must believe that Dariusz was close to finding whatever it was that Ania knew. So now, he had to be silenced as well.

He stood to one side of the window and peered out. He couldn't see anything, but that meant very little. He was beginning to imagine things, picturing armed police officers pressed against the wall beside his door, one of them counting silently to the others: three, two, one…

Paranoia. His security was good. He had to trust it. He forced himself to relax, knowing that the tension and the uncertainty would exhaust him faster than anything. He was already tired from his night in the cells and the day spent on what was beginning to look like a wild goose chase. He was weary beyond belief.

His hand was hurting. He looked at it and saw it was cut, a jagged tear that was probably from the glass on the cemetery wall. He washed it with water as hot as he could stand then, gritting his teeth, he poured neat antiseptic into the cut. He put a pad over it and secured it with a bandage, pulling it tight with his teeth.

He made himself coffee, and realising he was ravenous, put together a sandwich of rye bread, salami and pickle. After he had eaten, he leaned back in his chair and let his eyes close.

Ania was walking ahead of him down a long corridor. He was trying to catch her up, calling out, *Wait for me!* But his voice was only a feeble whisper. She was walking into the shadows and he had to stop her. She looked back as if she had heard him, but her eyes contained only cold rejection. *I could never let a child killer walk away*, she said.

'I didn't do it!' The effort to make his voice struggle free of the restraints on it woke him up. The coffee was cold on the table in front of him. Dawn was starting to break and the day stretched ahead of him, empty and bleak. He had slept in his clothes and he smelled of smoke and sweat.

His hand throbbed. He pulled himself to his feet, every joint in his body complaining and went to the window. There was no sign of the car that had followed him the day before. There was no one on the green spaces and paths that surrounded the block. The waiting and the anticipation would destroy him. He had to do something.

The idea that had been forming in his mind the day before was coming back to him.

Chapter 60

Dariusz showered and changed the bandage on his hand, then sat at the window with coffee and his first cigarette of the day. He knew what he had to do. He had to access the files he had downloaded. He was mulling over the best way to do this – get his hands on some money and buy a new laptop, or borrow one from someone – when there was a knock at his door. He checked his watch. It was eight. He'd been sitting there and thinking for the better part of two hours.

A quick check through the spy hole gave him the second worse news. It wasn't a stranger with a knife, but it was the police. There were two of them waiting outside the door. He thought about the files on his pen drive, and his heart thumped. 'What do you want?'

'The Komendant wants to ask you some questions.'

'Just a moment. I'll get the key.'

If they searched the flat, they would find the drive anywhere he chose to hide it. But they probably wouldn't carry out a search – they'd done that yesterday. They hadn't arrived mob-handed and they weren't beating down his door. He made a quick decision and slipped it inside the bandage on his hand, tucking it down into his palm.

He opened the door. The two men waiting for him were polite enough – a good sign. One preceded him down the stairway, the other flanked him. 'What you done to your hand?' he said.

Dariusz lifted it up and showed him the bruised fingers. The man grinned. 'Been fighting?'

'No such luck. I fell down.' The man's grin broadened but he didn't say anything else. He seemed to have accepted Dariusz' explanation. They remained polite as they assisted him into the car. He had no option but to cooperate.

***

Will's phone woke him and he sat up, disoriented until memory flowed back. He was in the bed in Ania's flat. A dim grey light was shining in from the window, and the phone at the side of his bed was ringing. He checked his watch. It was after nine. He'd slept for ten hours straight. He sat up, rubbing his face and trying to collect his thoughts. 'Will Gillen.'

'Will. It's Sarah. Sarah Ludlow. I'm sorry I didn't call you back. I was busy. I've got some news. It's…'

He interrupted. He didn't know if Ania's phone line was bugged, but it could be. 'I'll come in. We can talk then.'

'Not the office. I'll meet you at the university, the School of Languages, Linguistics and Cultures. It's on Oxford Road. Ask for Martin York. Can you get there for twelve?'

'I'll be there.'

The news from Euan Kingsley was sitting in his mind like a toad, waiting impassively for him to take it out and observe it, to take on the full implications of what he had heard. He could only do this by keeping it distant, by turning it into an academic problem he had to work out. It was nothing to do with Ania, nothing to do with anyone. It was simply that: a puzzle.

Why would someone twist another person's fingers until they dislocated? He knew the answers and rehearsed them like pages from a text book: sadistic murder or coercion. Sadistic murders were carried out for the satisfaction of a sexual perversion or for revenge. There was no evidence of any sexual element to the crime. Could it have been a revenge attack carried out by Haynes' friends or family? It was unlikely.

It had to be the second option: coercion. Ania had information someone wanted, so that person had twisted her fingers out of their joints one by one until she told him. It was as simple as that. And then? The window. A fall was a good way of concealing pre-mortem injuries. If it hadn't been for the sharp eyes of a doctor at Łódź Hospital, the anomaly of those injuries would have gone unnoticed.

Ania's attacker had killed her, which meant he thought he had the information he needed. She had kept her wits about her even in extremis, and she had misled him. He remembered the frustrated anger of the man standing over her body in his dream. Her killer must have realised what she had done almost immediately after he had – somehow – forced her out of the window.

Small Bear has a secret.

The secret she had died for was in the cassette tape and later that day, he was going to find out what that secret was.

Chapter 61

The School of Languages, Linguistics and Cultures was housed on the main university campus. The buildings were elegant, their Victorian facades and neo-Gothic architecture reminiscent of medieval Prague. It was an Arcadian retreat in the middle of the urban sprawl.

He had to drive round until he found a car park. He made his way back onto the campus, and orienting himself, cut his way across to the building he wanted. It was just on twelve as he came through the door, and saw Sarah waiting in the entrance lobby for him.

She looked the way he remembered her from St Abbs, her hair loose and tied back with a scarf, younger and more relaxed than she had appeared yesterday. She smiled when she saw him, then tilted her head in query at his guarded response. 'Problem?'

'No. I'm fine.' He wasn't going to share his doubts with her. If he had cause to worry, he didn't want her to know he was concerned.

'OK. I had a long talk with Martin yesterday. Now I understand what Ania meant when she said to get the tape authenticated. I'm not sure how far it gets us, but Martin can tell us which machine was used to record it. It's like guns – each recorder leaves a distinctive trace on the tape. I talked to the Senior Investigating Officer on the case and he sent the recorder he used to me. I got it to Martin last night. He's been working on it since then, and he's got some results for us. If it's the copy Cathcart made, if it's the actual tape, we can prove it. Come on.'

That must be what Ania had meant when she asked for the tape to be authenticated. They would be able to prove that this was the one, extant copy of the original recording. He wondered what it contained, to make it so dangerous.

The building reminded him of the university in Łódź. There were the same high ceilings, the same long corridors. Sarah led him along one corridor, down another until she stopped at a door. The plate read *Professor Martin York*. She knocked and a voice said, 'Come in.'

Martin York stood up as they entered the room. He was a tall man, thin with a slight scholarly stoop. His hair was so fair it looked grey and his eyes were colourless behind gold rimmed glasses. He held out his arms to Sarah who greeted him with a kiss. 'Martin. You don't know how grateful we are. This is Will Gillen.'

York nodded in a way that suggested he had recognised Will before Sarah spoke. 'I did some work with your daughter a couple of years ago. She was a very talented woman.'

'Yes. She was.'

The two men studied each other, then York turned back to Sarah. 'It's an interesting problem. I didn't get the recorder until late last night.'

'I had to be very tactful,' Sarah said.

'Mm. Tiger by the tail country, take my word for it.' His gaze met Will's again. Behind the nondescript exterior, there was a shrewd mind. 'Would you like some coffee?'

Will shook his head. He didn't want to go through the social negotiations. He tried not to let the impatience show on his face, but Sarah said quickly, 'Maybe later. Perhaps if you tell us what you found?'

'Of course. Of course. Well, I worked on it last night.' Another quick glance at Will. 'Our Ms Ludlow can be very persuasive. I started by checking the machine. This cassette…' He held up the audio tape. 'This cassette was recorded on this machine, and nothing has been done to the tape since then. I take it the recorder has been in police possession since the recording was made?'

'I asked Cathcart to check, and preserve it as evidence when I called him. It's been in the supplies store and no one has used it since the Haynes investigation.'

'Good. Good. So what we have here is a copy of the original sound file the police took from Derek Haynes' computer. You're with me so far?'

'Yes. It's the copy of the recording that Cathcart's team made.'

'Exactly. Now the next stage was to compare it with this one. He gestured to a sound file on his computer screen. 'This is the one that Ania returned to the police, the one that was used in court. I wanted to see what she'd done to it, OK?'

Will nodded, trying to conceal his impatience.

Martin York looked at them. 'This is where it starts to get interesting. The two recordings are identical.'

Chapter 62

Will stared at York blankly. He tried to account for what he had just heard. It had to be the wrong tape. Someone had got to it before Ania posted it. It...

Sarah's voice cut into his confusion. 'So you're saying there never was a fabrication – the tape was authentic all along?'

'No. Not at all. The original recording is the fabrication. It was done long before Ania got her hands on it.'

Jesus Christ Almighty. It hit Will like a physical blow. All this time he'd believed – he had accepted without question that his daughter, that Ania, had fabricated evidence that had sent a man to jail. He had built up a whole story to account for it, to justify her actions and all he had needed from the beginning was to have faith in her.

She'd told him. She'd warned him. *Occam's razor, Dad.* The explanation that requires the fewest assumptions is usually the right one.

'She never did it.' His lips felt frozen. He was aware of Sarah watching him, and he couldn't bear to see the compassion on her face. He'd rather face Erland's contempt: *so now you know your daughter again*

Maybe I never knew her. Maybe I never knew her at all.

Martin York was speaking again. 'The only difference is that on *this* one, on the one she used in court, she's smoothed out some fuzz, some glitches. I've enhanced it – it's almost unnoticeable. Listen.' He pressed a key and a voice spoke:

Not... Over here. Like that.

I can't...

Great. Great. You're a star.

He pressed another key and it played again. This time there was a faint, barely audible click between the words *that* and *I*. He looked at them to check if they'd heard it, then played it again. 'She must have smoothed it out for the court.'

Will could remember Oz Karzac saying, *she got Shaun to complete the last bit of the fabrication and now I'm going to have to work hard to convince the police he wasn't in on it.*

'What sent the defence team back to it?'

'Oh, that's simple enough. Even with Ania's evidence, the case against Haynes was never that strong. If Haynes managed to convince them he was innocent, hers was the evidence they had to attack. It isn't obvious, but if you look at the acoustics closely, there's just a trace of glitches here and there, and then you know, of course. It's one of the best fabrications I've come across. Even so, I would have expected Ania to spot it. I don't know why she didn't.'

She hadn't spotted it because she was too close to it. He could remember the time they'd argued about the case.

You shouldn't get personally involved. You have to be dispassionate. The best expert witnesses are impartial.

I am impartial. I'll do the analysis and tell them what I find.

And she had done, but her partiality had made her miss one vital thing: the recording she was working with was a fake.

'So Derek Haynes…'

'May well be innocent. The voice is almost certainly his. Ania knew her stuff. She wasn't wrong. But this recording has been pieced together – what from, I don't know. I'll have to take this to the police, you understand?'

'Of course.'

Half an hour later, Will stood in the courtyard outside the building. The campus spread out around him. The sun was low in the sky, casting the early glow of the sunset on the sides of the buildings. He could feel its warmth on his back. Sarah was beside him. She turned her face to the light and shook out her hair. It gleamed gold in the brightness. It was an irony that a city with a name for grey skies and rain should shine on them with such promise and such optimism. She looked at him. 'What are you going to do?'

'I don't know.'

'Ania's death – it doesn't look like suicide any more.'

'I don't think it ever did.' Only he hadn't seen it. *I know you again*, he reassured her silently.

'This changes everything. I have to talk to Nadifa. I have to find out what was going on.'

'And I need to talk to Cathcart.'

'Are you sure? Don't you want to wait?'

'For what?'

'I don't know. I work for the defence. I'm always leery of sharing with the police.'

'I am the police.'

She grinned. 'I know. I'm consorting with the enemy. Do what you think best. Shall we meet later, compare notes?'

He arranged to come to her flat later that evening, and they parted. He thought about what they had found as he walked back to the car. The tape, the fabrication – Martin York's findings had felt like a breakthrough, but now he realised he only had half the story.

Ania had been accused of fabricating the Haynes recording. Her response to this, when she had spent some time revisiting her work, had been to run. That made no sense. She'd had the proof all the time that she had worked with the material Cathcart had given her, that she had done nothing wrong. The worst she could be accused of was making an error in her analysis. She hadn't tried to falsify anything. So why run away?

He unlocked the car door and sat in the driver's seat, thinking. He took out the note Ania had sent him and read it again.

I've got a better idea of what's going on now. I can't get this done here – my mistake. If it goes through official channels, I'm afraid it might disappear.

He was struck again by the sense of coming into a conversation half way through. She wrote as though he knew what was going on. The only reason she would assume that was if she had told him. Somewhere there had to be an earlier communication.

And there was something else he'd lost sight of. A child was dead. The body had been well hidden, and hidden in a way that would have destroyed any forensic evidence. This was why the police case against Haynes had been so weak. Martin York's analysis showed that someone – presumably the killer – had fabricated evidence that pointed to someone else.

That was dangerous and it was also stupid. There was no obvious killer on the scene, no helpful uncle, no released paedophile with access to the centre. An anonymous abductor was almost impossible to identify. There had been no need to frame anyone. An intelligent killer would have sat tight.

He tried calling Dariusz Erland. Now that the tape was in the public domain, now that it had been analysed by an expert witness, he felt safe letting Erland know about it. Frustratingly, Erland's phone was switched off. Will left a message: *Will Gillen here. That thing of Ania's you were looking for, it's turned up.*

Now all he had to do was contact Cathcart. He keyed in the number. He wasn't looking forward to this.

Chapter 63

It was late afternoon before Dariusz was released from the police station. He had been kept waiting, questioned, kept waiting and questioned again. They didn't have the power to keep him there – he could have insisted on his rights and left, but that might have pushed them into arresting him if they thought they had enough evidence.

He needed to know how much they had against him, so he sat it out through a process that seemed designed to wear him down. The focus was constant: why hadn't he found the files on his hard drive sooner – why had he only claimed to find them now, just before the police were planning to raid him? Why hadn't he reported the break in at the time?

This time, he was more honest. He told them about the locked computer, and about the signs that something had been moved in the wardrobe. He admitted it was very slight evidence. 'That's why I didn't come to you. I thought someone had searched my flat. Nothing was missing. What would you have done?'

He was aware of the door opening. Król came into the room and stood in silence, watching.

Why did he assume someone had searched his flat? Why would anyone want to search his flat?

I thought it was you, he told them. Because of Ania, because she'd been murdered and someone was trying to hush it up.

Why hadn't he told them about this before?

He hadn't said anything because he had been alarmed and angry about his treatment and hadn't felt like cooperating. He'd had time to think about it now and realised he should have told them the first time.

That was his story and he stuck to it. Most of it was true so it was easy enough to keep up. He just had to remind himself not to elaborate, not to explain. He was sitting in the interview room towards the end of the day. The two men who had been questioning him had left with a promise to be back, but that had been an hour ago. He checked his watch. It was after four. He'd been here for over seven hours, and he was just about done with cooperating.

He stood up and stretched. The man waiting at the door stirred restlessly. 'OK,' Dariusz said to him, 'I'm ready to go. How about you get onto your bosses and tell them that if they need to keep me any longer, they'd better get back here now and give me a good reason.'

The man studied him in silence, then gave an abrupt nod. He used the phone on the wall, and after a slow fifteen minutes, they came back, just as Dariusz was about to assert himself again.

'Mr Erland,' the first man said. Dariusz was pleased to hear he was Mr Erland again. If they were being polite to him, they were unlikely to throw him in a cell for the night. 'You are free to go. Thank you for your cooperation. This matter might have been settled sooner if you had been more frank with us two days ago.'

Dariusz nodded. He wanted to know what, if anything, they knew. 'My computer and my phone – when can I have them back?'

'They're in our laboratory. They aren't available now but you can have them back tomorrow. Mr Erland, one last question: is there someone who doesn't like you?'

It took Dariusz by surprise. If he could take the question at face value, it meant they believed him. 'I don't know.'

'Your hand…'

'I fell. I was walking in the cemetery at night and I slipped.'

'It's odd to be walking there in the dark.'

It was ironic that something truthful – if not the whole truth – should sound so fabricated. 'Ania, my… Ania. That's where we met.'

There was a moment of silence, then the man said, 'I'm sorry. You're free to go.'

Dariusz found himself on the street with some loose change in his pockets and his pen drive still tucked into his hand. It looked as though the police had accepted his story.

The streets were busy enough. The working day was coming to an end and people were heading for home. The light was fading and soon the streets would be empty. He looked round. All he could see were groups, or individuals walking alone, everyone apparently intent on their own business. Was there someone in that crowd watching him – from a shop doorway, from a corner, walking casually past with no detectable glance – someone who had unfinished business with Dariusz?

He checked the time to disguise his indecision. He had almost no money on him. He could get a taxi – the driver would be pissed off when Dariusz had to go into the flat to get the cash to pay, but there wouldn't be much he could do about it. And then what? Hide behind his locked door for the night? And the next night and the next night? He couldn't live like that.

He started walking as he thought, lighting a cigarette, keeping a surreptitious watch on the road around him. He had enough cash to go to a café where he could get a sandwich and some coffee. He needed time to think.

What he had to do was to flush his attacker out. He needed to present an opportunity that was too good to miss. The idea that had come to him a couple of days ago was now formed clearly in his mind. He knew what he was going to do.

Chapter 64

Sarah Ludlow's flat was in Hale, south of Manchester. Will drove through the quiet roads, past houses set back behind trees and hedges. The address she had given him was for an apartment in a development called The Oaks. He pulled up at the gates, wound down his window and pushed the intercom for Apartment 3. After a few seconds, the gates swung inwards and he found himself driving towards a Victorian mansion with oak trees shading it on two sides.

One wing had a cupola, there were pointed dormers in the roof, and huge bays on the front. It was very different from the apartment where Ania had lived. He remembered Cathcart's words about Sarah Ludlow. Being a human rights lawyer clearly did not mean living from hand to mouth. He followed the driveway round until he found the parking bays. He parked in a space marked *visitors*, and walked to the front door.

She must have been watching him, because she buzzed him in before he rang the bell. He went up a flight of stairs, and she was waiting for him at the entrance to her flat. An image of Ania leaning in a doorway waiting for him flickered across his vision and he had to stop and wait until it cleared.

'Will. Are you all right?'

'Fine. I'm fine. This is a beautiful place.'

'Isn't it? I bought it two years ago, at the top of the market.' She made a rueful face. 'It's a good thing I have no plans to move. Now, come in and let me get you a drink.'

She ushered him in, and steered him into a huge, airy living room with off-white walls and a white floor that extended through into the kitchen. Chairs and a sofa made splashes of red, floor lamps and table lamps threw pools of light.

He sat back in one of the chairs that managed to be both elegant and exquisitely comfortable. She poured him a glass of wine and sat down opposite him. She raised her glass. 'To... What shall we toast?'

'Progress?'

'To progress.' They drank. 'How did you get on with Ian Cathcart?'

'I think I just made his life more complicated. He needed the information, but he wasn't pleased.'

In fact, Cathcart had sworn vilely when Will gave him the news. 'You're sure?'

'The expert witness is sure.'

'So you're telling me that the sound file on the Haynes video was a fake all along. Why didn't… Why didn't FLS spot it?'

He'd avoided saying Ania's name, avoided direct criticism of her. 'She got too close to it, I think,' Will said.

'Fuck. This is… OK. Thanks for letting me know.'

Sarah circled her finger round the base of her glass. 'There are implications for Nadifa as well.'

'Yes.' The bleak satisfaction of knowing her child's killer had been brought to account was taken away by this news. Will could see the problems Cathcart was facing. There had been no trace of another killer at the time, and after all these months, any trail that might have been there would be long gone. It was unlikely the case would be solved now, unless the killer struck again.

She changed the subject. 'Have you eaten?'

'No. I…' He was never hungry these days. He ate to keep himself alive. 'No, I haven't.'

'Me neither. Wait.' She went into the kitchen and came back with a dish of small meatballs, lentils and flatbreads. 'I think we've earned something.'

He had been indifferent to food for the past couple of weeks, barely aware of what it was he was putting in his mouth but the spicy, exotic fragrance made him realise how hungry he was and he found himself eating with something like enthusiasm. 'These are very good,' he said, when they'd finished.

'I like to cook. I learned a lot when I was travelling in Asia, and in Africa.' She cleared the plates away then came back and poured him some more wine. He wasn't used to being looked after. Elżbieta used to do it sometimes – when she knew he had been working hard, she would encourage him to sit down and put his feet up, then she would bring him a glass of whisky and sit with him while they talked about the day. She would keep the twins with their clamour and their boundless enthusiasms at bay for half an hour until he'd had a chance to relax, then…

He realised he was staring blankly at Sarah, lost in thought. She tilted her head in query. 'What?'

'I was thinking you look lovely.' She was wearing a grey silk blouse and a full black skirt. Her hair was hanging loose.

She smiled as if she knew he wasn't telling her everything. 'You don't have to fight all the time,' she said. 'You can put it aside sometimes, just for a while. It doesn't mean you've forgotten.'

He shook his head. He wasn't sure if he could.

She came across and sat next to him on the sofa, kicking her shoes off and tucking her legs under her. 'We missed an opportunity in Scotland,' she said softly. 'We could make up for that now.' She leant forward and her lips brushed lightly across his mouth. 'You can stay, if you want.'

She was a beautiful woman. There was no reason to walk away. He put his hand behind her head and kissed her.

They drew apart, and she took his hand. As she led him through another door into the hallway, he looked back and saw her shoe lying on the floor, an insubstantial object with a web of fine straps.

Not a shoe for running in.

He would find out what he needed. He would find Ania's killer. He realised he didn't care how he did it, and felt a sudden sense of liberation. With Ania's death, with his work gone, he had nothing left to lose. He could do what he liked.

And then…? He could feel the wheel of his boat under his hands and see the waves foaming as the bow cut through them. He would turn the boat north and sail as far as he could in the spring storms. If he shut down the radar and left no route, then no one would endanger themselves by coming to look for him.

Something dark threatened at the edges of his mind. He pushed it away and turned to Sarah. All he wanted now was this moment of oblivion.

Chapter 65

Dariusz left the cafe. He stopped at the small supermarket on the corner, and used most of his remaining cash to buy a quarter bottle of vodka, then he walked to the university. It was still busy, with groups of students streaming in and out so he walked round the corner to a coffee bar and ordered an espresso. He needed to be alert tonight. What he was planning could be dangerous. He picked up his phone and after a moment's hesitation, keyed in his father's number.

'It's Dariusz. How are you?'

'Dariusz! Why haven't you called before?' His father sounded anxious.

'I could ask why you haven't called me.' He had to get this out into the open between them. 'Ania died. You know that.'

His father was silent for a long time. 'You cared very much about her?'

'You know I did. We were getting married.'

'Beata said it would all…' His father made a sound of self-deprecation. 'I should know better. You should have brought her to see me, then.'

'I know.' He should have. He'd put it off, discouraged by Beata's hostility and his father's indifference. He'd allowed the rift between them to grow.

'There's something… I….'

'What is it?' The uncharacteristic hesitation alarmed him. 'What's wrong?'

'I did something I… I should have told you but I couldn't understand what she was saying.'

'For God's sake, Dad, what are you talking about?'

'She made me feel like a foolish old man,' his father said with a return to his usual asperity. 'She left you a message. That night.'

Oh, Jesus. A message from Ania, one he'd never got. 'Why didn't you give it me? Why didn't you tell me? What did she say?'

'I couldn't understand her. She kept saying it – accuse, she kept saying tell him it is to accuse someone. It made no sense. I couldn't…'

The old man had been ill and running a fever. He let his breathing steady. 'Try and remember, Dad. It could be important.'

'Beata doesn't want me to…'

'I don't want to know about Beata. I want to know what Ania said.'

'She said someone was to be accused… I don't know. I told you, it made no sense. I thought… He'll talk to her. I can't understand. I said you would be back in thirty minutes, and she said, *Tell him*, and then she put the phone down. Like I was a stupid old man. I couldn't understand her accent. She just said something was to be accused and I was to tell you. And to call her. I told you that.'

His father might have been confused and upset, but he'd kept it to himself all this time. Dariusz could imagine Beata encouraging him: *it's too late now, don't worry about it, it isn't important.* 'I can't talk about it now. I'll call you – I don't know. Sometime.' He cut the call off on his father's *Dareczek*… and sat in the dim corner of the coffee bar, oblivious to the people around him, remembering.

If his father had told him, he would have called her back at once. Those few minutes… Would it have made a difference? He'd never know. And Beata, making trouble, stirring things up. He remembered his last phone call with his sister – she'd talked about their father being worried. She must have encouraged the old man to keep quiet, hoping Dariusz would never find out, would forget… He couldn't forgive her. He couldn't forgive either of them.

Something is accused? What had she meant? That she was accused? She wouldn't have told his father that, wouldn't have left that message. It must have been something else, something his father had misheard. It had to have been something urgent, something important that couldn't wait… *accused*… What could she have said?

He checked his watch. He didn't have time to puzzle this out now. He needed to go. He walked back through the cold night air to the university where it was quieter now. He went in and made his way to the library. He'd waited here often enough for Ania when she was working late and they had plans to go out in town. He stopped at the drinks dispenser to get a cup of coffee, then found himself a desk at the far side of the room. Here, he could observe people coming in and leaving, but no one could approach him unseen. He was safe here until nine o'clock.

He had come equipped. In one pocket he had the small bottle of vodka he'd just bought. In the other, he had the lock knife he'd carried with him since that night in the cemetery, and he had Ania's keys, the ones that had been left in his flat. He had keys to all the rooms in this building where she had worked.

He pushed the conversation with his father out of his mind. That was for later. He had to concentrate now.

He went to the shelves where the law books were stacked and found a dictionary and a thesaurus. He could work at the problem here. He also found a journal article on laws relating to downloaded internet material. He put that on the desk beside him with the title visible.

He was pretty sure his stalker was watching him. If he wanted Dariusz out of the way, here was his chance. *It's going to get better*, Dariusz promised, as he tipped a generous measure from the vodka bottle into his cup. The fumes reached his nose and he saw a fellow reader glance round in irritation.

He concealed the bottle in his pocket and skimmed down the dictionary entries for 'accused'. Whatever it was Ania had said seemed to be lost in the maze of his father's confused mind. He closed the book in frustration and let his gaze wander round the room, drinking the vodka-laced coffee. He couldn't see anyone watching him, or anyone who turned away or tried to conceal themselves behind a book or periodical, but he was certain the man from the cemetery was there.

There were no familiar faces that he could see, but some of the tables were in shadow and some of the readers had their backs to him. Then shortly after eight, he saw someone he knew. Konstantin Jankowski came into the library, scanned the room without apparently noticing Dariusz, took a book off the shelves and left after getting it stamped out.

Jankowski? Why would it be Jankowski? Dariusz hesitated, but couldn't decide. Jankowski had a legitimate reason to be here.

He waited until quarter to nine when a man in security uniform came in at the start of his rounds. He recognised Jerzy Pawlak who spotted him and gave him a puzzled look. Dariusz swore under his breath. He didn't want anything to deter his stalker tonight. He drained the coffee cup and stacked the books on the table in front of him. He pulled on his coat, staggering a bit as he did it. *The bleating of the goat attracts the tiger.* The man who had observed him earlier saw this and looked disgusted.

He was among the last people to leave the library, walking with the conspicuous care of the drunk. The building was almost deserted now. There were still one or two people drifting along the corridors, but the place was shutting down for the night. The air felt cold as though the heating had been switched off. A cleaner passed him, rattling a trolley with a bucket and an array of brushes.

When he got to the entrance hall, the stairs were empty. As he'd hoped, the caretaker's booth was deserted. Pawlak would be doing his rounds now, seeing the last stragglers off the premises and locking up. Dariusz took his chance. He ran up the first two flights quickly, relaxing once he was out of sight of the main lobby. He didn't want to get thrown out by security, but he didn't want his stalker to miss him either.

He continued up the stairs to the top floor. Up here, it was dark and silent. The door of Jankowski's office was shut, and there was no gleam of light underneath it. Moving quietly now, he went through the door to the left of the landing and found himself in the narrow corridor that led to the computer room, the classrooms and the small office where Ania had died.

He let himself into the computer room and closed the door behind him. The Yale clicked home. Nothing would happen yet. If anything was going to happen, it would be later, much later, after everyone had left. Until then, Dariusz was alone up here.

He didn't turn on the lights. He didn't want to be disturbed by anyone with a legitimate reason to challenge him. He closed the blinds to shield out the glow from the computer monitor, and switched on one of the machines. He turned the sound low – the heavy door would muffle it but he was playing safe now – and took the pen drive out of his pocket. It lay in his hand, an innocuous piece of white plastic. It wasn't like a book or a film. Its outside gave no hint of its content.

He slipped it into the port and waited for the files to appear on the screen. He opened the video and pressed *play*.

Again, the camera wobbled and fuzzed, then steadied onto the scene in the basement, the metal shelves lining the walls, the damp making the stone floor shine. Again the child stared at the camera with frightened eyes.

There was a click and the film flickered. A voice spoke off camera. 'Not... Over here. Like that.'

The child's head turned to the camera. Her voice. It was quiet, barely above a whisper, the English accented. 'Please. *Please*. Listen. Please. I can't...' Her lips were quivering and tears were starting to spill out of her eyes. Dariusz wanted to turn away, but he kept watching.

There was the same slight flicker, and the man's voice spoke again with a feigned enthusiasm that was more chilling than anger. 'Attagirl! That's right.'

The screen flickered again and the sound fuzzed then cleared. 'Great. Great. You're a star.'

'I can't...' She was crying in earnest now.

'Star.' The child tried to choke back her sobs, her eyes enormous as she watched whatever was going on behind the camera. Then the man spoke again, mildly irritated, mildly put out. 'Look you'd better be quiet. We're going to get into trouble here. I'm not telling you again.'

She gulped and swallowed. 'Please. Please. I'm sorry. I can't...'

The camera steadied and framed the child. Dariusz braced himself. It was coming.

'Jesus.' The same tone of mild irritation. 'You don't listen, do you?' Then music played, the sound crackled, the image faded and was gone.

Dariusz stared at the screen. It was the same as the one he had watched before. The files couldn't have corrupted in the second sending, or not in exactly the same way. This must be it. This must be all there was.

Chapter 66

Will opened his eyes in the darkness of a strange place. The bed was soft and the air smelled faintly of perfume. He lay still as the evening before came back to him.

There was no one in the bed beside him. He became aware of the faint murmur of a voice, almost undetectable beyond the closed door. He lay there, listening. There was just the one voice, speaking, then stopping, then speaking again. Sarah was talking on the phone. He looked at the luminous numbers on the clock. Two thirty-one.

He was wide awake now. He listened as the voice went on and on, just on the edge of hearing, too soft for him to pick up individual words. After about ten minutes, there was silence. He waited. The bedroom door opened, and her shape was outlined in the doorway. His eyes were accustomed to the darkness, and he watched her as she felt her way across the room and back to the bed. The mattress barely moved as she slipped in beside him.

'Will?' It was just a breath of sound in the darkness. He didn't reply, just muttered something and turned over. He was aware of her watching him, and he made himself breathe evenly and slowly, like someone in deep sleep.

She lay down carefully, and he waited until he felt her relaxing, waited until her breathing became slow and regular, and waited half an hour beyond that, counting off the time by the faint illumination of the clock.

The moon was bright. He could see her where she lay asleep. Her hair was spread out across the pillow, and as she breathed, there was a faint catch in her throat. Her face looked soft and defenceless, but all he cared about now was the possibility of deceit, the possibility that behind the warmth, she concealed the secrets of his daughter's death. If she did, and if it was her actions that had taken Ania to that drop, then he swore to himself he would break her neck.

Once he was sure she was asleep, he slid out of bed. The door to the en-suite bathroom was just by the bedroom door. He reached in and switched on the light, pulled the door to, then he went out of the bedroom into the hall, where he had heard her talking.

The phone was on its stand on the side table. It was as simple as that. He took it into the room where they had been the evening before. In the dim glow of the moon, he saw their wine glasses on the coffee table, still half full. Her shoe lay discarded on the floor. This time he let the darkness in and saw another shoe in another place, lying where it had fallen beneath the desk. It had an impossibly high heel and a filigree of fine straps. 'Not a shoe for running in.' He looked out onto the street beyond the metal gates. It was silent and empty.

It was easy enough to get the information he wanted. The number she had called was listed, with the name and the time clear to read: JMB, 02.25. He pressed the call button and waited. After a couple of rings, the voice he had been expecting answered. 'Sarah! Is there a problem?'

Blaise. Sarah had been talking to John Blaise.

'There's a problem,' Will said.

***

Dariusz sat at his desk staring at the blank screen. The video he had just watched was disturbing and horrible. It was a record of fear and intimidation. It carried implications that made his stomach twist with nausea. But nothing happened, nothing to satisfy people who had such tastes, nothing marketable, nothing for a predatory paedophile's private collection.

He opened the images Strąk had sent and looked at them again. They were the way he remembered them. Overtly, they were innocent enough, a little girl dancing in her party clothes, but they carried the same disturbing overtones as the video. The fear was missing, but the promise of further revelation was implicit.

He let his mind work at the problem, listening all the time for movement outside, his ears attuned to the slightest sound on the stairway.

Images of child abuse were all over the web for those who went looking. The hardcore sites had to offer some level of security to their users who wanted to view images, to exchange images, to share incidents of live abuse on request, an à la carte of perversion and cruelty. How were people with such tastes guided to the sites?

Photographs such as these might do it. To the casual observer, they were innocuous enough, but to a paedophile the skimpy top, the swirl of the skirt revealing lace on the child's panties would tell them all they needed to know.

Even her smile… It wouldn't have been hard to coax that look of promise into a child's eyes. He had seen it in Beata's eyes when she was small and trying to wheedle her way round their father. He had seen it in the eyes of his nieces as they tried to persuade him to buy them sweets or take them to the playground or the fair, an innocent precursor of one of many adult behaviours, one he had, until now, found engaging rather than disturbing.

He couldn't remember all the details of the case. Ania had talked about it, but mostly in relation to her anger at men like Haynes, not the specifics. He began opening the other files Strąk had sent: newspaper reports, miscellaneous texts that he must have collected in case the story went big in Poland.

He found an article about the trial the day the pathologist gave evidence. *The child's body was too badly decomposed to establish the cause of death. There was no evidence of stabbing or blunt force. Sexual assault could not be confirmed, but it could not be ruled out either.*

He remembered the feeling he had had when Will Gillen had told him about mysterious Facebook sites and cryptic references to old stories, the feeling that someone was sending up smoke, was trying to make him look in the wrong direction.

It wasn't just the Facebook link that was a con. The whole thing was a con. Nothing was what it seemed. The only constant, the only thing that mattered, was that two people had died. He stared at the screen in fierce concentration, trying to force the images to give up their secrets. He was so focused that he missed the faint sound of footsteps in the corridor outside the door, moving along the passage and fading away into silence.

Chapter 67

'What are you doing?' Sarah was standing in the doorway, tying the belt of her robe round her waist. She looked dazed with sleep, but her daytime face, more guarded, older, harder, was in place. When he didn't answer, she said, 'Will, you are seconds away from me calling security. What are you doing?'

He met her gaze. 'If it comes to that, they won't get here in time.' He pressed the button to put the phone on loudspeaker. 'John Blaise,' he said.

She sank down onto the sofa. She must have seen the capacity for murder in his face. She was very pale, but when she spoke, her voice was steady. 'This is... different. This is something else.'

'Is it? I'm going to need some convincing. Let's start with Blaise. What's his involvement with this?' He spoke at the phone. 'Are you hearing me?'

'Loud and clear, Will. I trust you not to do anything stupid.'

He kept his gaze on Sarah. 'I'll ask you again. What's his involvement with this?'

'I've been in contact with him since I started representing Nadifa. Her husband...'

Nadifa's husband had been suspected of terrorist activity. That fitted. 'Go on.'

'Blaise wanted to find out how much Nadifa knew. Cooperating seemed like a good strategy.'

'Where was her husband?'

'He'd been deported by that time.'

'And Nadifa?'

'She was in detention. She and the children would be gone by now if Blaise hadn't put a hold on it.'

'And Sagal would still be alive.'

'Don't lay that on me, Will. If they'd gone back, they'd all be dead by now.'

'Like her husband?'

'I don't know. I think he must be. No one's heard anything of him since his deportation.'

'I very much doubt that.' Will knew he had very little time. He addressed Blaise. 'Who took François Akindès into custody? Where is he?'

'That's information I don't have.'

'OK. Where *was* he? What happened to him after he was deported?'

'My jurisdiction ends at our borders. You know that, Will.'

'I don't. Not any more.'

He heard Blaise sigh. 'It was in the hands of the authorities in Côte d'Ivoire. Will, where is all this going? What's the point of this?'

'Ania was murdered. I don't think she was the main target of this. I think she was collateral damage, but she's still dead. Someone planted a faked recording on Derek Haynes' computer. Ania was the fall guy who identified his voice. Then the appeal came along. Ania held the only evidence that showed when the fake had been made.'

Blaise's voice was flat. 'Go on, Will. I'll need more than that to convince me.'

'It starts when François Akindès was accused of belonging to a terrorist organisation. He was a Christian convert to Islam, and he'd had contact with some radical groups. He hadn't committed any offences in this country, and my guess is, he wasn't amenable to bribery. You offered his family immunity in return for his cooperation, right?'

'You're assuming I have that kind of clout. Go on.'

That was bullshit. Blaise had all the clout he chose to take. 'We've already established that Akindès was an exceptional man, who would go a long way to protect his family. So what happened next? He agreed to help you and they were given leave to remain.'

'They had a good case. Akindès had a good case. The wife and the children weren't so clear cut. Go on.'

'He became your informer. He had the contacts, he had the credentials. He kept an eye on the radicals in...' The implications of what he was saying hit him. 'He was your informer in Birmingham, wasn't he? The raid. Akindès was the source of that intelligence.'

The misinformation that had led to the Birmingham raid had had repercussions beyond the death of the young man at the station. The way the information had been used had revealed structures in the network that had left other informers vulnerable. British intelligence and British policing had been made to look incompetent. As Blaise had said at the time: *if someone had set out to damage us deliberately they couldn't have done a better job.*

He was feeling his way now. 'Your people thought Akindès had set them up. After the raid, he was taken into custody. A few weeks after that he was deported. Did he ever arrive in Côte d'Ivoire? Or was he sent somewhere else? Afghanistan? Pakistan? Jordan? Syria? Egypt?'

'If that's what happened...' Before Will could interrupt, Blaise said, 'And it may have done. I'm not disagreeing with you, Will. I want to know why you think I'm involved.'

Because you've been looking over my shoulder from the start. 'Who else?'

'I wouldn't have hurt Ania. Christ, Will, you worked with me for long enough. Do you really think I'd have run such a botched-up, amateur operation?'

That was the rub. If Blaise had been in charge of whatever it was that had led to Ania's death, there would have been no trail of evidence to follow. Will looked out of the window. Two cars had drawn up in the road outside the apartment block. He looked at the door, and at the window opposite wondering who was waiting outside. He was perfectly framed for a shot: Will Gillen, driven mad by his own mistakes, by the disgrace and death of his daughter, caught in the coils of his own conspiracy theory and shot when he tried to hold a woman hostage.

'Akindès was taken from the detention centre and disappeared. Did someone at the detention centre see him go? Haynes? Did he see too much? Is that what this is about?'

'It's about a murdered child and the death of your daughter. That's all it's ever been about. Leave it Will. It's not your investigation.'

***

Dariusz sat in the dark in the computer room. The temperature was dropping. A cold draught was coming from somewhere. It was a freezing night outside, and the building had been constructed in days when insulation had not been a priority. The huge windows leaked warmth, and they were ill-fitting and poorly maintained. His fingers were starting to lose feeling at their tips. He could feel the heaviness in his eyes that said he needed – desperately – to sleep. The draught swirled round his ankles.

It was like a river of ice in the darkness. He came alert.

That wasn't there before. Something's changed.

Something was causing the draught. Someone had opened a door or a window to make that current of air flow. He sat up, listening to the small sounds that were part of the silence around him. He switched off the computer monitor, and he was blind. His fingers wrapped round the knife in his pocket as he waited for his eyes to adjust. He slipped the blade open and felt it lock. *I'm ready for you, you bastard.* The darkness and the silence were complete.

He stood up and moved towards the door, treading carefully, testing the floor before he put his weight down to make sure he didn't stumble. The key turned silently. He let the door swing open onto the windowless corridor. He could feel the current of cold air more strongly now. To the right was the way out to the landing and stairway. That door was shut, and he was pretty sure it would be locked.

To the left... The door to the small office stood open, a pale outline in the darkness.

It was here. Ania had walked along this corridor in this darkness all those nights ago. It was almost as if he could see her there in the cold night, her arms held out, drawing him on. There was no point in running away. He had stepped into this trap deliberately.

He let the adrenaline and the fury hold him, then he walked along the corridor and through the open door to confront Ania's killer.

Chapter 68

Jerzy Pawlak was sitting by the desk, waiting. The window behind him was open to the night, and the cold air flowed in, flooding round Dariusz' ankles, chilling his body to the bone. The gun in Pawlak's hand was small, but it was pointed directly at him.

'It's going to make a sad story, isn't it Erland? Drunk and disgraced and you follow your girlfriend out of the window.'

'It's not going to look very convincing if I've got a bullet through my chest.' He hadn't anticipated a gun. His legs felt like water, but he managed to keep his voice steady. Pawlak? Why would Pawlak have killed Ania?

'The jump would be better but you probably haven't got the guts. You came here with the gun. You blew your own brains out.'

'From a distance?'

'I can get close enough if I have to. Don't move!' He had seen Dariusz brace himself for a lunge. The gun stayed steady, the gun was the only thing that mattered. He could feel the weight of the knife in his pocket, as useless as if it had been a hundred miles away. He hadn't expected the gun.

'I'll take the tape first.'

Dariusz understood why he was still alive. 'I haven't got it, not here. What did you think? That I was going to bring it as a present?'

'You aren't drunk either, are you?'

'No. I filled the bottle with water. It still smelled of vodka, but...' He shrugged. He might as well have got drunk. Maybe an erratic, roaring charge would have worked. Sober, he couldn't make himself do it, not into certain death.

'Wherever you've put it, no one's going to be looking for it now. Gillen's left. It doesn't matter anyway. Not really.'

'I'm not going out of that window. You'll have to shoot me. They might have covered up Ania's murder, but they won't cover up this one.'

There was something strange about the light. It seemed to come and go, a pale, sickly glow in the night that cast almost no illumination. Pawlak made a sound that was more like a titter than a laugh. His rat-like face contorted into a gleeful grin. 'I didn't murder your girlfriend. She jumped, Erland, just like they said.' He pushed the gun forward. 'Don't!'

'She... you lying piece of shit!' But Pawlak's voice held the note of truth. For the first time, a terrible doubt began to fill his mind. *Kiciu*?

'She wasn't going to tell me where that tape was. That's what I wanted, the tape. I had to give her some encouragement. She knew she couldn't hold out. She knew she'd tell me in the end.'

Pawlak had been a member of Służba Bezpieczeństwa the SB, the secret police. He would have known the techniques of swift, harsh interrogation. What had he done to her, up here, alone in the vast, empty building?

He could see the retrospective frustration in Pawlak's face. 'She got away from me and she went out of the window. I didn't expect that. She tried to climb across to the fire escape.' Then he grinned. 'She screamed. When she fell, she screamed.'

He knew he was going to die, but he was going to destroy Pawlak first. He was across the room before the words were out of Pawlak's mouth. He saw the gun jump and it was as if he had hit a brick wall. He was thrown backwards and a rod of agony rammed itself through his arm. All the strength drained out of him and he was on the ground.

'Stupid cunt!' Pawlak spat. 'Look what you made me do. Doesn't matter. You attacked me. I had to defend myself. That's it. You're dead, you're...!' His head whipped round and he froze.

Dariusz' ears were ringing, but he could hear it too, voices calling, as if they were cheering him on. As the darkness bloomed at the edges of his vision, he though he heard Ania saying his name. *Dariusz*. It was her voice. She was there. He tried to reach out, but his arm was too heavy. Pawlak lifted his gun, and in the light that glowed and then waned, Dariusz could see the weapon was shaking. The shouting rose towards a crescendo and Pawlak jumped onto the desk, his eyes fixed on

the door. 'Dead,' he spat, 'like your fucking whore, you're...'
The crash echoed in Dariusz' ears.

Time stopped.

Then there was nothing.

Chapter 69

The drive from Hale to Birmingham took Will just over an hour. It was early in the morning and the roads were quiet. He'd left Sarah without any further discussion – there was nothing left to say – and headed south. Face to face, Blaise would tell him what he knew. Will had nothing left to lose. Now it was too late, now it didn't matter any more, he had all the power he needed.

He arrived at Colmore Circus shortly after seven. He parked under the glass cube of the shopping plaza where the day's commuters were already starting to gather, and walked across to the blank-faced building that was the West Midlands Police HQ. Blaise would be there – he would be expecting Will. In all the years Will had known Blaise, he had never been able to surprise him.

He went to the desk and gave his name, getting a respectful *Sir* from the young constable on duty. The security here was low key but no less rigorous for that. He knew that CCTV cameras were focused on him and that his every action was being observed and analysed.

Five minutes later, he was escorted into the main building, taken quickly and efficiently through the various security procedures and found himself on the familiar staircase leading down to the below-ground offices from where Blaise ran his operation. Blaise's office door was open. There were no flunkies or flappers to impede Will's progress. Blaise didn't play power games. He had no need to.

Blaise stood up to greet him. 'That was quick, Will. You must have had a good journey. Coffee? It's been quite a night one way and another.'

'Yes. Thanks.' The last time he had been in this office it was to accept the offer of early retirement, an offer that, at the time, he could see no way of refusing.

Blaise nodded at the constable who had accompanied Will, and the man vanished, returning a couple of minutes later with two polystyrene cups. Once the door was shut and they were alone, Blaise leaned back in his chair and studied Will over steepled fingers. 'You haven't exactly covered yourself in glory this past twenty-four hours,' he said.

'I'm doing what I have to do to find out what happened to my daughter. I'm getting close.'

'You are, Will, and closer than you think. Actually, I was thinking about Sarah. She didn't deserve all that. She doesn't know anything about Ania's death. She's just trying to protect her client.'

'She could have trusted me more.'

'Like you did her?'

Will shrugged. *Touché.*

'You'd better tell me what you know.'

This was where the bargaining began. 'I can pick up the story when François Akindès was deported to Abidjan. He was arrested as soon as his plane touched down there. Officially, he's still in Ivoirian custody, but my guess is he was flown from Abidjan to somewhere he could be questioned more efficiently.' He looked at Blaise, but the other man's face was unreadable. 'I can take it that far, but I'm not sure I understand.

'You do, Will. But before you go on, there's information I have that you need.' He picked up the phone. 'Get me Piotr Król,' His gaze met Will's. 'There's been another death in Łódź.' He waited with the phone held to his ear then grunted in some kind of acknowledgement. He put the phone on loudspeaker and handed it to Will.

Will took it, a sense of foreboding clenching his stomach. 'Will Gillen.'

'Gillen. It's Dariusz Erland. I'm under arrest. I don't know why they're letting me talk to you.' His voice sounded lifeless, like someone who had experienced an immense shock.

Will was surprised by the flood of relief he had felt as he heard Erland's voice. 'They told me someone was dead. I thought it was you. What's happened.'

'I went to the university last night. Jerzy Pawlak put a bullet through my arm.'

'Pawlak?'

'Pawlak. Then Król's men are hammering on the door and Pawlak goes out of the window.'

'The... Why?'

'I think he was trying to get away. I think he was trying to reach the fire escape, but something... I don't know.'

Will could hear the confusion in Erland's voice. 'Where are you?'

'In Król's office. For now. I'll be in a cell as soon as we're done.'

'Pawlak killed her? He killed Ania?' Jerzy Pawlak, the man who 'found' Ania's body, the ex-SB agent, the police informer. Will had talked to Pawlak, observed his shifty hostility and seen no sign of guilt, but then a man like Pawlak wouldn't feel guilt.

He had met enough Pawlaks in his time. It was only the blindfold of grief that had stopped him from seeing the man for what he was. At last, he knew the name of Ania's killer. There was no comfort in the knowledge, just the bleak satisfaction of knowing her killer was dead. 'What happened?'

There was a long silence. Will knew there was something Erland wasn't telling him. His eyes met Blaise's, but he couldn't read the other man's expression. This had to be part of Blaise's game. Not shifting his gaze, he said, 'There's more, you know that don't you?'

'Yeah. I think I'm the price they're willing to pay to keep the *more* quiet. They're planning to charge me with Pawlak's murder.'

It was a charge that would never stick, but Król could make Erland's life very uncomfortable if he chose. 'And you...?'

'I'm not cutting any deals Gillen. I don't work with the good wardens.'

That meant nothing to Will, and he didn't have time for Erland's scruples now. 'Listen. I found the tape.' He filled Erland in quickly about what he and Sarah Ludlow had found. 'There never was a fabrication. The tape Ania analysed was the one taken from Haynes' computer. That was the one that was faked.'

There was silence at the other end as Erland absorbed what he had said. 'It was all a fake, right from the start.'

'A child was murdered. That was real.'

'The reason she was killed was real. Have you watched the video, the Haynes video?'

'No.' That was one piece of evidence he couldn't bring himself to look at. The recording had been bad enough.

'Nothing happens, Gillen. It's just the kid being threatened.'

Blaise reached forward and took the phone out of his hand. 'OK.' He spoke to someone at the other end, then hung up. He looked at Will. 'You've got everything you need now, Will. I'm told it's a lovely day out there. I've got some calls to make. Go for a walk, and we'll talk later.'

Chapter 70

Blaise was right. By the time Will left the building, the sun was up. It was a clear winter day with blue skies and small white clouds. The sun cast a warm glow over the city. He walked away from the main road towards the cathedral. He knew this area well with its mix of old and new, of Victorian stone and 21st century glass and steel.

He felt oddly detached. He had a name for Ania's killer, and her killer was dead: Jerzy Pawlak, a police informer and an ex-member of the Communist secret police, the SB. Pawlak had fallen on hard times under the new regime, a regime that was slow to forgive the past because it was easier to focus on old grievances than try to correct the new. Pawlak's death should be a closure, but it wasn't.

Pawlak may have killed Ania but he was just the weapon. Will needed to know who Pawlak had been working for.

Who had paid him? Who had paid him to rip information out of Ania then kill her when he got it? Blaise? No. Blaise knew what had happened, he knew the whole story, Will was certain of that, but if Blaise had run this operation, there would have been no evidence, no trace, no tape.

His wanderings had brought him to the Cathedral Church of St Phillips. He walked along the pavement under a row of trees, gnarled and leafless. The railings of the graveyard were black tipped with gold. He went in and found a bench where he sat in the quiet and studied the grave stones as the bustle of the early rush hour gathered beyond the gates.

Eighteen months ago, the Birmingham raid had damaged the credibility of the Birmingham anti-terror squad and had effectively cost Will his job. The raid had led to a needless death – a seventeen-year-old youth, shot dead on the platform at New Street Station, his hand in his pocket reaching for his ID card. It was after the raid that François Akindès had been arrested and his wife had absconded with the children.

He took out his phone and keyed in Sarah Ludlow's number. He wasn't sure if she would talk to him, but he had to try. 'It's Will Gillen,' he said when she answered.

Her voice was cautious. 'Will. I... What do you want?'

'Why was François Akindès was deported?'

'You know that. He got involved with a bunch of Jihadists. It was a crazy thing to do.'

Crazy was not the word. Akindès had taken great risks to protect his family. It didn't make sense that he had thrown it all away to get involved with an extremist group. 'And then?'

'He was arrested. Nadifa panicked and ran. They picked her up a few weeks later – it's hard to go into hiding when you've got dependent children. She was arrested, he was deported.'

'Hang on – they didn't deport him until after they'd got his wife and children in custody?'

'No. They were all supposed to go, but Sagal was ill. She wasn't fit to travel.'

'And then Blaise stepped in. Nadifa Akindès should have been sent back with her children. What was she prepared to do to keep them safe? What deal did you make, Sarah?'

'The best deal I could,' she snapped. 'Her husband had decided to put politics before his family. I told her Blaise would help her if she cooperated with him. He promised he'd get her and the kids leave to remain if she told the police what she knew. That was the deal.'

'OK.' She'd tried to her best for them, he could accept that. 'One more thing – what was wrong with Sagal Akindès? Why was she too ill to travel?'

'Asthma. She suffered from asthma.'

Asthma. It was slowly coming together. 'OK. Thank you for your help.' As he put the phone down, he saw Blaise walking towards him. He stayed where he was, watching the familiar figure, tall, grey-haired now, his heavy overcoat slung round his shoulders. 'It's a good place for thinking,' Blaise greeted him as he joined Will on the bench. 'Have you got there yet?'

'Almost.'

'Good man. I was sorry to lose you.'

'After the Birmingham raid... These are all the repercussions, aren't they? I thought the information for the raid came from someone who'd already been deported, someone who was – what's the phrase? – being robustly interrogated. Akindès didn't get involved with a terrorist group, he infiltrated one. Was that his choice, or did you persuade him – safety for his family in return? What really happened? Was his cover broken, or was he angry enough to feed you misinformation deliberately? I can't see him putting his family at risk.'

'Neither can I. I think they knew he was working as an informer and they used him to get at us.'

'And the guarantees you'd given Akindès?'

'They only stood if he played by the rules. Someone decided he hadn't.'

'OK. You let Akindès go, but you stopped his wife and the children being sent back to Côte d'Ivoire. Sarah's grateful to you. She's been keeping you updated on everything because you've convinced her it will help Nadifa and the children. Why did you want his family?'

He could sense Blaise weighing things up in his head. He seemed to come to a decision. 'Whoever fed us the information that led to the raid set us up. They knew far too much about how we operate – they had a line right into our system. We had to find that and cut it off, and François was the one who knew. He had the names and the contacts but he was too scared by then. They knew he was a plant. It wasn't just him, it was his family. He wasn't talking. He was afraid of reprisals. You've got to remember I didn't know for sure Akindès had played straight. He might have turned double agent. Having his family seemed like good insurance to me.'

'So you threatened him through his family.'

'That was going to be the deal. Tell us, and we'll protect them. Keep quiet, and they'll have to take their chances back in Côte d'Ivoire.'

'Going to be?'

'After that, I moved on. Someone else took over the case.'

'But it was still your plan, right? Only it wasn't just deportation – it was a different level, wasn't it? If Akindès thought his daughter was in the hands of a paedophile ring and he was the only person who could save her, then he'd talk. Was that your idea? It's your style.'

Blaise gave a thin smile and quoted, apparently from memory: "*"Inducing* unfounded *fear, physical discomfort, isolation can lead a suspect to cooperate with the authorities, and such methods have provided our own security forces with valuable, sometimes life-saving, information.*" It is my style. It's what I believe. But the key word is *unfounded*. I would never have sanctioned what they did to that child.'

'Sarah Ludlow thought you were protecting them.'

'Maybe I was, Will, as best I could. It wasn't good enough as it turned out.' Blaise paused and studied the inscription on the gravestone in front of the bench. 'Read that. Two kids under ten dead, and the mother dead at forty. *Autre temps, autre mœres.* After the raid, I had to move on.'

'Who gave the orders for Sagal Akindès to be abducted?'

'It wasn't an abduction. The child's mother cooperated. It was done through Haynes. She trusted him because he'd helped her. She thought he was in touch with a support group who were going to get the child out of there. She let them take the kid. There was supposed to be a video, but just of the kid dancing. Someone got too clever.'

'The child was murdered! For Christ's sake…'

Blaise sighed. 'She died, Will. She panicked when they started setting her up for the video. She died of an asthma attack.'

'Where's Akindès now?'

Blaise shrugged. 'Who knows? It stopped being our operation once he left these shores. You're looking at cock-up rather than conspiracy. If I'd known, I'd have stopped it. As it is, it's my job to pick up the pieces. You know that.'

'And Ania?'

'I can promise you – you can believe it or not – that no one sanctioned any action against her. The files should never have been on Haynes' system. He should never have been charged. Given that he was…'

'Ania was the fall guy.'

'I didn't know about that video. Something went badly amiss and people have got some questions to answer. Ania would never have gone down for it. I could have handled that.' He sat in silence, his gaze still on the gravestone. 'One more thing you might need to know, Will. Pawlak was under investigation in

Łódź. Child pornography. Seems he was moving into the supply side. He got a bit too clever and they tracked some stuff back to him.'

They sat side by side on the bench in a parody of companionship. The weight of it, the sheer weight of the useless, pointless mess made it hard for Will to move. He forced himself to his feet.

Blaise didn't look at him. 'Goodbye, Will.'

Will nodded and turned away, moving like an old man. The recording was running through his head as he left the graveyard and went out onto the busy streets of Birmingham. *I can't... I can't... I can't...* Over and over again, she had struggled to say it, and the person behind the camera had just not been listening. *I can't breathe.* No one had listened, and Sagal Akindès had died.

Then the cover-up had begun.

Chapter 71

Will waited in his car for an hour before Dariusz Erland called him. 'They let me go. You're doing what they wanted? I didn't ask for that.'

'There was no need. Blaise knows I can't talk – I can't prove a damn thing.'

'So you're giving up?' The jeer was back in Erland's voice, but it had lost its power to sting.

'No. There's one more thing to follow up. Who paid Pawlak? Who wanted that recording enough to pay Pawlak to kill her for it?'

There was silence as Erland absorbed this. 'Your people over there. They paid him.'

'No. The cover-up was complete when Sagal Akindès' body stayed hidden long enough for the forensic evidence to be destroyed. The video wasn't the responsibility of the UK intelligence people. That was someone else.'

'You believe that?'

'I know that. It wasn't necessary. It was enough that Akindès' family was in UK custody and under the control of John Blaise. Akindès worked for him. He knew what Blaise was capable of. The outcome of the trial didn't matter. It didn't matter if Ania was able to show she hadn't tampered with the recording, that it was a plant from the start. All that would happen was Haynes would be released and the case would drift into the unsolved files. If Ania had spotted the fake at the start, then that's what would have happened anyway. But she didn't.'

'You're saying she worked for all those weeks on a recording that was a fake and she didn't spot it?'

'She was too close to it. She let herself get too close.'

He heard the hiss of exasperation as Erland let out his breath. 'Jesus, Gillen, you don't give up, do you? Sure, Ania had a rough time about her sister. Sure, she was still working through it. But she'd survived. She was a strong woman, your daughter.

Your expert spotted that fake at once, right? There was no way, *no way* Ania didn't see it.'

He was right. Of course he was. He had to get out of this pattern of thinking, of seeing Ania as a frightened, damaged child. He had to see his daughter as a woman who had survived everything fate had thrown at her and who had made a success of her life: a woman who was liked and respected, a woman who was loved. A woman with a future.

Erland was speaking again, and he had to backtrack quickly to catch what he'd missed.

'...a message with my father. I was out when she called. She said something about being accused.'

'Being accused? Was she talking about the Haynes case?'

'I don't know. He didn't understand it so he didn't pass it on. She said something about someone being accused. That's all I know.'

'Telling you that she'd been accused? Hadn't she already...'

'Told me? Yeah. We'd already talked about it. That's why it doesn't make sense.'

She must have been talking about herself, but why would she ask Erland's father to tell him she had been accused? Why the urgency? Had there been some contact from the police in the UK, making formal charges? Had the Polish police been in touch with her? Will looked down the street ahead of him, a city street with shops and cars, a vista drawing his eye to the high tower of glass in the square at the end. As he watched, it seemed to fill with people wandering aimlessly along its length.

Then, at the far end, he saw a woman with fair hair. She was walking towards him. She vanished among the crowd, reappeared, was obscured briefly as someone walked across his line of vision, then she was gone. He blinked. The street was empty, but her voice was still there in his memory. *Occam's razor, Dad.*

'Something must have happened, something she needed to tell you at once.'

'But she couldn't because I wasn't there. And then she died.'

There was nothing Will could say to that. Could Erland have prevented her death over those hundreds of miles, if he had taken the call, if he had got the message? But there was something else now, something he hadn't realised before. 'You're right about the recording. She must have known there was something wrong with it. I need to work out why she didn't say anything. I need to talk to some people. I'll call you later.'

Before Erland could respond, he put the phone down, and walked back towards his car. When his phone started ringing again, he switched it off.

Occam's razor. He knew who he had to talk to. He had to get back to Manchester.

Chapter 72

DCI Cathcart didn't look happy to see Will. He was at his desk in the small office where he had talked to Will last time, working his way through a pile of papers. He frowned when Will was shown through the door. 'Mr Gillen,' he said. He didn't stand up.

'I won't keep you. I just need to know if there've been any developments.'

'Apart from your causing a disturbance in Hale, you mean, sir?'

'Apart from that, officer, yes.' The two men locked gazes, until Cathcart looked away.

'There's nothing new.' A muscle in his jaw was working. Will couldn't understand what was making him so angry – the news about the tape? The events at Sarah Ludlow's flat? Whatever it was, it was clear Cathcart wanted Will gone.

'What's the next stage?' Haynes' team would be pressing for a date for the new trial.

'There isn't a next stage. In the light of your recent findings, the investigation is being scaled down.'

'And the trial?'

'Probably won't happen. Haynes' conviction will be declared unsafe, and he'll walk free.'

It was the worst outcome for everyone. Will began to understand Cathcart's manner. He'd put all the effort he could into the case, into looking for new evidence, and now the whole thing had fallen apart. From Cathcart's point of view, it was an expert witness fiasco, and Will was the closest thing he had to a target for his anger. 'I need to know what Ania told you about that recording – not what she told you in her report, what she told you off the record – the things she believed but couldn't prove. Tell me that, and I'll get out of your way.'

Cathcart stayed at his desk, resting his chin on his hand while he studied Will. 'She told me she was certain it was Haynes.'

'I know that. Was there anything else?'

'We talked about a lot. What did you have in mind, exactly?'

'The recording's been cut. She can't have missed that.'

'She didn't. But that's in her report.'

'It's…?'

Cathcart went through the out tray on his desk and found a sheaf of papers that were stapled together. He flicked through them then held them out to Will, folded back to show a specific page. 'There. At the bottom.'

Will realised he had never seen Ania's report on the case. He read through the paragraph Cathcart had indicated: *there is evidence that small sections of the recording have been cut. These relate to cuts in the video that has been lightly edited to remove unwanted material.* 'Why didn't the defence go after this? It's wide open.'

'They did a lousy job. They thought the case against Haynes was so weak, they didn't expect the recording evidence to carry much weight. They thought the fact you can't pin a voice to an individual would be all they'd need. But if they had gone after it, Ania was ready for them. She'd worked on the video as well. She'd got an expert opinion that the recording wasn't dubbed. Cuts or no, it was still Haynes' voice and the jury would have to wonder why the cuts had been made – because the killer came into shot, that was Ania's opinion, or because the kid named him.'

'So it's still Haynes. You've got him. And you've got another expert to identify him. Where's the problem?'

'Your new expert doesn't agree. He's had the whole thing checked, and the so-called cuts turn out to be a complete fake. The voice on the recording was superimposed after the video was made. Not the kid, the abuser. The voice may well be Haynes. He might have been there, but the recording doesn't prove it. You'll understand I don't put a lot of faith in anything your daughter told me now.'

A complete fake. How in hell had she missed it? But Haynes had been involved in Sagal Akindès abduction. Blaise had told him that. Haynes had been a key figure because both the mother and the child trusted him. He remembered the photographs of Sagal dancing. She had looked happy and carefree, not a child acting under any kind of duress.

'You know why the whole thing was set up?' He felt no obligation of secrecy to Blaise.

'I've been advised that I don't need to look into that too closely.' Cathcart's tone was flat.

'Haynes was involved, for God's sake. If he wasn't there, if he wasn't in on the death, why didn't he start talking once he was charged?'

'That's a good question, Mr Gillen, but one that I'm not getting the chance to ask. If you ever find out, let me know. Now if you'll excuse me, I have things I need to get on with.'

Will didn't move. 'Ania knew. By the time she died, she knew. She didn't kill herself, she died trying to get the information out to someone like you, because she thought you needed to know. She thought you'd do something.'

For a moment, Cathcart's face showed regret, then he was the professional police officer again. 'Like I said, if you find anything, we'll do what we can.' From his voice, Will knew that Cathcart believed all the routes into the investigation were now blocked.

He could feel the pieces of the story starting to fall apart in his head. York's report had removed any chance of Haynes being found guilty again. The trial would not even take place. Maybe that was Blaise's way of handling it – leaving Haynes to live with what was effectively a not-proven verdict hanging round his neck. York was Sarah Ludlow's expert, and she was in Blaise's pocket. He felt the familiar weariness engulf him. Had Blaise tangled him in a web of deceit that he would never escape?

Cathcart was watching him, waiting. Cathcart, too, had his own agenda. There was no one Will could trust – just himself, possibly Dariusz Erland, and…

Occam's razor, Dad.

There was one other person.

Chapter 73

It was early evening when Will left Cathcart's office. The city centre was a maze of lights, orange, green and red against the night sky. The full moon hung pale and remote above him. As he drove away from the centre, the streets became darker. The streetlights were intermittent, shops were barricaded and locked up. He saw a group of people spilling out of a brightly lit chip shop, and later, a small group of smokers huddled in the dim light of a pub sign. He drove on past rows of terraced houses with shut doors and dark windows. Then the houses were boarded up, and the signs of demolition were all around him.

He pulled in at the kerb and got out, wondering briefly as he locked the car if it would still be there when he came back, then dismissed the problem. It wasn't important.

The FLS building looked derelict now. The sign above the door was broken, the carved *Infants* on the lintel fully exposed. Will wasn't certain if he would find anyone here. The move might be complete, the staff might be gone. He had come to find the last link in the chain.

Occam's razor…

He picked his way round piles of discarded junk to the main entrance and tried the door. It opened. Someone was here. It was probably just a security guard. The place wouldn't have been left to the mercy of the local vandals. He went in.

The reception window was shut and the office behind it was in darkness. The gallery of staff portraits was still on the notice board. The pictures were dusty and starting to curl at the edges. He could still see the lighter square where Ania's photo had been. He let his fingers drift across the space, then he reached into his pocket. He took out the picture of Ania he carried in his wallet and, using a spare pin from the board, put her image back in its rightful place.

There was no one to stop him, so he went on through to the back of the building, past rooms that were empty apart from discarded furniture – a battered plastic chair, a desk with a broken top, an old phone – until he saw the closed door of Oz Karzac's office. Light leaked from under the frame.

He pushed the door open without knocking. The books had gone from the shelves and the filing cabinet drawers stood open and empty, but the desk was still there, and the high backed chair. Karzac sat at the desk, his forehead resting on his hand. He looked up as Will came into the room. 'Gillen.' He spoke as if Will was expected. 'I heard.'

'About Ania?'

Karzac nodded. 'Are you all right?'

'What do you think? Jerzy Pawlak murdered my daughter.'

'I... It's weird. I must have seen the guy a hundred times, but don't remember...'

'You don't remember him?'

'Who notices caretakers, people like that? What happened? Did he come onto her or something?'

'She was murdered because she had something he wanted. Something someone wanted. Pawlak's job was to get hold of it.'

'Look, Gillen, I'm out of the loop on this one. You're going to have to explain it.'

'Then you don't know she's been exonerated? That she didn't fabricate anything?'

'How do you...? Oh, I get it. You found the tape.'

'You're not surprised? You were sure she'd done it.'

'Nothing surprises me about this any more. I'm sorry. I should have trusted her.'

'So should I.' And he should have listened more carefully. She'd tried to tell him.

Karzac's hand covered the lower part of his face. His voice, when he spoke, was muffled. 'So what's it all been about? If there was no fabrication, Haynes' conviction stands. Why did anyone care?'

'Oh, there was a fabrication. It was done long before the recording ever landed on Ania's desk.'

Karzac shook his head. 'And she missed it. If she'd picked it up at the time, none of this... I blame myself. I should have insisted on taking the case. She wasn't focused on the work. If she had been, she would have spotted there was something wrong with it. Well, I guess that's...'

'Maybe she did. Maybe she talked to someone about it.'

Karzac was silent.

'Who would she have gone to if she wasn't sure, if she wanted some advice?'

He could see Karzac's tongue move to moisten his lips as if his mouth was suddenly dry. 'I don't know. Any of us.'

'No. Not anyone. She'd have come to you. You were her mentor, weren't you? You were the person who had picked her out, started her off in her career. If she had worries about that recording, she would have come to you.' It was getting clearer as he spoke, as if he'd finally found the loose end, and as he pulled, it started unravelling into a long, straight thread – a thread that led to Ania's death.

'What are you saying, Gillen?'

'I'm saying Ania came to you with the Haynes recording. She knew who the speaker was, but she could tell the recording had been cut. She wanted to know if there had been any funny stuff with the video. You were the film expert. She wanted to know if her speaker profile would stand up.'

'I know you're having a hard time, Gillen, but there's only so much I'm going to… I wasn't here, remember?'

'And Cathcart wanted Ania on the case. You tried, didn't you, to get that changed. I thought it was an ego thing.'

'I understand why you're doing this, Gillen. Believe me, I do, but you've got to accept what happened.' Karzac pressed on, urging Will to listen to him. 'Yes, I wanted to take the case over. I wanted to do it because she wasn't coping. My concern was for FLS. If she got it wrong, it would be bad for us, and I have a lot of people relying on this company, Gillen, in case you've forgotten. I spent years building this place up, and Ania's mistake nearly sent it down the toilet.'

The thread was starting to tangle. Why would Karzac have put his own company in jeopardy by misleading Ania? Will kept his face expressionless, not wanting Karzac to see his doubt. Occam's razor. First principles.

François Akindès had been subject to extraordinary rendition. He had been sent to Côte d'Ivoire, apparently as a failed asylum seeker. He had been taken into custody, and probably transferred to another country where the interrogators were waiting.

Unfounded fear. The photographs were supposed to be Blaise's message to Akindès: *we have your child.* Sagal and her mother trusted Haynes, who had befriended them. Had Haynes known what he was doing, or was the story Nadifa had told the court true, that Haynes was working – or thought he was working – for Nadifa's supporters? With the photos maybe, but the video? Haynes must have known.

The images were as vivid as if he held them in his hands: the dancing child, twirling round, caught at the moment her skirt snapped round, with the teasing flash of lace – so much innocence and so much promise.

Attagirl! That's right.

Haynes' voice, callous in its spurious note of encouragement as a child pleaded for breath.

Please. I can't...

You're a star.

Blaise said the video was supposed to be of the child dancing, not a film of abuse – an innocent image whose sinister overtones would only be clear to the man it was targeted at: François Akindès, who knew only too well what Blaise was capable of.

The thread began to run free.

'What happened to the first video? The one of the dancing child? The one the images came from.' He slipped back into the interrogation techniques he knew so well. Don't ask questions, don't let them know you aren't certain. Present your suspicions as facts.

Haynes' encouraging voice was just that – he had been calling to Sagal as she danced, cautioning her when she got too boisterous, a man interacting with a child he knew well.

Karzac's mouth opened to speak, then closed again. He shook his head. 'You're crazy, Gillen. You need help.'

'I have help. Ania called someone the night she died. If she'd called me, I might have understood, but I don't think the phone she was using would make international calls. She'd worked it out, you see, what had happened with the Haynes recording, and she wanted to let someone know. Even then... I wonder if she ever realised how much danger she was in.'

Karzak's gaze met his. 'Worked it out? Worked what out?' His tongue flicked across his lips again.

'She tried to leave a message with a friend's father. But she spoke Polish with an English accent and he couldn't understand her. He thought she said, *Oskarżać*. To accuse. She didn't. She said, 'Oz Karzac.' She said, 'Tell Dariusz it's Oz Karzac.'

Chapter 74

Karzac sat in frozen silence. 'She can't have…' he said again. He looked directly at Will, challenging him. 'It's Haynes' voice on that recording!'

'It's Haynes voice, but it doesn't belong with that video. It belongs with the one of the child dancing. It would have been simple enough – for someone with your skills – to take Haynes' voice from the first video and put it onto the second one. It's over, Karzac. They're taking the whole thing apart right now.'

Karzac's hands moved over the surface of his desk, as if he was searching for a piece of paper he had just mislaid. 'I'm not prepared to listen to this. I want you to leave. I'll call the police if I have to.' But he didn't move.

'Nadifa Akindès claimed Haynes was working for her supporters, that Haynes said he'd handed the child over to them. The investigating team thought she was lying but maybe she wasn't.' Will kept his voice calm, a simple recitation of obvious facts that were not in dispute. He'd done this before and he'd trained others to do it. 'He was there when the first video was made – you can see the child looking at someone who's just off camera – but he wasn't the one doing the filming. The question is, how involved was he with the second video? That video… I haven't seen it. I never will. But I saw a still. That scene was made by someone who knew what he was doing, someone who knows about those films.

'It was you, wasn't it, behind that camera.'

Karzac was on his feet, his hand moving like lightning, gripping something, sweeping towards Will's chest. Will sidestepped in a movement that came back to him from his time as a young policeman, and pulled Karzac's arm up behind him, immobilising him. Something clattered to the floor. Will glanced down and kicked it out of the way. 'A paperknife. Did you really expect to stop me with that?'

'Let me go!' Karzac was struggling. 'You were threatening me. I had to defend...' Will pulled his arm further up his back. '*Shit!*'

'Does it hurt? Does it hurt as much as having your fingers broken, one at a time? Do you want to know?'

'Gillen, for Christ's sake, you're crazy, you're...'

'You're right, Karzac. I am crazy. I can do what I like. You need to cooperate with me.' He yanked Karzac's arm again, hard.

'*Shit*! What do you want? What do you want to know?'

'First question: you knew Pawlak. You recognised the name at once. Right?'

'Yes. Christ, Gillen, go easy. Yes, I knew him.'

'See. It's simple. Now the next one. Pawlak was a fixer. He was ex-SB, he'd fallen on hard times but he still had all his contacts. He got stuff for you, didn't he?'

Karzac didn't reply. Will gave his arm another twist. 'OK! You don't have to... Give me a chance.'

'What? What did he get you?'

'Nothing much. Cheap booze, cigarettes... *Shit!*'

'Don't lie, Karzac. I'll break your arm, then I'll break your neck. Was it drugs? Coke? Heroin?'

'Yes. *Yes!* I have a bit of a habit...'

'You have a lot of habits. Expensive habits. How do you afford them? The car? The drugs? FLS doesn't bring in *that* much. How much do you get for those Home Office contracts? The ones that never give them an answer they don't want to hear? I don't care about the drugs. That's your problem. It's your other habit I'm interested in. Pawlak was able to supply stuff for that as well, wasn't he?'

'I... I don't know what you're talking about!' Karzac's sudden panic was as good as an admission. 'Haynes...'

'Didn't they tell you, Oz, confession is good for the soul? Don't lie to me. I know. I know exactly what you are. It wasn't Haynes. It was never Haynes. He knew about the asthma. He'd never have let her die. '

Karzac's breath came in sobs.

'Don't worry. I've almost done. It's the last bit I'm not sure about. Were you making the second video for the same people, or was it a bit of private enterprise? They must have known. They did the cover up. You were in the clear. Until images from the dancing video appeared on the net. How did that happen?'

'I don't know. I don't... *Christ, Gillen. OK! OK!!* Pawlak. It was fucking Pawlak put them there.'

The thread was running free now. The original plan had gone horribly wrong; but Karzac had been left in possession of a valuable commodity. He must have doctored the video to remove any evidence of his own presence and put Haynes there – a safeguard before he passed on the material to whoever had commissioned it.

How much money did Karzac owe to Jerzy Pawlak? Or had Pawlak been blackmailing him? Will didn't know, and he didn't care. What mattered was the video had a particular and perverse value. Sagal Akindès might have died before any abuse took place, but Ania's instincts had been right. She had said to him: *Haynes probably filmed her death.*

Only it hadn't been Haynes, it had been Oz Karzac, her mentor, the man she trusted. Karzac had sold a copy of the videos to Pawlak who had cashed in, and the dancing images had been discovered.

Nadifa had told Cathcart the truth, that Haynes was taking her daughter to 'Dave.' No one had believed her and Haynes had been convicted. Even so, Karzac must have lived in dread of discovery.

Karzac was talking freely now. 'Ania told me she had the audio cassette, and she was going to get that authenticated so she could show she hadn't tampered with anything. I told her we'd have to be careful, we didn't want stuff going astray. I suggested she get out of the way, go to Łódź at once and do her analysis there. I told her to leave the audio tape with me – I'd deal with it – and she said she would. She knew things were going to get very nasty. She told me to be careful, and said she was going to keep her head down. I thought we were in the clear then.'

'We? You mean you. But you weren't.'

'No. When I got in the next morning – I got there early because I wanted to make sure everything was sorted – no cassette, just a note from her saying she was going to get it authenticated independently so that FLS weren't open to any more accusations of tampering. She'd taken it to Łódź with her. I was in the shit.'

'So you had to stop her.'

Karzac nodded. 'I wiped her system – I had to overwrite all her data. It took hours. I destroyed all her post – I didn't know what she'd written and I didn't have time to go through it. Then all I had to do was get the audio tape back. Only...' His face darkened.

'She spoke to you, didn't she, from Łódź.'

'I tried to persuade her to send it back. Maybe I overplayed my hand there, maybe that was what first started her thinking. The irony is, she couldn't have got it authenticated there. Their expert had left.'

'And you'd warned Pawlak. If you went down, he was going to go down too.'

'That wasn't my fault. I never asked him to... All I wanted was the audio tape. That's all. You have my word...'

'Which is worth how much, exactly?'

'I'm telling you the truth! I never meant... I know you blame me, but...'

'You let Pawlak loose on her. You knew. You wrote the suicide note, didn't you, or you gave him the wording for it. I should have realised sooner. She never called me "daddy," not since she was small.' He released Karzac's arm. The feel of the man disgusted him. He wanted to be as far away from him as possible. 'Blame you? Oh, I blame you. Give me one good reason not to kill you, Karzac. One.'

Karzac sagged against the desk, breathing hard. 'The tape,' he said after a moment. 'Where is it?'

'It's with Cathcart.'

He saw an expression – he couldn't quite define it. Relief was the closest he could manage, a smug relief – that flickered across Karzac's face. Karzac knew. He knew Cathcart had been told to wind the case down, put it in the tombs of the cold cases files. There would be no clamour for an answer to the death of Sagal Akindès. If one monster – Haynes – was released, there was another monster – Nadifa – to hate. Karzac would not have to answer for what he had done. In the end, he would have the protection that had been denied to Sagal Akindès and to Ania.

'But Pawlak told me he'd found it. I paid him.'

'She set up a decoy in case she was being watched – she knew the significance of the audio tape, you see. That's what he found, and it didn't take him long to realise he'd been fooled. She didn't reckon on Pawlak. Even then, she didn't think you would do that.'

'She knew…' Karzac slumped in his chair. It would have been simple for Will to deliver the blow, the one that would bring the story to a close. It was what Blaise wanted. It was what he had set up. *There's one more thing you need to know...*

Will didn't work for him any more. Blaise could do his own dirty work.

He walked away.

Chapter 75

Dariusz was clearing his desk. He was moving clumsily. His left arm was immobilised in a cast and would be for weeks. The orthopaedic surgeon couldn't promise that his arm would ever fully recover. The bullet had torn the muscles and shattered the bone.

It was a week after Jerzy Pawlak had fallen to his death from the top floor of the university building and Dariusz had – briefly – been arrested and charged with murder. Mielek could barely conceal his pleasure, but Dariusz wasn't giving him the opportunity to do anything about it. He resigned.

He was finished with Łódź. He had to get away if he wanted to put his life back together. He had several job applications out which were already generating interviews. There was one that interested him in Warsaw – he'd always wanted to move back to Warsaw, but he was beginning to wonder if that was far enough. There was an academic post in Birmingham, at the university. They wanted to interview him as well, and sounded very interested. Dariusz' experience in EU employment law made him versatile and marketable.

He packed away the last of his books and looked round the room to make sure he hadn't left anything. There was just the photograph on his desk, of him and Ania the day they had danced on Piotrkowska, a snap taken by a street photographer. He slipped it into his bag.

'Dariusz?'

He turned round. Krysia was standing in the doorway, looking uncertain.

'I wanted to say goodbye. And I'm sorry. About… You know. Ania.'

He nodded. The verdict on her death had been changed to manslaughter. Król's men had investigated again, and they had found a print on the fire escape rail. She had tried to escape from Pawlak by the only route available, trying to scramble across to the fire escape just a few short feet away, but with her damaged hands, she had been unable to grip and she had fallen, Ania, with her fear of heights. 'She wasn't going to let him have the information about the tape,' Gillen said when he told Dariusz what he had found out. 'It was the only way to stop a paedophile. She trusted me to do that, and I came so close to letting her down.' He cleared his throat. 'Thank you for... you know.'

There was an awkward silence. It had been a series of illusions, of one thing masquerading as another – even the deaths were not clear cut murder, and the truth, Gillen was telling him, would probably never come out. 'Karzac walks free?'

'For now. Without Ania's evidence, without Pawlak, the law can't touch him.'

'Yet.' Dariusz had his own plans. He might be in the UK soon.

'You won't do anything.' Gillen's voice was suddenly authoritative. 'Do you think Ania did this to see you in jail for the rest of your life? It'll be taken care of.'

'Taken care of? You mean he'll get early retirement and a pension?'

'I mean it will be taken care of.'

And Dariusz realised, to his surprise, that he trusted Gillen to make certain of that.

He realised Krysia had been talking. '… you again?'

'Sorry? I didn't…'

'I said, shall I see you again? Maybe we could have a drink. Before you go…'

'No. I don't think that would be a good idea.'

She bit her lip. 'OK.'

'You can make Mielek's life difficult, if you want. I'd like that.'

He smiled at her and after a moment she smiled back. 'I'll try.'

He carried the rest of his possessions out to his car. He had a bit of time off before his interviews. He could go and see his family. His father was getting more and more frail. He had barely spoken to Beata since the party. There were some bridges to mend on both sides.

And then? Anything was possible.

Chapter 76

When Will arrived back in St Abbs, he went straight to Jack's caravan and collected Keeper who greeted him with hysterical joy. 'She's been fine,' Jack said. 'You OK?'

'I'm OK.' Will knew that would be the only reference between them to the events of the past few weeks.

He took stock as he walked back along the cliff path to the village. He'd called Blaise after leaving the FLS building where Karzac still sat at his desk. 'I won't do it for you,' he said.

There was silence, then Blaise said, 'That's your choice. It always has been.'

'Listen to me. Karzac isn't going to die. He's going to be exposed for what he is. He's going to jail. That's what Ania wanted.'

'My hands are tied, Will. You know that.'

'There's a way round everything – isn't that what you used to tell me? That video is still out there – the undoctored version. I want your word you'll support me, let me search for it – I can find it. And then...'

There was silence on the other end of the line, then Blaise said, 'I trust you, Will,' and Will knew he had, once again, done exactly what Blaise expected him to do.

And that was enough.

Dariusz Erland was coming to the UK in a couple of weeks. He had an interview in Birmingham. Afterwards, he had promised to come north to St Abbs. He wanted to see the places that were important to Ania, and he seemed to think that they should keep in touch. Maybe he was right.

Will threw a stick for Keeper and watched her as she vanished into the long grass. Her coat was soaking when she emerged. She'd need a good brush later. He stopped and looked out across the sea. The sun was low and the water reflected the light, the grey turning to silver as the sun set. He had to get the boat ready. The funeral was in a couple of days and he'd need to take her out to do what he had promised. He could see the wake of the boat and the stream of grey ashes falling into the water, dancing on the surface in the turbulence, then sinking away.

He was almost back at the cottage when his phone rang. He answered it. 'Will Gillen.'

It was Sarah Ludlow. They exchanged cautious greetings, then she said, 'I thought you'd want to know that Nadifa's going to get leave to remain. Blaise came through. She can stay. And they've found out what happened to François. He's alive. He's in a camp, but they're going to try and get him out. It won't be easy, and it could take some time. Blaise is prepared to say François was working for him. I don't think it will get him any medals.'

'Blaise will survive.'

Silence fell between them. 'I'm sorry,' Will said, 'for what I...'

'It's OK. I understand.'

She probably did – understood a lot, and forgave a lot.

There was a lot to be forgiven, a lot to atone for. To do that, he had to live, he had to endure. Just now, it seemed unbearably hard, but he couldn't let Ania's courage down by taking any easy ways out.

He was at his cottage. He unlocked the door and pushed it open. Keeper bounded in ahead of him, and he followed her, picking up the post from the mat, checking the phone, following the familiar routine. 'I'm back,' he called into the waiting silence.

And in the silence, he could sense she trusted him enough to say goodbye.

Epilogue

The sky was a clear blue, and the small yard was awash with sunlight. Nadifa turned her face to the warmth and closed her eyes. With the brightness against her lids, she could be walking along the shore at Grand-Bassam where the trees grew through the decaying colonial buildings, and along the beach where she and François used to walk together, before rebellion tore their lives apart.

The flies started to drone and her eyes flew open.

The yard was filled with colour. Her friends had brought tubs and pots that had blossomed in the sunlight. Leon was kneeling by a tub of bright blooms that looked too exotic for an English summer. He was digging, his face serious and absorbed. Bees burrowed industriously into the flowers.

She let her eyes close again, but this time, she was back in Danané, filling a plastic bowl with water. Sagal stood beside her, holding the jug. Her small hands were steady. Nadifa kept her eyes focused on her daughter as the shouting and the gunfire came closer.

The water kept pouring and pouring.

And the flies...

'Mama?'

Leon's hand tugged at her skirt. He climbed onto her knee and knelt up, looking at her face. One muddy finger traced the tear that had run down her cheek. 'Mama?'

She looked into his eyes. They were dark, like Sagal's, and for a second, she thought her daughter was looking back at her, then it was Leon again, holding out a flower to her. She took it.

He smiled, and she could see the way his cheeks had plumped out and his eyes had brightened since they left the detention centre. He looked so like François, the way he was when they first met, when he was a young man.

François was coming back. In a few days, he would be here. She didn't know what would happen then. She had no inclination for thinking or for making plans. The warmth of the sun was enough.

Leon slipped off her lap and ran back to his digging.

She let the quiet of the day close over her, drifting on the murmur of the bees.